THE SPACE BETWEEN US

MELANIE SUMMERS

Books by Melanie Summers

SPICY ROMANCE

The Full Hearts Series

Break in Two (Full Hearts Book One)

Don't Let Go (A Full Hearts Novella) – Prequel to Breaking Love
– E-book only

Breaking Love (Full Hearts Book Two)

Letting Go (A Full Hearts Novella) – Prequel to Breaking Clear

Breaking Clear (Full Hearts Book Three)

Breaking Hearts (Full Hearts Book Four)

ROMANTIC COMEDIES

The Crown Jewels Series

The Royal Treatment

The Royal Wedding

The Royal Delivery

Braniacs in Love

The Space Between Us

Love Signals (Coming Soon)

Paradise Bay Series

The Honeymooner

Whisked Away

The Suite Life

Resting Beach Face

Pride and Piña Coladas

Beach, Please

Crazy Royal Love Series

Royally Crushed

Royally Wild

Royally Tied

Stand-Alone Books

Even Better Than the Real Thing

A Hollywood Ending

WOMEN'S FICTION

The After Wife

I Used to Be Fun

Dear Lovely Reader,

I am what you could call an optimistic skeptic (if such a thing exists). As a young child, I was like a yellow lab, bouncing around, assuming everyone I met wanted to be my friend, only to have life teach me that some people won't like me no matter what, and that sometimes nasty things happen for no reason at all. So, I pretty much spend my time navigating between my gut reaction, which is to welcome everyone and each new experience with open arms, and that alarm going off in my brain that tells me to BE AFRAID BECAUSE SOMETHING COULD GO WRONG.

I'm guessing a lot of us are like this. Being human is hard. But it can also be wildly fun if we let it. These days, I'm doing my best to say yes to the new. New people, new experiences, new foods (so long as they aren't laden with onions). None of this is easy, but it's totally worth it.

This book is about learning to say yes. It's about learning to trust again. And it's about just how damned important acceptance is. It's also about sex. (Well, not really, but there is one long, sexy sex scene that I hope is tastefully done. Also, you'll note that I don't mention the use of condoms, but trust me, they're using them. If opened-door scenes aren't your thing, please skip chapter 25 and chapter 26 up to the scene break.)

Anyway, happy reading, my friend, and thank you for being here.

I appreciate you.

xoxo,

mel

A Short-but-Powerful Motivational Speech from Your Hero...

Ty Sterling

TIMING IS EVERYTHING. That, and relentless pursuit of your goal. When those two things come together, one can achieve what others would consider impossible. It's not luck. It's not magic. It's not the cosmos or the alignment of the stars, or whether Mars is in retrograde. That's all bull-shit—excuses people give themselves when they don't have what it takes to make it.

The truth is this: achieving your dreams is a matter of putting in the work that no one else will. It's that simple, and it's that hard. And that's why most people accomplish far less than they could in their lives. Because they're not willing to grind it out day after long day until they get where they're going. It becomes too hard or too boring or they feel like they're missing all the fun, so they quit. They give up and accept an ordinary life when they could be living an extraordinary one, like the one I'm leading now. At thirty-six, the corporation I started with my best friend was a Fortune 500 company and I had already made my first billion. At forty-one, I have enough to make my one real dream come true.

I didn't start out rich. In fact, I grew up in a lower middle-class family until my shitty excuse for a father abandoned our family when I was eleven (which meant we went from poor to really frigging poor). My mother died when I was nineteen and overnight, I became the sole caregiver of my little brother, Michael. Did I give up my dream? No, I did not. I worked harder than I thought possible, juggling his needs (which were many considering he's on the autism spectrum) with my need to educate myself, start a business, and make a disgusting amount of money in the shortest amount of time imaginable.

I did it all because I know the meaning of the word relentless. When I set my mind to something, I *will* make it happen because, if there's one thing life has taught me, it's that no one is going to hand you anything. You go out and get it. When you've actually gotten your shit together and you're poised and ready to pounce, *that's* when the timing comes in. Because when the opportunity of a lifetime presents itself, if you're not prepared, you'll miss it.

My opportunity of a lifetime is happening right at this very moment, and I can tell you one thing—there's no way in hell I'm going to miss it. It's taken surgical precision and putting myself in exactly the right place at precisely the right time, but basically I'm at the finish line. I'm one signature away from having my dream come true. Well, technically two signatures, an enormous transfer of cash, and then the actual purchase itself, but the point is, I'm so close, I can almost taste victory. Unfortunately in this case, it smells like a sweaty locker room after the Super Bowl.

"It's done," I say into the phone as I climb into the back of the limo. The driver shuts the door and I settle myself against the leather seat and finally let my shoulders relax.

"Wow. That's … quite an accomplishment, Mr. Sterling," Donna, my assistant, says.

Donna's amazing. She's my calendar, my bouncer, my memory, and at times, my conscience all rolled into one. Other than my brother, Donna is the closest thing I have to family. I can tell by that little pause between the word 'that's' and 'quite' that she disapproves of what I'm doing. She shouldn't bother to say anything though because I'm not going to change my mind. Not after over twenty years of planning and working towards this moment. And certainly not after spending the last five days in Dallas flattering the insufferable Mrs. Muffy Bowles-Tillington to get her to sell. I'll finally own the only thing that my father cares about. And I can make sure he never gets to enjoy it again, which will be worth every fucking penny. If any man deserves it, it's him.

"Have the contract sent to the printer on the jet."

"Certainly, Mr. Sterling. And before you ask, the money hasn't been deposited into the foundation's trust account yet," she says. "I spoke with Rohan, who told me those papers haven't been signed either and that Dr. Napper doesn't want to be bothered with that today."

Dr. Richard Napper—or as the world knows him, Dr. Dick Napper—has been my business partner for the last eighteen years, during which time we've taken a simple idea of his (at-home DNA testing kits) and turned it into a multi-billion-dollar bio-tech corporation. I'm the money guy, he's the inventor. It's a match made in heaven, or I should say it was until we made so much money, he decided he'd rather galivant around the globe than show up to work.

"It's been three weeks. I hope Rohan told him that I

really will pull my half of the money out of the trust account. I don't want to do it because it'll really hurt the foundation, but if I have to I will."

"I made sure to tell Rohan to impress upon him what was at stake."

"Thank you. What's he doing that's so important?"

"At the moment, he's on a helicopter in Tanna, Vanuatu."

Of course he is, because he couldn't be on *this* side of the planet when the most important deal of my life is teetering on the edge. "What is it this time?"

"He's about to be dropped onto one of the planet's most active volcanoes so he can set some sort of world record."

"For what? Most insatiable need to overcompensate?" As soon as I say it, I feel bad. Richard's one of the very few people I can trust in this world. I'm just mad that he's dragging his feet on something so important to me.

She snort-laughs, then says, "Something like that. If you get to the plane in the next fifteen minutes, you'll be able to watch it live on the Dick Cam."

"As much as I wish I could, I'll be busy running the company we started together."

"Are you still planning to come home tonight or do you want me to have your flight rerouted to Vanuatu so you can apply pressure in person?"

"I'll go home. I've already been gone too long," I tell her.

Whenever possible, I try not to be gone for more than three days. It's too hard on my little brother, Michael. (Sidenote: Michael would be highly irritated that I've just called him 'little,' on account of him being an adult. He takes everything quite literally. Because he's the same height as me and weighs ten pounds more, he'd tell you,

I'm actually the little brother and he is the younger one. But since I'm seven years older than him, and I raised him since he was twelve, he'll always be little to me.)

Despite having a live-in caregiver, Greta—who Michael adores and vice versa—he gets upset when I'm away too long. He manages three days quite well without me, but much longer than that and he struggles. The truth is, I struggle too because I can't sleep anywhere other than my own bed. Not in the world's finest hotels, or on the biggest, most luxurious yachts. Not even on my jet (which I've had fitted with the exact same mattress, pillows, and bedding as my bed at home). Certainly not at a girlfriend's house, when I've had one. This means that other than a few short catnaps taken while sitting up, I have been awake since Sunday. And it's now Thursday. But it's totally worth it because … revenge. "Find out where Richard's going to be tomorrow and arrange for me to go there in the morning."

"If I had to guess, I'd say he'll be at the morgue," Donna says dryly.

"He'd better not be. I need him alive to sign the papers and buy me out of the trust already."

When she doesn't offer a quip back, I know she's got something to say.

"What is it, Donna?"

"Nothing."

"It's something, so out with it."

"It's just that you're about to spend more than the entire GDP of Albania to buy a football team just to spite a man you haven't spoken to in over twenty-five years."

"Donna, did you do a Google search for countries with gross domestic products under five billion to try to get me to change my mind?"

"Yes," she says, sounding sheepish. "Wouldn't it …

wouldn't it be better to, I don't know, let it go maybe, sir? You don't even like sports."

"True, but it's a good investment with a side bonus of allowing me to devastate my father."

"Okay then," she tells me, her tone filled with the disappointment she normally saves for her husband.

I glance out at the *Ripley's Believe It or Not!* Museum as we zip past it. (And no, I do not believe it, Ripley. Not even for a second.) "Look, I know you're not a fan of what I'm doing and believe me, I understand. But it's literally been my main driving force throughout my entire adult life. I'm not going to abandon it now. So just say whatever it is you want to now, then forever hold your peace."

"Fine. It won't make you feel better. I know you think it will, but it won't. You won't get back the love you and Michael should've had. It won't bring your mom back. You'll get your revenge, I guess, but you'll also be out five billion dollars."

"You guess? I *will* get my revenge. It's going to kill my father. Hopefully literally. His one true love in this life is that team. He's had the same seats for every game for the last twenty-eight years, and unlike my high school graduation, he'd never miss it. I'm going to ban him from the stadium permanently and have his seats donated to the Dallas Autism Society so they can either be used by members or auctioned off. He will *hate* the idea of someone like Michael sitting in his beloved seats, which makes it all the more delicious. He can never high five the other fans or hold out his hands in hopes of catching a t-shirt from one of those ridiculous t-shirt guns. He can never drool over the cheerleaders in person. And when he sees all the public photo ops with his own sons hanging out with the players, knowing that if he'd just been a decent human being, he'd be right in there with us? He'll lose his will to live. It's going to be glorious."

"Okay, but Rohan said Dr. Napper is extremely disappointed that you're pulling out of the foundation. Is it really worth upsetting your partner?"

"If Richard actually wanted me to be part of it, he wouldn't have chosen the world's most ridiculous non-profits to back. He would have gone with worthy causes, not the ghostbusters or those weirdos who walk around with tin foil on their heads hoping to meet little green men."

"All right then," she says, but I can tell by her tone she thinks this is anything but all right. "The contract should be printing on the jet already. I'll have Josh put them on the table, then I'll find out where Dr. Napper will be tomorrow. Is there anything else you need?"

"No, thanks. That'll cover it for now."

"Very good, Mr. Sterling. Have a safe and pleasant flight." She hangs up before I can say goodbye, which is Donna's version of flipping me the bird.

I toss my phone onto the seat next to me and sit back, closing my eyes for a few seconds. The truth is, she doesn't get it, which is to be expected. Donna's parents are still together. I think. I mean, if they're still alive, they're probably in their nineties. But I seem to recall her saying something about a happy childhood. Or a normal one. Something like that. Donna doesn't know what it's like to hurt the way we hurt. She didn't see how awful my father was to Michael when he was a little kid—yelling in his face to 'just act like a normal human!' while my brother went stiff with fear. She wasn't there when he packed his bag and left us on a random Tuesday night in November, never to even try contacting us (or providing financial support) again. Donna didn't see how much my mom struggled to put food on the table while taking care of a little boy she couldn't send to daycare on account of his behavior being 'too unpredictable.' Donna's dead wrong. I *will* feel better —so much better knowing that Patrick Sterling is going to lose the only thing he's ever cared about.

Picking up my phone, I call Michael, knowing he'll want an update as to my estimated time of arrival.

"Hello, Ty," he says.

"Hi, Michael, how was it at the museum today?"

"Excellent. The IT technician, Tony, managed to get the interactive Jurassic game working again, so that's a big relief for the staff and patrons alike."

Michael works at the Museum of Natural History, Monday through Friday, from nine until two, through a work program that links neurodivergent people with jobs to which they're well-suited. Michael helps out in the back with planning displays, tagging and organizing items, and other jobs that don't require people skills.

"I'm glad to hear that," I answer. "I know it's really been bothering you."

"Well, of course it was bothering me, Ty. It's a vital part of our dinosaur display. Most people choose not to read the signs next to the dinosaur models, so without that game, they're not learning anything," he says. Michael is big on learning, and he wants everyone else in the world to be equally as passionate about expanding their knowledge, especially when it comes to dinosaurs.

"You know one of the many things I admire about you, Michael?"

I'm about to tell him when he interrupts. "Over the years, you've told me many things you admire about me, Ty. Are you asking me to name them? Because that will take quite a while."

I smile to myself, knowing I walked into that one. "No

need for you to list them. I was going to say your passion for learning."

"Ah, yes, that is one of my best attributes, along with my keen ability to solve puzzles and my honesty."

He's right about that last one. Michael is incapable of lying, which, in my opinion, is one of the gifts of the way his brain works. Most people are capable of such deceit— saying what you want to hear, omitting pertinent details, flattering you when they would much rather punch you in the face. At least that's how people are with me. They're either a little scared or they're desperate to get something from me, both emotions allowing them to justify lying to my face. With Michael, however, I know I'm getting the truth, even if I don't want to hear it.

"And Ty, how was your day? Did you get what you went to Dallas for?" he asks.

"As a matter of fact, I did," I tell him.

"So Mrs. Bowles-Tillington has sold the Destroyers to you."

"Not yet, but she's agreed to sell them to me. I still need to deal with some paperwork and shift some money around, but it's basically as good as done."

"I still don't understand why you are buying a football team. You don't even watch it," he says.

"It's a good investment," I answer vaguely. I can't explain the real reason I'm buying the team to him. Revenge is not exactly something of which he'll approve. "Plus, maybe you and I can start going to games once in a while. We can sit in the owner's box so you won't have to hear it, and they serve really great food. We could fly straight home as soon as the game ends."

"If it would make you happy to do that, I'll go along with you, but I won't watch the game. I'll eat the food though."

"I don't want to push you to go," I tell him. "But maybe we could try it once and see how you like it. If it's not your thing, we could even leave at halftime."

"Or sooner?" he asks.

"Sure, or sooner."

"What time will you be home, taking into account any traffic issues, both air and motor vehicle?"

"Taking all of that into account, I should be back by seven."

"I'll ask Greta to have the cookies ready for seven, then. Or maybe three minutes to seven so they can cool a little."

"That sounds perfect. I can't wait to get home."

"All right. I should go. Greta and I are playing Rummy and I paused our game to take your call."

"Of course. Have fun. I'll see you in a few hours."

As soon as I hang up, I get a text from Donna.

DONNA

Dick'll be staying in Vanuatu for the next five days. Something about a lava dance ceremony tonight. Tomorrow, he's going to an island called Malekula to visit the former cannibal sites and be inducted as an honorary chief in the Big Namba tribe (Namba being the name of the penis sheath worn by the men. There is also a Small Namba tribe, but apparently he didn't want to join them).

Book me to Vanuatu. Get a yacht to take me to Malekula and find out if he's willing to meet me on board for a few hours.

DONNA

Aye, aye, captain.

I should be happy. Thrilled even. This is it—the

moment I've been waiting for my entire adult life. All I have to do is get one little signature from Richard removing me as co-chair of the foundation and get him to pay me out, then swing back to Dallas to get Muffy to sign off, transfer five billion dollars to her, and boom! I'll be the new owner of the most expensive football team in history. As Michael would say, easy peasy, lemon squeasy.

So why do I feel absolutely dead inside?

2

Stupid Human Tricks

Gwendolyn Fox - Mountain View, California

WHEN YOU GROW up in a house full of very serious scientists, you learn two things: 1) How to argue any topic into the ground in an attempt to prove you are, indeed, the biggest brain in the room, and, 2) the scientific method (obviously).

My parents met one November morning in the PhD students lounge at Yale. At the time, my mother was studying condensed matter physics while my father was getting his doctorate in Analytical Chemistry. They had a huge argument over crystal growth (my dad believing that it was both a controlled and predictable experiment, while my mom insisted it was about as scientific as witchcraft). They fought until the custodian came in to clean up that evening, then continued their argument at an all-night Denny's, finally reaching the following conclusions at eight o'clock the next morning: 1) They were going to have to agree to disagree, and 2) They should get married. Which they did that afternoon, after each going home to shower and change first. They've been happily arguing ever since.

When it was time for my older brother, Benjamin (a total people pleaser), to choose a field of study for his doctorate, he decided to go for a double in both Analytical Chem *and* Condensed Matter Physics. He works for NASA and is married to a psychiatrist, Carla, who he never argues with, on account of them having developed 'healthy communication boundaries for which to create a safe space for growth.' I'm happy for him, I really am, but honestly, their relationship sounds boring as fuck. Give me a hot debate every day of the week and twice on Sundays because to debate is to truly be alive. Luckily, Ben still brings his A game when we go visit our parents at Thanksgiving, Christmas, and Independence Day. The volume and vitriol around the dinner table has scared off more than a few boyfriends in the past. But that's okay. It only means none of them were the right ones for me. Forget love at first sight. It'll be love at first fight for this girl. He's out there somewhere. I just haven't fought him yet. But when I do, it'll be glorious. He'll hold his own without getting nasty or personal. He'll also know when to back down, which will be as soon as I prove him wrong. And he'll know it's all in good fun.

Speaking of fights, and more specifically, things over which to fight, my career of choice has become a rather large bone of contention between my parents and me. Because I have a bit of a rebellious streak in me, or maybe it's because I'm unusually optimistic for a scientist. After completing my PhD in astrobiology, I went immediately to work for the SETI Research Institute. If, on spec, you're not sure what SETI stands for, allow me to jog your memory (because you most definitely have heard of it).

The Search for Extra-terrestrial Intelligence.

My parents, who were already telling the neighbors they were about to have *two* children over at NASA, have been cycling through the first several stages of grief ever since. Shock. Disappointment. Sadness. Anger. Bargaining. Nearly ten years on, they haven't reached acceptance, but what can I really expect from two people who fought for twenty hours straight (minus bathroom breaks and time spent ordering food) about crystal growth? Apparently, not a change of heart. It's been especially hard for my mom, who, let's face it, as a physicist, barely even believes that chemistry is a pure science. Imagine finding out her youngest child is dedicating her life to the possibility that she'll have a gab sesh with E.T. one day.

When 'it first happened' as she puts it, she was certain I was having a quarter-life crisis. After six years, however, she developed a new theory: I must have suffered a severe, untreated and asymptomatic concussion. She even booked me an MRI. I did not show up.

The truth is, I just really believe in what we're doing. I love it. I love my team (well most of them—not Chad. He's the worst, as are most Chads). The rest of them? Chef's kiss. My boss, Dr. Keenan Edwards, is incredible. Not only off-the-charts intelligent, but kind too. He looks just like Morgan Freeman, and has a deep, rich voice, except with a British accent, since he hails from across the pond. He's also absolutely full of faith in his staff, which makes the entire team want to do our very best.

Us SETI researchers are an odd bunch because, in order to do this type of work, you have to embody a strange combination of logical, scientific reasoning with the utmost in faith—not exactly the usual mix. A lot of the science-minded folks (read: my parents and brother) think what we do is a total joke, which it most definitely is not. The ultra-faith-based people of the world don't necessarily care about proof (which is something we are *rigorously* seeking). And of course, they're not concerned with proof, because faith is all about belief in the absence of evidence. If you had proof, you wouldn't need faith.

Anyway, the chances of making contact in my lifetime are low (in fact, it's most likely going to be approximately 400 years from now). I get up every day knowing that it's a distinct possibility that I won't actually witness the wonders of that first message from a far-off galaxy. There's about a 99.999991% chance I'm just a runner who will hand off the baton in the longest marathon in human history—a mere footnote in some textbook written half a millennium from now.

But on the other hand, it could happen tomorrow.

And *that* is the thought that gets me up every morning, rain or shine. I bounce into the office praying that today will be *the day*.

In truth, today's work will likely be far less glamorous. It's going to be interrupted by a school tour that I have to lead. I drew the short straw. Again. If I didn't trust my team so much, I'd probably be wondering if the game is rigged because this is the *third* time this year that I've had to host a group of seventh graders—which is widely known to be the worst age. They come in two packages: either completely apathetic or totally rowdy. *Any* group is better than teenagers, including the California Keenagers (senior citizens who pretty much complain the whole time about it being too hot/too cold/too loud/and, inexplicably, too quiet at the same time), and the ever irritating 'moms with bright babies' group that shows up once a year with children under the age of two. Let's face it—the babies aren't getting anything out of my talk on radio versus laser telescopes, and neither are their Starbucks-fueled, Lululemon-clad moms who are basically just using us to jockey for the position of 'best of the best smug moms who will do *anything* for their little cherubs.'

But I digress, which I better not do when the teens are here, because if you lose them for even a second, *anything* could happen. Take last month, when my best friend, Allie Camereri, was taking around a class of sophomores from Palo Alto. She lost their attention early on, and when it was time to put them back on the bus again, the teacher discovered that two students were missing. The entire staff had to stop what we were doing and conduct a thorough search of the three-story building until we located them in the custodial supply closet, high as kites. Apparently they brought a dab pen on account of thinking they were going to one of those laser music shows popular at planetariums the world over (which even today, for some unknown reason, go super heavy on Pink Floyd). Let's just say it was a massive waste of time for everyone and no one was particularly happy with poor Allie.

The kids from Mountain View Middle School will be here for exactly two hours and forty-six minutes, and I have every one of those minutes accounted for with one goal in mind: Keep their minds busy so their bodies don't start to cause trouble. Each time I do one of these hellish tours, I learn a little something that I can use the next time. It's still a nightmare of gargantuan proportions, immediately transporting me back to my days of wearing braces, spitting when I spoke, and having one boob significantly larger than the other (the right one was the lag-behind). Kevin Parker, a scrawny bully, nicknamed me Wonder Boob, as in, I wonder when her other boob will come in? But don't worry, karma got Kevin, who now works as a night shift manager at a twenty-four-hour car wash.

Anyway, even though this tour will be a sweaty, soul-sucking endeavor, I always go in hoping for at least one promising young mind to be among the group. So far, I'm 0 for 27 tours, but that's no big deal because I know those minds are out there, just like I know for certain there is other intelligent life somewhere in the universe. They just don't come here. They visit NASA instead.

I usually have my routine down, but today, because of an important event in the auditorium, we won't be able to watch a thirty-two-minute video on Frank Drake (the father of SETI). Dr. Drake, of the Drake equation (which is the second-most famous mathematical equation, right after Einstein's $E = mc2$), isn't exactly a household name, even though he absolutely should be. The reason he's not is because a lot of people dismiss anything to do with the search for extra-terrestrial life to be a bunch of nonsense. We've gotten a lot of bad press throughout the years because of all the crazies out there running around claiming to have been abducted and probed. (Why always the probing, people? Why couldn't at least one of them say they were subjected to a Rorschach test or a lovely four-course meal and some friendly chit chat?)

But I'm off topic again, which tends to happen when I feel passionately about something. I was talking about Frank Drake and the video I usually show students. Truth be told, they couldn't care less about him, but if there's one thing I've figured out about this next generation, if you stick them in front of a screen, they're helplessly frozen in place like Han Solo in carbonite. Just stuck there with their mouths agape until I shut it off and turn on the lights.

Lucky for me, I can bring the class to today's big event. There's about a sixty-one percent chance they might even enjoy it, although I'm guesstimating a ninety-four percent chance that even those who do find it fun will pretend they thought it was 'the worst.' At exactly 2:00 p.m. P.S.T., our major financial backer, bio-tech billionaire Dr. Dick

Napper, is going to be attempting to set another world record, so at exactly 1:54 p.m., I'll be herding the class into the auditorium for freeze-dried ice cream while they watch the video on the Dick Cam (an unfortunately-named live-streaming video feed that Dr. Napper uses whenever he's out doing something daring). Apparently, he's volcano surfing today, which sounds terrifying enough to keep the kids quiet for a good fifteen minutes.

The bus is going to be here in two minutes, which gives me just enough time to run to the ladies' room (a must on account of my nervous bladder). Who knows? Maybe today will be the day when I meet the promising young mind who will one day take over our very important project…

———

Newp. Not one promising child in the bunch. We've pretty much completed the entire tour and not even one measly question. Very little eye contact either. I feel like the weirdo boy with chronic halitosis at the prom trying to get someone, anyone, to show even a tiny hint of interest. But the floor has become suddenly fascinating to all the girls.

"No one? Not one question for Gwen?" their teacher, Mrs. Jones, asks.

"I've got one," a kid in a Metallica hoodie says.

I smile at him, hope building in my chest. Maybe I'm wrong about this group.

"Have you met any little green men?" he sneers.

I weep for the future.

"Dillion! That's not polite," Mrs. Jones says. "Gwen has given up a lot of her time today to share her knowledge with us. We owe her our respect."

"That's fine, Mrs. Jones," I say, keeping my smile in

place. "Dillion, here's my answer. Not yet, but with persistent application of our knowledge, someday, we will definitely make contact with intelligent life on another planet. Consider this: In all the years that SETI research has been happening, it's the equivalent of taking a close-up photo of a single leaf in the Amazon rain forest and determining from that picture that there are no animals living there."

"Ooh! Really?" Mrs. Jones exclaims. "Did you hear that, children? Write that down in your notebooks because that is a very interesting fact."

Tilting my head a little, I say, "It's not a fact so much as an analogy."

I should not have said that. The excitement in her eyes just dies completely. *Stupid, Gwen. Stupid. You know teachers do not like being corrected in front of their students.* "But … an important analogy. Definitely worth writing down because it really illustrates just how narrow our search has been so far." I smile at her but she's not having it. Glancing at my watch, I see we've got another five minutes to kill before we can swing by the lunch room for the snacks. "Any other questions?"

A girl in a half shirt (or is that a sports bra?) and baggy pants holds up her hand. "My dad says this isn't a real science and that the money you get for your fake research should be given to some better cause."

Your dad should shut the hell up and stick to things he knows like watching football and finally fixing up that old Trans-Am he bought when he was sixteen. You know, the one he knocked up your mother in on his parents' driveway. "Interesting take. What does your dad do for a living?" *Come on, Gwen, do not go down this road. It will help nothing.*

"He owns a lube shop," she says, snapping her gum at me.

"I see. And before he got into the lube game, did he get

his science degree? A master's maybe or a PhD?" *Stop now. Right fucking now.* "I'm only asking because I'm trying to ascertain his understanding of what science is. I'm assuming it went beyond the rudimentary teachings of secondary school, since he obviously holds such a strong opinion on the matter."

She chews her gum with her mouth open while she shakes her head. "No. My grandpa owned the shop first and gave it to him."

"Is he a big reader then? Like maybe he's got some Stephen Hawking and Carl Sagan books hanging around the bathroom that he just ... devours every chance he gets?"

"He mostly just listens to the Joe Rogan podcast."

Don't say it. She's a child, Gwen... "Okay, well tell your dad to head on back to school, get his PhD in ... any science at all, but preferably astrophysics, astrobiology, or astronomy, then come find me so we can have a talk about what is and what isn't a science, because there's no point in debating someone who lacks even a base knowledge on the topic."

Dammit. I said it. But at least I didn't let the Trans-Am thing slip out...

Mrs. Jones is full on glaring now. Like, death glare. I swallow and offer the girl an apologetic smile. "What I meant to say was that the work we do here adheres to the strictest scientific methods in the world. We're using a multi-disciplinary approach with a team of engineers, astronomers, astrophysicists, and biologists. I can assure you that the answer to the age-old question of 'are we alone' is a resounding *no*."

She snaps her gum at me and shrugs. "Whatever."

I glance at my watch again. 1:52 p.m. Sweet. We're rounding the corner to the exit of this shit maze. I lead the group over to the lunch room and stop in front of the door, smiling dramatically at them. "Okay, who wants to try a very special treat that normally only astronauts get to enjoy?"

A girl directly in front of me who has the most eyeliner I've ever seen says, "As long as it's not freeze-dried ice cream. They always serve it at the planetarium and it's so *boring*. I've had it, like, a thousand times already."

Butts.

Mrs. Jones sighs. "Candace, that's not polite. Gwen here is offering us a special treat and we need to accept it graciously, no matter how boring it is." She turns to me with a slight wince and whispers, "Is she right?"

"Yes, as a matter of fact, my young friend Candace here has guessed it. It is freeze-dried ice cream," I say, still smiling even though I'm simultaneously wishing a sinkhole would open up and swallow me. Hmmm … make that Candace. "There will also be a super exciting live event happening that you'll all get to watch while you eat your snack."

"Somebody kill me now," one of them murmurs.

If you say so…

I lead them into the lunch room and walk directly over to the cupboard that I labeled 'Freeze-dried NASA foods.' I hear some snickering and when I turn, I see that I have completely forgotten about the dartboard. On it is a photo of Ty Sterling, Dr. Napper's business partner, soulless billionaire, and hater of all things SETI. His face is full of holes made by angry darts thrown at him. On the counter, under the board, is a tall stack of photos of him, all of which have been defaced in some way. My favorite is the long, twirly mustache version that makes him look like a villain from an old timey cartoon. Too bad that one's not up there now because the one that *is* on the board says

"ASSHOLE" in bold, red Sharpie across his forehead. Shit. Mrs. Jones does not look pleased.

Candace turns to me with her eyes wide. "Oh my God, it says asshole on that guy's picture!"

Triple shit. "Er, yeah, that's not a nice word, is it? I'm not sure who wrote that."

It was me. *I* wrote it. But I had a very good reason. "But I'm sure whoever it was, they had a very good reason. Who wants that ice cream?"

A bead of sweat rolls down my spine as I rush over and tear the photo down from the board, then flip over the other photos. The last thing I need is one of these kids to start videoing this and upload it to social media. I quickly grab the box of ice cream and rush to the door. "Let's take this into the auditorium so I can get the video feed set up in time for the big event."

A few minutes later, the kids are all seated, ripping into their packages of ice cream while I fire up the computer and start the Dick Cam.

Laughter breaks out across the room, accompanied by a loud gasp. Mrs. Jones rushes over to me, whispering furiously. "What exactly are you about to show us?"

"It'll be fine, I promise. It's just a poorly-named live feed. Dr. Dick Napper is our major sponsor. He spends most of his time doing daring things around the world and he has set up a live feed system at all of his foundations and corporations so he can share his adventures with us. Today, he's aiming to set a Guinness World Record for Volcano Surfing."

She gives me a hard look. "It better be fine, because after that whole dartboard incident, I'm not so sure this is an appropriate place for children."

"It's totally appropriate. In fact, it'll be *inspiring*. Dr. Napper is one of the leading minds in the bio-tech industry. He's a true philanthropist and is overall a very interesting person."

"Children, stop laughing," Mrs. Jones says. "The dick in this case is a man's name. It's short for Richard. Dr. Dick…" She looks at me for help.

"Napper. Dick Napper," I tell them proudly. "He's not only a genius, but a hero. Dr. Napper is one of the world's most generous humans. He backed our research facility nearly ten years ago and has just agreed to give us another hundred million dollars in funding so we can continue our work for another decade."

I'm so excited just saying it, I want to start clapping, but I won't because these kids don't give a flying fuck. They also won't care that as soon as Dr. Napper had the Zoom call with our team to share the good news, I was finally able to put an offer in on my very first house—a cozy bungalow that's only a forty-minute commute to work. I'm not sure what you know about real estate in Silicon Valley, but it's a tad bit pricey, so it's taken me close to ten years to scrape together enough to get me in the game. That Zoom meeting (which happened three weeks ago) was absolutely a best-case scenario for our team because not only are we getting the funding, but ASSHOLE Ty Sterling will no longer be a financial backer of the Napper Sterling Foundation. He's moving onto more evil pursuits, I'm sure, while Dr. Napper is taking on the foundation himself, which means no more public criticism from a guy who, frankly, doesn't have the first clue what we do. I mean, I can see him criticizing some of the other projects, like the ridiculous Yeti Research Institute or those crazy telekinesis people, but our project? One-hundred-percent solid.

Most of my team files in, except Allie, who must be delayed. They all take seats near me at the front of the room. Behind me, I hear one of the kids say, "Bet you ten bucks I can spit in that nerd's hair from here."

"Which one?" his friend asks.

I whip my head around and glare in their direction, giving them the international sign for "I'm watching you" made popular by the great Robert De Niro in *Meet the Parents*. They both do their best to look innocent, one of them looking up at the ceiling and pretending to whistle, as if I don't know that little trick. He's probably the spitter. But he won't be spitting on anyone today. Not on my watch. Or, I suppose I should say, not on my listen, since it's my hearing that saved the day this time. After a decade listening for the faintest of sounds, I've developed what my brother calls my bat hearing. And he's not wrong either. I can tune into more than one conversation at a time while conducting my own. I'd make a great principal at a school for troubled youth. Or an on-top-of-it mom.

The feed starts up and the sound of a helicopter fills the room. Dr. Napper smiles at the camera. "Hello, world! I am Dr. Dick Napper, coming to you live from Mount Yasur in Tanna, Vanuatu. Today I'm not only inventing a new sport, but I'm also going to set my fifth world record. I'm about to become the first-ever person to attempt Heli-Volcano Surfing which means I'll be dropped from this helicopter onto an active volcano with my feet hooked onto a snowboard that has been coated to withstand the heat of the terrain. No one has ever volcano surfed from a helicopter before. Mount Yasur is one of the most active volcanoes on the planet and could erupt at any moment which would mean almost certain death for me. There's also the danger of me succumbing to the toxic fumes before I can reach the bottom, but don't worry. I'll be fine. Because today is simply not a good day to die."

Mrs. Jones glares at me and I give her a sheepish look.

"He'll be fine. He's always fine," I assure her, even though his logic of 'today not being a good day to die' isn't exactly sound.

I'm just sitting down in the empty front row when Allie hurries in and takes a seat next to me. She pulls her slightly wild, light brown hair into a scrunchie. "Oh good, I didn't miss it."

"You're right on time."

"How's the tour going?" she whispers as we watch the Dick Cam switch to show a quickly approaching volcano.

"You know, the usual."

"Have you met E.T.?" she asks.

"Yup. And the b.s. about it not being a real science."

"Of course."

"Oh, and Chad forgot to put the pics of the devil in the drawer like I asked him to, so when I took the kids into the lunch room, they all saw it."

"Blerg," Allie says. "That's rough."

"Yeah, the kids loved it, but the teacher, not so much." I shake my head a little. "We should have gone with the twirly mustache instead of asshole this week."

Dick's grinning face fills up the huge screen again. "Okay, this is it! I'm ready to jump. I'd like to dedicate today's world record to the great Daryn Webb, who invented volcano surfing to begin with. Daryn, if you're watching on a Dick Cam somewhere, I hope to do you proud. And remember kids, don't try this at home." He salutes, then the feed switches to a drone shot of the outside of the helicopter, which is hovering above the volcano.

Dick dons his goggles, gives two enthusiastic thumbs up, then hops the board to the edge and wiggles until he's out far enough for the nose to tip down and for him to free fall onto the dark grey gravel as the sound is overlaid with the techno beat of "Born Slippy" by Underworld.

Allie glances at me. "Doesn't this seem like one of those sports that started with some guy saying, 'Hold my beer.'"

I laugh. "Right? You wouldn't catch me doing this for all the ore on Mars."

We watch as Dr. Napper hits a big bump, both of us wincing. "So? Did you hear back from the realtor yet?" Allie whispers.

"Nothing yet." The inspection on the house showed some wood rot on the exterior trim of the house, so I had the realtor ask if they'd be willing to either fix it or knock twenty grand off the price.

"I wonder what's taking so long for the homeowners to decide?"

Shrugging, I say, "Good question. I just hope it doesn't mean another offer came in."

"Well, even if it doesn't work out, another house'll come up soon."

"Not in my price range," I tell her. "It's either this one or I'll have to give up the idea of having my own yard and just settle on a condo."

"Either way, I'm completely jealous that you're going to have your own home." Allie lives with her parents. She and I used to be roommates, but her dad had a stroke three years ago so she moved back home to help out.

"You can stay over as often as you want," I tell her.

"Believe me, I'll be there," she says. We're both quiet for a moment while we watch Dick traverse the rocky decline.

The beat continues and when I look around at the kids, they're completely riveted, some of them even dancing in their seats to the music. A smug smile crosses my lips. Best. Tour. Ever. This is a day these kids won't soon forget.

"He's moving fast," Allie says.

I watch as Dr. Napper hits a bump and is lifted into the air. He lands hard, spraying rocks to both sides. "Yeah, it's almost like he's just on this side of being completely out of control," I tell her, my stomach clenching with nerves from just watching.

I glance at Mrs. Jones, who shoots me a look that says, 'this better turn out all right.' I nod and offer her a confident smile, even though, to be totally honest, I'm suddenly terrified on his behalf. But it'll be fine. Dr. Napper does some seriously dangerous stuff, and he's always fine.

———

Turns out he is not fine. Not at all, actually.

In fact, Dr. Dick Napper, bio-tech genius, inventor, and philanthropist, is most definitely dead. And I, in my infinite wisdom, just showed a group of minors a live death. On an enormous, 'you can't miss it because it's in HD' screen.

Which I just shut off.

One of the boys yells, "Whoa! That dude died! No cap!"

"No, he didn't!" I squeak.

"He totally died," Candace drawls.

The girl next to her says, "He's like … *super* dead."

I blink back tears, my voice all squeaky as I say, "I'm sure he's just fine. Probably a few bruises, maybe a broken rib or something, but Dr. Napper is going to be a-okay."

"Then why'd you shut the video off?" the lube shop heiress asks.

Crap. She's got me there. "Umm … because it was done. So…"

"Turn it back on then," the boy says.

"What?" I ask, a cool sweat forming, oh, everywhere.

"If he's fine, turn it back on again so we can see him get up."

"I would because he's definitely alive, but um, because of the time…" I glance at my watch, even though my eyes are too blurry to see what it says. "We should get you all back on the bus."

Mrs. Jones stands, her face white. "Yes, everyone file out. We need to leave immediately."

"I'm so very sorry," I whisper to her.

"If he's actually dead, you will be sorry," she whispers. "Half of these kids' parents are lawyers. You're going to get your ass sued from here to the end of the galaxy and back if you just showed these children a live death."

So, that's just great…

3

What Was That Thing I Said About Timing?

Tr

I know something's wrong the second I step out of the jet. Donna is standing at the bottom of the staircase, and even though the sun is setting behind her, making it difficult to see her face, I can tell by the way she's standing that she has something to tell me that I won't want to hear.

I jog down the stairs to her, inhaling the cool breeze off the Santa Cruz Mountains and start toward the limo while she falls into step with me. "Please tell me you didn't make the long drive because you think you can talk me into changing my mind. Because if there's one thing I won't do it's—"

"Dick is dead."

I stop in my tracks, my heart free-falling to the asphalt under my shoes. "What?"

She turns to me. "Dick died. About two hours ago."

My brain feels as if it's going to shut down. My entire body goes numb, but I somehow manage to turn toward Donna. "The volcano?"

She nods. "The gas got him."

Blinking hard, I try to make sense of what she's saying. "What are you talking about? What gas?"

"The fumes. From the volcano. He passed out, then started to roll, then hit a boulder. It was pretty awful actually."

"You watched?" I barely manage to get the words out.

Nodding again, she clears her throat and I can tell she's trying not to cry. I let out a long sigh, telling myself to keep it together. "Christ, I'm… I can't… Are you okay?"

"I'll be fine," she says, turning back toward the limo and walking briskly. "There will likely be reporters camped out in front of your house, hoping to get your reaction."

"Is that why you came? To warn me?"

"Yes. Well, and I didn't want you to find out about it from your news feed."

"I appreciate that." Rubbing my jaw, I allow the news to sink in a little more. Richard is dead. My best friend in college, who I could always count on to be kind to Michael, my partner with whom I started with nothing and built a Forbes 100 corporation, is gone, in an instant. Shock vibrates through me.

"Obviously this is going to change everything with your … plan."

"It'll change everything with everything," I tell her as we reach the car. "I guess I won't be going to Vanuatu tomorrow." I know it's stupid the moment the words leave my lips, but somehow, my brain is only allowing me to see from here to the next step.

"No, that won't be necessary. You'll need to get out in front of this thing to protect the company. I've already got the team started on writing up a statement on your behalf. They should finish it within the hour and I'll send it over for your approval."

"Thanks."

"I've also been getting calls and emails from the directors of each of the foundation's projects. They all want to make sure you're not going to back out on the next decade of funding. I'm assuming you are, but I need to know what you want me to say. So far, I've been ignoring them."

"For now, nothing," I tell her, my mind swimming in sludge. The plan was never to shut down the foundation, only to extract my money from it. Richard was going to take half a billion from his personal assets to shore up the difference. "I'm assuming he's left everything to that awful nephew of his."

She nods. "Based on an Instagram post Skip put out a few minutes ago, it sounds like it."

"Shit." I rub the back of my neck, knowing that Skip Napper, Richard's only living relative and useless douche bag extraordinaire, is about as likely to put a dollar into a non-profit as I would be to invite my father and his common law wife, Chastity, to move in with me.

A glimmer of hope crosses Donna's face and I know she thinks I may have to abandon my plan.

My phone buzzes in my pocket at the same time that Donna's makes a loud pinging sound. She digs around in her bag while I pull mine out. It's a text from Richard.

> To everyone I know and love, please turn on your Dick Cam in exactly two hours for an important message from me. Forever Yours, Dick

Donna lets out a shaky breath. "What the actual hell?"

"I take it you got the same message?" I ask. She glances at my phone and nods.

My heart beats wildly as I stare at the text. "What if this whole thing is a hoax? That's totally something Richard would do."

"I don't see how he could've survived that."

"What if none of it was real?" I say, allowing just the tiniest bit of hope to enter my mind. "Has an official announcement been made?"

She nods again. "Paramedics were on standby and they pronounced him dead at the scene."

Another text comes through on my phone.

ROHAN

> Mr. Sterling, Dr. Napper instructed me to write you the following message: "Ty, It's real. And no, I wouldn't pretend as some sort of grand hoax (although, I wouldn't put it past me either). Please, for the love of God, stop being so damn cynical. It's ruining all your fun. Dick"

ROHAN

> I'm sorry about that last message, Mr. Sterling. He insisted I send it in the event of his death. I hope you're not upset with me.

> It's fine, Rohan. You're only doing what you've been told to do.

ROHAN

> I appreciate that, sir, because this is the least strange of all the things Dr. Napper has asked of me.

Donna, who has been reading over my shoulder, looks up at me. "Oh God, what do you think is coming next?"

———

I arrive home thirty minutes later. I'm a total mess, my mind whirring along with all the thousand things that have now changed and the million things I have to deal with now that Richard is really gone. On top of all these responsibilities, I also have a pile of emotions swirling inside me. Grief at losing one of the only people in this world I know I can trust, shock at this all happening so fast, guilt for allowing us to grow apart over the years. But I can't think about that now. I have to stay focused or everything we built together is going to slip through my fingers like dry sand.

Michael, who must have been watching on our security screen in the kitchen, opens the front door as soon as the limo passes by the gates to the estate. The gates slide shut, blocking any view the reporters would have of me exiting the car.

I open the door before the driver can get to it and hurry to greet Michael as he carefully makes his way down the front steps of our sprawling Spanish Revival home. The sun has set over the ocean in the distance, and the hills are dark except for the lights of the few homes in this area of Woodside.

Michael's face lights up. "You're home. Finally."

We give each other a quick hug—nothing tight and never longer than a couple of seconds, even though, at the moment, I could use something longer. When I pull back, I put my hand on his shoulder as we make our way up the front steps. "I'm glad to be home."

"I heard about Richard and I'm very sorry. How are you?" he asks.

"I'm okay. A little sad and there's a lot I have to do now that he's gone."

Nodding, Michael says, "I'm sad too. Dead is forever."

His words are a punch to the gut, but I offer him a small smile. "Yes, it is."

The smell of freshly baked gingerbread cookies greets me as soon as we step inside. Greta, our housekeeper and

Michael's caregiver, pokes her head out of the kitchen. "Welcome home, Ty. Come have a snack."

When we reach the kitchen, I see she's got two plates with cookies and two mugs of cocoa set up at the table. Michael and I settle ourselves at the table, and I reach for the mug, letting it warm my hands that I didn't realize until now were cold.

"I'm sorry to hear about your friend," Greta says. "He was a great man. So full of life."

"Thanks. That he was," I answer, completely numb.

"I imagine your life is going to be turned upside-down for a while."

Michael cocks his head to the side. "Greta, Ty is very much sitting upright at the moment and I doubt very much that he could live upside-down, no matter how sad he is."

She and I exchange an amused glance and she says, "It's one of those strange expressions, Michael. It means that a lot of things will change very quickly for Ty."

I break off a piece of the soft, warm cookie. "Yes, I'll be really busy making sure the company can continue to run smoothly and dealing with a lot of paperwork."

"Hmm, that means you will probably have to be traveling quite a bit again."

I nod and sigh, then pop the cookie in my mouth and let the blend of sweetness and spice soothe my nerves.

Michael gives me a pointed look. "Can you please try to keep your trips down to three days? Because it's really not that fun for Greta to have to deal with me every day for an entire week. I get quite agitated when you're gone too long."

I smile at him. "I'll do my best, Michael. I promise."

"That is all anyone can ask of anyone else," he says. "That they do their best." He pauses, then says, "Actually, that's not true. You can ask them to do their *very* best."

"Good point. And I promise to do my very best."

———

It's funny how you can be so close to someone, then gradually, time and circumstances (or perhaps stubbornness and differing priorities) can cause you to grow apart to the point where you don't feel like you know the person anymore. Not really. Not the new version of them. The Richard I partnered up with was a nerdy college kid, like me. Ambitious, determined, and laser-focused on becoming wildly rich. He knew what it was like to not fit in, which I think was one of the reasons he was so good to Michael. He took notes for me when I had to miss classes because Michael was sick or his school was closed for a holiday the university didn't have.

But people change. I wanted to stay put and continue to grow our fortune while he wanted to see every corner of the planet and break as many world records as possible. We both did what we set out to do, but it was at the expense of our friendship. Little irritations grew bigger each year until we barely saw each other anymore. Only when necessary. But the friendship was still there underneath it all. The honesty. I can (and did) say that he let me down, but he also was the reason I have what I have today. And that's a hell of a lot more than most people get.

His final message is about to start and I am sitting at my desk sipping a cocoa with a generous splash of whiskey in it while I wait for the Dick Cam to boot up. Michael is watching a nature documentary in our home theater, which means I'll have at least ninety minutes to myself.

The screen lights up. Richard is sitting at his desk in the office, dressed in a fleece jacket and a t-shirt, looking like a hiking guide instead of a COO. He smiles, salutes and starts talking. "Hello, team, if you're watching this, it means I must have gone off on life's final—and greatest—adventure today. I'm sure I still had much to do on my list, but I died knowing I had already accomplished more and lived enough for a dozen men. I truly had it all and did it all so don't grieve for me. Instead, I want you to take this time to celebrate. Not just me, but the opportunities that I have afforded you as well. All the ways that I made your life better through my money, my advancements in the bio-medical industry, and hopefully, the inspirational example I have set for you." He picks up a glass of champagne and holds it up. "To a life well-lived."

I tip my mug to the screen. "Modest, as always, Richard," I mutter.

He has a sip. "Mmm, that really is good. 2013 Taste of Diamonds. Just over two mil per bottle." Setting the flute down, he says, "Now, onto the exciting news. In a couple of days' time, my sendoff will commence, and no, it won't be some drab funeral. It's going to be a five-day epic trek kicking off in Lima, Peru. Because of the scope of this adventure, and the fact that we can't very well shut down all of our businesses and projects for that length of time, each team will be required to send a delegate—someone who will well represent what Napper-Sterling Bio-Tech Inc. stands for—innovation, integrity, and wellness for all. Because of the physical requirements for parts of the trek, only those who are in good health will be able to attend. My ever-faithful assistant, Rohan—I'm assuming Rohan is still with me at this point, if not you'll be hearing from whoever his replacement is—will be contacting you shortly to provide details of the event and to arrange logistics. If this is far enough in the future, perhaps you'll be taking flying cars to Lima, although it's highly doubtful that they'd have the range required. It's a fun thought, anyway."

He pauses and has another sip of his drink. "Ahhh. Well, that's it for me. I shall sign off one last time. I wish you all the best in life—wealth, health, and experiences. And remember, the key to life is to stay curious and be brave."

The screen goes dark and I sit, staring at it, half-expecting him to reappear and say, "BOO!" but he doesn't.

This is really happening.

I close my eyes and rub my face with both hands.

My phone buzzes and I open one eye, thinking it might be another message from Richard.

DONNA

A five-day trek in Peru? Seriously?

Apparently.

DONNA

You go stock up on sleep. I'll find out whatever I can about what you'll be doing.

I appreciate that. Good night.

DONNA

'Night, boss.

I get up and wander through the house and down the stairs to the theater, then sit on the sectional next to Michael and watch the rest of the documentary with him. It's on the spiders of the Amazon rain forest and just the sight of them makes my skin crawl. I have a very bad feeling I'm about to end up seeing one up close and personal.

4

The Science of Beauty

Gwen

"OKAY, team, I know it's been a turbulent fifteen hours so I wanted to make sure to meet with you all first thing this morning. Did anyone *not* watch Dr. Napper's final video last night?" Keenan asks.

When no one seated around the large table says they missed it, he nods. "If anyone needs to speak to a counselor about what happened, please let me know and I'll arrange for someone to come in right away."

Chad, the assistant manager and world's biggest buttsmoocher, says, "Or come see me. I can also help you in finding a therapist."

"Thank you, Chad," Keenan says. "Now, with Dr. Napper's untimely loss, I'm sure you're all wondering if Ty Sterling is still one of the heads of the foundation, and as of this moment, the answer is yes. We don't know why, but we *do* know the paperwork wasn't completed before Dr. Napper passed away."

Groans can be heard around the room, and sweat

forms under my arms. My dream of homeownership is about to go up in smoke, isn't it? I'm going to be stuck living in my cramped apartment with a view of the dumpster forever, aren't I?

"Nobody panic, though," Chad says, holding up both hands in a way I'm sure he believes is reassuring. "Dr. Edwards and I have a plan."

Keenan smiles at him. "We certainly do. Now, is it bad that we've lost our biggest benefactor and the man left in charge has publicly and repeatedly stated how much he hates our project? That would be a resounding yes. But fear not because there's still much we can do to make sure we keep our funding."

"That's right," Chad adds. "All is not lost."

"Oh, for God's sake, Chad," Tina, our chief engineer, mutters. "Let the man talk."

Chad shoots her a look while Keenan continues. "The first thing we need to do is choose the right delegate from our team to go on the trip to Peru. That person will have access to Mr. Sterling for the entire time. If handled correctly, it is certainly long enough to convince the man not to pull our funding."

"So who are you going to send?" Allie asks.

"That's what we're here to decide," Keenan says. "My hip precludes me from going, but really there's no reason any one of the rest of you can't go."

"I nominate me," Chad says. "As second in command, it just makes sense."

Some low murmurs of dissent can be heard around the room.

Keenan just smiles at him. "Thank you for volunteering. I think before we choose someone, however, we need to decide what our goal for the mission is."

"To get the money," Chad answers.

"Yes, that's one reason." Keenan writes the word *Mission* on the whiteboard, then writes *secure funding* underneath it. "What else?"

"To represent the team," Allie says.

Keenan writes that up while Chad sits forward in his chair and says, "But that's just so we can get the money."

"No, it's not," she tells him. "It's also so we can do some networking with some of the other—"

"Who? The ghost idiots?" he sneers.

"And that's why you're not going," Keenan tells Chad.

Chad's face turns red. "Why? Because I'm honest?"

"Because you'll have difficulty showing the proper respect for the other delegates."

"Come on, *nobody* respects the ghost busters."

"Dr. Napper did," Keenan says. "Now, back to the mission. What other goals do we have?"

"To pay our respects to Dr. Napper," I say.

"Exactly."

"So we can get the money," Chad puts in.

I roll my eyes. "It's also because Dr. Napper was a great man, a visionary, and someone who believed in what we do. We owe that to him."

"Very good, Gwen," Keenan says. "Thank you. Now, who will be our best representative?"

Chad sits up. "Well, if we go back to my point of getting the money, we need to pick the person who has the best chance of convincing Mr. Sterling to hand it over. As a master debater, I believe I have the best shot."

Allie leans in and whispers, "He's a master debater, all right."

I stifle a laugh, then murmur, "Yes, I'm sure he master debates at least twice a day."

Virgil, an astrophysicist in his fifties, puts up his hand. "I think we should send a woman."

"Interesting," Keenan answers. "Why?"

"Because Sterling is a straight, single man. A woman will have the best shot."

"At what? Seducing him?" Allie asks, looking as horrified as I feel.

"No, at convincing him," Virgil says.

"You know, if we're going to go with a woman, we should choose the most attractive option," Edward, one of our astronomers, adds.

"*Option*?" I ask, wrinkling up my nose. "What are we? Used cars?"

Edward pushes up his glasses on his nose. "Of course not, Gwen. I didn't word that properly."

"I should say you didn't."

"Studies show that attractiveness is strongly correlated with obtaining positive results, such as being selected for a job or getting a bank loan."

"But how do we choose the most attractive woman on the team?" Virgil asks him. "What is attractive to one person won't be to another."

"Simple: we go with the one with the most symmetrical face," Edward answers. "That is the most accurate way of determining attractiveness. And no offense to Tina, but we should also choose someone within her child-bearing years."

"That's ridiculous. I'm not going to have his baby," I snap.

"No, but Mr. Sterling is forty-one years old and his best friend just died. That's the type of event that can get a man thinking about how short life is and what legacy he's going to leave behind," Virgil says.

"So, if we pursue Virgil's line of thinking, we're down to Allie and Gwen," Keenan says.

"This is completely sexist," I say.

"And ageist," Allie adds, pointing at Tina. "I can't even believe we're talking about this."

"It's neither ageist nor sexist," Edward says. "We're simply looking for the strategy that will ensure the best outcome, which I think we can all agree is the most important variable we need to consider."

"I'm afraid he's right," Keenan says.

My heart starts to pound. "Okay, Keenan, please say you're not seriously listening to this. I mean, we can't throw poor Allie—who definitely has the most symmetrical face—to the wolves like this, based purely on gender and attractiveness."

Allie raises an eyebrow at me. "I have the most symmetrical face? I'm pretty sure that's you."

"You're so sweet. But even if I did, Allie, the sale on my house is about to go through. I have way too much packing to do to go traipsing off to Peru to beg some giant asshole to let us keep our jobs."

"If we can't convince that giant asshole, you won't need to worry about moving because you'll lose your house," Chad says.

Edward snaps his fingers. "Oh, here it is! There's an app that measures facial symmetry. Let me download it."

No! This is not happening. "Look, of everyone on this team, I think we can all agree I hate Ty Sterling the most. I mean, whose idea was it to put up the dartboard?"

"Yours," Tina says.

"And who takes the time to print the photos and draw on them?" I ask.

"You," Virgil answers.

"That's right. It's me, and you may not know this, but there is very little in this world that gives me as much pleasure as sketching devil horns on that man's face."

Edward points his phone at me. "Here. Stay still and don't smile."

I stare into his phone, lifting my right eyebrow slightly while attempting to drop the left side of my mouth.

"Stop making that face," Allie says.

"What face?" I ask, tilting my head to the side.

"That face! You're totally drooping your mouth on one side."

"She's right, you definitely don't look like that," Edward says. "Let's start over."

"Let's not," I tell him, holding up my hand to block his camera. "I will completely blow it for the team. For one thing, I have a terrible habit of saying exactly what's on my mind. Remember when Chad got highlights? We *all* thought he looked ridiculous, but I only held my tongue for, what? Thirty seconds before I asked him where the other New Kids on the Block were." I glance around wildly. "Let's just say it, people. I'm rude."

"You're not rude," Allie says. "You're just ... exceedingly honest."

"And honestly, what's on my mind when it comes to that man? Just pure, consuming hatred. There is *literally* no way I'll be able to hide my feelings."

"We *all* hate him," Tina says.

"But I hate him the *most*."

"You can't quantify hate," Chad says.

"I'm sure we can," I tell him. "Edward, see if you can find an app that quantifies hate."

"Stay still and look at the camera," Edward says.

"No way." I shake my head then start moving my head in big circles while I talk. "Now, let's pursue another method of determining who should go, like ... who's the best public speaker on the team or umm, maybe we go back to Chad, who's a master debater. A *master*, people. We can't overlook that."

"Oh," Tina says, pointing to an open page in the information package. "It says here that due to parts of the trek being through the Amazon rain forest, the delegate will have to be fully vaccinated for Hepatitis A and B, typhoid fever, and rabies."

"That means I'm out. I only have my hepatitis shots," Allie says with a grin that I am not too fond of at the moment.

"Who has had all of the shots listed?" Keenan asks.

I have, but for once in my life, I'm keeping my big mouth shut. Heads around the table shake while I stare down at my fingernails, hoping against all logic that he won't remember.

Keenan clears his throat. "Gwen, you went to Puerto Rico when you were in grad school to study at the Arecibo radio telescope, yes?"

Shit. He remembers. "Yes."

"And I assume you had all the vaccinations before you went?"

Fucking shitballs. "Uh-huh."

"It's decided then. Gwen is going."

———

Fox Family Chat

BEN

Gwen, Carla and I saw the video of Dick Napper. Did that actually happen or was that some crazy fake?

Sadly, it was very real. A huge loss for our foundation and the world, to be honest.

MOM

Dad and I were both sorry to hear about it.

Thanks, Mom.

CARLA

How are you doing with all of this? It's got to be a shock. I'm here if you need to talk.

Thank you, Carla. I appreciate it. It's definitely a shock, and I'm worried about what's going to happen to my job without him here as our champion, but I'm all right.

BEN

Don't be a hero, G. You should really talk to Carla.

CARLA

If not me, someone else who can help you process your feelings.

Don't worry, I will. Although, I won't have time for now. Dr. Napper asked for a representative from each team to attend his big send off, and I was chosen to go. In a couple of hours, I'll be heading to Peru for a week. I'll be in touch when I get back.

Okay, so I'm deliberately omitting the fact that I'm only going because of my vaccines in an effort to make it sound like I'm going because I have some special skills or talents that no one else on the team possesses. But if you knew my parents, you'd understand. They're highly competitive, overly critical, and are always keeping vigil for the next disappointing thing their daughter is going to do. Therefore, I have to take every opportunity I can to pump up my own tires.

As soon as I hit send, my mom's face lights up the screen. Crap. "Hello?"

"Gwendolyn, *Peru*?"

"Yes, he has some sort of adventure planned."

She makes a *tsk*ing sound, then says, "That man always did have a flair for the dramatic."

"I appreciated that about him. He really lived."

"Well, all that living just killed him. I hope it's nothing dangerous," she says in that dry voice of hers. She would never stoop to allowing herself to sound worried because she says worrying is the most useless way to spend time and energy. But her words get the message across. She's worried.

I think about the fact that no one with heart conditions or high blood pressure is allowed on the trip, then say, "Nope. He would've known that the kinds of extreme stuff he does wouldn't be safe for most people. I'm sure it'll be more of a sightseeing thing."

"What about your nervous bladder? Aren't you worried about holding people up?"

"Mom, it's not like I have to pee every five minutes. I'll be fine."

"I hope so. Disneyland was an absolute nightmare with you—rushing you off to the bathroom after every ride."

"I was eight and Disneyland is overstimulating."

"You were nine, and it didn't affect me like that when I was a child."

"Well, I'm not you, Mom."

"I'm aware of that, Gwendolyn. Now, what's going to happen to your job?" Her tone isn't that of a concerned mom, it's more … hopeful that her only daughter will finally switch to a respectable career.

"I don't know," I tell her. No sense in pretending I do. She already knows the Sterling half of the Dick Napper and Ty Sterling Foundation has been jonesing to shut us down for years. "At this point, I can only hope for the best."

"Sitting around hoping isn't going to get you anywhere. You need a plan."

"I won't be sitting around. I'm going to Peru where I'll have a meeting of the minds with Sterling."

"He's not the type of man to be talked into things." What she really means is she doesn't think *I* can talk him into it. I've long been considered to have the lowest intellect in the family, which isn't exactly a badge of honor in a clan whose family crest might as well be *We're smarter than you*. My choice of career definitely sealed my fate as 'not quite as bright as her big brother.'

"All I can do is give it my best shot," I answer, knowing how much she despises sports analogies. "And hope I don't strike out," I say, adding another sport to the mix just for funsies.

"Hmph, I suppose," she says, then her tone lifts. "I can probably get you a junior professor position here. Or I'm sure Ben can get you on at NASA"

"I don't want to work at NASA, Mom. I love what I do, and I honestly don't have time to debate it right now," I say before she can open up the discussion about the lack of merits of my career. We've been around and around this topic, only to have to agree to disagree every time.

"Fine, I understand, but let me just say this: It might not be the worst thing in the world if you move on to something else." She means something she can tell all the other profs about at the next faculty Christmas party. "Broaden your horizons, do work that will actually reach its crest during your lifetime."

"Or, it could be tomorrow," I tell her for the hundredth time.

"It won't be, Gwendolyn."

"Mom, I really don't have time for this."

"I just can't understand why you insist on—"

"Wasting my life, I know. I've heard it," I quip. "The crazy part is every time you say it, you expect me to change my mind even though past history should indicate that I won't."

"Are you suggesting I'm crazy?" she asks, her tone cool, even though I know she's miffed.

"Well, you know what Einstein said about insanity."

"Oh, nice, thank you, Gwen."

We've now reached the passive aggressive portion of our program.

"And thank you for your support, as always," I tell her. "Gotta go. I need to finish packing."

"Fine, we'll discuss this when you get back."

"I'd rather not."

"And yet, we will. Have a safe trip. I love you."

"I love you too."

I hang up and growl at the phone. "Narrow-minded and judgmental, that's what you are, Mother," I mutter as I open my sweater drawer. How come I couldn't have gotten a nice, supportive mom? The kind who bakes cookies and thinks the sun shines out of my fingertips?

———

ALLIE

How's the packing going?

Crappy. Just got off an irritating call with my mother.

ALLIE

Let me guess, she's already suggesting you jump spaceship?

Yup. Which is the last thing I need right
now. Not while I'm packing for every
possible climate. Do you know how many
there are in Peru? Beach, jungle, crazy high,
cold mountains. Plus, I need funeral
clothes. And we're only allowed one large
backpack. How, Allie? How?

ALLIE

Start by picking out what you're wearing on
the plane. That's one less outfit to go in
the bag.

Okay. Good idea. Cargo pants, a tee, and a
fleece.

ALLIE

Newp. You should dress up for the flight.

Why?

ALLIE

Because when you get to Lima, you'll be
making your first impression on Sterling.
And there's only one shot at that so you
better go professional. Wear whatever
you're bringing for the funeral.

Seriously? But I like to be comfortable
when I fly.

ALLIE

Sterling is a suit. You need to be a suit, too,
or he'll never respect you/give us the
money.

Okay, fine, but I won't like it. Also, now that
I'm swapping out my heels for my heavy
hiking boots, I have no idea how I'm going
to get this backpack closed.

ALLIE

I wish I could come over and help instead of being stuck in the lab with stupid Chad (who is TOTALLY pouting because you're going instead of him).

He was probably too upset to master debate last night.

ALLIE

Bahaha! Probably.

You know what's funny? Chad and I finally agree on something. He totally should be going instead of me.

ALLIE

No freaking way is that true.

It is. I'm going to mess this up so badly, Allie. I know you think I won't, but I will. And we are all going to be out of jobs. And I'm going to lose my house before I can even move in.

ALLIE

It's a lot of pressure, I know, but you've got this, Gwen. I know you do. You are the smartest person I know, and you can win an argument against anyone anytime on any topic. Forget Chad. You're the masterest of the master debaters. You know, in actual debates. Not the other thing…

Thanks, but that's actually my Achilles heel, not my greatest strength.

ALLIE

Not true.

Totally true. I have literally never been able
to stop the thoughts in my brain from
coming out of my mouth when I disagree
with someone. And I cannot think of anyone
I will disagree with more than Ty Sterling.
I'm going to wind up telling him exactly
what I think about him. We are all going to
end up out on our asses and it'll be all my
fault.

My phone rings. It's Allie. "Chad went on his coffee break, so I can chat a bit. Look, I know it's going to be hard for you, but you're so smart. Just constantly tell your sense of logic to override your need to be right."

I plunk myself on my bed, next to the pile of clothes I'm bringing. "I don't know how! Seriously! I am freaking out here, Allie. This is *way* too much pressure. Just think of Keenan. He's in his late-seventies. If we get shut down, who's going to hire him at his age? He'll be done, and SETI is his life."

"You can't think about that. Instead, you have to focus on how to get the job done."

"Which I have no clue how to do. How am I supposed to convince Ty Sterling, human gargoyle, who's been gunning for us for the last nine years, that he should fork over another hundred million dollars?"

Allie lowers her voice a little. "Okay, I've been giving this a lot of thought. The two quickest ways to a man's heart are through his stomach and his pants. And since I doubt the opportunity to whip up a gourmet meal is going to present itself…"

After a full body shudder, I say, "Gross. Yuck. NEVER EVER EVER. Next idea."

"I'd do him. He might be a narrow-minded asshole, but he's got that whole McDreamy vibe going on. Besides,

I don't mean you should *actually* sleep with him. Just make him think it's a possibility."

"You just set feminism back by fifty years."

Allie sighs. "Well, desperate times call for desperate measures."

"Like prostituting myself?"

"No, just make him *think* you're willing to prostitute yourself."

The truth is—and I would *never* say this out loud—Ty Sterling is undeniably hot. He absolutely looks like McDreamy from season eight of Grey's Anatomy. And if I thought I had *any* chance at seducing him to save our jobs, I'm not even ashamed to admit I would consider it. Does that make me a bad feminist? 100% yes, but then maybe I'd rather be a bad feminist with a job and a house than a good one who's homeless and broke. But, just no. No. Way. Never. A wave of desperation hits me again for the thousandth time today. "There's got to be some other way. Let's think."

Allie clicks her tongue a few times, which is her thinking sound. "All right, so this is a definite opportunity. You're going to have access to the guy day and night for almost a week. Actual in-person, face-to-face time, which is so much better than if we were just trying to set up a meeting with him."

"Right. Okay, that's good. An opportunity. That feels better," I say, getting up and opening my underwear drawer. I pick out three pairs of seamless grannies, two boyfriend shorts, and, after a moment's hesitation, one thong.

"Mind you, the competition is going to be fierce. There will probably be dozens of other people there all vying for his time. And you know those Yeti quacks are going to send some hottie with totally toned legs from all that hiking in the woods."

Side note: we hate the Yeti team the most on account of their name sounding almost exactly like ours. We're the SETI Research Institute, and, in an attempt to give themselves some street cred, they named themselves the Yeti Research Institute, which is an insult to both research and institutes everywhere.

"True, I bet they send Miss Canada."

Karen Taylor, the face of the Yeti team, is a former Miss Canada, so not only is she beautiful, she's also annoyingly congenial, hailing from the nicest country in the world. I want to hate her, but there is literally no way to do so because she's just the sweetest, most sincere person on the planet.

"Allie, I can't compete with that," I say, tossing the thong back in the drawer and grabbing another pair of grannies. I shake my head at myself. "Not that I want to compete in that way. But, you know, trying to get his attention long enough to convince him."

"Oh, I know!" she says, sounding excited. "Maybe your first job should be to try to reduce the competition."

"Oooh! Good. This feels good. A plan is forming. How would I do that?"

"I have no idea," she says.

"Butts."

"But maybe it'll become obvious once you're there."

"It better or we're all screwed."

"You can't think like that," Allie says. "If you do, you'll beat yourself before you even get there. Now I know there are a lot of things that are not within your control in this situation ... lots of competition, some of whom will be quite possibly much hotter and more willing to do stuff you clearly aren't, projects that he actually believes in, people who aren't as likely to offend him, not to mention that some of those people are going to be a lot better at the outdoorsy stuff than you because that's really not your forte either."

"Are you going somewhere with this? Because so far, I do not feel better."

"Yes, bear with me," Allie says. "You know how, on *The Bachelorette*, the guy who wins isn't necessarily the hottest guy or the smartest guy or even the nicest guy?"

"Like Roberto in season six?"

"Yep. The winners are always the ones who don't think about the other bachelors. They play their own game. They draw on their own strengths. They have confidence that they can do it, and it's really that confidence that convinces the bachelorette to choose him. It's like it somehow rubs off on her like a Jedi mind trick."

"You want me to Jedi mind trick him?" I roll a pair of my grannies into a tight roll. "These aren't the projects you're looking for."

"Okay, make fun of me if you want, but I'm right about this. Confidence is key. If you go in there believing that you're going to get that money—better yet, that he *wants* you to convince him—you're going to make him do it."

"Yeah, I think this is why you're a radio astronomer, not a business mogul."

Allie lets out a little grunt. "You are the best person to be going on this trip. Out of the whole team you have what none of the rest of us do."

"Yeah, the necessary vaccinations."

"No, *passion*. No one believes in SETI as much as you."

"Sure, but I'm passionate about something that he thinks is a joke."

"No, Gwen, you're passionate about something he just

doesn't understand yet. But you're going to *make* him understand. You'll use logic, reason, and every ounce of faith that you have to prove that what we're doing is real and important. You'll talk to him about the legacy that he could leave behind as the person who allowed one of the greatest advancements in human history to happen. And for the first time in his life, Ty Sterling is going to have to admit he was wrong about something. He's going to give us the money, and it's going to be because *you* convinced him to do it."

I allow a surge of hope to flow through me. "Do you really think it could be that simple?"

"It has to be. Because if it isn't, we're all screwed."

5

Heavy is the Head That Wears the Crown...

Ty

To-Do List:

- Emergency Board Meeting (Goal: Reassure board everything is fine/try not to offend anyone)
- Emergency Shareholders Zoom Call (Goal: Reassure shareholders everything is fine/try not to offend anyone)
- Pack for trip to Peru (Michael is doing this for me—thank God!)
- Call Muffy (see if a quick stop in Dallas is necessary)

"Muffy, I'm so glad I caught you," I say as soon as she answers my call. I'm not lying—I am glad I caught her, but not for the reason she thinks. She thinks I enjoy spending time with her when really I just need to make sure she knows the deal is still on even though Richard is gone.

The truth is, Muffy Bowles-Tillington is one of the worst humans I've ever met. She's one of those ultra-phony people who only save their smile for people they deem worthy (i.e. the rich and powerful). She can't be bothered to be civil to anyone she considers 'low class.' Trust me, I've been to multiple restaurants with her. She was so rude to the staff, *I* wanted to spit in her food. The irony of it all was that her husband, the late Turner Tillington the Third (who hailed from an old oil family), met Muffy when she was working at a bikini car wash back in 1968. That was her first and only job, other than 'lookin' pretty and being a trophy wife.' But since she's the only thing standing between me and my dream, I have to play nice and pretend she's my people, which is extremely problematic for me because I loathe phoniness with every fiber of my being. Just not as much as I loathe my father. That loathing is why I've managed to successfully pull this whole thing off.

"Oh, Ty, my dear, sweet boy," she drawls. "I heard about Dick, may God rest his soul. How are you holding up?"

"It's tough, but I always knew there was a chance this could happen. There was a reason he couldn't get life insurance."

"Yes, I suppose so," Muffy says. "How was your trip home?"

"Fine." Until I got off the plane. "Listen, I'm not sure if you heard that Richard has a rather... *involved* funeral planned, and I'm afraid I've got to leave for Peru in a couple of hours. Apparently, he's sending us all on some sort of five-day adventure as his final hurrah."

"He was a strange little man, bless his heart."

"Er, yeah. There was certainly nothing conventional about Richard. Anyway, I wanted to touch base and reassure you that nothing has changed as far as my plans for the team go."

"Oh, did Dick sign off before he…?"

"No, but it's really not a problem. Just some paperwork on my end and we'll be good to go," I answer, hating myself for lying. "Obviously with the trip and shifting things around with the corporate structure, we'll be delayed a bit, but hopefully not more than two weeks."

"Hmmm." She sucks her teeth, then says, "Well, that's not at all convenient. The Ortegas are selling their superyacht and I really don't think they'll want to wait that long to sell it."

Perfect. I know where this is going. "Oh, is that so?"

"Uh-huh. It's the only one I've found with furnishings and lighting that make the most of my complexion," Muffy says. "Honestly, I look a good twenty years younger on it. You should just see me."

I rub the bridge of my nose and put on a flirty tone that makes me want to flog myself at dawn. "How is it even possible for someone to look any younger than you do? I thought you were Turner's granddaughter when I first met you."

She laughs, sounding positively giddy. "I remember. Now, about that yacht I've got my heart set on."

"Why don't I see what I can do?" I ask, writing 'Superyacht' at the top of my already insane to-do list.

"Are you sure, shug?" she says. "I know you've probably got a whole plate load of things to deal with right now."

Yes, Muffy, I do. I'm absolutely buried at the moment. "It would be my pleasure to make this happen for you," I tell her. "I'll put in a call and see if I can't convince them to wait until our deal goes through."

"I don't know, I really was hoping to go out on it next week with my girlfriends. We're all celebrating our fiftieth birthdays again," she says with a laugh.

Closing my eyes for a second, I hold in the heavy sigh that's brewing. "Right, well, okay. Why don't *I* buy the yacht and we'll call it a down payment on the team?"

"Oh, I like that idea a whole lot," Muffy drawls. "It'll feel like I'm getting a great, big, shiny present from a handsome man."

"Perfect." Actually, not perfect at all. Huge pain in my ass. "I'll get back to you as soon as the deal is done. And in the meantime, if you don't mind keeping this whole thing just between the two of us, that would mean the world to me."

"Oh, of course, Ty. Mum's the word. I know how important it is to you to surprise your daddy."

"Exactly. Thank you." Surprising the old bastard is a key element of my plan. Hopefully it'll be a big enough of a surprise to kill him.

***

"Is everyone here?" I ask Donna as soon as I step off the elevator.

"You have enough for a quorum. Everyone's here except Mr. Dumphey, who is at some sort of silent retreat in India."

"Poor India," I mutter. "And they all understand that I need to be out of there by ten, so there won't be any time for chitchat or long tangents?"

Donna hands me the agenda for the emergency board meeting as we walk swiftly to my office. "I have explained that the voting must happen in time for the shareholders meeting or they're all going to stand to lose millions by lunch time."

"That ought to do it," I tell her with a grin.

"It would work on me," she answers. "Did you get any sleep?"

"Three hours. It was glorious," I tell her. I worked last night until nearly two a.m., along with several members of our legal department. Even though we had a contingency plan in place in case either Richard or myself left the building, there is still a surprising amount of scrambling that has to be done. Our Chief Science Officer, Dr. Anika Gupta (double PhD in Genetics and Medicine), will slide over into a dual role as CSO and interim COO (replacing Richard). Since she's already taken on a lot of his work over the last few years, it'll basically just be a massive pay bump for her.

With any luck, the board will approve everything in the next twenty minutes, which would be just in time for the shareholders meeting. This all has to happen at lightning speed or the shareholders will get nervous, and that's the last thing we want. Nervous shareholders equal mass sell-offs equal my personal fortune being cut, possibly in half (or worse). I don't even want to think about that, and I really don't have to, because I won't allow that to happen. To say I'm tired would be a gross understatement. But such is life. You can't expect to run a billion-dollar corporation and have lots of 'me time.' That's not a thing. No matter what billionaires in romance books are doing these days. "And you? Did your head even hit the pillow?"

"I got in a solid twenty."

"Minutes?"

"Yup."

"Ouch. Please make sure I buy you something extra terrific for Christmas this year."

"A Tesla X ought to cover it."

"Is that all?" I ask as we round the corner.

Giving me a wry smile, she says, "Should I have gone for a Gulfstream?"

"For one night of lost sleep? That might be pushing it."

"That's why I went with a Tesla."

"Smart. We should be promoting *you* to COO."

"I wouldn't say no."

She opens the outer door to my office, where her desk sits, and I drop my briefcase on it. Her assistant, Willow, hands me a freshly brewed espresso and I suck it back in one gulp. "Thank you, Willow. Make one for Donna while you're at it."

Willow's eyes grow wide. "Another one?" she asks Donna.

"He's just joking," she says. "Listen, I've been thinking about this trip to Peru. What if you just meet them there in a day or two? The timing couldn't be worse to have you go A.W.O.L. Besides, it's going to be god-awful. You stuck out in the jungle surrounded by who knows how many people with their hands out for cash."

My gut tightens. She's right. This is literally the worst day possible for me to disappear into the jungle or up a mountain where there is likely no cell reception. And almost everyone on this trip will definitely be trying to 'get on my good side' in an effort to change my mind about the foundation. It'll be my job to steer them in the right direc-tion—directly at Richard's nephew, Skip, because there's no way I'm going to hand over another ten years' worth of funding for projects I consider absolutely useless. I mean, come on, telekinesis? I don't know what Richard was thinking.

But I can't be a no-show for the trip, no matter how badly I want to right now. Shaking my head, I say, "I owe it to Richard to be there."

Donna nods. "Yeah, I suppose it would also look bad if you didn't go."

"Honestly, I couldn't care less about what it looks like. Richard and I were partners. He's asked for one last thing and I'm going to do it. Speaking of which, did Rohan give you any idea as to what's in store for me?"

"Not even the smallest hint," Donna says. "But he did say that the attendance would have been heartbreakingly low for Dr. Napper. He wanted a little over two-hundred people, but apparently he didn't take into account the fact that the majority of people wouldn't have the proper travel vaccines."

"How many are coming?"

"Apparently, it'll be under thirty. Rohan is gutted."

As bad as I feel for Richard, this is very good news for me. It'll be awful enough being chased around by a couple dozen of these wackos while I smack mosquitoes in the discomforts of the Amazon jungle, or try to think straight at the oxygen-depleted altitude of Machu Pichu. Two hundred would've been unbearable. "I'll talk to Rohan. We should plan a memorial for him here when we get back. Something ridiculously big. Over-the-top. Star-studded."

She gives me a dirty look from the top rim of her glasses. "Sounds like a Gulfstream-sized amount of work for me."

I shake my head. "Find a planner and we'll let Rohan be the point person on it. It'll give him something to do when we get back."

Donna nods, then taps her watch. "Go give 'em hell at that board meeting. You've got eighteen minutes until the shareholders call."

"Will do," I say, saluting her, then turning to leave. I call over my shoulder, "We're just joking about the Tesla, right?"

"Of course we are."

"And you won't hate me for it?"

"Only a little," Donna says. "Besides, I'm planning to sleep for twenty-four hours straight as soon as I get you on the plane. But don't tell my boss. He's a bit of an asshole."

I snort out a laugh and head down the hall to the board room, calling over my shoulder, "That he is."

I turn back. "Oh, I almost forgot two things—I need a dossier on everyone who will be on the trip so I can read it on the plane."

"Security's already on it," Donna says. "Second thing?"

"I need you to get in touch with the Ortegas and buy their superyacht, then have it sent to wherever Muffy wants to ship out from next week."

"She gets a yacht and I don't even get a car?" Donna asks.

"Yes, but trust me, it's not because I love her more. It's a down-payment on the team. Apparently it flatters her pasty complexion and she was planning to buy it as soon as our deal went through, only now we're delayed and … and it's a whole thing," I say. "Just make it happen, okay?"

She salutes me. "One superyacht, coming up."

"Oh, Richard, you weird, weird man," I mutter, glad that I've got the entire cabin of the jet to myself so no one can hear me.

My flight to Lima will land soon, and I'm planning to stay on-board until the very last possible second to soak in the silence before embarking on a five-day fresh hell of Richard's choosing. I'll be thrown in with an odd mix of corporate suck-ups and representatives of quite possibly the worst ways to waste money known to man. Richard was big on searches for things no one will ever find—the Search for Intelligent Extra-Terrestrial Life (too far away, even if they do exist), Big Foot (imaginary), the Lost City of Atlantis (spoiler alert: it was never there to begin with), and ghosts (again, not real).

I absolutely hate the fact that I have no idea what we'll be doing or where we'll be going for the next five days. What I do know is we're not going to spend it sight-seeing and eating at Michelin-star restaurants in Lima. That wasn't Richard's style. Whatever this is, it's likely going to be borderline dangerous and will most certainly involve posthumously inflating his sizable ego.

This is going to suck hard. And not only that, but it really does come at the worst possible moment of my life. Just when I'm about to grab the brass ring for which I've been reaching. Just as things between Muffy and I are at our most delicate—right before the sale. Donna's still working on the yacht. Apparently the Ortegas are harder to reach than I thought. The clock is ticking fast on closing the deal, and every minute that I'm out of reach is sixty seconds too long. I need to be present, on it, and available to Muffy around the clock in case she gets cold feet, which is an absolute possibility. Not only that, but I really should be there for our first week with a new Chief Operating Officer. Anita's got it handled, but it's all about the public perception. The media is going to be sniffing around for signs of trouble. Any whiff of a lack of confidence in the leadership, and our stocks will tank like a lead ball tossed from the Empire State Building—fast and hard—which is why I've spent the entire flight studying for the trip. I need to be a leader out there, in case people post parts of our 'adventure' on social media. I've been reading about the climate, dangers, sights, and culture. I've also been studying the people with whom I'll be traveling so I can figure out who to avoid.

I close the dossier I've been reading on one Karen Taylor, Cryptozoologist of the Yeti Research Institute with offices in British Columbia, California, and Bhutan. Karen hails from Canada and, when she's not out hunting Big Foot, she loves to knit. She also collects cocktail napkins.

But more important than what I've learned about Karen (who sits firmly in a pile I'm making of 'people to avoid'), I've noticed a pattern. Almost every team in the foundation has elected to send a woman, generally attractive, and on the younger side. So far, only one project is sending their actual director—Niles Thompson, of the Paranormal Investigation Team (or Ghost Hunters R Us, as I like to call them). If I had to guess, I'd say the only reason they aren't sending a young, good-looking woman, is because the team doesn't have one. All dudes, just like the original Ghostbusters. I bet they're kicking themselves for not letting a girl play, because if they're anything like the rest of these quacks that we've been funding, they're also assuming that I'll be more likely to say yes to a woman if I want to sleep with her.

Frankly, it's insulting. First off, you don't get where I am in life by letting your johnson do your thinking. I'm a little smarter than to get drawn in by a pretty face and fork over a few hundred million in a moment of post-coital bliss. Second, it's not like I'm desperate for love or something. I'm not sure if you know this about billionaires, but we have a pretty easy time finding women. Even the ancient ugly ones (billionaires, not women). I definitely don't need to be set up because if I wanted a wife, I'd have one. I know that sounds cocky, but it's just reality. I'm rich, I'm in my prime, I keep myself in great shape, and I'm not awful to look at (according to Michael). And if I did want a wife (which I don't and never will), it certainly won't be some pretty idiot who believes she can bend spoons with her mind (Savannah Stevens, parapsychologist who specializes in telekinesis).

And it one-hundred-percent won't be this next woman, Gwendolyn Fox from the SETI team. I open her file and stare at her picture for a moment. Okay, I do have to admit that the SETI people have done the best job of selecting someone attractive. Big, pouty lips, bright green eyes, dark brown hair that falls below her shoulders and has a bouncy look to it. "Too bad she's a gullible weirdo."

"What's that, sir?" Josh, my flight attendant (and master at sneaking up on people) says.

I jump a little. "No, nothing, Josh. Just talking to myself."

He leans over my shoulder and stares at the page. "Ooh, she's pretty. Look at those full lips. I think you should give her a chance, even if she is a gullible weirdo. After all, there are worse things than being gullible. Or weird, for that matter."

"These aren't dating profiles."

"Oh, well, that's good because this woman clearly hates you."

"What?"

He points to a paragraph near the bottom of the page.

Use extreme caution around Ms. Fox. She is not a friendly. Defaces and posts photos of you onto a dartboard in staff lunch room for team to throw darts at you. Each week, she provides new photos. This week's had the word "ASS-HOLE" written across your forehead.

What the…? Seriously?

"It's lonely at the top, isn't it, sir?" Josh asks, patting me gingerly on the shoulder.

I shut the folder and look up at him. "It's got its perks too. Speaking of perks, I could use another coffee."

"Certainly," he says with a nod that verges on a sarcastic bow. I never know with Josh. He might absolutely despise me or he might be my biggest fan.

As soon as he walks away, I reopen Ms. Fox's folder.

Gwendolyn Fox

Age: 36

Place of Birth: Pittsburgh

Siblings: Benjamin, age 39

Parents: Dr. Jeff Fox (Director of Product Development at Draper Labs Inc.) and Dr. Stephanie Tatum-Fox (Professor of Condensed Matter Physics at M.I.T.)

Education: Completed high school in two years and graduated from St. Mary's Girls Academy with a 4.0 average. 1570 on SAT. Received double doctorate from M.I.T. in Aeronautics and Astronautics/Statistics.

Work Experience: Hired directly out of university, Ms. Fox has worked as a SETI Researcher at the Dick Napper and Ty Sterling Foundation in Mountainview, California, since the program's inception.

Personal Information: Relationship status—single. No evidence of significant past relationship found.

Hobbies/Activities: All staff-related, including: Karaoke night on the last Friday of every month and Wednesday night bowling. Her go-to song is "You're So Vain" by Carly Simon (which she dedicates to you). Her average bowling score is 65.

Financial: Just put in an offer on her first home, a 3-bedroom, 2-bath, 1965 bungalow in Pacheco for $639,499 (with a down payment of $87,000). Owns a Kia Soul outright. No other debts.

I stare at her picture for another second before I put her folder with the rest of the 'to avoids.'

"Here's your coffee. The captain wanted me to let you know we're landing in fifteen minutes."

"Perfect. Thank you." I have a sip, then pick up the last folder: Skip Napper, Richard's horrible nephew. I open the folder and am faced with Skip's shit-eating grin. There is no family resemblance between Richard and his brother's child, unless you count narcissism.

Skip Napper

Age: 26

Place of Birth: San Francisco

Siblings: None

Parents: Wanda Prince-Napper and Peter Napper (both deceased)

Education: Completed one year of philosophy at NYU before being kicked out for poor grades and selling prescription drugs to fraternity brothers.

Work Experience: Several failed start-up attempts including: Amazon affiliate, a MLM selling manscaping equipment/oils, and his own cryptocurrency (Napper Bucks).

Personal Information: Single, although it appears as though his ex-girlfriend (out-of-work actress, Jerri Pete) has come back into his life as recently as yesterday.

Hobbies/Activities: Avid Formula One fan (and amateur racer), avid mixed martial arts fan (and amateur fighter), and attends several beer festivals around the globe each year.

Financial: Lives off trust fund Dr. Napper set up for him and is rumored to inherit the bulk of his estate.

As badly as I want to stick Skip in my 'to avoid' pile, he's really the only person on the trip that I need. By the time we're on our flights back to the US, he must have agreed to slide a cool half billion out of his inheritance to keep the foundation going. It's either that, or I shut the entire thing down and all my 'to avoid' people turn into unemployed people. And that is not the goal. I only want to hurt one person—Patrick Sterling. But if other people get caught in the crossfire, I suppose that's something I'll have to learn to live with.

The plane starts its descent and knots form in my gut. This trip is going to suck *so* hard. I'll be stuck with twenty-eight people who desperately want something from me I can't give them, and one lazy, selfish person who's about as likely to honor his uncle's wishes as I am to bend this spoon with my mind.

I sit back in my leather chair and let out a heavy sigh, then give myself a mental pep talk. *Okay, Ty, you've made it this far. You're so close to getting your revenge, you can almost smell those sweaty football players. All you have to do is get through the next few days, buy one little superyacht, convince Skip to fork over half a billion dollars … oh, and survive whatever the fuck Richard has in store for us.*

If only I could get the 'to avoids' to leave me alone.

A smile crosses my lips. I *can* get them to leave me alone. All I have to do make sure they understand Skip is their only hope, not me.

6

Never Check Your Bags. And
I Mean Never, Ever…

Gwen

"What do you mean, it's lost?" I ask the flight attendant. "When you asked for volunteers to stow their bags under the plane, you told me that it would be waiting right here when I got off the flight." I stare down at the empty gate floor again. "It must be there. In that special compartment where you said it would be safe and sound."

She shakes her head. "I guess not. The guys checked and your bag is not there."

"But you said—"

"It's not there," she tells me with an icy look that says 'back off, bitch.' "The only thing you can do now is go to the lost luggage counter and give them the information about where you're going to be so they can get it to you when it arrives."

"I don't—!" I stop myself and lower my voice. "I don't know where I'm going to be because I haven't been given an itinerary. I'll be on a tour but the destinations are going to be a surprise."

"Well, that's not going to help you at all," she says.

Yeah, kind of like you… I swallow my words, then manage to replace them with, "Where's the lost luggage counter?"

"It's downstairs, to the left."

"Thank you." *For exactly nothing.*

In Lima. Backpack has been lost. Waiting in line-up at luggage claim counter with crying baby in front of me. I'm completely panicking. I have to be at the meeting point in ten minutes, and according to Google maps, it's a six-minute walk from here. So far, Peru and I aren't exactly tight.

ALLIE

Oh no! That sounds awful.

Can I come home now?

ALLIE

I wish. Hang in there.

I'm trying.

Oh God, that baby is loud. Poor thing. She's so tiny. And her parents clearly have no clue what to do for her. Her mom just keeps patting her back and shushing. Totally useless. The mom turns a little and looks back at me. "Sorry. I think she has gas."

I offer her a smile. "That's okay."

"The truth is, I feel like crying. I'm so exhausted. My husband wanted to come on this trip. I knew it would be too hard. And the airline lost our stroller."

"They lost my backpack too," I tell her.

She gets back to bouncing and shushing the baby, which I know won't fix the problem, based on my TikTok-knowledge of how to get babies to stop crying. I should help her. It would actually be doing a favor for everyone in the vicinity. I tap the woman on the shoulder. "Can I try? I have a great hack that ought to do the trick."

"Really?" she asks.

Nodding, I gently take the baby from her, hold her little bottom with one hand, then wrap her tiny arms together, carefully turn her so she's leaning forward and start to bounce her gently in midair. The baby stops crying immediately and her mom gasps. "It worked!"

Offering her a knowing smile, I say, "Works every time." I think. According to that pediatrician on that video anyway. Really, parenting is probably a lot easier than most people make it. You just have to do your research, people.

I turn the baby so she's facing me and hold her up above me. "See? That's better, isn't it?"

The baby looks down at me.

And pukes right in my hair.

The man behind the counter shouts, "Next!"

———

I arrive at the meeting point ten minutes late, drenched in sweat and reeking of what I'm pretending is spoiled formula, because being covered in spoiled stranger's breast milk is a little more than I can handle right now. I also feel like I have to pee really, really badly, only I'm sure it's just nerves on account of the situation. But there's no time for that. We're right outside the airport, where the shuttle buses pick people up. I frantically search the sidewalk for my group, then let out a huge sigh of relief when I see a massive sign with a picture of Dr. Napper's face on it. It reads: The Dick Napper Farewell Tour.

Dammit. I never should've let Allie talk me into looking professional. I'm the only one in a stupid skirt suit and heels while everyone else looks like they stepped out of an

Eddie Bauer catalog. Except Ty Sterling, who I spot immediately. He looks like he stepped off the cover of GQ, if GQ were featuring asshole billionaires who also look rugged and sporty. He's surrounded by a group of women, who all seem to be vying for his attention. He's smiling smugly, of course, and I'm sure he's just loving the attention as they all stroke his giant ego. The thought of stroking his giant anything makes me feel physically ill. Well, sort of. Not really.

Before I can stop gawking at him, he glances in my direction, his eyes stopping as he stares straight at me for a second. A look of recognition crosses his face but that's impossible. He doesn't have the first clue who I am. Now he's scowling a little, which I assume is what he does whenever he sees someone new, because again, he can't possibly know who I am. He's still staring. And I can't seem to tear my eyes away even though I most definitely should.

Is it hot out here? Is my heart pounding extra hard? Wait. Am I ... *attracted* to the worst human to ever live?

I hold two fingers up to my neck to take my pulse, then remember that of course I'm hot and my heart is pounding. I've run more in the last five minutes than I have in the last five years combined. Which means, I haven't inexplicably gone completely and utterly insane. Phew!

Okay, back to the problem at hand. I need clothes, hiking boots, a toothbrush, and a whole bunch of other shit so I can go on this trip. Glancing around, I see a man who I'm pretty sure is our guide based on the fact that he's standing next to the shuttle bus door holding a clipboard. He's wearing a golf shirt, cargo pants, and a name tag that says, *'I'm your Tour Guide, Thiago. How can I help?'*

Oh, thank God. Someone who wants to help. Things are looking up already.

His smile fades as soon as I'm close enough to smell. "You must be Gwendolyn Fox," he says. "Our straggler."

Straggler? That makes it sound like I've been just moseying around the airport chatting people up. I pant and nod at him. "The airline lost my backpack and a baby threw up on me and I had to run all the way here," I say, holding my side to soothe the horrible stitch in it.

"Why would you check your bag? They always lose checked bags."

I narrow my eyes at him. Obviously, I'm smart enough to know you don't check your bag if you don't have to. "I didn't check it." Pant, pant. "They ran out of room in the overhead bins and asked for volunteers to put their bags under the plane." Pant. "Anyway, it's lost and I only have this … outfit, and it's covered in baby vomit so I need some time to go buy some clothes and hiking shoes and toiletries."

He shakes his head. "No time. We must leave now so we can do the first activity before dark."

"But I'm—"

He holds up one hand. "There are stores where we're going. You can shop there." Lifting a whistle to his lips, he blows it so loudly, my eyes are vibrating. "Everyone! Our straggler is here. Get on the shuttle bus."

"Wait, where are we—?"

"No clues. Dr. Napper wanted all surprises to be *surprises*, which means you won't know where we are going until we get there. Now, hurry up because we need to get to the other airport where the helicopters are waiting." He balls up his fist and shakes his head, looking annoyed with himself. "Stupid, Thiago. You weren't supposed to say that."

I hurry onto the bus and make my way to the back, hoping that whoever gets stuck next to me has no sense of smell. Settling myself onto a seat by the window, I watch as everyone gets on and selects their seats, a lot of them seeming chummy already. A couple of other participants come close to sitting next to me, then wince and move to other spots on the bus. I can't blame them though. I am *ripe*.

Mr. Sterling gets on and immediately several hands go up and I hear offers for him to, "Come sit here."

Let the sucking up begin. It's just all so disgusting. And the worst part is I'm going to have to do it too. I picture myself motioning at him with my finger. *Come sit by me, you big, strong, hot piece of man candy.* Blech! No! Never.

Not right now, anyway. I'm not going to be winning any points with him smelling like I do. Lucky for me (and him, I suppose), he chooses a seat halfway down the aisle with an empty seat next to him. The disappointment in the air is palpable. As is the desperation. But I'm hardly one to judge—I'm every bit as desperate as these other people. Women. I'm desperate as all these other women. Now that I look around, there are only a handful of men—Thiago, the devil, Niles Something-or-other from the ghost busters group, and Rohan, Dr. Napper's faithful assistant who appears in lots of his videos. Allie was right. All the groups did exactly the same thing. Sent hotties. Not that I'm a hottie. I'm not unattractive, you know, for a science geek. But if this whole thing did come down to the power of seduction, I'd definitely lose to most of these women. First of all, I don't want to seduce him, which I imagine will be fairly obvious to him. Second, it's not like I'm exactly experienced in successfully hitting on guys. I've had exactly three boyfriends—one in college and two since. In all three cases, *they* were the ones who asked *me* out.

The bus starts up and I sit back in my seat listening in to various conversations, tuning my ears into different ones as we embark on our journey. Shameless flirting with Mr. Sterling by a woman across the aisle from him. I recognize her to be part of the 'parapsychology' team (which is totally not a real field of study no matter what they want everyone to think). He has already completely tuned her out and is staring intently at his phone. Rude. I can totally understand why, but still—because it's him, rude.

Thiago's voice comes over the audio system. "Good afternoon, everyone. Who's feeling good?"

A spattering of low murmurs can be heard around the bus.

"Okay, I get it," he says. "You are sad because the world has lost a great man. I am also sad, even though I didn't know him. But I'm an empath so I feel your pain. You wish you could still touch him and hug him and hear his voice and see his smile." He pauses, then says, "The good news is, Dr. Napper will be with us for the entire adventure."

He holds up an ornate gold urn.

"Sweet Jesus," Mr. Sterling mutters.

"He's not only in here, but he has also recorded videos for us. So, even though we can't hug him or touch him or smell him, we can see him and hear him."

My jaw drops as my brain begins to process what Thiago is saying.

"We'll watch the first video after we get to today's location. Dr. Napper didn't want you to miss the sights of this vibrant and beautiful city," Thiago says. "So, make yourselves comfortable and try to relax a little because you're about to embark on the adventure of a lifetime."

I stare out the window for a minute, watching the buildings whip by, listening to the conversation happening in front of me. One row up, three women are talking in low voices. "Do you have all of them?" one asks.

"No. Just the hepatitis. But what are the chances we're even going to come into contact with some of those other diseases?"

"I don't know. I'm hoping there will be zero chance."

"Like, who even gets rubella anymore anyway? Have you ever heard of anyone who got it?"

And I think I just found a way to get rid of some of my competition…

The Anti-Santa Claus...

Ty

OKAY, it's only been forty-five minutes since I got off the plane, and I'm already regretting having decided to come. Not just because of the company I'm surrounded by (who are all every bit as phony as I expected). To be honest, I've rarely met such efficient gold diggers, and yes, I know I'm not using that phrase in the traditional sense, but digging for gold, they are. I've already been invited back to one woman's yurt anytime (Savannah Stevens, who would like to 'show me how she can make anything rise, just with her mind'). She's either making the offer on behalf of her team, or she's looking to land a billionaire for herself. And she's about to be wildly disappointed. There are a few high-level managers I recognize—none of whom I'd ever actually choose to have a beer with, let alone travel with for days on end.

Notably absent is Skip Napper, Richard's awful nephew who is set to inherit his fortune. Apparently, the bum couldn't be bothered to show up to honor the uncle he's been sponging off his entire life. According to Rohan, Skip might join us later, but at the moment he's grieving on his own in Las Vegas. You know, because that's a natural place to go when you're despondent. So, the one person I actually need to be here isn't here and I'm stuck with a bunch of Savannah Stevens-types and one ghost buster. Oh, and this is just perfect—another young woman from my 'to avoid' list is smiling at me. She glances away coyly, and back at me again. Karen Taylor, the Canadian cryptozoologist in search of Big Foot. Well, you won't find him here, Karen, so take a hike.

Blech, at the back is Gwendolyn Fox. Defacer of photographs, hater of all things logical and despiser of me. Why is she dressed like that? In a suit and heels? She clearly doesn't know the first thing about the man we're all supposedly grieving if she didn't realize she needed hiking clothes.

Too bad she's cute. People should look exactly like they act. If that were the case, she'd look like the bridge troll she is—with a wart-covered face, a hunchback, and … I don't know, scraggly hair or jet-black teeth. Whatever, you get the point. She wouldn't be able to fool the gullible people of the world into thinking she's got any human decency whatsoever. But I'm sure she can't fool them long since she's so awful. That's probably what's got her so desperate to find E.T.—everyone on *this* planet already hates her.

But it's not the people who are (or aren't) here that are making me regret coming. I already knew what would happen when I got here. What I *didn't* know was what might be happening back home. Or more accurately, in Texas.

I just got a text from Donna that requires me to be state-side putting out a small fire with a high potential to become a raging inferno any second.

DONNA

> Mrs. Tillington called me to see if I can find you. Apparently the Ortegas are entertaining other offers on the yacht, and it got her thinking that if they can get a higher offer on the yacht, maybe she can get a higher offer on the team from someone else?

At five billion, I'm already at the top of the top end of my budget. I need to get this deal done now for the price we agreed on. The last thing I need is for her to go public with the fact that the team is up for sale. So far, she's been touched by my whole 'I'm buying the team for my dad' thing. If word gets out, it'll lead to a bidding war, and there's no way I can or will go higher. But I can't leave, because … Richard.

Hmm … what if the trip were canceled entirely? That would mean I could leave without all the guilt of having flaked out on my business partner's last request.

So, new goal for me—somehow put an end to this trip (without actually being responsible for it) so I can fly straight to Dallas. But first, I need to talk to Donna.

The bus pulls through the gates of a small airport where I see a line of five helicopters ready to go. As soon as I'm on the tarmac, I walk away from the rest of the group and call her. Donna picks up on the first ring. "Took you long enough."

"Is she actively seeking other buyers or just trying to get me to negotiate against myself?"

"Hard to say. You probably want to treat it like there's another fox circling the hen house."

I turn and look behind me, only to see a fox—but in this case it's a Ms. Fox of the SETI group watching me.

She quickly turns away, her cheeks slightly pink. Hmm, those pink cheeks don't exactly say she hates me.

Seriously, Ty? You're thinking about a woman right now when the deal of a lifetime is about to go up in smoke? "Okay, I'm not proud of what I'm about to tell you to do."

"Great," Donna says sarcastically.

"I want a security detail on her. Make it subtle, but I want intel on who comes and goes from her house, who she sees when she goes out, and if possible, phone records," I say, hating myself for what I'm doing. "And buy her the biggest bouquet of flowers in Texas. Or better yet, a puppy. Something white and fluffy."

"I'm on it."

"In the meantime, I might have a way to get back to the US, by tomorrow morning if at all possible."

"What about Dr. Napper's last wishes?"

"We can't have a farewell trip if I'm the only one left to take it."

"Oh, Ty, no," Donna says. She only calls me Ty when she's especially shocked by something I'm about to do.

"I don't have a choice. Besides, other than Rohan, none of these people give a shit about Richard. They're all here for one reason only."

Thiago blows his whistle and out of the corner of my eye, I see him waving furiously at me. "Gotta go. I'm not sure when I'll have cell reception again, but hopefully later today when I'm back on the jet."

I end the call, then stride over to the group, only to hear Ms. Fox saying,

"…for a *week*. The abdominal pains are supposed to be unbearable. Apparently, most people actually *wish* for death. And that's not even the worst part because once the initial symptoms go away, it gets much worse. Bleeding gums, blood in your vomit and stool, rapid breathing. It takes ages—sometimes months—to feel even remotely human again."

Gross. What the hell is she even talking about? And why does the rest of the group seem so interested? And what is that in her hair?

One of the women says, "And it's *that* common?"

"*So* common. In fact, the travel advisory board recently issued a warning about an outbreak in the Amazon. Just takes one little mosquito bite," she tells her. "But we'll all be fine because we've had our vaccines." She shakes her head, then says, "If a person hasn't though … wow."

Oh. My. God. She's trying to talk people into leaving. And based on the terrified faces of a few of our fellow travelers, I think she's going to manage it. She really is evil.

An evil genius who is unknowingly doing me a massive favor.

The woman who asked if it's that common blurts out, "I haven't had mine and neither have they!" She points to two other women standing beside her.

One of them gasps. "You snitch!"

"I'm just trying to save your life!"

Thiago, who looks thoroughly annoyed, steps forward. "Who all hasn't had the required vaccinations?"

More than half of the people put up their hands, prompting him to swear in Spanish. "Get back on the shuttle bus. You're going home. The rest of you board the helicopters. We need to leave now."

I clear my throat. "I'd like to say something before we leave … in honor of Richard." I pause for a second, trying to think of how to word this. I'll need to be delicate, to say the least, but Richard would understand—he knows what it's like to have vultures circling. Or I suppose, I should say, he knew. "I'm sure most of you are here because you want to honor Dr. Napper. He was a great man, a philanthropist, and an adventurer. However, I also know you're all very busy people, and the last thing you thought you'd be doing today was embarking on a five-day send off in a foreign country. If you are here because you are worried about funding for whatever program you're part of, you need to know the truth right now. I am not going to fund you anymore. As you all know, Richard was planning to take over the foundation entirely, but the final paperwork and the actual transfers didn't happen. My own money is about to be tied up in a business venture that has been twenty years in the making. The ball is in motion and I couldn't stop it now, even if I wanted to," I say, glancing at Ms. Fox. "I don't want to, but even if I did, I couldn't. It's over. So, if you were sent here to try to convince me, you might as well get back on the bus and go home. No one will think less of you. In fact, it would be the smart thing to do because the man who is set to inherit Richard's fortune is his nephew, Skip Napper. Your time would be better spent going to find him so you can talk him into giving you the funding you need. Apparently, he's in Las Vegas at the moment."

"Seriously?" one of the women asks.

"Seriously. I need to be clear—the money is not coming from me. So there is no need to try to suck up, cajole, entice, or otherwise talk me into it. I promise."

"No chance at all? Really?" someone in the back asks.

"It's a zero percent chance. Zero," I answer. "We're talking a 'when hell freezes over' scenario." Okay, this next bit is going to sound cocky, but I'm only saying it because I really do need to get back to the U.S. "I should also note that I am in a very serious relationship as well, so ... in case you are here husband-hunting, that also is not going to happen."

I glance at Savannah Stevens, whose face turns bright red. And … now we know why she came.

"This sucks," one of the women says, poking her head up so she can make eye contact with me. "I came all this way for nothing!"

"If you're only here for the money, I'm afraid so," I answer.

"Of course I'm only here for the money. I didn't know Dick. I've never even met the man!"

"How can you just shut us down like this?" Niles Thompson asks.

"I'm not shutting you down. It's just a matter of unfortunate timing," I tell him.

"But *come on*, you're a billionaire. You must have the money."

"As I said, it's been spoken for. So, if you'd rather not put yourself through this grueling and potentially dangerous trip, please get back on the bus. If you're staying, please … don't waste the next week trying to get blood from a stone."

Murmurs ripple through the crowd. Thiago looks panicked and furious at the same time. "Every trip I do, there is one problem. I thought it was the straggler," he says, pointing at Ms. Fox. "But now, I think it's *you*. You are the problem!"

"Yeah, he's the problem. He's a greedy fucker," someone hiding at the back mutters.

And that's what it's like to be a billionaire…

———

Six people. That's how many of the thirty are still remaining. Six bloody people including Rohan and me, which means I was *so* close to putting an end to this insanity. Our group has whittled down to Savannah Stevens, Gwendolyn Fox, Niles Thompson, former Miss Canada Karen Taylor, Rohan, and me, of course.

So, inexplicably, the trip is still on. Seriously, why would *any* of these people have stayed? Other than Rohan and me, none of them knew Richard personally. And I couldn't have been more clear about my intentions.

Thiago is beyond furious. Rohan looks dumbfounded. But I can't think of that right now. I did what had to be done, even if I failed. Besides, I was just being honest, which under the circumstances is the right thing to do. No sense in giving these people false hope, especially when they should be either out looking for jobs or finding some other sucker to fund them.

Rohan walks up to me, then turns and takes a few steps away, then comes back. "You know…" He shakes his head, then says, "Forget it."

"Say it," I tell him. "You know you want to."

He shakes his head again, looking at me through glassy eyes. "You had to do it. You had to ruin the last thing he wanted."

"I got rid of the phonies," I tell him. "The people left here actually care about him, and shouldn't those be the people who are there in the end?"

"He wanted…" Rohan throws his hands in the air. "He wanted this big, glorious send off, and you literally just chased away almost all of the few people who could actually make it!"

Guilt stabs at my chest. "I'm sorry, Rohan, but if it were my funeral, I'd only want the people who actually gave a shit about me to be there. Not all the fuckers looking for handouts."

"But it's *not* your funeral!" Rohan says. "It's Dick's."

He storms off before I can say anything, but honestly, I have no idea what I would say anyhow.

Thiago is deep in conversation with one of the helicopter pilots—likely explaining that we have to cancel most of them because at most, we'll need two. I watch as Ms. Fox interrupts to ask where she can go shopping. Oh, that did not go over well. Thiago is yelling at her for being 'the problem.' I can't blame him though. Now is not the time to shop.

8

Free Falling...

Gwen

"But you said I could shop at the next location."

"This isn't the next location! We have to get on the helicopters to get to the next location."

"Oh, sorry," I answer, feeling suddenly sheepish. "It's just that when you used the word next, I took it to mean the next place, not the place *after* that."

Thiago closes his eyes for a second, then exhales loudly through his nose. "We're on a tight schedule, okay? I don't have time for this."

"Sure, all right," I answer with a nod that says, 'Don't worry about me, I'm not a problem.'

He returns his attention to his clipboard when I realize I absolutely must use the bathroom before we get on the helicopter. I lift my hand to tap Thiago on the shoulder, then change my mind. I can wait.

Umm, no, I really can't. I lift my hand again and poke him on the upper arm. "Excuse me."

"Yes?"

"It's just that, I have this…" Lowering my voice, I continue, "Nervous bladder condition. When I'm in high stress situations, I have to … use the ladies' room more frequently."

He stares at me for a second, then sighs. "Everyone, listen up! If anyone else here needs to use the toilet before we leave, you have exactly three minutes before we're leaving! Go!"

I glance around, hoping there will be a group of us, but apparently it's just me because nobody moves. Nuts. I'd feel a lot less silly if I had someone else to come with me. Thiago gestures for me to get going and I all but spring to the hangar, returning with ten seconds to spare. I didn't even have a chance to wash the vomit out of my hair, but I did have the opportunity to see what I look like right now. Insane. I look completely insane.

When I get back, he's making an announcement. "We can fit the group into two helicopters—this big one and that smaller one. Four plus me here. Two on that one," he says, gesturing to the aircraft to his right. He points to Mr. Sterling and me, then says, "You two—other helicopter. You are the problems and I don't need problems right now. Everyone else, with me!"

I open my mouth to object, but then remember I'm not supposed to insult Sterling. I'm supposed to be sucking up. And since this will allow me to have him all to myself, I guess I better just cooperate. I look up at him and see he's staring at me with a strange look on his face. Contempt? Amusement? I honestly cannot read him at all.

He slings his backpack over his shoulder and strides over to our chopper, looking all dapper and confident, which is *completely* annoying if you ask me. I hang back for a second, then force my feet to start moving, my toes already cramping up in these stupid heels.

Mr. Sterling steps aside to let me get on first, which I imagine is supposed to make me think he's a gentleman. Obviously, I'm not buying it. After listening in on part of his phone call, I now know he's not only an asshole, but he's a controlling monster too. Having his girlfriend tailed? Asking for her phone records? Wanting a list of everyone she sees? I mean, seriously, that's some stalker bullshit right there.

I offer a smile to our pilot, who is standing next to the helicopter. "Hola."

"Hola, you are a light traveler."

"Excuse me?" I ask.

"You have no luggage. Did you forget it?"

"The airline lost it."

He shakes his head at me. "I never check my bag. They always lose it."

I almost tell him what happened, but then just smile instead. "Good tip. I'll remember it for next time."

"Yes, you will, because that skirt is going to give you some trouble where we're going," he says.

My pulse races a little. "What kind of trouble? What are we doing?"

He shakes his head. "I'm not allowed to say. Just … some trouble. You'll be okay though."

"Thank you, that's very reassuring."

"You're welcome," he says, clearly not picking up on my sarcasm.

He holds out one hand to help me get on, which, it turns out, is necessary because this skirt is already causing me trouble making this high step up. Mr. Sterling is right behind me, and I'm pretty sure my butt must be in his face. My cheeks flame at the thought of him so close to my behind.

Oh God, can I please go home now?

I settle myself into my seat and put on a headset, trying to act like I ride on helicopters all the time. Somehow, I feel embarrassed that this is my first time and it has to be with someone who probably fires up a chopper every time he wants to go to the corner store to buy a pack of gum. The truth is, I find flying a little nerve-wracking in the first place. But at least airplanes are big and they feel solid, whereas helicopters seem like all window, which won't protect you at all in a crash scenario. An airplane gives you the impression you'll have a chance. Chopper? Not so much.

But I don't have time to think about my impending doom because *he* is getting on. I do my best to scooch over to the right side of my seat so as to stay as far away from him as possible (which, as it turns out, is only about three inches, tops).

He puts on his headset, then, out of the corner of my eye, I see him wince. "Good God, what is that smell?"

Keeping my eyes trained on the seat back in front of me, I say, "Baby vomit."

"Perfect."

"Try having it in your hair."

"Hard pass. It's bad enough from here."

A smile builds inside me at the thought of him having to deal with this stench too. I hide it of course, but I cannot wait to tell the gang at work about it. *Ohh, we're going to have such a laugh.*

My surly seat mate turns his head to face the window, and I can't help but notice he's got his fingers under his nose. Good. I hope he gets a crick in his neck. Grabbing my phone out of my handbag, I shoot Allie a text.

In helicopter sitting next to the devil himself. Still covered in baby vomit with a sprinkling of B.O.

ALLIE

What?! You're joking, right?

Wish I were. This is very real. Can I come home now? I'm done.

ALLIE

You can do this. Think positive. This is an opportunity. You've got Sterling all to yourself. Use this time to get him to warm up to you.

Do I have to? He's scary and awful and I hate him. He's seriously so much worse than we thought. I overheard him on the phone telling someone to have his girlfriend followed and to get records of her phone calls.

ALLIE

NO!!!! Really???

Yup. Who does that? Psychos, that's who. And talk about an ego - he told the entire group he's in a committed relationship so not to bother trying to 'get with him.'

ALLIE

He didn't!

Not in those exact words, but that's what he meant. Also (and probably most importantly), he told everyone he isn't going to fund any more projects so if that was the only reason we were here, to just leave now. He claims he has a business deal that's been twenty years in the making and the money's gone.

ALLIE

Shit. Seriously?

I'm not buying it though. Twenty years ago he'd have still been in college. He just wanted to get rid of people.

ALLIE

Why would he want to do that?

Because he hates people. Speaking of getting rid of people, I figured out how to weed out some competition. I told everyone there was a dengue fever outbreak and all the people who were faking their vaccinations fled like rats on a sinking ship.

ALLIE

Score one for SETI!

I'm honestly not sure it'll help. I don't think it's possible to get through to this guy.

ALLIE

If anyone can get through to him, it's you. Now, plaster a smile on your face and be charming.

I'd have a better shot at charming a rabid dog into giving me his last bone.

ALLIE

You got this, Gwen. I believe in you.

Thanks. But just in case I don't, he also said that Dr. Napper's nephew, Skip Napper, is supposed to inherit his fortune. Apparently, Skip is in Vegas. I think the team should send someone there to find him. Pretty sure the other teams are sending people and we don't want to miss out.

ALLIE

Seriously? He's not on the trip?

Nope. He clearly loved his uncle a great deal.

ALLIE

Wow. Okay. Is there anything else we can do from here?

Pray.

Sliding my phone back in my bag, I stare out the window as we fly over the expansive city. The coastline runs all along to my right. It's actually quite breathtaking now that I've bothered to look up. But I'm not here for sightseeing. I'm here to get a job done. One that may be impossible, but I have to try anyway. I sit, desperately trying to think of something to say. Am I sweating again? Oh wait, I don't know if I ever stopped. Honestly, I have never felt this awkward in my entire life. I'm going to be alone, sitting next to Ty Sterling, for the next … well, I have no idea how long. Even another five minutes seems like an excruciatingly long time with a man like him.

Okay, say something, Gwen. Anything. Be witty. Smart. Enchanting.

Finally, I turn to him and say, "I'm Gwen."

He either can't hear me or he's ignoring me. My heart pounds in my chest as I reach up and tap him on the shoulder. He turns, and I can see he looks slightly pale. "Yes?"

"I was … just going to introduce myself. I'm Gwen."

He nods impatiently. "Yes, I know. Gwendolyn Fox. Researcher on the SETI team."

"That's right. And you're Ty Sterling. CEO of Napper-

Sterling and vice-president of the Napper-Sterling Foundation."

"Yes."

I glance down at his hands, only to see he's gripping his knees, his knuckles white. And that's when I realize it. Ty Sterling, heartless business mogul, is afraid of heights. Or helicopters. Or crashing. He's afraid of something anyway, which means he has emotions after all. Well, at least one— fear. "Are you all right?"

He turns back to the window. "Never better."

"It's just that you seem … a little unwell."

"I'm fine. And I'd rather not talk about it."

"You're fine or you'd rather not talk about it?" *Whoops, that sounded argumentative. Charming, Gwen. Be charming.*

"What?"

"It can't be both. You're either actually fine or you're not and you don't want to talk about it, but it can't be both." Apparently my brain doesn't have a charm setting.

He glares at me, his deep brown eyes making me squirm a little in my seat. "I don't like helicopters, but as long as we don't crash, I'll be fine."

"I don't like them either," I tell him. *Ooh, much better— you're finding common ground.* "They really are the motorcycles of the sky. Say, I wonder if that's why they're both referred to as choppers?"

He swallows hard. "I have no idea."

"It kind of feels like we're flying around in a giant fishbowl, and I don't know about you, but I cannot see how all this glass would protect us from anything if we do crash."

He turns slightly green and closes his eyes.

"Sorry. I shouldn't have said that. I tend to have trouble keeping my opinions to myself, even when I should. It's a bad habit."

"It certainly is," he says, turning back to the window.

In my brain, I'm mocking his voice, making him sound like the snootiest of all the snooty billionaires in the world. *It certainly is.* But on the outside, I'm offering him a sympathetic smile just in case he turns around. "Anyway, I'm really sorry about Dr. Napper. I'm sure this must be just awful for you—losing your business partner and probably your best friend."

He stiffens a little, then says, "Thanks, but I'm fine."

"He was an incredible human," I say, glancing out to see that we're no longer flying over Lima, but are now at the base of the mountains. "Not only generous, but so full of life and really incredibly inspiring. I watched every one of his adventures on the Dick Cam."

Mr. Sterling blinks slowly, then says, "You needn't bother. I meant what I said earlier—about there being absolutely no chance of me funding any of your projects."

"I know you did. You hate what we do, even though SETI is a real and highly respected line of research. Not like a lot of the other projects in the foundation." Leaning toward him a little, I say, "I mean, come on, the search for Atlantis? Might as well look for King Arthur's sword. Embarrassing."

His lips curve up ever so slightly, and I'll be damned if those aren't a nice set of lips. "Let me get this straight. *You* look down on *them?*"

My face heats up with humiliation, which turns instantly to rage. Doing my best to stay icy calm, I say, "I assure you what those other teams do and what we do are nothing alike. Ours is a very real science based on facts and certainty. Theirs is a fairy tale."

"I have news for you. You're not that different."

Okay, now I'm mad. "We most certainly are nothing like those crazy Yeti people."

"You most certainly are. You all employed exactly the

same strategy when it came to sending someone on this godforsaken trip to try to handle me."

"Which is…?"

"Sending a young, attractive woman to convince me not to shut you down." His eyes sweep over me. "It's insulting really."

Attractive? Did he just call me attractive? Is my face bright red right now? Because it feels ridiculously hot. Stupid face. "That's not why I was picked."

He arches his left eyebrow. "Really?"

"Yes, *really*," I answer, sounding haughtier than I should. "There was a very good reason my team sent me."

"What? Are you the only one who speaks Klingon or something?"

I narrow my eyes at him. "Obviously not. I'm the only one who had the necessary qualifications."

He looks impressed for a second, but then I realize he's just pretending. "So *you're* the brains behind the whole operation then?"

"No, *everyone* on the team is … the brains behind the operation. We're all one big brain and together we have all the skills and knowledge needed. Honestly, the whole thing would fall apart if you got rid of any of us," I say, laying the groundwork in case he does give us funding but then decides to turn around and downsize us. Well, he could let Chad go. That would be fine. I'm about to say as much when the helicopter suddenly seems to be lifted up out of nowhere, pushing me into my seat with a terrifying force.

Without thinking, I reach for Mr. Sterling's hand and he does the same to mine. We grip each other as the nose of the aircraft pitches up violently and the engine stalls. Closing my eyes, I feel panic take over me as it feels like we're about to drop out of the sky. Without a parachute in sight. Thank God I went pee back at the airport…

9

Flirty Banter, Adrenaline Rushes, and Soft, Warm Hands...

Ty

"SHHHIIITTTTTT!" I tighten my grip on her hand and place my left one over top. I can't die this way. Not holding the hand of a smelly woman who hates me so much she defaces my photo every week. My heart pounds out of my chest, adrenaline surges through my veins, and I sit, helplessly awaiting our fate. Instruments beep loudly. The pilot starts muttering in Spanish, and I have no idea if he's praying or swearing.

After a few more terrifying seconds, he manages to right the helicopter, the engine kicks back in, and we continue flying as though nothing just happened. The pilot glances back at us with an easy smile. "Sorry about that, folks. We're fine now."

"What the fuck was that?" I demand.

"An updraft. It happens sometimes over the mountains," he says with a shrug.

"Well, it better not fucking happen again," I tell him,

even though if it does, really, what am I going to do about it?

"Thank you for getting us out of that," Ms. Fox says, giving me a dirty look.

I roll my eyes, then look down at our hands, only now realizing I still have a death grip on her. She glances down too, then at the same time, we both let go, her looking like she was just holding a fresh turd.

Clearing my throat, I say, "Well, that was … something."

"Yes, it really was. I didn't know that could happen."

"Neither did I or I never would've gotten on this stupid thing to begin with," I say, my heart still pounding.

"If you thought you were scared of helicopters before," she says, "I'm sure that didn't help."

"I'm not scared. I just don't *like* them."

"Right, yeah," she says. "On account of them feeling like deathtraps. But you're not scared."

"Exactly," I tell her, letting a tiny grin escape.

I look outside for a second, only to see the mountain we almost crashed into, then decide I'm better off looking at her. There's something about her that's very distracting, and if I need anything right now, it's a good distraction. Otherwise, I'm going to wind up curled up on the floor in a ball, not being scared. I stare at her for a second, taking in how incredibly green her eyes are. They're bright and shiny against her pale skin. Her white blouse is a bit rumpled and I can see the top of a lacy soft pink bra. Well, that's certainly distracting. *Hello, Ms. Fox.*

No, not hello, Ms. Fox. She is the enemy. Not only that, she was sent here to part you from a cool hundred mil that you need.

I stare at the back of the pilot's head for a second to avoid getting drawn in by … whatever those thoughts were.

But looking at him only reminds me of the fact that we're flying a thousand feet above a very hard mountain in a giant fishbowl that almost crashed a few minutes ago.

My eyes are begging me to look to my right and down a little for a sight of her … shirt again. *No way, eyes. We're not getting suckered in here. No way, no how. No matter how soft her skin is.*

I allow them to focus on her face again. Better. Very calming for a woman who can't stand me.

She offers me a reassuring smile. "We're going to be fine."

"You sure?" I ask, allowing myself to exhale fully.

"I am." The way she says it makes me almost believe her. She's so confident about it.

I take another deep breath and feel myself relaxing slightly (which is to say, I've moved from full-on terror to my original state of 'I hate this with a passion, get me off this thing.') My mind searches for something to think about other than death, and the conversation we were having just before my life flashed before my eyes comes back to me. Swallowing hard, I say, "So, what exactly makes you so qualified that no one else could've come in your place?"

"What's that?" she asks, giving me a blank look.

"Earlier. You said you were the only one who had the qualifications to come on the trip. Remember? You were a little put out that I suggested you were only sent because you're attractive."

"Wouldn't you be insulted if I said that to you?" she asks.

"If you said I was attractive?" I say with a smirk. "I honestly don't think that would bother me all that much."

"You didn't say I was attractive," she says, taking a big breath. "You said I was *only here* because I'm attractive, which negates my intellect, education, and skills and reduces me to some sort of … Playboy pin up."

"Playboy pin up? That's not what I said. Not even close," I tell her, trying not to imagine her in one of those poses with red lips and very little covering her. Too late. "Obviously I know you're smart. You wouldn't have gotten through school if you weren't."

"Damn right, I'm smart."

"But look around. All the foundation's projects—every single one—sent a young, relatively attractive female. Except the Ghostbusters, but that's just because they've got a total sausage fest going on over there."

She snort laughs, but then quickly recovers, and when she talks, she's all business. "I can assure you my looks have nothing to do with me being here."

"So? Tell me then. Why you? Are you the genius with the highest IQ on the team or something?"

"Not exactly," she says, glancing out the window, then back at me. "It's less to do with my IQ and more to do with my … umm … vaccinations."

I pause for a second, sure I heard her wrong. "Come again?"

Swiping her tongue over her front teeth, she says, "I was the only one who had all the necessary travel vaccinations to go into the jungle."

My mouth drops, then I burst out laughing. She turns to face the other way while I try to get my laughter under control. "The only one … bahahaha!"

"I'm not sure why you find that so funny," she quips.

"It's because you were so haughty about it." I raise my voice so I sound vaguely like her. "I'm the only one with the necessary qualifications."

"That *is* a qualification."

Okay, this is definitely working. I've completely forgotten where I am. Well, almost. "No, it's not. A qualification is something like a skill or an attribute that allows you to do a job. It's not a shot in the arm."

"That's not true. It's any condition that must be met in order to qualify you for something. Take the presidency. One of the qualifications is that you must have been born in the United States, which is neither a skill nor an attribute. It's just … luck."

Damn. She's got me there. I stare down at her, thoroughly enjoying the smug look on her face. "All right, Ms. Fox. I concede on one condition."

"Which is?"

"That you admit you were trying to make it sound as though you had some personal attribute that led your boss to choose you."

She glares at me for a second, and damned if she's not actually really beautiful with that look on her face. "And why exactly do you think I care if you concede?"

"Because it means you win," I tell her.

"I already won. I proved my point. I don't *need* you to concede. Besides, that wasn't about winning. It was about accuracy. Your definition of the word 'qualification' was too narrow and required expanding, which I was able to do with my example," she says, reminding me very much of a stern English teacher I had in high school. "You know I'm right, so there's no need to agree to your condition."

I sit quietly for a minute while I consider her words. She's smart. Really fucking smart. A force to be reckoned with. To be honest, I'm not sure I can keep up with her mentally, which is not something I've encountered often. This is all horribly inconvenient because I'm not supposed to enjoy sparring with someone who hates me the way she does. Oh, and I hate right back because … nasty and all that. What the hell. This is fun. "I don't believe you. I think that was about winning."

"I know my own mind, Mr. Sterling. Certainly better than someone who met me less than an hour ago. It was not about winning. It was about accuracy."

I'm tempted to tell her to call me Ty, but there's some weird part of me that enjoys hearing her call me Mr. Sterling. Besides, I should keep it professional. That would definitely be the smart thing to do. The last thing I need is to get all confused about a woman. That's a road I'm never going down, but if I did, it certainly wouldn't be right now. In fact, I should shut this conversation down. Only no part of me wants to. "Admit it. It was a little bit about winning."

"Why on earth would you think that?"

"Because someone who argues like that must be doing it for the thrill of victory."

A reluctant grin escapes her lips even though she's trying very hard to look serious. "Fine, yes. I do like to win a good argument, but other than that, I'm not really much of a competitive person."

"I beg to differ," I tell her, unable to wipe the smile off my face. "Only a highly competitive person would try to scare people off with a fake dengue fever outbreak. Nice work, by the way. Very effective."

Her cheeks turn bright pink. "That was for their own good. I overheard them saying they didn't have the vaccinations and they really would've been putting themselves at risk."

Narrowing my eyes a little, I say, "But that's not why you did it, is it?"

"Of course it is," she says, having the nerve to look offended even though we both know she's lying.

"Liar. You sent them away because you needed to

narrow the playing field, and now you're pretending you were just making a public service announcement."

"It was in all of our best interests to send them home. We're going to be out in the middle of nowhere. We can't afford to have someone get gravely ill."

"But that's not why you did it."

She opens her mouth to say something, then clamps it shut.

"It's impressive, really. While all those other women were trying to suck up to me, you were busy figuring out a way to remove them from the equation. You're a bit of an evil genius."

Ms. Fox purses her lips, then says, "Look, this is life or death for our program. I need every advantage in case you're willing to fund, say, one extremely valuable project for all of humankind."

My smile disappears and my gut tightens as I remind myself she's only after one thing—my money. "It's not going to happen, Ms. Fox. I'm not going to lead you on by making you think it might."

She gives me a defiant look that says she really doesn't believe me. I'm ready for her to tell me she intends to change my mind, but she doesn't. Instead she just offers me a slow smile that says, 'we'll see about that,' then she turns to look out the window. I sit back in my chair, thinking about our conversation and about how unpredictable she is. The fact that she's not trying to convince me right now shows a restraint that few people have. I know it's not over. She's just biding her time, waiting for the right moment. Too bad it's never going to come. Because I'm not changing my mind.

The helicopter slows to a stop mid-air—a little trick they do that I despise. Then it makes a soft landing on the top of a mountain and I let out an exhale, my shoulders relaxing finally. Ms. Fox takes off her headset and places it back in its holder. Her hands really are quite delicate in addition to being incredibly soft. And warm.

And what the actual fuck am I thinking right now?

10

Thiago is a Big, Fat Liar...

Gwen

WELL, as far as I'm concerned, we're at the second location. Only there's not a shop to be seen from here. Unless I pull out a pair of binoculars and look way down into that village below. There might be one there. But there sure as shit isn't one up here. There's only a small shack and a cold breeze blowing up my skirt. Oh yeah, and a zipline. I suddenly understand why the pilot said I was going to have trouble. I'm going to chafe like a mother. My inner thighs hurt just thinking about it, as does my sense of decency because everyone up here and on the way down is going to get a good look at my grannies.

At least I can put some distance between myself and Ty Sterling. That whole ride was intense, and to be honest, I'm a hot mess right now. The entire time, my body felt alive in a way it never has. All tingly and weird with butter-flies in my stomach. Although, that was probably just what it's like to ride in a helicopter, right? Because no man can have that sort of effect on anyone. Certainly not an asshole like him. Right?

Right. It's fine. I'm not losing my mind or anything. It was the helicopter and the near-death experience. And the holding hands. Wow, he's got some big manly hands. All veiny and warm and muscular and … *stop thinking about his hands! He's the enemy.*

Maybe I *am* losing my mind because I'm not disgusted by him at all. Not in the least. In fact, he smells so good he should be kept on some island somewhere—away from all us unsuspecting women who might fall prey to his good looks and delicious scent, like those children in the Pied Piper story. It's ridiculous. I'm all hyper-aware of where he is. Like right now, he's to my right, holding his phone up looking for reception. Probably so he can check in on his girlfriend who he clearly doesn't trust. Which reminds me to snap the hell out of it because the man is trouble with a capital TROUBLE.

So why did I keep getting flashes of climbing into his lap when I was sitting next to him? It's got to be the altitude. I look over at him again. He's given up on his cell and is shoving it in his pocket, looking totally pissed. Monster. There's no way I want him. It's definitely the altitude. And the almost dying. It heightens all your senses.

Thiago ushers us all into the shack where harnesses and helmets are hanging neatly on one wall. "Time for the first video."

He puts his iPad on a small wooden table and presses play. I stand off to the side, trying to ignore the fact that Mr. Sterling is standing right next to me, his arms folded across his chest.

The screen lights up and Dr. Napper's smiling face appears. "Welcome to Peru! Thank you all for making the trek to South America to honor me. I have traveled to every country in the world, but none has spoken to me in the way that Peru does. I found myself returning to it time and time again because of its history, beauty, and magic. It connects to my soul in a way no other place does. And it is because of this that I wanted my final adventure to be here with you all. This is going to be a transformative trip for each and every one of you. You'll make friends, meet yourselves for the first time, and go home a changed person. I guarantee it."

Next to me, Mr. Sterling mutters, "Sounds like summer camp."

I try not to smile, but it's what I was thinking too.

"I'll be coming along, too, in this special carrier," he says, holding up what looks exactly like a Baby Bjorn. "It was built to fit my urn's exact specifications so it won't fall out and is extremely comfortable to wear. Now, I know everyone is going to want to have a chance to wear me during the trip, so Rohan has made up a schedule to make sure you all get equal time. Because there are so many of you, it'll only be a few minutes each, but please take that time to say what you need to, and feel free to talk to me about what's happening and how much you're enjoying your time in Peru."

Blerg, the guilt at getting rid of so many people washes over me. Not too nice, Gwen. I look over at Rohan and see he's currently wearing the Baby Bjorn with the gold urn stuffed into it. I half expect him to start bouncing up and down a little and shushing it. Oh, this is weird. Just so very weird.

On the screen, Dr. Napper is still talking. "As you've guessed, our first adventure is ziplining down to the incredible Sacred Valley of the Incas. This is going to be the first of several challenges I will ask you to undertake with me. Each one will stretch your mind, push your physical limits, and lift your soul to new levels. Please use this trek as a chance to open your mind to the possibilities of the universe, broaden your boundaries, and test your mettle. Let the trip unfold as it will and trust me, you'll be better for it. Also, please note this will be the easiest leg of our adventure, so buckle up. Things are going to get interesting. But that's really the point. For me to show you life truly is about the journey, not the destination." He grins, then says, "I'd like you to choose a buddy for the trip. Someone to watch out for you and who you will watch out for in return. To my business partner, Ty, assuming you're here, everyone needs a buddy, including you. And to whomever gets Ty, don't be intimidated. It's all just an act. He's like an M&M—he's got a hard outer shell but he's soft and sweet on the inside. Now, stick together and get to know each other and yourselves. Peace out."

I glance around to try to find a buddy, only to see Sterling pointing to Rohan, who shoots him a dirty look, putting his hand on the urn as though protecting it from the mean man. Niles, Karen, and Savannah are all holding a hand up in Ty's direction while I try to get Karen's attention. She completely ignores me. I know I should be trying to pair off with Mr. Sterling too. It would be the smart thing to do, but he really is the last person who I would ever want as my buddy in an actual life and death scenario (which could very likely happen out here). Ty taps me on the shoulder. When I look up at him, his expression is passive, although I think I can see a hint of desperation in his eyes. "Will you be my buddy?"

"Me?"

He rubs the back of his neck. "Yes. We've already nearly died together and we got through that, so…"

You have to do this, Gwen. You know you do. Offer him a toothy smile. No, that's too much. He looks scared. There. Much better. "Sure. I'd love to."

Disappointed grunts and groans are heard around the shack, then I watch as Niles and Rohan pair off, and Savannah and Karen do the same.

A man in a windbreaker and cargo pants comes to stand next to Thiago. "Welcome. I'm Luis and I will be your guide today. We are going to take five ziplines, which together make a total descent of 3000 meters. The entire thing will take just under an hour. When we get to the bottom, there will be a bus waiting to take you to the village of Yanque where you will stay the night. If you need to use the toilet, now is the best time."

Thiago snaps his fingers at me. "You, nervous bladder, you should go now."

Oh, thanks a lot, asshole.

Luis shoots Thiago a dirty look, then glances at my legs. "Miss, you might want to put some pants on."

"I totally agree. Unfortunately, this is all I have," I tell him, pointing to my clothes.

Luis looks at the other women. "Might one of you have some pants for this poor woman? She is going to chafe very badly," he says, gesturing to his inner thighs.

Savannah looks at me, then wrinkles up her nose. "I don't think I'll have anything that'll fit. I'm just so small-waisted."

Karen smiles at me. "I have some pants you can wear."

"Really?" I ask her.

She nods. "We girls have to stick together," she says, glancing at Ty. "Especially in this situation."

I nod and let out a sigh of relief. "Thank you."

She crouches and pulls a pair of leggings out of her backpack. "They might be a little long, but you can roll them up."

I take the pants and smile at her, feeling guilty for how much shit I've talked about the Yeti people over the last decade. "Thank you. You're very kind."

I search the shack for the bathroom, only to spot it through the window. It's an outhouse. Awesome.

A few minutes later, I've peed (yes, again), changed into the world's tightest leggings (because of course Miss Canada is super thin), and returned in time to see Mr. Sterling being fitted for his harness. *And hello, Mr. Sterling! Nice to meet all of you.*

When it's my turn, I feel heat rising up my neck as Luis lifts the harness up my legs and tightens it around my waist. Oh my God, I bet I have a serious case of camel toe on account of the crazy tight leggings and the harness. Can this be over now?

He stands up and selects a helmet off the wall, then when he's about to hand it to me, he looks at my hair and narrows his eyes. "What's in your hair?"

"Dried baby vomit."

He wrinkles up his nose. "We better get that cleaned up."

"I would love that."

He walks over to a cooler on the table and opens it, taking out a bottle of water. "Come on. Let's do this outside."

So now, I'm outside on a windy mountain bent over with the outline of everything my pants should be hiding on display for the world while a complete stranger rinses vomit out of my hair. What was that thing I was thinking earlier about being enchanting?

11

The Joys and Pains of Being a Gentleman...

Ty

I STAND off to the side watching Rohan, Thiago, and Niles as they gawk at Ms. Fox getting her hair washed. I forget all about trying to get a cell signal so I can check in with Donna and find myself striding over to the trio, my hands balled up in tight fists. "Enjoying the view?"

"Yes, it's beautiful," Thiago says.

Niles just nods and continues staring while Rohan, who knows I'm not just making conversation, turns his attention to me with a guilty expression. "The valley? Yes, it's really something. I can see why Dick loved it here so much."

I glare at him, then snap my fingers several times at Thiago and Niles. "Hey, you two, stop being disgusting."

They both straighten up, Niles looking sheepish while Thiago turns his gaze to the ground. I shake my head at them, then walk over to Ms. Fox, who is now wringing out her long, dark hair. Between the skin-tight pants and the harness, you can basically see her entire ass. And it's a Very. Nice. Ass.

One that is about to be covered up because I'm sure she doesn't want it on display. She turns around to face me, shivering a bit. "That wind is brisk when you have wet hair."

I tug off my fleece pullover and hand it to her. "Here. Take this."

"No, I couldn't possibly," she says, trying to give it back.

"I insist."

"But then you'll be cold."

Shaking my head, I say, "I'm fine. I run hot anyway." As in, hotblooded enough to knock some heads together if those idiots start staring at her again. *Okay, seriously, Ty? You're turning into a neanderthal now?*

She nods and offers me a smile that does something to me. "Thank you. That's very kind. Honestly, I'm feeling a little exposed in these pants."

I put on an innocent expression. "What? Oh, don't worry. You're fine."

Ms. Fox gives me a skeptical look, then pulls the shirt on over her head. "I am, now, thank you."

She looks ridiculously small in my pullover. Like she's drowning in it. I'm tempted to roll up her sleeves for her, but then I remind myself of all the ways that would be completely inappropriate. Besides, she's rolling them up herself, you know, since she's not a toddler. Smiling up at me, she says, "I'm starting to wonder if Dr. Napper was right about you."

My face heats up a little at the memory of him calling me an M&M. I roll my eyes. "Don't believe it. I'm neither soft nor sweet."

"Well, this was not exactly awful of you."

If she only knew why I did it, she wouldn't think so.

You know what's really uncomfortable? Ziplining with a hard-on. Yeah, not great, if I'm going to be honest. The harness made it so that pullover rides up and my buddy's bottom was showing the entire time, and being the gentleman I'm pretending to be, I let her go first on each leg of the trip which meant I had the world's best view the entire time. I'm honestly not sure I'll ever recover.

The sun is just setting as we pull into the village, everyone around me chatting away about the experience we just had, while I sit at the back of the bus, looking for a few bars of cell reception. So far, nothing, which really sucks because I have to let Donna know I'm stuck here, and I also really must get ahold of Muffy and check in with Michael.

The village looks like a place that time forgot. Stone walls surround the entire place, the dirt streets are too narrow for two vehicles to pass each other, and based on the lack of signs, I'm guessing the locals 'just know' which way to go. The houses and buildings are all one or two stories, allowing for a view of the surrounding mountains to be seen no matter where you are. We pass through town, cross a river on an old bridge that doesn't exactly inspire confidence, then pull up in front of an expansive lodge.

Thiago stands and says, "This will be our stop for the night. The Colibri Lodge is the best place to stay in the entire valley. The food is delicious, the hospitality is top notch, and the best part? Natural hot springs to rest your weary bones. Follow me to the front desk to get your rooms sorted out."

I stare out at the stone building, admiring the old-world construction. I expected we'd be stuck in tents, or worse, sleeping up in a tree somewhere, but this is a place I would actually pick for myself. *Well done, Richard. This is a pleasant surprise.*

I follow the group into the lobby, checking my cell phone again. Still nothing. Thiago stands at the desk and assists with checking everyone in and giving instructions. Ms. Fox approaches him carefully when it's her turn. "I hate to bother you, but I really do need to do some shopping."

"Yes, of course," he says, turning to the clerk and saying something in Spanish.

The clerk shakes his head at her while answering Thiago.

"What did he say?" Ms. Fox asks.

"He said you should never check your bag because they always lose them."

She flares her nostrils a bit, then closes her eyes for a second, which I take to be what she does when she's about to lose it. The clerk and Thiago go back and forth for a minute, then Thiago says, "They can give you a toothbrush and toothpaste here. The only store that is open at this hour is a quick walk. You just cross the river, then turn right. It's a tourist trap but they have clothes."

"It'll have to do," she says.

The clerk hands her a room key (not a key card, an actual room key), along with a toothbrush and a tube of toothpaste. She pops everything in her hand bag, then walks out, while I impatiently wait my turn. When I get up to the front, I ask Thiago about internet access.

"I'm afraid there is no internet here. No cell reception either."

Of course, there isn't. "Is there a phone in the room I can use? I have an important business call that can't wait."

Thiago shakes his head. "No. No phones."

The clerk, who clearly understands more English than

he's letting on, points outside and says something to Thiago, who turns to me. "That store across the river has a phone. You can use theirs."

Well, that's just perfect. I take my key, thank the clerk, and hurry out the door.

Once I'm outside, I can see Ms. Fox's outline as she crosses the bridge. It's already getting dark out, and I don't love the idea of her walking alone into town, so I jog to catch up with her, telling myself I would do the same for any of the women on the trip. And I would too, just maybe not as fast.

She must hear me coming because she turns quickly, looking slightly startled.

I wave to her. "It's just me."

Without breaking her stride, she says, "You really don't have to come with me. I know we're supposed to be buddies and all, but I can handle a quick walk to the store."

"I need to use their phone," I tell her as we fall into step with each other. "I have an urgent business matter to attend to."

"I bet you do," she says under her breath.

"What's that supposed to mean?"

"Nothing. I shouldn't have said that."

"But you did and you clearly meant something by it."

"It's none of my business," she says.

"Agreed," I say, still feeling irked.

We walk for another minute, the only sound is our feet crunching on the gravel, then she says, "Maybe you shouldn't be in a relationship with someone you can't trust."

"What?" I ask, stopping in my tracks.

She stops and turns to me. "Your girlfriend. Clearly you don't trust her if you're having her followed, which honestly gives me the creeps just thinking about. You should probably consider going for therapy based on that alone, but while you're there, maybe do some digging into why you'd even want to stay with someone you can't trust."

"Girlfriend? I don't have a girlfriend," I say before remembering that I indeed told everyone I was in a committed relationship.

"Really? Because you made a big thing about it back in Lima, remember? And I couldn't help but overhear you ordering someone to be watched. I put two and two together."

"Wait—couldn't help but overhear or were purposely eavesdropping?" I ask, feeling slightly pissed.

"I can't help it. I've spent years training my ears to listen for the slightest noise for my work. Now it just … sort of happens, even when I don't mean for it to."

I stare down at her, trying to decide if she's telling the truth. It sounds plausible enough for someone who's spent the last decade listening for chit-chat from outer space. Although it's more likely complete bullshit. She has every reason to listen in on my conversations, and even more reasons to lie about it now.

Shrugging, she says, "I'm telling you the truth. I didn't mean to hear you when you were on the phone."

She starts walking again and I do the same.

Rubbing the back of my neck, I say, "That wasn't what it sounded like."

"No? Then what was it? Because where I come from, people don't have each other followed."

"I don't even have a girlfriend. I lied because the last thing I need is some gold digger trying to mine me the entire trip," I say. "The call had to do with a very important business deal. I need to make sure there aren't other offers coming in while I'm out here in the … 1830s." I glance up for the first time, only to be struck by how incredibly bright the stars are. "The entire thing is very delicate and if someone else swoops in, it'll be a disaster for me."

When she doesn't answer me, I say, "Do you believe me?"

"I guess so. It still seems to be all kinds of wrong, even in a business setting."

"It is," I answer. "I'm not proud of what I'm doing, but my whole life … this is the only thing that has mattered. I've wanted this since I was a kid. Before I was even out of high school. And now that I'm so close I can taste it, it might get ripped away. And this might be me justifying my actions, but I believe that there are a few situations in life when a person has to use every advantage they can find."

"So it's your dream then?" she asks, her voice softening.

"You could say that," I tell her, then for no reason at all, I find myself trying to convince her not to think less of me. "Some dreams are worth fighting for, aren't they? Even if you have to bend the rules?"

Ms. Fox looks up at me, her eyes searching mine in the faint street light. "Yes."

I smile down at her, relief washing over me.

We round the corner and the store comes into view. It's brightly lit up, giving it a warm feeling against the dark evening. I hurry ahead a little so I can open the door for her. A bell rings, notifying the sales clerk that we're here.

"Hola!" We're greeted by a woman in a pink blouse and a black skirt with bands of various colors around it— traditional Inca clothing, which I wonder if she's wearing for the tourists.

Ms. Fox and I both say hola back. As soon as she hears

our accents, she starts to speak in English. "Are you looking for anything in particular this evening or just browsing?"

"I need to use a phone," I tell her.

She nods at me, then turns to Ms. Fox, looking her up and down. "And your wife? She looks like she could use some new clothes."

Ms. Fox and I exchange a glance, and I wait to see if she's going to correct the woman on her assumption. She smiles up at me sweetly. "Yes, sweetie, I think I could use some clothes, you know, since my bag got lost and all."

I grin down at her. "Of course. Anything for my girl." Turning to the clerk, whose eyes are lit up like the sky on the Fourth of July, I say, "She's going to need everything—pants, shoes, undergarments…"

The woman smiles at Ms. Fox. "He's a very good husband. Not cheap like so many of them."

"If there's anything Ty isn't, it's cheap," she answers.

Huh, she called me Ty. I actually do like the sound of that better.

"You look around while I help your husband make his call," she says. "We have more sizes in the back, so if you don't see the right one, I can check. My name is Marisol, so just yell, *Marisol!* if you need me."

She gestures to me. "Come on. The phone is back here. But I need your credit card."

Of course she does.

12

Shopping with the Enemy...

Gwen

OKAY, if there's one thing this store has a lot of, it's colorful ponchos. I reach out and touch one of them, then mutter, "Oh, that is *so* soft."

"It's real baby alpaca wool," Marisol says. "A lot of stores say they use baby alpaca, but it's a lie. They only use maybe one percent. Ours is one-hundred percent."

"That's good to know," I say, flipping the price tag over on the poncho. It reads $100 USD/375 SOL. Yikes, that's a lot. "As beautiful as this is, I need to be practical. I have to get a jacket, some pants, shirts, underwear, socks, and hiking shoes."

"I have everything you need. Don't worry."

Within a few minutes, I'm in the dressing room, my arms loaded with clothing. Not my usual style—everything is very bright. Nothing black other than if I wanted to buy a traditional skirt, but even those have bands of color. The T-shirts all say Sacred Valley or Peru on them, but they're nice, soft cotton and will be a hell of a lot more comfortable than wearing this silk blouse everywhere. There is one style of denim jeans—boot cut in a medium wash. Luckily, she also has cargo pants. But as far as jackets go, it's really just the ponchos or wool cardigans.

On the other side of the dressing room, I can hear Ty on the phone. *Okay, Gwen, do not listen. Do not. Although if you do listen, you might hear something that'll come in handy when you need it.*

So, yeah, I'm listening.

"It didn't work. I'll be stuck here the entire time." Pause. "Well, that's certainly not the news I was hoping for, but it's not worst-case scenario."

Hmm… I wonder what the worst-case scenario is?

"I'll call her right now. What did you send her?" Pause. "Really?" Pause. "No, that's great. Very … out-of-the-box. I'm sure she'll love that." Pause. "Thanks, Donna. I have no idea when I'll be able to reach you again, but I'll—"

"How's it going in there?" Marisol asks, interrupting my eavesdropping.

"Great. I could use a bigger size in the jeans, if you've got them."

She pulls the curtain to the side a bit and pokes her head in. "Okay. I'll be right back. But first, you need a chullo and a bowler. The chullo will keep your ears warm and the bowler will keep you from getting wrinkles." She thrusts several hats at me. The chullos are like wool beanies with ear flaps and pompoms. The bowlers, are … well, bowler hats, which are apparently as popular with people in the Andes as they were with city gents in the late 1800s. No way am I buying two hats for a five day trip.

I take them and thank Marisol, wanting her to leave because I can hear Ty on another call. "Muffy, I'm sorry I missed you. I'm in the most beautiful little village in the Andes right now. A place that Richard loved. I'm afraid I won't be able to get in touch with you over the next couple of days, but I hope you'll enjoy your time with Bobbie Brown. According to my assistant, she's *the* makeup artists to the stars. I hope our deal is still on. As I've told you, I've been wanting to buy—"

"Here are your jeans!"

Dammit. "Thank you," I whisper, taking them from her.

"…a little kid with big dreams. No one will do a better job of looking after the club than I will. And that's a promise. I'll try you again as soon as I can get to a phone. In the meantime, if you're not happy with our agreement, I hope you'll give me a chance to make it right, without involving other people. Take care. Talk to you soon."

Huh. A club? His big business deal that is going to cost in the billions is some sort of club? What the hell? Also, that just doesn't help me at all.

I tug off the tight jeans and try on the other pair. Much better. Pulling a poncho with stripes in various shades of red over my head, I then look at myself in the mirror. Not half bad. Now I add the bowler hat. Oh, wow. Who is this bold woman?

Ty places another call. "Hey, Michael."

Oh, Michael! Who's Michael?

"It's been a little strange." Pause. "Unpredictable. I'm actually in a tiny village in the Sacred Valley." Pause. "That's right, Michael. Did you see that on one of your documentaries?" Pause. "Of course, I remember now. What did you and Greta do today?"

Long pause while I pull my poncho off my head and try on the cargo pants.

"Did it help?" Ty asks. Then he says, "I'm glad you had fun. What was your favorite part?" He waits for an answer, then I hear him say, "The jellyfish really are the best thing there, aren't they?"

He chuckles a little, and it's a deep, low sound that I kind of don't hate. "Right, I remember you told me that. Just jellies."

Another pause, then, "To be honest, I don't know. Richard wanted everything to be a surprise."

"A little, yeah, but don't worry about me. The people running the trip are top notch professionals," he says, pausing for a second, then adding, "Don't worry, you know me. I can handle myself."

I just bet he can handle himself.

"What are you having for supper?" he asks, sounding like he's not ready to hang up just yet.

"Yum. I'm missing out." Pause. "Greta's the best." Pause. "I love you too, Michael. Sleep well."

He chuckles again. "Right. That's what I meant. Good night."

Okay, so now I feel totally guilty. Listening in on a business call that might help me save our team is one thing. Listening in on a personal call? That's a whole different level of … wrong. Especially such a sweet call. But who the hell is Michael? Does he have a son no one knows about?

"How's the shopping going?" Ty asks, his voice now coming from the front of the curtain.

I'm standing in just a poncho and hat, no pants, so I instinctively cover up my thighs with both hands, even though there really is no need. "Good. Having lots of luck."

Marisol pokes her head in. "Are you ready to show your husband what you're buying?" She glances down. "Where are your pants? Did they not fit?"

"They're fine. I was just about to try on another pair."

"Okay, then come out so he can see how beautiful you look. So colorful! And that hat…" She does a chef's kiss.

"Umm, that's okay. I think we should skip the fashion show. We need to get back to the lodge for supper."

"No, babe, I'd love to see what you're wearing. Come on out," he says, and I can almost picture him with a big stupid grin on his face.

I pull on the cargos, then slide the curtain, expecting him to laugh.

"Very nice. You look good in red. You should wear it more often." He turns to Marisol. "I've literally never seen her in anything other than black and white."

"So boring," she answers, shaking her head. "We'll fix that."

"Yes, let's. I want to see my lady in lots of colors for a change," he says. "Oh, and she's going to need a backpack and a swimsuit. You don't happen to have those, do you?"

"I certainly do," she tells him. "Sexy bikinis."

He grins at me and my stomach does a little flip without my permission. "She's got bikinis, babe."

———

Twenty minutes later, I walk out of the dressing room in my new jeans, a long-sleeved tee that says, "Life's better in the Sacred Valley," and the red poncho.

Marisol is humming to herself while she rings everything up and packs it carefully in my new backpack. Somehow she talked me into the bowler hat *and* a chullo. I stare, horrified at the amount of money I'm about to spend. I wonder if Keenan would let me expense it? Or maybe the airline will reimburse me? I'll have to figure something out because this is going to cost a fortune. My face heats up with embarrassment and fear while I watch her ring it up. The heat is probably also because of this super warm alpaca wool poncho and socks. But, mainly, it's embarrassment. I'm hoping he doesn't notice. I also hope my credit card goes through because it's due next week and I've charged it up something fierce this month.

"Three-thousand, two-hundred and twenty-nine."

My jaw drops. "Dollars?"

"Soles." Doing the math in my head, I feel my heart sink. I'm about to spend almost twelve hundred dollars which I know isn't going to fit on my already-stretched card. I dig around in my purse for my wallet, preparing myself to ask the dreaded question of 'can I put it on two cards?' but when I look up, Ty's already handing her his black card.

"Oh no, I can't let you—"

He grins down at me. "Of course I'm buying. You're my best girl."

Marisol beams at us. "He's a keeper, this one! Don't ever let him go if you know what's good for you."

"Oh, I won't," I say, adding, "He's my boo."

Ty snorts out a laugh, then wraps an arm casually over my shoulder. "And you're worth every penny I make."

"So romantic!" she squeals, handing the backpack to Ty.

I grin up at him, then turn to her with a sassy look. "Well, it's not like he's a billionaire or something…"

As soon as we walk out into the night air, my heart lurches. What am I doing? Flirting with the enemy like this? Shamelessly, I might add. And even worse—I *like* it. I mean I *really frigging like* flirting with him. It's the most fun I've had in … well, years, really.

What would Allie say? She'd be horrified. And the rest of the team would ice me out if they knew that I was feeling all sorts of feelings I shouldn't be. It hasn't even been one day. I am a weak, weak woman, turning into putty in the hands of a very evil man. Well, not evil. But certainly selfish to put that stupid club ahead of the foundation. Plus he said all that awful stuff about us to the media—how he never would have put in a dollar if he'd known the types of projects Dr. Napper was funding. I hate him, right?

Yeah, I still hate him. Now that I remember all his criticism over the years and what he said earlier today about shutting everything down. He's the worst person ever.

Only maybe he's not…

13

And Back to Our Regularly Scheduled Program...

Ty

Whatever weird spell we were under in the store ended the second we stepped outside. Gone is the flirty Ms. Fox, replaced by the serious version again. We walk along in an awkward silence for a couple of minutes while I go over what just happened. I have no idea why I decided to pretend we were married. No clue. I guess I thought the whole thing would amuse me. Or maybe it's the altitude playing tricks on my brain, but the thing is, I didn't mind having Marisol think Gwen Fox was my wife. Even though I don't now, nor ever have, wanted one. But obviously, the whole thing was a mistake in judgment because now things are strained.

We're just about to the bridge, when she clears her throat. "Look, Mr. Sterling, I intend to pay you back for the clothes. I shouldn't have let you pay for them in the first place. I don't know why I did it, actually."

"You don't have to pay me back," I say. "It was nothing. And I think we should dispense with the formalities, Gwendolyn. We were just married, after all."

She grins for a second, then as quickly as it comes, it disappears. "No, it was definitely something. Maybe not for you, but for me. Besides, accepting them sends the wrong message."

"What message is that?" I ask, stuffing my hands in my pockets to warm them up.

"I don't know. That I'm the type of woman who lets men buy her expensive things?"

Raising one eyebrow, I say, "Is that a thing?"

"Yes, it's a thing. I believe you referred to them as gold diggers earlier."

"I don't think you're a gold digger. Not in the traditional sense, anyway."

"What is that supposed to mean?"

"You're here to get money, but not for yourself. It's for your whole team."

"Yes, I am, which is why I'm going to pay you back."

I stop walking and she does the same. "Look, I didn't want to embarrass you back there, but I could tell that it was an amount of money you weren't comfortable spending."

"I have the money, I just…" She trails off and starts walking again.

Catching up, I say, "You just what?"

"Would've needed two different cards to pay for it," she says, her tone telling me she did not want to admit that. "I've had a lot of expenses lately, not that I expect you to understand."

"I understand what it's like to cut it close every month."

"You do not."

"I do. I've lived paycheck to paycheck."

"What? Were you spending seven figures a month or something?"

"No, I didn't exactly grow up with much, and when I was in college, I was so broke I worked at a bar just so I could get free food. And the first few years that Richard and I were building our company? Totally broke ass broke." I smile, remembering the crappy basement suite he, Michael, and I shared. "If I had seven dollars at the end of the month, it was a hell of a good month."

"Oh, I didn't know that about you."

"Did you assume I was born rich?"

She nods.

"Most people do," I tell her. "But I wasn't. Lower middle-class family until my father left us. Then we became a lower low-class family."

Gwen looks up at me and I can see she's almost as surprised as I am that I'm saying any of this. "I'm sorry to hear that."

"Don't be. You weren't the dirt bag who abandoned a wife and two sons—one of them autistic and needing special care."

"Was that who you were talking to earlier? Your brother?"

I raise an eyebrow. "Were you accidentally tuning into my conversation?"

"I really couldn't help it. That wall was very thin."

"Yes, that was Michael. He lives with me."

She's quiet for a moment, and I know she's absorbing this information. Part of me hopes it'll change her opinion of me, even though I really shouldn't care what she thinks. "Where's your mom now?"

"She died when I was nineteen."

"I'm sorry," she says. "That must have been awful—

being so young and suddenly having to care for your brother."

There's a gentleness in her voice that makes me want to wrap my arms around her and tell her all about every shitty thing I've ever been through. "It wasn't easy, but I managed okay," I say, offering her an easy smile to lighten the moment.

She doesn't smile back. Instead, she says, "You don't have to do that. You can just be real with me. It's okay."

"What, are you a soft place to land?" I ask, verging on sarcastic to avoid how I'm actually feeling.

"I could be."

Somehow I know she means it, and to be honest, this whole thing is suddenly extremely confusing. Here's a woman that I met a few hours ago, who I can't seem to stop breaking all my own rules for—oversharing, flirting, wanting her opinion, and wanting to change her opinion of me. And I don't want that from anyone. I need to get away from her right now so I can get my head screwed on straight again.

We walk back through the gates of the lodge and up the long, paved driveway. When we reach the lobby, I pull the door open for her and we walk inside, the warm air welcoming us. Gwen stops and looks up at me, her green eyes melting my resolve. "Would you like to grab a bite of supper with me? I'll treat."

Yes, I would. "I think I'll eat in my room. I have some work I have to take care of."

I can see the disappointment in her eyes but she keeps her smile in place. "Right. Yes. Well, thank you," she says, reaching up with her right hand.

For a brief second, I think she's going to pull me toward her for a kiss, but she doesn't. She puts her hand on the strap of her backpack. "I should take this then."

"Right, yes." My first response is disappointment which is swiftly followed by shock. There's no way I should want that. There's no way I should want her.

"I'll see you tomorrow," she says. "Good luck with your work."

"Thanks. Have a good sleep."

"I will."

I turn and walk down the long hallway to my room and unlock the door. When I'm inside, I let out a long sigh, then open the room service menu and call down to order the fish carpaccio and two bottles of beer. After that, I wander around my room for a minute, and decide to take a shower while I wait for my meal to arrive.

As the hot water washes over me, I feel agitated. Alone. No, more than alone—lonely, which is crazy because I like being alone. Love it, in fact. Alone is my happy place, other than when I'm at home hanging out with Michael. I'm just tired. That's all this is. Tired and maybe a little mixed up. But the fact that I'm so mixed up is exactly why I *should* be alone right now. I need to concentrate on the important things in life—how to safeguard the corporation now that Richard is gone and make sure I'm the next owner of the Destroyers. Gwendolyn Fox is one distraction I don't need. Or want. No matter what her ass looked like in those leggings.

14

Heating Up the Hot Springs...

Gwen

I SHOULD BE SLEEPING. It's been an insanely long day. I'm exhausted. Except, I'm not. My whole body feels like it's vibrating, as if I'm hooked up to some sort of motor with no off switch. I've just been lying here, my mind going over every minute I spent with Ty Sterling today. It feels as though I've always known him, even though I really don't know him at all. And what I do know, I don't like. He's a cynic. A critic. And worse, he's one of those awful critics who's vocal with his opinion even though he's never stepped foot in our facility to see what we do, how we do it, or why. Instead, he sits in judgment of us from a place of ignorance and skepticism (two things the world really doesn't need more of right now).

For the life of me, I can't reconcile that version of him with the one I met today. The one who gave me his pullover when I was cold and exposed. The flirty, fun version pretending to be my husband. The caring one on the phone with his brother. The one holding my hand on that helicopter. The man that, in just a few short hours, stirred all kinds of feelings in me that I haven't had since my college days. I grab my phone to text Allie, even though I have no idea when it'll get to her.

Super confusing day. Spent the entire time with Ty Sterling. He was actually oddly amazing. Not sure he's who we think he is.

I stare at it, then delete it. I can't send that to her. Not after years of us having so much fun hating him. The thought of Allie makes me realize what's at stake—our jobs, my house, my entire social circle. It'll all come to an end and it'll be because of him. No. It'll be because of me if I can't convince him.

Come on, Gwen. Get your head in the game. Because this is a game to be won or lost by me. I know I can change his mind. I can see it in his eyes when he looks at me. The way his focus is only on me, how his pupils get a little bigger, the way he held my hand—with such warm comfort. I can use this to save us all. And isn't that exactly what someone like him would do? He said it himself. Use every advantage you can find. Bend the rules. So maybe that's what I have to do too.

Picking up my phone, I write: *I was wrong about him having his girlfriend followed. It's to do with a business deal—the one he's using as an excuse to shut us down. Please Google the name Muffy and club, see if you can make sense of it. He's buying some sort of club that must be worth billions. He needs to keep it a secret or it sounds like the whole deal will go up in smoke. If we can figure it out, maybe we can find a way to use the information to get our funding.*

I press send and hope that sometime tomorrow, it'll go through. Throwing the covers off, I walk over to the window, the hardwood cool against my bare feet. The stars are unbelievably bright here, reminding me of my time in Puerto Rico back in grad school. When I look down, I spot one of the hot spring pools. It's empty and the steam rising into the dark night air looks extremely inviting. That'll help me fall asleep.

I quickly change into the new bikini Ty bought me, pull on a plush white bathrobe and hotel slippers, pocket my room key and head outside. The air is much cooler now and I bundle the robe tighter around my waist while I make my way to the pool. Sloughing off the robe, I slide into the steamy water, feeling the silkiness against my skin. "Ahhhh."

I sit back against the side and stare up at the stars, feeling both small and connected to the universe at the same time. We're not alone. I know we aren't. If only I could convince Ty of the one thing I can't convince my family—that there is life out there and one day we will know each other, maybe even be friendly but distant neighbors.

I think about all the steps between now and then— thousands of them—securing our funding, updating the technology so we can make faster progress, expanding our search. But it all starts with me using whatever advantages I can to change the mind of one very stubborn man. One very stubborn, chivalrous, sexy, fun man. Guilt comes over me about the text, but then I remind myself why I'm here and who's going to get hurt if I can't figure out a way to get this done. I picture Keenan puttering away in his garden, lonely and lacking any purpose. I picture myself staring at the dumpster outside my kitchen window until I'm fifty.

My mind wanders back to Ty and I can see his smile in my mind. "I'm so confused," I say, even though there's no one here to listen.

"About what?"

I start and turn, my heart pounding as I take in the sight of the man himself standing beside the pool wearing only swim trunks and a smirk. Oh. My. That is one manly man. Everything about him is sculpted to perfection and for lack of a better word—big.

"Mind if I join you?" he asks.

"Yes," I say, before I realize what his question actually was. "I mean, no. I don't mind." My face warms up with more than just the heat of the water.

He grins, then steps into the pool and sits down on the opposite side facing me. "Ahh, that's nice."

"It's great, isn't it?" I ask, glad that he seems to have forgotten about me being confused. "I couldn't sleep so I thought I'd give this a try."

He nods. "I tend not to sleep when I'm on the road."

"At all?"

Glancing up, he says, "A few minutes here and there."

"Sounds rough."

"It's one of the reasons I try not to travel much."

I fill in the blank—it's also because of his brother.

His eyes light up and he says, "What are you confused about?"

Damn. He remembered. "Umm … it's one of those things that's hard to explain."

"Try me. I've got time and maybe I can help," Ty says with an easy smile. When I don't answer right away, he adds, "I'm going to be up all night anyway."

Turning my attention to my fingernails, I try to quickly think of something that would be confusing because I can hardly say I'm talking to the night air about him, now can I? "I was just thinking about how … they get the caramel into the Caramilk bar."

He lifts one eyebrow and that damn smirk is back.

"Really? You're an astrobiologist and you're confused by that?"

"Yes," I say, lifting my chin defiantly. "Total mystery."

"Liar."

"Maybe, but only because it's none of your business. I wasn't talking to you."

He stares at me for a moment and honestly, the intensity of it is enough to melt the rocks surrounding the pool. He knows. He totally knows I was talking about him. It's written all over my stupid face, isn't it? "Can I guess?"

"What?"

"If I guess right, will you tell me?"

"That's not a game I'm willing to play," I say, my voice coming out breathier than I intend.

"Too bad. I have a feeling that would've been fun," Ty says. "What game are you willing to play?"

The words *hide the sausage* pop into my mind. Newp! Not that. Boy, it's hot in this hot spring. Like ridiculously hot. They shouldn't make them so damn hot. Electing to ignore his question, I say, "Did you get your work done?"

A flash of guilt crosses his face, and I know it was just an excuse. "As much as I could without internet access."

"So, approximately nothing?" I ask.

"Yeah, about that much. Maybe less."

We both laugh, then, when it all starts feeling like too much, I look up at the night sky. When I glance back at him, I can see Ty is doing the same thing.

"Is that the Milky Way?" he asks, pointing to the band of light to my left.

"Uh huh. It's beautiful, isn't it?"

"I've only seen it once before. It's hard to forget."

"Did you know until the 1920s, people believed the Milky Way contained all the stars in the whole universe?" I ask.

"I did not know that," he says, looking back at me again.

Nodding, I say, "It's true. It was Edwin Hubble who proved that it was just one of many galaxies."

"Edwin Hubble of the Hubble telescope?"

"Yup. 1920 really wasn't that long ago, in terms of human history," I say. "Our knowledge can change in the blink of an eye. Technology too."

"Gwen, I'm not going to change my mind."

Offering him a guilty grin, I say, "I wasn't trying to. I was just making conversation."

He raises one eyebrow at me, and I squirm on the stone bench a little before looking back up at the stars. I'm just in time to see a meteor. I make an involuntary "ooh!" sound and point up as it leaves a long, bright tail against the darkness.

He swivels around and looks up. "Was that a shooting star or one of your friends doing a fly-by?"

I give him a glare, but not a real one. A real flirty one. "A meteor, yes."

"Oh, sorry, a *meteor*. Only us laymen call them shooting stars, right?"

"Well, technically they're not stars, so…"

"Accuracy."

"Exactly," I say, trying to suppress a grin (and losing badly). "Actually, it's the Geminid meteor shower right now, so we should see more. You'd have to come sit on this side of the pool though because they're generally in the northern quadrant of the sky." I blush a little, hoping he doesn't notice on account of my cheeks probably already being bright pink. Shrugging, I add, "I mean, only if you're into that sort of thing."

He glances at my lips, then stands up and strides toward me, allowing me the perfect view of his naked torso. Am I biting my lip while staring shamelessly at his chest and abs? Yes, I think I am. I should stop. I clear my throat and turn my gaze back to the sky, even though it's the last thing I want to look at right now. Ty sits next to me, so close that if I shift just the slightest to my left, our arms will be touching. My heart pounds wildly in my chest and I swear he can hear it in the silence. "Umm… so, do you see Orion's belt right there?" I ask, pointing up.

Nodding, he says, "Is it that group of stars that looks like a belt?"

I turn to him with a small smile. "You're a bit of a smartass, aren't you?"

"Uh-huh," he answers, looking down at me.

"No one ever writes that about you. In any of the articles I've read."

"You've read articles about me?" he asks, looking awfully amused.

Looking back up at Orion, I try to sound very professional. "It's good to know everything you can about the man who signs your paychecks."

"Of course. Smart," he says, but I can tell by his tone he doesn't believe me.

"What? That is absolutely why I looked you up. Because you're my boss. Sort of. I mean, a boss is more like someone who actually *knows* what you do for a living. You're more of a reluctant patron."

He ignores the subtle dig, which I thought he'd jump on. Instead, he says, "And in all those things you read about me, what did you learn?"

I pause, trying to decide how much to say. "That you're a skeptic. You don't believe in anything you can't see, touch, or hear."

He glances down at me and I very stupidly look up at his gorgeous face. "Don't forget about taste."

Swallowing hard, I say, "Right. That too."

"And even if I can do all those things, I still only believe half of it," he says, his eyes flicking down to my lips again. Oh my God, is he going to kiss me? Because I wouldn't say no to that. Wait, yes, I would. Wouldn't I?

15

When the Brain and the Body Totally Disconnect...

Ty

OH wow, do I ever want to kiss her. I can't remember a time when I wanted to kiss a woman this badly. Probably not since I was a naive teenager who didn't know any better. This woman—this feeling—is nothing but trouble. The smart thing to do would be to excuse myself, get out of this pool, and go the hell back to my room. But I won't. Not just because I only came out here because I saw her and didn't like the idea of her being out here on her own, but also because I don't want to. There's a defiant part of me that is insisting I stay right here next to her, despite how stupid it is.

I force myself to look up at the sky. "What else do you know about me?"

"You graduated at the top of your class at Harvard business school. You and Dr. Napper were college roommates and you started your company together as soon as he finished med school. The business flailed for the first six years until he came up with the idea for the DNA testing kits. Then things just sort of took off."

Nodding, I say, "Yes, we were one of those overnight success stories that was years in the making."

She chuckles a little, then says, "Does it bother you? When people assume it came so easily?"

"It would if I cared what people thought."

Gwen turns and looks up at me. I can feel the skepticism on her face without bothering to look. "Everybody cares what people think of them."

"I don't."

"Now it's my turn to call you a liar."

I glance down at her with a half grin. "What? Did one of your articles suggest I spend my nights stewing over public opinion of me? Because I'd caution you not to believe everything you read."

"No, you gave it away yourself."

"How?" I ask, pulling back a bit.

"Because you wanted to explain yourself to me earlier —when there was the mix up about you having your girlfriend followed."

"I was merely trying to correct a false impression. That kind of thing could start a rumor that would follow me for years."

"If you didn't care what people thought of you, you wouldn't care if they believed a rumor." Her grin says, 'Beat you again, sucker.'

Narrowing my eyes a little, I smile back, then shake my head. I let out a sigh and stare up at the stars again. "You're too fucking smart." And too fucking gorgeous. And too fucking sexy in that bikini. I haven't even seen her full body in it, just her bare shoulders and the top of her chest, and even that's got me undone.

"I'll take that as a compliment even though I'm not sure that's how you meant it."

Just then another meteor shows itself. I point up to it. "There's one!" Okay, I sounded way too thrilled about that just now. I'm supposed to be playing it cool.

"They're amazing, aren't they?" she asks, her voice suddenly all dreamy and doing things to me it shouldn't.

"Surprisingly exciting." As in, I better not stand up right now.

We sit in silence for a moment, the tension between us growing thick. Needing a distraction from thinking about all the things I want to do to her, I say, "So after all the articles you read about me, what conclusion did you reach about who I am?"

My mind wanders back to the word ASSHOLE across my forehead. *Good, Ty. Think of that. Not what's happening right now.*

Gwen pauses, then says, "To be honest, my opinion of you was on the low side."

"You probably thought I was a real asshole."

A flash of guilt crosses her face. "You did say some pretty awful things about our program—that thing about us wearing tin foil hats? Or when you told GQ the entire foundation is a massive embarrassment to you and that you couldn't wait to distance yourself from every single one of those 'ridiculous time and money-wasters.' I'm sure you can understand how people on my side of those comments would feel threatened."

"And hurt?" I ask, guilt coming over me as I reflect on my own words.

Nodding, she says, "That too. But now that I know a little about your background, I think I can understand what made you this way. Nobody's born cynical. They get that way by being hurt themselves."

"Wow, you cut right to the heart of the matter, don't you?" I turn to her and prop my arm up on the side of the pool so I can focus on her.

"You asked," she says, looking up at me from under her thick eyelashes. "Were you expecting a less direct answer?"

"Yes," I say, and we both laugh a little about it. "I thought you might say something about me being a self-made man or how impressive it is that Richard and I turned one little idea into a fortune."

"You assumed I would flatter you," she says, touching her collar bone with her fingertips.

"That's what usually happens in these situations."

"Is this a typical situation for you? Alone in a natural hot spring with a woman late at night?" Gwen asks, pushing away from the side and turning to face me from the middle of the pool.

"I didn't mean that. I meant … when I'm dealing with someone who wants something from me."

Her smile fades and she says, "I'm guessing that's almost everyone you meet."

"You'd be right about that."

She spreads her arms out to the sides, skimming the top of the water. "You didn't answer my question."

"The one about whether I frequently find myself alone with a beautiful woman?"

"I never said anything about beautiful."

"My mistake. I thought you did." Not my mistake. Just my way of telling her she's beautiful without actually saying it. You know, since I really shouldn't be saying it again.

"Well, I didn't. You still haven't answered."

"I don't want to."

She grunts a little, then says, "I'll take that as a no."

I laugh at her answer. "Why wouldn't you take it as a yes?"

"You don't want to lie to me because you know I'll see through it, but you also want me to think you're some sort of player, because deep-down, you want to impress me."

Grinning at her, I push myself away from the edge and swim toward her a few feet. "I'm not trying to impress you, but would that really work? If you thought I was a total dog?"

"No, but *you* might think that would work better than letting me believe you spend most of your nights hanging out at home with your brother."

"I do spend most of my nights at home with my brother," I tell her, moving a little closer. "We play cards and watch a *lot* of documentaries."

"Let me guess—in your home theater with a massive screen, huge leather recliners, and one of those big red popcorn machines?"

"Home theater with a relatively large but not ridiculous screen, a big, comfy sectional—velvet, not leather—and gingerbread cookies."

"Gingerbread? Really?" she asks.

"Yes. Soft ones. Fresh from the oven."

She smiles, looking slightly surprised. "And do you bake them yourself?"

God, this is fun. So very much fun. "Greta makes them. She's my housekeeper, and she looks after Michael for me when I can't be home. Your turn."

"My turn for what?" she asks, swimming a little closer to me.

"I've just told you a lot of private information about myself. The fair thing to do would be to reciprocate with similarly private information."

"Is the fabric of your couch really that private?"

"For me it is."

"In that case, I have a microfiber sofa. It's gray. And as much as I like gingerbread, I'd choose chocolate chip every time," she tells me. "But then, I've never tried one of Greta's fresh-from-the-oven gingerbread cookies."

"Well, that's why you'd choose a lesser cookie then."

"Chocolate chip is in no way lesser. Especially mine."

"You bake?"

"Only when I'm feeling happy."

"And is that very often?"

Her smile falters a little, but just a touch. "Often enough, I suppose."

Something about her answer bothers me. It's like I instinctively want to find a way to make her happy all the time. But that's crazy. I don't even know her. "How do you decide what's often enough when it comes to happiness?"

"I don't know. Nobody gets to be happy all the time. Most days are just sort of … normal, right?"

"Agreed," I tell her, moving toward her again. "And what would you call today?"

Glancing up, she says, "Strange."

"Agreed."

"Ooh! There's another one!"

I look up to see the tail end of a meteor.

"This is definitely in my top three night sky experiences."

"Top three?"

She nods. "Puerto Rico as a college student and a family vacation in the Canadian Arctic—northern lights. You?"

I stare up at the millions of stars. "I'm going to say this tops the list."

"Really?" she asks.

I watch her as she moves toward me again, wanting

very much for her to close the distance between us completely. Wanting to feel her wet body pressed against mine and to taste her lips. "Definitely."

I propel myself to her with my arms, too caught up in the moment to care about the consequences. She looks up at me, her lips parting, her eyes wide. She glances at my mouth, then licks her lips, and I know she's feeling this too. The same pull that I am. It's magnetic. Irresistible. And completely wrong. I cannot be the one to make the first move. Not with her. Not with who I am to her. Not with what I'm about to do to her and all her teammates.

The tension between us builds to a breaking point. My heart pounds in my chest. I move ever so slightly toward her again, leaving a couple of inches between our mouths, waiting for her to make the decision.

She swallows hard, then flops onto her back and swims away from me, leaving me standing here hard as a rock and totally gutted. "We should get some sleep."

"Good idea. I think we have to be up early."

Swimming to the steps, she saunters up them, giving me the view of a lifetime—the curves of her almost-naked body, dripping wet. If I were one to pray, I'd be praying for her to turn around and invite me back to her room. But she can't, and even if she did, I couldn't go. All too quickly for my liking, she's pulling on her robe and sliding into her slippers. She turns around and smiles at me. "Are you going back to your room too?"

"In a bit." As soon as my obvious attraction to her is no longer so obvious.

"You won't sleep anyway."

"Exactly."

"Good night, Mr. Sterling."

"Good night, Ms. Fox."

16

Pancakes, Bacon, and Unwanted Girl Talk...

Gwen

Is THIS HAPPENING? All of this crazy, wonderful, sexy stuff? With the last person I would *ever* have thought it could happen with? It's got to be because of the near-death experience. That happens in movies all the time. The couple is about to be killed so they confess their love to each other only to survive and live happily ever after. Side note: I'll be getting back on a helicopter in exactly NEVER days.

But, back to the problem at hand, because it is a giant one that needs solving, like right now. I can't have feelings for him. I simply can't. And I'm sure I don't. It's just exhaustion from the last few days. Or maybe, they pumped something into the air in that helicopter because there is no way this is actually happening. I'd sooner believe that I got knocked out somehow back at the airport in Lima and I'm actually in a coma having weird, lucid, steamy dreams than think for a minute that this is real.

Yet, it all feels pretty damn real. I check my phone again to see if it's time to get up yet. I've been awake since four o'clock, having managed about three hours of solid sleep before a very spicy moment with my arch nemesis woke me up all hot and bothered. We were right back in that hot spring about to kiss, only instead of swimming away, I wrapped my arms around his neck and planted the mother of all kisses on him. I can still feel it now, even though it never happened. And in my dream, it was amazing. He pulled me close, our bodies pressed against each other, as we kissed some more, his tongue doing all the things I needed, my legs finding their way around his waist. His swim trunks miraculously dissolving in the water. My bikini bottoms yanked out of the way. Just as the first big thrust was about to happen, I woke up with a gasp.

And haven't slept since. That was over an hour ago, so I might as well just accept that *that* was the start of my day. A sexy dream about a man I love to hate. Seriously, hating Ty Sterling has been my favorite pastime for years. If I stop now, I don't know what I'll do with my free time.

I take a quick shower, eager to go in search of some coffee. After getting dressed in my new jeans, a long-sleeved tee, and my hiking boots, I decide to throw on my poncho. What the hell? I'm in Peru and that lady in the store said red was my color. So did Ty, but obviously that's not why I'm wearing it. It's because ponchos are surprisingly practical, especially up in the mountains when the sun is barely up and the air is cool.

Making my way down to the lobby, I smell the aroma of freshly brewed coffee. It's too early for the full breakfast buffet to be out, but I'm pleased to see there is already a table set up against the wall with carafes, juices, muffins, and fruit. I walk over and pour myself a steaming cup, adding lots of cream and sugar so I can get some carbs, sugar, and caffeine to make up for my lack of sleep.

Honestly, I'm a little peeved. Stupid sexy Sterling

stealing my sleep. That's just like him. The original version I have of him in my mind, that is. Making us poor unsuspecting women feel … whatever it is I'm feeling so we can't sleep or think straight. That's how he gets what he wants. In this case, it's to prevent me from stopping him from ruining my life. Asshole.

That's better, Gwen. Get mad. Anger will fuel your brain. That, and this deliciously sweet nectar of the gods. Aahhhh…

Okay, all I need is a plan. With any luck, the team back home will soon be searching for Skip and trying to find out about this mysterious club Ty's buying. (My current theory is it's some sort of secret billionaire's club where they make poor people wrestle for dimes.) Aside from trying to get any information I can on the club, my main job is to stay close enough to Ty so I can influence his decision, yet far enough away that I keep my heart safe. That shouldn't be a problem, right?

I'll be polite, but slightly aloof so he knows that what almost happened last night is *not* going to almost happen again. Then I'll spend the rest of the trip looking for an opportunity to pry open his very closed mind. He responds to logic and reasoning, both of which I can do. He has already admitted when he was wrong more than once, so I know he's not an impossible wall of a human. I hope.

An hour later, the rest of the group starts to trickle down to the lobby, all looking a little worse for wear. That is, except for Ty, who looks completely refreshed and ready to take on the world. Bastard.

Okay, Gwen, artfully avoid him without making it seem like you're avoiding him.

I wait until he's nearly done loading up at the buffet table before making my way over to do the same.

He glances up from in front of the scrambled eggs. "Good morning, Ms. Fox. I trust you slept well."

Ms. Fox? Oh, I see he's going for polite-but-aloof as well. "Yes, thank you. That soak in the hot springs put me right to sleep." Oh, I am *such* a liar. "I trust you didn't sleep at all."

"Not a wink," he says before walking away.

Adding a stack of tiny hot cakes, fresh fruit, and bacon to my plate, I then go in search of somewhere to sit, only to see Ty settling himself at a table with Niles, Rohan, Thiago, and Dr. Napper's urn.

I guess it's girls versus boys at breakfast this morning. Suits me just fine. I make a beeline for the table that Karen and Savannah are at. "Mind if I join you?"

"Sure," Karen says with a smile. I know she's basically an expert at smiling, but honestly, she really does seem to mean it. Canadians are so nice. Also gullible. Well, this one anyway.

"Thank you so much for your leggings," I tell her, pulling them out of my backpack and placing them on top of hers. "You're a real life saver."

"You're welcome. How'd it go at the store last night? I see you found at least one nice outfit."

My face heats up at the mention of my shopping trip with my 'husband.' "I managed to find a few things that should work."

"I see that," Savannah says. "Cute poncho."

"Thanks," I tell her. "It's so soft."

She reaches out and pets my arm. "My goodness, but that is the softest thing ever!"

Karen does the same. "Ooh, wow."

"It's real baby alpaca."

Savannah's jaw drops and she pulls her hand away. "They killed a baby alpaca for that?"

Oh dear. "No, they just shear them down. Like they do with sheep."

She lets her shoulders drop. "Thank heavens! Here I was starting to think you were a real Cruella de Vil."

"Nope. I'd never make a coat out of puppies." I add some syrup from a small bottle at the table and slice into my pancakes. My stomach grumbles at my first bite, reminding me of how long I've been awake already.

"You certainly got lucky yesterday," Savannah says.

"How so?" I ask, wondering if she's referring to being vomited on, losing my luggage, or almost dying in a helicopter.

She gives me a 'you know what I mean' look. "Mr. Sterling picking you as his buddy? All that extra time together?"

I set my gaze on my breakfast to avoid eye contact. "Umm, yeah, I guess so, but it's not like he's going to change his mind about the money."

She purses her lips together. "You certainly seemed to be doing your best to convince him in the hot springs last night."

"Hot springs?" Karen asks, her eyes growing wide.

A little louder, Karen. I'm not sure the entire restaurant heard you. I glance at Ty, who is looking over at me with his eyes narrowed a little. Oh, perfect. Now he's going to think I'm spilling the tea over here, which I definitely would never do.

"Uh-huh, real late last night too," Savannah says, stabbing a piece of melon with her fork. "I woke up and there they were, nearly naked as jay birds. And from the looks of things, you two left that pool hotter than you found it."

"What?!" Karen whisper-yells.

"Nothing happened," I whisper, leaning in. "Nothing at all. Just … talking."

Savannah glances at Karen. "They almost kissed."

"No," I say, chuckling like it's the craziest thing I've ever heard. "We definitely didn't… Is that what it looked like from your vantage point?"

"It looked like it because that's what was happening." Glancing at Karen, she adds, "You should've seen them, all snuggled up together."

"There was a meteor shower and I was showing him the meteors. That's why he was so close to me." I take a gulp of water, hoping to cool down my flaming cheeks.

"You were showing him your meteors all right," Savannah says. "I know what I saw, honey, but don't worry. I'm not mad. We're all out here playing the same game. You just got a head start on us is all. Now, my big question is who asked who to meet out there?"

"Neither." I shake my head vigorously. "It just sort of happened. I was there, then a little later, he was there too. Then I left. Alone. Went back to my room and straight to bed. To sleep. Alone," I ramble. "Look, I don't know what you thought you saw, but believe me, I am not interested in him that way. Obviously I want the money. We *all* do," I tell her. "But I'm not about to prostitute myself to get it."

"I don't think we're supposed to say prostitute anymore," Karen says. "The correct term now is sex worker."

"Really? I thought we weren't supposed to say sex worker. I read an article that suggested the rebranding of it has hidden dangers."

"No, I think that's the new term," Karen says.

"Okay, well, either way, I'm not going to do any…" I lower my voice so I can barely even hear it myself, "…sex working. No sex work at all. None."

"It wouldn't exactly be a job," Savannah says, gazing across the restaurant at him. "Not with a man that fine."

Karen and I both look over too, and of course, he sees us, which means he totally knows we're talking about him. Gah! This is brutal. Why don't we just pass him a note in bio class that says, "Which of us would you want to marry, kiss, or kill?" I look back at Savannah. "Even with a man that fine, sleeping with him to get money from him would be the definition of … either of those terms."

"So you have no interest in him then?" Savannah asks, popping a grape into her mouth.

"No interest whatsoever. I could never be with a man that cynical."

"You won't mind if I take a swing then?"

"Obviously not," I answer, scoffing a little as if the thought of being with him never crossed my mind.

"Good, because I'm definitely going to swing," she says, staring at him while she plays with her necklace. "*Hard.*"

Hmm, I'm having an interesting reaction to that idea. I kind of want to rip her face off right now. When I have a quiet moment, I should probably dig in and analyze why.

Karen looks over at him too, then back at us. "Do you really think sleeping with him would get him to change his mind?"

"Oh, I don't care about that," Savannah says. "Unless it's changing his mind about that girlfriend of his."

The girlfriend he doesn't have.

Karen looks at me like I just kicked a baby alpaca. "I forgot he had a girlfriend. I wonder how she would've felt about you two being in the hot tub alone in the middle of the night."

She would've felt nothing, Karen, because she doesn't exist. But, not my secret to tell, even if this does make me look like a woman with what my grandma would call 'loose morals.' "I … have no idea, but like I said, I was there first, so it's not like I went looking for him to try to start something."

Karen makes a little *hmph* sound, then concentrates on eating her one tiny pancake while I shovel my six into my mouth, feeling like I should have a scarlet A sewn to my poncho.

Thiago stands and walks over to us. "I hate to interrupt, but we really have to get going to our next destination and before we can do that, we have a video from Dr. Napper. So please finish eating, then come over to our table to watch it."

I scarf down the rest of my food, not sure when we're going to eat again, then wipe my mouth with my napkin.

Karen carefully folds up her napkin and puts in on her plate. "Look, I didn't mean to sound judgmental there. This is a strange situation. We're *all* desperate here. All of us are going to be out of our jobs in a few weeks. I really think the best thing would be if we put our heads together and work as a team."

Savannah smiles at her. "Oh, sweetie, you're so naive. Gwen's been playing the game since the moment she showed up at the airport and scared off half the women."

Karen gasps a little. "You did that on purpose?"

Guilty as charged. "Well, I mean … they would've been putting themselves in a dangerous situation. Dengue fever is no joke."

Savannah gives her a 'See? I told you so' look. "She's way ahead of us, but that doesn't mean we're out of the running."

From across the restaurant, Thiago clears his throat loudly. "Ladies, please! Is there a problem?"

Yes, Thiago, at the moment I have about ninety-nine problems, but a bitchy tour guide ain't one.

We hurry over and stand behind Niles and Ty, facing the screen.

Thiago presses play, and Dr. Napper's face appears. "Good morning! I hope you all enjoyed the hot springs last night and slept well. Today is going to be a big, amazing day, and I'm glad I can be both the reason for and a part of it. As you've no doubt learned by now, the people on this trip are varied in terms of beliefs, talents, education, and vocations, but you all have one thing in common. No, not me, although you do have that. What I'm referring to is the fact that you will all, like me, die one day."

Wow, that is not where I thought he was going with that.

He pauses, then says, "I know. It's a lot to absorb. But it's something we all must face. We will all die. That's one of life's only certainties. The question you have to ask yourself is, what will your legacy be? Today, you will learn about an ancient people who were far ahead of their time in terms of agriculture and feats of engineering. Although the Incas have died off, many of their advancements and much of their knowledge live on today. Over the next few hours, I want you to consider what you will leave behind for humanity, whether it's something grand—such as I have done—or something small like passing along your favorite cookie recipe so your grandchildren's grandchildren can enjoy them. Think about what you will leave behind. What will you want people to remember about you? How will you leave the world? A little better than you found it? Or worse off? The choice is yours. Now, make sure you gather your things because the fleet of helicopters is about to arrive. By the way, don't you just love traveling in a helicopter? It's my absolute favorite on account of how nimble and convenient they are. Anyway, time is ticking so I'll stop talking. Now, let's go have an adventure."

17

Lessons in Leadership...

Ty

SO FAR SO GOOD. I'm playing it cool. Creating a safe distance. Shutting down any thoughts she has about seducing me out of a hundred million. Because that's all this is really. No matter how things felt last night. She's here for one reason only—to get my money. She as much as said it. And this morning, she was definitely engaged in some serious girl talk about me. I wish I knew what she told them. Not because I care, but because it would be helpful for me to know. Strategically.

Last night was two beers too many and a lack of sleep affecting my brain. I never should've gone out there, never should have gotten in the water with her, and definitely never should've almost kissed her. No matter how badly I wanted to. But the good news is, I didn't kiss her. There was no kissing. Or pulling her to me and pressing her body up against mine. Or running my hands along the curves of her hips and up to her...

"Mr. Sterling? Is there a problem?" Thiago barks,

snapping me out of that thought.

When I glance around, I see I'm the last man on the helicopter. I get up and hurry to get off, only to notice we've landed on top of a mountain with ruins and agricultural terraces cut into it that seem to go on for miles.

"Okay, thank you for joining us," Thiago says to me. "Everyone has heard of Machu Picchu, but few people come to see Ollantaytambo, which was just as sacred and important to the Incas. In the valley below, is the ancient town of Ollantaytambo, one of the few places that managed to fight off the Spanish Conquistadors. The streets are made of the original cobblestones from the time of the Incas. Up here, we will visit the unfinished Sun Temple—a wall of six monoliths, including the second heaviest Inca monolith. As you will learn, this remains a great architectural mystery. Stay together, oh, and put on some sunscreen because the sun is strong up here and you will burn."

I grab my Oakleys and my ball cap out of my bag. When I glance back at Gwen, she's got her felt bowler hat on and she's squirting some sunscreen into her palm. The first word that pops into my mind is not a welcome one (or one I use often): adorable.

What is with me today? Pathetic. I need to get ahold of Donna and Muffy, not waste my time flirting. I hold up my phone, only to discover there is—surprise!—no cell reception. Mother fucker.

We head up the path as a group. Savannah is wearing Richard's urn and smiling at me while she pats it like a baby, presumably so I can imagine her as a caring mom. Well, I'm not imagining that, Savannah, because it's not a baby. It's my quite possibly insane business partner's ashes.

I slow down a little to put some distance between Savannah and myself, only to wind up walking beside

Gwen. Oh perfect. Just what I don't want. Thiago is telling us all about the Incas who lived here back in the mid-15th century. "The ninth Inca ruler, Pachauri, was not only a great military strategist, but also was very wise. He decided to have these terraces built into the side of the mountain to take advantage of the sun and produce more food than they needed. He knew that an empire is not only about land, but about the people, so he chose to take care of his people and make sure they always had more than enough. This is true of all great leaders. They know the value of those who work for them and live under their rule."

"Hmm... that *does* sound very wise. Don't you think?" Gwen asks me.

"There's a difference between valuing your people and valuing what they do," I tell her.

Thiago shoots us a look, then continues. "And here is the Sun Temple—a great mystery to this day because the stone used to create the wall was made of six parts, each one weighing around fifty tonnes. Because this stone is from the next valley over, the question remains of how they managed to drag them up here without modern equipment."

"Maybe the aliens did it," I whisper to her.

Gwen purses her lips at me, then mutters, "They obviously used lots of people, rope, and probably rafts of some sort to bring them down the river."

"Lots of well-fed, valued people, I'm sure," I say.

When we reach the wall, I check my phone again (as discreetly as possible). No bars. You know what would make me believe in miracles? If the Incas had set up cell towers. The rest of the group walks up to the wall for a closer look while Thiago comments on how each stone would have taken several decades to smooth with the hand tools they would've had back then. "Imagine that.

Spending your entire life just working on one piece of this stone, knowing the work would have to continue after you die?"

He lets that question linger in the air as we stand around staring at the wall. Gwen saunters back over to me. "What do you think? Talk about a legacy…"

"Meh. Sure, they worked hard, but at the end of the day, what even was the point?" I'm winding her up a little, but only for my own amusement.

"It was an important religious temple that took generations to build. It's still here after thirty-five-hundred years!"

Shrugging, I say, "They didn't even finish it."

"But that's only because they had to abandon it before the project was done," she says. "Sad, really. I wonder what it could've become if time had permitted."

"A bigger wall," I say, shaking my head. "What's sad is the lives they had."

"What do you mean?"

"Think about it. You spend your entire life—day after day—sanding down one little piece of a big rock, knowing you'll be long gone before it's finished."

She stiffens a little, then lifts her chin. "I don't know, I think it gave them a sense of purpose. And maybe they felt good knowing they were an important part of a lasting legacy. They knew they wouldn't see it to completion, but that their work would always be here—as proof that they lived."

"Where's the glory in that?"

"Not everyone cares about glory," Gwen answers. "Some people care more about being part of something bigger than themselves—something that will move humanity forward."

"Why do I take it we're now talking about you?"

"Not just me. Everyone who does SETI research. We

all know it's a total long shot that contact will be made in our lifetime, but someone's got to keep the work going. If we don't, we'll never get there."

I stare down at her for a second, then say. "Can I ask you an honest question? And I'm not trying to be an asshole here, okay? I just genuinely want to understand."

"Sure," she says, but I can tell by the wary look in her eyes that she won't like my question.

"Why SETI? When you could've dedicated your life to anything?" Before she can answer, I add, "I mean, you're clearly brilliant. You could've done anything, worked anywhere. Somewhere with prestige and *way* more money than you're making."

"Because this project could be the greatest thing to ever happen to our species. Think of how boring your food would be if there had never been any explorers throughout history. Or how limited our knowledge would be, or the lack of variety in the music we'd have or all the medicines that wouldn't exist," she says, her eyes lit up with excitement. "It's the sharing of knowledge and culture that makes life rich. Imagine how rich we'd be if we could share that with beings from *another planet*. It would be incredible."

"Or maybe when they find out we're here, they'll swing by with a laser and wipe our planet off the face of the universe…"

A look of understanding crosses her face. "Oh, I get it now."

"You get what?" I ask.

"Why you hate us so much," she says, turning from me as if she's bored. She pulls her phone out of her pocket and takes a close-up photo of the wall. "You're scared."

"I'm not *scared*," I say, jamming my hands in my front pockets.

"Sure you are. I should've guessed based on your reaction to riding in a helicopter."

"We almost *died*. Besides, I wasn't the one gripping my own hand on that thing."

"Yeah, but even before that. The white knuckles, the slightly pale face," Gwen says, glancing up at me and shrugging. "It's okay, really. Lots of people get scared. They like the familiar, whereas the work I do is all about the unknown. It's a rare person who is comfortable with it."

"I am perfectly comfortable with the unknown. I just don't like helicopters."

"And you're afraid the aliens are going to attack us."

"I was just playing devil's advocate."

"Really?" she asks, wrinkling up her nose a little. "Because you seemed worried about it."

"I was joking," I say, feeling more agitated by this conversation than I should. "Look, I'm nothing if not a risk taker. If I weren't, I wouldn't be where I am today."

"Oh yeah?" she asks, turning to face me. "If you're such a risk taker, what's the biggest risk you took?"

I narrow my eyes, coming up completely blank. Other than some high-risk investments, I haven't done anything that wasn't a sure thing in years. "Starting the company with Richard."

"Okay, but that was decades ago. What's the last big risky thing you've done. Or … what's the next big risky thing you're going to do?" she asks. "Come on, wow me with how comfortable you are with the unknown."

"Are you *taunting* me?"

"No, I'm not taunting you. You're the one implying your middle name is Danger, so I'm just asking you to provide examples."

The football team will be a risk. Well, not really. It's been the most profitable team for three decades, so it's pretty much sure money. It's just *a lot* of sure money. But I can't talk about that anyway, so it's time to deflect. "And you're such a risk taker, sitting at a computer all day listening to static? What? Do you spend your weekends base jumping or something?"

Jutting out her chin, she says, "No, I don't. But that's only because I don't have a death wish."

"Okay, so what's the last big risky thing you've done?" I ask, taking two steps closer to her. "Or the next one?"

Shit. My eyes keep flicking down to those full lips and now we're in perfect kissing position again. I swear the heat between us must be visible to the naked eye. If anyone is looking at us right now, they're going to know exactly what this is. And for some stupid reason, I can't stop myself from staying exactly where I am, focusing every bit of my attention on her beautiful face. "Come on, Ms. Fox, what's the next big risk you're willing to take?"

She licks her lips, and I'm positive she's about to kiss me. My entire body hums with excitement. But she doesn't. Instead she seems to be able to resist whatever this pull is between us. Clearing her throat, she says, "I don't know about the next one, but I've risked my entire career and my reputation on the bet that we're not alone in the Universe."

A sense of full body disappointment comes over me as the moment slips away. "That's … actually a pretty good one."

"I know," she says, glancing at my mouth.

Wait, maybe the moment is back…

Before I have a chance to find out, Thiago blows his whistle. "Okay, everyone! We need to hike down the mountain. Our next stop is a real alpaca farm!"

"Hi, Michael, how are you doing today?"

"I'm a little peeved, actually. Some child climbed on Tessy the Triceratops and got her all sticky with a blue gooey candy."

"Oh dear. Is it fixed now?"

"Yes, but it took a total of thirteen minutes for Jane and me to wipe it down, and now my hands smell like the cleaning product, even though I've washed them three times already."

"What if you use some vinegar? That's supposed to help with smells."

"Because, Ty, if I do that, my hands will smell like vinegar, and I hate vinegar."

"Right, I can see the problem."

"Greta's warming some water and putting lemon in it because I do like the smell of lemons. She thinks that will help, but I'm not convinced."

I stifle a laugh, then say, "It's worth a shot."

"Yes, I suppose. And where are you today? Are you in the Andes or the Amazon? I assume it's one of the two."

"We're in the Andes. Still in the Sacred Valley."

"Machu Picchu is in the Sacred Valley. Is that where you are?"

"No. We're in a different place called Ollantaytambo right now. I'm not sure if we'll go to Machu Picchu or not."

"Well, if I were you, I'd be hoping to go there rather than to the Amazon. Did you know there is a tiny fish in the Amazon River that some people call the vampire fish?"

"I did not."

"I will tell you about it then, in case you end up there."

"Thank you." I smile, knowing how much he loves teaching me new things.

"Apparently, the vampire fish, which interestingly

enough is also called a toothpick fish, is attracted to the scent of urine and is capable of crawling into the human urethra and lodging itself in there, which would be very bad."

Wincing, I say, "Yeah, that sounds bad."

"There is one documented case from 1997 in which a man claims he was standing in the river urinating when one jumped from the water into his urethra where it chewed its way to his scrotum. Although his story is disputed by some, his doctor claims to have removed the fish himself and put it in a specimen jar."

"That is really gross, Michael," I say. "Probably don't tell that story to too many people."

"I am aware that it is likely offensive and was not planning to tell it to anyone else. Only you so you will understand the dangers of that river should you go there."

"Well, thank you. I appreciate the heads up."

"You're welcome. Now, will you be able to call me again tomorrow? You know how I do better when I can talk to you."

"Honestly, I'm not sure. Richard wanted everything to be a surprise, so I have no idea where I'll be going. I promise if there is phone reception of any kind, I'll call you. But there's a good chance we're going to be in places without it."

"I don't like that idea *at all*, Ty," he says. "That will completely throw off my routine, and you know how I like my routine."

"I know, Michael, and I promise I'll do my very best to get a hold of you every day," I tell him. "But in the meantime, did you know it's the Geminid meteor shower? Maybe if it's a clear night, you can sit out by the pool tonight and see if you can spot any shooting stars."

"That sounds like something I would like, but how do

you know about it? You're not interested in space."

"Umm, my new friend Gwen told me about it. In fact, we watched it for a bit last night."

"New friend? I haven't heard you use that phrase for a long time indeed."

"Well, I haven't made any new friends in a while," I say, trying to sound casual.

Michael lets out a little *hmm*, then says, "That's what you say about a woman you want to date. Do you want to date this Gwen person?"

Yes, very much. "Oh, I don't … I mean, she's … it wouldn't work out, so…"

"You didn't say no."

He's got me there. "I'm not her type." Her type is probably not going to be a man who causes her to lose her job, and likely her new home.

"Why? What kind of person is she looking for? Someone poor and ugly?"

"No, just … someone else who isn't me. Listen, Michael, I have to hang up. We're about to leave for the next part of the trip and everyone is waiting for me."

"I will say goodbye then because it is inconsiderate to make people wait."

"That it is. Goodbye, Michael. Love you."

"I love you too. Have a safe journey and call me as soon as you can."

"I will."

———

"Finally," Donna says as soon as she picks up the phone. "I was about to send the security team over there to find you."

"Muffy hasn't called me back and I have a feeling this

isn't one of those 'no news is good news' situations."

"Yeah, I'd have the same feeling. Apparently, she and Bobbi Brown didn't hit it off."

"Crap."

"I guess Ms. Brown said something about her having mature skin, and things went downhill from there."

I glance over at the rest of the group, all of whom are across the field, fawning over a brown and white baby alpaca. I needed to make sure I was too far away for Gwen to 'overhear' me. She's crouched down, petting the fuzzy animal on its long neck. I'd take some of that petting action, no matter how mad she makes me. *Come on, Ty. Get your head out of your ass.*

"Apparently someone else is in the mix now and a serious offer is being prepared."

"Shit," I mutter. "And I'm sure he knows exactly what the current offer on the table is."

"Yup. Looks like it's Hail-Mary-pass time. If I was you, I'd be zipping to Texas for a couple of days."

I run my hand through my hair, my gut tightening. How the hell do I get out of this without looking like the world's most heartless man? "That's going to be tricky."

"I know you're concerned about doing the right thing by Dr. Napper, but honestly, Ty, he knew how much this meant to you. I think he'd understand."

I look over at Rohan, who is holding Richard's urn. Rohan would never forgive me if I left, not after chasing away half of the people who actually showed up for this thing. And it would be exactly the kind of thing Gwen Fox would think an asshole like me would do. "No, I can't. I need to be here."

"Okay, but there's only so much I can do."

"I know," I tell her. "I'll find a way to make it work."

"You're going to have to because the clock is ticking."

18

The Right Tool for the Job...

Gwen

Fox Family Chat

DAD

Gwenny, how are things in Peru? Your mom and I would like to hear from you so we can ascertain your whereabouts and have an update on your status.

MOM

Yes, Gwen. Please let us know where you are.

MOM

Gwen, it only takes a second to send a note. Please be more considerate in the future.

Hi, all. I literally haven't had cell reception since we left the airport in Lima. We spent the night in a tiny village in the Sacred Valley. Quite safe and beautiful. Amazing stargazing last night from a natural hot spring. We're now in another small town—Ollantaytambo—but will be leaving here in a bit for destinations unknown. The entire trip will likely be in places with spotty/no cell service, but I am in good hands. Our tour guide is quite knowledgeable and so far, we've been traveling via helicopter, so all very lux. No need to worry. I'll check in with you again soon. Love to you all!

MOM

I'm not worried. In the event of your safety being in jeopardy, we simply need to know if some sort of action is required from our end.

BEN

Sounds suspiciously like worrying, Mom.

MOM

It is nothing of the sort. Worrying is the world's biggest time waster.

CARLA

With all due respect, Stephanie, allowing yourself to label your feelings is both healthy and productive.

MOM

How's this? I'm feeling irritated.

CARLA

Excellent work! You'll get the hang of it.

———

"Where are you?" I ask, pressing the phone to my ear so I can hear Allie over all the background noise on her end.

"Vegas," she shouts.

"You went?!"

"I'm here with _____ !" she yells, but I can't hear the name.

"With who?!"

"VEGAS, BABY, WHOOHOOOO!!!!" a man hollers, pretty much directly into my ear canal.

"Can you get somewhere quiet so I can hear you?"

"Sure, one sec!"

I glance around the quiet street here in Ollantaytambo —a place about as far from Las Vegas as you can get, and not just geographically. I'm not even sure if they have any stop lights, let alone all the bright lights of The Strip. The rest of my group is seated around a long table inside the restaurant I'm in front of, waiting for the dessert course of our lunch. I came out here because there is no way I want anyone to overhear my conversation—especially not Ty, who, now that I look, is watching me through the window. Or maybe he just looked up at this very second and I only think he's watching me because some sick, twisted part of me wants him to be.

I give him an innocent smile, then turn back toward the sun.

"Okay, how's this?" Allie asks in a normal tone. The sound of a toilet flushing tells me where she went.

"Much better. Tell me everything."

"Skip's going to be easy to find. He puts out Instagram stories every couple of hours so Chad and I drove up this morning. We're currently at the Hard Rock, which is the last place he posted."

"Eww, you had to go with Chad?"

"Yeah, but honestly, I think he might be the best option

on account of Skip most likely being a total douche canoe as well," she says, sounding slightly tipsy.

"Ah, they speak the same language."

"Exactly. You should scroll through his Insta feed. Wow, douchey."

"And you're there in case the situation requires someone with a very symmetrical face."

She laughs, then says, "I super wish you were here with me. Vegas is surprisingly fun."

"Huh, I hadn't heard that about Vegas," I answer, my heart squeezing to be able to talk to my bestie when I'm feeling so alone. "Did you guys find anything about Muffy and the club he's buying?"

"Hard no. Do you know what comes up when you google those two words together?" she asks.

Shuddering, I say, "I can imagine."

"I don't think you can," she says. "So, *so* bad."

Dammit, that means I'm back to square one—no leverage whatsoever.

"How are you making out there?" she asks.

Not 'making out' nearly as much as I want to. "Umm, I don't know. It's umm … he's…"

"Even worse in person than we thought? Completely arrogant? Rude beyond comparison?"

All the moments we've shared in the last twenty hours zip through my mind—the good, the sexy, the funny, the crazy hot banter, the almost kissing… "Challenging. That's probably the best word I can think of to describe him."

"Hmph," she says, sounding disappointed.

See? I can't go messing around with him. Allie will never look at me the same way again. Neither will the rest of the team. They'll all think I'm a complete idiot if I turn around and say, 'Turns out he's a pretty good guy' or worse, 'I think I might have feelings for him, even though I met him less than twenty-four hours ago.' And let's face it —that *does* make me an idiot. Nobody meets and falls in love that fast. Well, I suppose my parents, but they're freaks of nature. Needing to change the subject, I say, "Is the rest of the group looking for a different backer?"

"Yup. In fact, they've turned the lunch room into a war room, and they're working around the clock trying to figure it out."

"Okay, that makes me feel better," I tell her. "We're really covering all our bases."

"Yeah, but honestly, Gwen, you're still our best shot. Trying to find someone who'll give us ten million a year is a total long shot, and based on the reels I've watched of Skip, I'd say there's a good chance we're wasting our time here. He seems like he'd be totally capable of burning through the entire fortune by the end of the year."

I close my eyes for a second, feeling the pressure pile back on. "I'm going to do my best," I tell her.

"That's all we can ask."

I walk back into the restaurant just as the server brings two long plates filled with something called picarones, which apparently are a lot like donuts. I take my spot at the long table between Karen and Niles. I originally sat between them because I needed a break from Ty. I was so hot and bothered during our argument earlier, I was tempted to pin him up against the Sun Temple and do all sorts of things that could get us arrested. I lied so hard when I was at breakfast with Karen and Savannah. I definitely have feelings for him. Big ones. Utterly wrong ones. Completely unsafe, about to get my heart stomped ones.

Ty elected to take an end seat even though there was

an empty chair across from me. My sense of logic is quite pleased, but my lady bits are complaining loudly. Richard's urn has been placed in the seat at the other end of the table, like a guest of honor, which I suppose he is, and I take a moment to marvel at the fact that none of us has said anything about how weird it is that we're having a meal with a container full of human remains. It's a bit gross, no? I can't be the only one who thinks this?

I take a picarone off the plate and dip it into the small syrup container in front of me. My first bite is sweet, but not too sweet, crunchy, and delightfully warm. "Oh wow, that's good," I mutter to no one in particular. I munch away while I listen to the conversations around the table. Rohan and Thiago are whispering about the next location, and damned if they're not good at being really quiet. I'm getting no clues at all. Savannah is cozied up to Ty asking him about his pet peeves.

Without missing a beat, he says, "People who ask too many questions."

I tuck my teeth between my lips to stop myself from laughing, then dip another section of my picarone and pop it in my mouth. Yum.

Huh, now that I think about it, I realize I've made a tactical error. I'm allowing Ty to see me with people in two of the world's most ridiculous projects, therefore, if I managed to make any headway at all with my speech about music, food, and medicine (which I sort of doubt), I could easily backslide if he starts to lump me back in with them. God, I hope he's not listening to their conversation because it's utter nonsense.

Niles seems to have a crush on Karen, by the way. He keeps talking around me to her about his latest paranormal contact. "A chill ran right through me."

For her part, she seems fascinated. "I've read that a chill is a sign of a ghost."

"Definitely. We can actually capture it on our equipment—the most I've had is a drop in temperature of two degrees."

"Wow!" Karen says.

"Was there a window open?" Ty asks.

Oh, I guess he *is* listening.

"What?" Niles asks.

"When the temperature dropped. Was there a window or a door open by any chance?"

Rude. Exactly what I was thinking, but still, rude.

Niles shakes his head. "No. The entire building was sealed up tight."

"Perhaps there's something wrong with your equipment then."

"The Spirit Sensor 5000 is state-of-the-art. The best money can buy," Niles tells him. "I assure you it's not the equipment."

"If I were trying to fool people into purchasing expensive equipment for searching for something that doesn't exist, I'd make sure it randomly changes readings," Ty says, tearing off a piece of donut and dipping it into the syrup. Holding it halfway to his mouth, he says, "That way the person using it would always believe there's a chance, so instead of getting bored, they'll keep it up and hopefully buy another one when it breaks."

"Trust me, the folks at Paranormal Monitors and More are the real deal."

I roll my eyes, then glance at Ty, only to see him watching me. He definitely saw that. My face heats up a bit and I return my gaze to my dessert.

"Niles, I've heard that you mainly use electromagnetic

readings for your research. Are there other types of readings you take?" Karen asks, batting her eyelashes at him.

Oh, get a room, you two.

He smiles. "Actually, we do a lot of work with rapid-scanning radio devices. Ghosts are able to rearrange words and phrases to communicate with us."

"Fascinating," she says.

"Say, Gwen," Ty says. "You use radio frequencies to search for aliens, don't you?"

I don't have to look at him to know he's smirking. I do look at him, of course, because I can't seem to not do that, and he is, indeed, smirking. My skin heats up another few degrees. "Yes, but it's hardly the same thing."

"Isn't it?" he asks. "AM/FM. Listening…"

"No. Not AM/FM at all," I tell him, feeling super defensive but trying to act like I'm not. "Our telescopes capture the radio frequencies emitted by astronomical objects. Things like nebulas, planets, and galaxies—which actually exist. No offense, Niles."

He gives me a glare that says, 'offense taken.'

Ty just grins at me. "And these galaxies, are they far, far away?"

"Some of them, yes," I say, ignoring the obvious *Star Wars* reference. Dammit, he's totally making fun of me. So much for making headway earlier…

"Wow, Gwen, I'm surprised a SETI researcher would have such a closed-off attitude when it comes to Niles's work," Karen says. "Do you also doubt the existence of Yeti?"

Crap. Now I'm going to have to go after the nice Canadian. "I believe in the *Gigantopithecus*, but they died out over 300,000 years ago."

"I agree, they probably did die out at that time, but that's not the same creature we're looking for now. The modern-day sasquatch is something different—possibly related, but potentially having evolved from a completely separate species," Karen says, narrowing her eyes a little at me. "But I can see by the look on your face that you think I'm insane."

"Not insane," I tell her, feeling Ty's eyes on me. "Just … wrong. I can't see how we wouldn't have found any real evidence of them yet. I mean, not one?"

"I could say the same about aliens," Niles says.

Stay calm, Gwen. Stay calm. Your entire life has trained you to win this argument, especially against such ill-equipped people. "Niles, we've long known that the universe is infinite and ever-expanding. The probability that Earth is the only planet to have the conditions for life on it is basically zero. Same with the idea that we're the only version of intelligent life in the universe. Granted, the other such planets are far away, that's true, and it may prove to be an impossibility to ever contact them, but they *are* out there, and with advancements in technology, we will likely find a way. Or they will find a way to reach out to us. Ghosts and Yetis, however? There really is no theoretical basis on which to believe in them, and there is no definitive proof of either. I'm sorry, but those are just facts."

"With all due respect, Gwen, you're wrong about ghosts," Niles tells me, setting down his fork. "There have been hundreds of thousands of documented sightings around the world—many of them eerily similar in nature, even though there is no way the people who reported them could've heard about each other's stories. And as to Karen's work, they—like you—are covering a vast area of unexplored territory. What if these creatures have senses that are so far superior to that of a human, they are able to avoid being found?"

"With all the trail cams that have been set out all over

the world, surely one of them would've caught sight of a Yeti by now," I answer. *Check and mate.*

Karen shakes her head. "Not true. What if Yetis are so intelligent that they figured out how to avoid trail cams?"

"That would require them to have an understanding of what a trail cam even is, which is an impossibility for an ape-like creature with no contact with humans or our technology whatsoever," I tell her.

Her face turns bright red, and I can tell I'm totally upsetting her, but I can't stop now. Not with so much at stake. I have to find a way to show Ty that what I do has value, which means separating me from them.

Niles comes to her rescue with, "What if the very act of putting out the trail cam leaves a human scent that lingers for years? Not one *we* would detect, but one that *they* would detect, therefore avoid? Look at cadaver dogs— they're able to smell human remains, even fifty years after they were buried, even at the bottom of a lake. We certainly can't detect that, but they can. And they're only dogs. A Yeti could have a far superior sense of smell than a dog."

"Human bones release a gas that the dogs can smell," I say. "If a human walks through an area of the woods, hangs up a trail cam, then leaves, they don't leave anything else behind other than the camera. A scent, yes, but after the first rain, it would certainly be washed away."

"But we have to go change out batteries on the cameras," Karen says, raising her voice a little. "Each time we do, we are leaving some type of evidence."

"Nothing that would last as long as the batteries."

Rohan taps his glass with his fork, making a loud dinging sound. "Okay, so we've got to get going now. Thiago is paying our bill and it's time to gather our things. I heard a lot of discussion around the table, but nothing about legacy, so I wanted to remind you that it was very important to Dr. Napper that you all think about your legacy. That was the whole point of this morning. Well, not the alpaca farm. That was just because they're so cute."

Heads nod around the table, and words of agreement are heard.

"Adorable, with the little humming noises?"

"So freaking soft and fuzzy."

"Anyway," Rohan says, "leaving a legacy was extremely important to Dr. Napper, and I know part of that legacy is to inspire others to do the same. So, what will your legacy be? What will people remember about you?"

Niles stands up and murmurs, "What's your legacy going to be, Gwen? Shitting on other people's dreams so you can get ahead?"

Karen stands too, and looks at me like I just kicked a baby alpaca. "I certainly know what I'll remember about you."

Savannah shakes her head at me. "I actually think you would make a coat out of puppies."

I sit for a second, my face hot with shame. I shouldn't have gone after them like that. I didn't have to do that. I have one last sip of water, remembering something my dad said when we were watching the news one night: *Desperation will turn even the best people into the worst versions of themselves.*

And I just allowed it to do that to me.

I linger a bit at the table, then head to the bathroom, hating like hell that I'm going to have to spend several more days with people I've hurt. I feel suddenly very alone, and it's all my own doing. I just want to go home and go back to my safe, ordinary life with my people.

When I walk out of the bathroom, I see Ty waiting in the hallway. My heart pounds a little faster as I look up at him, assuming he's about to give me a hard time about what I just did. Not wanting to hear it, I say, "You really didn't have to wait for me."

"Thiago said I had to. You're my buddy, and everyone else took off already."

"I'm sure they did," I answer, winding my way through the tables to the door. Ty quickens his last two steps so he can hold the door open for me.

Oh, stop being so gallant already.

As soon as we're out in the bright sunshine, I pull on my hat and start up the street.

"That was certainly an interesting lunch," he says.

Letting out a sigh, I say, "Unfortunately, I have a real gift for offending people sometimes."

"Yeah, you sure went in for the kill back there," he says, and I don't know him well enough to know if he's horrified or impressed. He's horrified, right? Yeah, he is. Dammit.

"I just … can't seem to help myself sometimes. I come from a long line of very logical, highly accomplished scientists who believe in good science. It's like … our religion. I was taught to follow it with great zeal and defend it to the death."

"Too bad they didn't teach you how to hold back when you're dealing with unarmed opponents. Talk about bringing a bazooka to a fist fight. That was … ugly."

Ugly? Gah! That is never a word you want to hear from a hot guy you can't stop fantasizing about. "Yeah, well, you're the one who started it," I say, sounding like I'm about eight years old.

"Me?"

"You were making fun of me about the radio equipment … and … and lumping me in with the ghost busters. The Spirit Sensor 5000? Come on."

"I was teasing you—which you deserved by the way, after implying I'm a total fraidy cat this morning."

"Fraidy cat?"

"Aren't we pretending to be in middle school right now, Miss You Started It?"

I let a tiny grin escape. "More like elementary."

"Right, elementary. But the point is, what I was doing was gently mocking you. You, however, decided to disprove their entire life's work over tapas."

"But what they do is ridiculous."

"True, but you don't have to be the one to tell them. That is not your job."

He's right. I didn't have to do that. I felt like I had to, but I really didn't. "I have trouble holding back, especially when the stakes are high."

"What stakes?" he asks, looking genuinely confused.

"I didn't want you to lump me in with them," I say with a sigh. "Just in case you'll agree to fund *one* project, I want you to know that ours is the one to back."

"But I'm not going to fund one project. I'm going to fund none of them," he says, his tone filled with irritation. "For someone so smart, you really seem to have trouble grasping that concept."

Ouch. That stung. My first reaction is to snap back, but I know I have to over-ride the system right now. *Stay calm, Gwen. Do not react to that. Let it roll off your back.* I say nothing and keep my eyes forward, stewing away in my sense of shame and humiliation. He as good as told me I'm being stupid, oh, and that my behavior was ugly. You know what? I don't care how hot Ty Sterling is. I was right all along. He is an asshole.

―――――――――――

19

Beam Me Up Scotty...

―――――――――――

Gwen

LONGEST FISHBOWL FLIGHT EVER. Apparently we were on some special chopper that flies faster and farther than the rest of them, meaning we've been up in the air for three whole hours. Three hours of me sitting in the back corner with only Dr. Napper's urn and my nervous bladder to keep me company while the rest of the group chatted and laughed together—including Ty, who seems to be more than willing to let Savannah and Karen flirt away with him. In fact, he seems to be *enjoying* it, while I sit here alone, disliked and seething with jealousy every time Savannah touches his forearm while she laughs (which is a *lot*). I started counting and we're up to twenty-four times already.

Oh, there she goes again. What could possibly be so damn funny? I mean, I get that the guy is witty, but he's no Nate Bargatze.

I sit back and close my eyes, wishing I could press a transporter button on my poncho and be instantly beamed

180

back home where people don't hate me. Oh, to be sitting at my desk in my cozy office with Allie right now. Hell, I'd even take a full shift in the server room with Chad because this sucks moldy fur balls. I've alienated everyone on this trip—Thiago because I'm 'a problem,' Rohan because I scared off half the group, Ty for showing my 'ugly' side and for pestering him for money, and everyone else for shitting on what they do. So, yeah, sign me up for four more days of this fun!

The worst bit (besides the guilt at hurting Karen, Niles, and Savannah's feelings) is that Ty is never going to look at me the same way again. I've totally blown it with him. Not that there was anything to blow. It's not like we were ever going to end up together, but somehow, I desperately want him to like me. And the crazy part is, it's got nothing to do with the funding. I want him to like me because I just do. He's a good man hiding out as a hardened, closed off one, and I need him to know I'm a good person too. Underneath the arguing and the defensiveness. And yes, what he said to me hurt, but if I put myself in his shoes, I can see why he'd be irked.

The fact that he thinks so much less of me now is killing me. I can tell he wants to be as far away from me as possible (given the fact that we're on an aircraft together), and all I want to do is get closer to him. He's like a black hole—he's got a gravitational pull so strong, I don't have the energy to fight getting sucked all the way in. Only now, he's repelling me. Or perhaps more accurately, he's repelled by me.

What I need is a plan. A good plan always makes me feel better. New goal: Keep my effing mouth shut and don't offend anyone for the rest of the trip. Shouldn't be a problem, now that I literally have nothing left to lose. There's no way I'm going home victorious, which removes the stakes, which means instead of feeling like I have to fight for every penny I might be able to get, I can just let that go and show the rest of the group I actually am an empathetic, kind human. I can do that. I won't correct anyone. I won't roll my eyes or scoff. When someone says something grossly inaccurate, I'll take a page out of Keenan's book, and say, "That's interesting."

Yes, that ought to work. And maybe, just maybe, after a couple days of that, Ty will see who I really am. Not that it matters, because when we leave here, I'll never see him again. But still, the thought of him being out in the world thinking so poorly of me isn't something I'm willing to live with.

Finally, the helicopter lands in a clearing just at the edge of the jungle. It's already getting dark and I'm really hoping that just inside those trees is a nice hotel so I can go to my room, take a long hot bath, and sleep for twelve solid hours.

I pick up my golden seat mate and make my way to the exit where the humidity and heat slap me across the face. When I get off, I hand the urn to Rohan, who is already wearing the Baby Bjorn. I tug off my poncho and shove it in my backpack while Savannah asks Ty to help her adjust her straps. "It's riding a little too low and when I try to fix it, I keep over or under-correcting it."

'Sure, thing little lady,' is what I expect him to say, followed by, 'we should get married and have babies who can move their sippy cups with their minds.'

But he doesn't say that. Instead, he fiddles with the straps on the lower part of her bag—which is about a tenth of an inch from her perky ass. "How's that?"

"Much better."

"Okay, people! We got here later than I wanted," Thiago says. "I need everyone to listen up. We're going to hike into the jungle for two hours. Headlamps are a must. If you don't have one, I hope you brought a flashlight because as soon as we get under the canopy, it's going to be dark. The Amazon is a dangerous place, okay? It's not just tripping on tree roots that you have to watch out for. There are deadly predators in here—jaguars, anacondas, black caiman. I don't need any problems, so no straggling," he says, glancing at me, because apparently he hasn't forgotten that I had trouble at the airport back in Lima. "No veering off the path to explore. We all need to stick together so keep up." He looks at me again, but this time he points as well. "If you suffer from a nervous bladder, you have to let the group know so you won't be left alone. Being alone out here makes you vulnerable."

I'm feeling vulnerable, Thiago. I really am out here alone.

"Okay, so get your headlamps on and let's go!"

Oh, Marisol, why didn't you talk my fake husband into buying me a headlamp?

Once Thiago has his on, he blinds me with it. "Let me guess. You don't have a headlamp."

"That would be correct," I tell him. "I packed one but…"

"But then you lost your bag."

"Technically the airline…" Nope. Do not say it, Gwen! "I'll be fine. I'll just … use the flashlight on my phone."

"It's not going to last two hours," Thiago says. "But use it as long as you can and stay close to your buddy."

I nod and give him a thumbs up even though my buddy has already started walking. The rest of the group starts to move and I find my place at the back, right behind Rohan. I use my phone, knowing that as soon as this dies, I'll be screwed. Thiago wasn't joking—it is freaking dark in here. Noisy too. The sound of insects is almost overwhelming at first. Add to it the frequent screeches of what

I hope are monkeys (and not tourists who are up the path from us being murdered) and you've got yourself one scary place to hike. I keep glancing behind me to see if there's anyone following me, like a jaguar, for example. That would be bad. But each time, it's just darkness.

I hurry up a few steps and walk beside Rohan. "It's super dark in here."

"Yup," he says.

"This must be so hard for you," I tell him, realizing it for the first time. "I mean, you and Dr. Napper were probably so close, and instead of being able to grieve, you're having to help make this trip happen."

He shifts the carrier a little and wipes his forehead with the back of his hand. "Doing this for Dick is an honor. Yes, it's exhausting, but it was always exhausting to work for a man with the type of energy and passion he had."

"Listen, if you need any help, I'd be happy to pitch in," I say.

Rohan glances down at me, blinding me temporarily. "Really?"

Sweet! I might be about to make a friend. "Yes, name it."

He unclips the baby carrier and holds it out to me. "Carry this for a while. My back is cramping up."

————

You know what's not a good time? Hiking through the dark, muddy, terrifyingly noisy jungle while carrying a gold urn on your front and a backpack on your back. I actually think this urn is made of solid gold. It's *that* heavy. And to be honest, I don't think Rohan even wants to be my friend at all because as soon as I took Dr. Napper, he rushed ahead to walk with Thiago. My phone died after about fifteen minutes, so I've been hot on Niles's heels the whole time, basically keeping my eyes on his feet and stepping where he does.

Just when I think I can't take it anymore, I spot something up ahead that looks like a fire, which I am really hoping means we're at the end of our journey.

We arrive at a clearing in the trees and see a large campfire with small stools around it. Off to the side, there's a table with a man standing at it, preparing food. God, I hope he's making picarones. When I glance to my right, I see the largest treehouse I've ever seen. I crane my neck to see the thatched roof at the top. Torches are lit on the corners of each of the three levels.

"Home sweet home," Savannah says, tugging off her backpack.

"Okay, everyone," Thiago yells. "Gather around. This is Ian. He's our chef. He is making our supper and our breakfast before we set off tomorrow morning. We will sleep in the treehouse tonight. Women on the top floor, men on the second. There are sinks on each level to wash up. Please be careful to only use water as needed and don't drink it. You will find water bottles next to your hammocks that you can drink and use to brush your teeth, etc. There is an outhouse back there," he says, pointing to the darkness. "Dr. Napper has a video for us to watch. Go get washed up and put your things by your hammock for the night. When we've all assembled here, we'll watch the video."

I turn to Rohan and unclip the Baby Bjorn. "What would you like to do with … er … Dr. Napper for the night?"

"Put him on that big stool by the fire so he can join us."

"Righto," I say, as if this is totally normal.

I do as Rohan said, then follow the crowd up the stairs

of tonight's accommodations. By the time I reach the third floor, I see that Karen and Savannah have already picked out side-by-side hammocks. Offering them a tentative smile, I say, "So I guess we're roommates tonight."

"Don't even," Savannah tells me. "In fact, you'll probably be more comfortable over there," she says, pointing to the hammock on the opposite side of the space.

Nodding, I say, "Sure, yeah," then I make my way over to the far side, mimicking her in my head. I put my pack down and pull out my hairbrush, then go to the sink to wash up and brush my hair.

Karen walks up and waits for me to finish, tapping her foot a little.

I finish up quickly, then step aside. "It's all yours."

"Thanks," she says, but based on her tone, that's Canadian for 'go screw yourself.'

Stepping aside, I say, "Karen, about our conversation at lunch, I never should've said any of that stuff. Not in front of Ty."

"But you did."

"I know. And I just wanted to apologize. I didn't mean to embarrass you."

"That's exactly what you meant to do," she says.

Okay, she may not be wrong about that. "Well, I am sorry."

"Be as sorry as you like, but it doesn't matter. It's game on."

Crap. Karen's not going to let this go, is she? "I don't see any reason for us to compete against each other, not when there's nothing to win. Mr. Sterling isn't going to change his mind about the funding."

"You'd like it if I thought that, wouldn't you?"

"It's the truth." I shrug.

"You know what's true? You've been gunning for us

this entire time while you cozied up to Ty. But that's over now. You've shown your true colors and it's my turn now, so step off."

Step off? Are we in a 90's dance movie? "Believe me, I have no intention of … stepping on."

"You better not." Glaring at me, she adds, "I didn't win Miss Canada by being nice."

"Huh, I would've thought that's exactly how you'd win Miss Canada."

"Well, it's not," she grinds out.

I hold both my hands up in surrender, then go put my brush away.

Seriously, why aren't transporters a thing?

20

The Sharing Circle (a.k.a. My Worst Freaking Nightmare)

Ty

I SHOULD NOT HAVE INSULTED Gwen like that. She's basically stopped talking completely, which I'm guessing is what she does when her feelings are hurt. Or she's pissed off. I never should have implied she was being stupid. And I know I upset her with everything I said about how she treated Niles and Karen. She certainly didn't have to go after them like that, but then again, I didn't have to go after her. Not when I hold all the cards. She's desperate and she's got a lot of pressure on her. Her entire team is probably relying on her to save their jobs. Plus, she's just bought a house she won't be able to pay for. Urgh, maybe I *should* be sporting a twirly mustache.

I'd like to make it right, but it really is a conversation that needs to be had in private, and privacy is a little sparse right now, and likely will be until sometime tomorrow, what with us all sharing an open-air tree house. So for now, I'm giving her some space and biding my time until I can get her alone.

I make my way over to Thiago, who is standing near the fire holding the iPad. Everyone else is already here except Gwen, who hurries over and takes a spot on the far side of the group. Yup. She's mad.

Thiago presses play, and Richard's face appears on the screen yet again. "Welcome to the Amazon rainforest, a magical, mystical place alive with beauty, danger, and life itself," he says. His smile is a slap to my soul, reminding me yet again that he's gone forever. "This is where you come when you want to connect with the planet, and with yourself. If there is any place on Earth that forces unabashed honesty, it's here, because it will challenge you in ways you've never been challenged and will force you to face your demons. With no television, no internet connection, and no ability to communicate with the outside world, you are stepping back even further in time than the Incas. Life out here is only about one thing—survival. You will be stripped of your ego and of everything you think you know. And tonight is the start of that. We will share this space around the fire, and you will enjoy the meal together that has been prepared with ingredients found only within walking distance. You will also share with each other who you really are, your essence when everything you have is stripped away and you are merely a human. Tonight, you are not a CEO or a researcher or an accountant or an assistant. You are just a human. Equals around *the sharing fire*. These are the questions you will answer: What's the one thing that hurt you the most and how does it still impact you today? What's the worst thing you've ever done? What are you most proud of? What are you most scared of?

"So, open up, talk, share stories, and I promise you, tomorrow, the world will be a little different. And Ty, of everyone here, you need this the most. So, be brave, share your story, and unburden yourself in this safe space. It's my last wish, so you have to do it."

Thiago shuts off the video. "Okay, first go get your meal from Ian. Then take a spot around the sharing fire."

The sharing fire? Really, Richard? If there is a heaven, he's up there right now laughing his ass off at me because he knows how much this whole thing is making my skin crawl. And believe me it's crawling like the rain forest floor, which is literally covered with, well, things that crawl.

I stand and wait in line for my bowl of wild boar stew, grumbling internally about Richard's video. Unburden myself in this safe space? The place is anything but safe. It's teeming with spiders. And pumas. And crocs. And probably some sort of land piranhas I've never even heard of that are going to hop up to me and attack my ankles. And as far as it being safe to 'share my story?' In front of people so desperate they'd probably resort to blackmail to get what they want from me? Yeah, no. I don't think I'll be sharing my story. Not tonight, Richard. You already got me out here. Don't keep nickel and diming me to death with your last wishes.

I take a stool in between Karen and Savannah, and across from Gwen, who is sitting alone on the other side of the fire. I almost feel sorry for her. Actually, I do, but it's not like I can act on it. I'm making smart decisions for the rest of the trip, which means hanging out over here, with women I have absolutely no connection with, and there-fore will have no trouble saying no to, and no problem forgetting when this whole thing is over.

We all eat quietly, listening to the sounds of the jungle —the cicadas chirping, the birds singing even though it's been dark for a long time now, and the buzzing of insects. After a few minutes, Rohan says, "I know some of you won't be comfortable with the sharing fire, but it really means a lot to Dr. Napper, so, someone needs to go first."

It sure as hell won't be me. I'm not even going to be offering any sympathy whatsoever because that might give them false hope. I'm just going to sit here and eat my stew.

"I'll go," Niles says. "The thing that hurt me the most was constant rejection when I was growing up. You can probably tell by looking at me that I'm not exactly the most athletic guy and I don't have buckets of confidence. School was hell for me. Pure hell. I was the perfect target for every bully, including my older brothers and my father, all of whom are now big, burly cops. I'm built more like my mom—small frame, shapely hips. It used to bother me, but I've gotten over it. I think the defining moment for me was when I asked my mom to let me try out for the boxing team. I was twelve and I thought that if I ate enough spinach and meat and started doing crunches, I'd magically become built like my brothers. I made a big deal about it at home, trying to make sure I was doing push-ups, sit-ups, or drinking raw eggs whenever my father was around…"

Oh God, this is so awful, I'd actually welcome a land piranha attack right now.

"…wanted so badly to belong."

And I want so badly to go home.

"… had to admit I didn't make the team, he said, 'Oh, you didn't think you were actually going to make it, did you? That's just sad. You need to learn to be more realistic, Niles.'"

Ouch. So, I guess I'm not the only one with a dickhead father.

"Oh, Niles," Savannah says, getting up from her stool and walking over to him. She tucks him against her like a mother would a small child, cradling him against her curvy body. "You poor, poor thing."

Smart, *smart* thing is more like it. He looks happier than a pig in shit right now. After a few minutes of fawning over Niles, she lets him go. "And how does that awful moment still affect you today?"

"Well, after that, I gave up on trying to impress him, which was a good thing actually because there is literally no way that man was ever going to be impressed by me. Clearly, I didn't take his advice because I certainly didn't end up in a field that he would consider 'realistic.'" Niles pauses long enough to glare at Gwen. "But I don't care what other people think. I'm living my own life. I met my best friend Ryan a week after I got cut from the boxing team. It was in a paranormal investigation chat room, and that was it for me. I just … found my place in this world. I found my people. I worked at a game café and we all used to investigate on weekends and evenings until Dr. Napper gave us the funding to make our passion a full-time gig. This last decade has been the best time of my life. Earning a decent living doing what I love and working with a team of guys who all really get each other, you know? It's been more than I could have hoped for."

"You found the camaraderie you were looking for," Savannah says. "That's beautiful, Niles."

"Yes, Niles," Karen says. "I love how your defining moment caused you to do the opposite of what your father wanted. You became your own person, instead of trying to follow in his footsteps."

Niles nods. "Thank you. I realized that trying was pointless when it came to him. I was never going to be another carbon copy of him, no matter what I did. So I gave up and I've been better off for it ever since."

Okay, so that is pretty damn impressive, even I have to admit that. "What's your relationship like with him now?" *Wait. Did I just ask that?*

He shrugs. "Irrelevant. My mom, who was always in my corner, is the one who matters to me. They got a divorce after all of us kids moved out, so I don't have to see him in order to see her. He and my brothers all hang out a lot and go drinking together. I meet him for lunch from time to time. And I couldn't care less. I have nothing in common with those people. I just happened to have been born into the same family."

"But, you must hate your dad, right?" I ask. *Umm, what happened to just sitting here eating my stew and staying out of this?*

Shaking his head, Niles says, "No. I still love him. I just … understand his limitations. He was never going to be a good parent to a kid like me, and that's okay. It's not his fault. He's just … weak. And because I know that, I was able to forgive him and move on with my life."

"Huh," I say, letting his words sink in.

"That's so wise, Niles," Karen tells him. "To just let it go instead of carrying that burden around."

"Thanks," Niles says. "But honestly, who in their right mind would spend their life being bitter about some shit that went down when they were a kid?"

Someone like me.

21

Feet to the Fire...

Gwen

THIS IS HELL. Pure and simple. So far, Niles, Karen, and Savannah have all taken their turn sharing, and with each word, I feel smaller. Honestly, they've all got such sad stories. Niles and his ultra-alpha, toxic masculinity upbringing. Savannah was raised by a single mom who was also a psychic—and not the 'good kind,' according to her (whatever that means). She had people in and out of their house at all hours, and honestly, it sounds like pure chaos. No bed times, no meal times, just a free-for-all of fending for yourself and doing whatever you want whenever you want. It was just the two of them, and her mom passed away when Savannah was twenty-one. She's been on her own trying to figure it out ever since.

Karen was a victim of some serious sexual harass- ment in her former job as a marketing assistant, and as weird as it sounds, she's made a pretty damn good argu- ment for how hard it would be to be that beautiful. The expectations on her have been sea-level low. People assume she's an idiot (an easy one at that), neither of which are true. So when she finally found her place among the strange-but-kind Yeti crew, she finally felt like she found a home.

Now that I've heard their stories, I feel *so* much worse than I already did about trying to make them look bad. The truth is, they're all really good people and they're not that different than me. We all had trouble fitting in as teenagers, we've all struggled to find acceptance. We all believe in stuff that other people find laughable. Only, *I* was the one laughing at them. And the truth is there's really no way to fix it. I can apologize again, but the damage is done.

Rohan, who is sitting next to the urn, turns to me. "Gwen, you and Ty both haven't shared yet. Who would like to go first?"

I look at Ty who shakes his head. My heart pounds in my chest. "Sure, I'll go. I think I'd like to answer the question about the worst thing I've ever done."

Rohan nods. "Of course."

"So, umm, it's actually how I've been acting since I met you all." I glance at Karen, who rolls her eyes at me. "I'd roll my eyes if I were you too," I say. "I was really nasty earlier and it was unnecessary. I'm sure you'd all prefer if I just left."

Nods are seen around the fire and Niles says, "Yes, that would be nice. Why don't you?"

Whoa, that felt like a splash of cold water. I didn't expect them to agree with me. "I could. That would be the easy thing to do, and probably the smart thing, given the fact that Ty has made it more than clear to me that there is literally no way he's going to change his mind."

"Oh, come on," Savannah says. "You're still doing it!"

"Doing what?" I ask.

"Trying to get rid of the rest of us so you can have him for yourself."

Shaking my head, I say, "No, I'm really not. I don't expect you to believe me, not after that whole dengue fever thing or after how I acted at lunch, but I've honestly given up on the idea that he's going to fund anything."

I glance at him and see he's staring at me, his expression unreadable.

Karen shakes her head at me. "So why do you even *want* to stay? You've burned your bridges with the rest of us, and you claim you don't think Ty's going to change his mind, so why put yourself through the next several days with a bunch of people who don't want you here?"

"Because I owe Dr. Napper," I tell her. "He believed in us. He saw our potential. He gave us a chance and really good jobs for the last decade. And not only that, he was *excited* about giving us another decade. The least I can do is give him a few more days, even if they're uncomfortable."

"He believed in *all* of us, not just the SETI people," Karen says.

"I know he did," I tell her. "What I realized this evening, sitting here listening to you all, is that for the last several years, I've been angry with people who judge my program without bothering to learn more about it, when really I've been doing the same thing to you all. Not only that, I went after Niles and Karen today just to make myself look better, and I'm sorry. I wish I could take it back."

I look at both of them, hoping that they'll accept, but based on their expressions, I can see it's a hard no. "I thought I was so much better than you. So much smarter, and I guess I was desperate to prove that to Ty, but the truth is, we're all the same—we're a bunch of dreamers trying to find our place in a cynical world."

"Isn't that funny, since just this morning you said you'd never want to be with a man like Ty because *he's* too cynical."

Fuuuckkk... My face turns bright red and I glance over at him just in time to see him blink a couple of times. "I … that is … absolutely true. I did say that."

"Well, I'd rather be a cynic than a total hypocrite," Niles says.

"She's actually both," Savannah adds.

"That is also true," I answer, my whole body feeling mushy. Owning up to your mistakes is kind of the worst, no? "Anyway, I am sorry and if I could take it all back, I would."

Karen squints her eyes at me. "What I want to know is what made you so mean?"

"What?"

"What made you such a nasty person that you would try to kill our dreams like that?"

"Yeah," Niles says. "I'd like an answer to that too."

Okay. Wasn't expecting that. "I guess I've always felt like I had to fight for every bit of respect I've ever gotten," I say. "I was raised by very logical, highly accomplished people. My father has his PhD in Analytical Chemistry— he's a pretty big deal in that world. The funny thing is my mom is a professor of condensed matter physics at M.I.T., and I don't know if you know much about physicists, but they're so serious about science, they think what chemists do is laughable. So for her, even what my dad does is a bit of a joke, so just imagine what she thinks about what I do…"

"Let me guess," Rohan says. "Your very logical, highly accomplished parents don't approve."

"Oh, they hate it. I'm a total disappointment to them

and they are both one-hundred-percent sure I'm wasting my life."

Rohan tilts his head. "That sounds like it could make for less-than-pleasant Thanksgiving dinners."

I nod, glad that he seems to get it. "And phone calls home, and Christmases, and our annual fourth of July week at the lake…" I say. "They're actually extremely embarrassed by my job. I happen to know that my mother never discusses me with her colleagues. I might as well be a stripper as far as she's concerned. Not that there's anything wrong with being a stripper, I mean, if someone enjoys stripping. But you know … it's not the dream most people have for their daughters. Anyway, lucky for my parents, they've got my big brother to boast about at the office. He has a double doctorate in both of their fields of study and works for NASA. They're constantly 'suggesting' I ask him to get me a job there." I look over at Karen. "I don't expect you to feel sorry for me and I don't mean to say I have an excuse for being so shitty to you. I just … think maybe this is why I turned out to be 'so mean,' as you put it."

She nods at me. "Yeah, that would do it. Sounds kind of awful, actually."

Shrugging, I say, "I know a lot of people have it much worse than parents with extremely high standards."

"No, that's hard, there's no two ways about it," Karen says. "I can see why it would make you defensive."

"And offensive," Niles adds.

"All right, Niles, no need to pile on," Savannah says. "The woman said she's sorry. Let's just let it go."

"I don't want to," he says. "She may have done a lot of damage to all of our programs. At the very least, she certainly didn't help. It's not like Ty needed more reasons to shut us down."

Everyone turns to look at Ty, and my heart pounds a little harder. Whatever he says next is going to either make or break me with these people.

He shakes his head. "To be honest with you, Gwen just said what I was already thinking, and even if she had managed to sway my opinion—which she didn't—the end result is the same. I'm pulling out of the foundation. I'm not going to pick a favorite project or two to save. So, for the rest of the trip, can everyone please just stop?"

Niles nods and gazes at the fire. "Yeah, I guess so. If life's taught me anything, it's to know when you're beat."

"But let's not give up," Karen says. "Who knows? Maybe Skip will honor Richard's wishes."

I nod and offer her a hopeful smile, even though I have a bad feeling that's not going to happen. "Anything's possible, right?"

She smiles back which I take as a sign that she's over what happened. "I like to think so."

Rohan yawns, then says, "Okay, Ty, you're the last one."

Ty looks around, then says, "You know what? It's been a really long day and it's getting late. I think we should all just turn in."

Rohan glances at the urn, then back at Ty and shakes his head. "All right then."

Dropping his shoulders, Ty says, "Right, it was his last wish, so I guess I have to. I'm going to answer what I'm most proud of."

"I know what I'd be proud of, if I were you," Thiago says, rubbing his fingers and thumb together like he's holding some cash.

Ty gives him a little nod, then says, "That's not it, actually. It's nice, but what I'm most proud of, or I guess I should say, *who* I'm most proud of, is my little brother,

Michael. Not a lot of people know I have a brother. I don't want to expose him to all the … noise of the world. Michael has autism and he lives with me. I've been looking after him since he was twelve and I was nineteen, and to be honest, it's been the greatest privilege of my life. Forget being in *Forbes Top 40 Under 40*, or meeting the president. None of that means anything, it's just…" he waves his hand, "…strange. But watching him start to open up and start talking or seeing him smile or making him laugh, now *that's* real. He's come so far since he was a little kid. So far, and now he's this funny, smart, surprisingly insightful, brutally honest person I get to spend my free time with."

The emotion in Ty's voice and the sincerity in his face is enough to bring tears to my eyes. He's completely lit up, like a parent is when they talk about their child, and in a way, I guess Michael is very much like his child. I just want to jump up and go hug him, and I'm guessing the other women sitting around this fire are having that same desire right now. He clears his throat, then looks at the urn. "There, I hope that counts."

Rohan nods at him. "I think Dr. Napper would've said it did."

"Good," Ty answers. "Because nobody here owes Richard more than I do, and we all owe him a lot."

———

Later, as I climb into the hammock and stare up at the thatched roof above, I think about everything that happened today, about what I learned, not only about the other people I'm with, but about myself too. I guess Dr. Napper was right—maybe we are meeting ourselves for the first time out here. And I don't like what I saw today. Yes, it's good to stand up for yourself, but not when it means putting someone down. Especially someone weaker than you.

My entire life, I've thought I was such a fighter when the truth is, *I've* been the weaker one, and my family has been putting me down. Instead of understanding how much that hurts and deciding never to do it to anyone else, I've been doing the exact same thing. I'm an elitist even though that's the thing I hate the most about my parents.

Silent tears roll down my cheeks as I think about how wise Niles has turned out to be, or how kind Karen is or how Savannah has been through some awful shit, and yet she still holds her head high and does her best. I think about how strong they all are—truly strong, not just pretending, like I've been doing. I think about how much Ty clearly loves his little brother and how his face lit up when he talked about him. He's not the man I thought he was. Not even close. Guilt creeps over me as I think about the pleasure I took in throwing darts at his picture or how many times I've gotten up on that stage and clearly told the crowd at the bar I was dedicating the song to the worst man on Earth.

Here I've been, spending my life judging others while simultaneously raging whenever anyone judges me. Talk about a foolish way to live. But maybe it's not too late to change. And I can start trying right now.

22

There's the Smart Choice, and There's the Tempting One...

Ty

ONE THING about being awake all night is it gives you a lot of time to think, which isn't always a good thing. If I at least had my laptop, I could make use of the time, catching up on emails and making sure things are going smoothly with the transition at the company. But instead, I lay in my hammock until the sun finally crept up through the mosquito netting, listening to splashes in the river nearby and the birds chattering away, my stomach tied up in impossible knots. Because without the distraction of a multi-national corporation to run or Michael to look after or the ability to help Anika in her role as COO, I have nothing to do but reflect on my own actions. The last two days' events are rumbling around relentlessly in my brain, as well as the knowledge of how the lives of the people with whom I'm surrounded right now are going to change permanently.

I'd rather *not* know their origin stories or what sad lives they had before Richard found them and gave them a sense of purpose and people with whom to share their days. I'd much prefer to forget what Niles said about bitter people stuck on childhood traumas (which I'm sure is true for most people, but in my case is totally different). I also absolutely don't want to think about what will become of the group when they lose their jobs. Because let's face it, they *are* going to lose their jobs. Skip is not about to come through for them and neither am I.

Even if someone does swoop in and buy the team out from under me, I can't exactly go back on what I've been saying publicly for years—that the foundation is an embarrassment, a waste of money, and that I'm out the first chance I get. How would that look to the other billionaires at the club? Just kidding. There is no billionaires' club, despite what people think. Although, I have been to a golf club on Maui that I don't think has members that have less than three commas in their bank account statements.

But I digress, which I suppose is what I want to do because *not* thinking about the lives of Nigel, Karen, Savannah, and Gwen is so much easier than thinking about them. It's easy to screw people over when you don't know them. Once you've gotten a glimpse into their realities, however, it's damn hard not to want to rush in and save them. Although I suppose one could make an argument that saving them would actually be a patriarchal thing to do, and that instead, I should trust them to save themselves because they're all competent adults. Huh, yeah, that feels better. In a way, it's actually *more* respectful to let them sort out their own lives. If only I could convince myself of that, I'd be able to offload a lot of the guilt I'm feeling right now.

Speaking of guilt, I still haven't made things right with Gwen, and after hearing more about her family, I feel much worse about being so hard on her, especially about calling her stupid. If I had to guess, I'd say she already feels stupid a lot of the time, even though that's the very last thing she is. Argumentative, feisty, and occasionally insensitive, yes. But she's something so much better than some vapid human with no opinions on anything. She's alive with passion and is unfailingly honest, even when it's the last thing she should be.

At least I'm going to have a lot of time alone with her to try to make things right. We're about to embark on a day-long canoeing trip down the Amazon, and we'll be traveling in pairs with our buddies. In Richard's video, he told us today's theme was survival. We've each been given a tent, sleeping gear, and food, and we'll be heading even deeper into the jungle, where we will spend a night without the 'luxuries' of the tree house, which I'm guessing means no outhouse and no cook.

The group is quiet this morning, and I'm sure it's because we're all a little worn out from the last couple of days. Gwen has barely said two words as we load up our canoe, which bothers me more than it should. I'm not one to care too much if people aren't happy with me. In fact, you can't be a people pleaser and a CEO—that doesn't work—so the fact that I'm so desperate to fix things with her is surprising, to say the least.

"So, I think that's everything," she says, glancing briefly at me.

"Yup, I think so." Remembering her nervous bladder, I say, "Do you want to … run to the ladies' room before we set off?"

She nods. "I better, thanks."

I stand by the shore and watch the other pairs as they prepare to set off. Thiago and Rohan have the canoe next to ours. They've got Richard's urn loaded up at the front of their canoe already, strapped in and ready to go. Niles,

Savannah, and Karen, who are all traveling together, look like they're ready to leave. The two women are sitting already as Niles pushes off from the shore and hops in, surprising me with how skilled he is at this.

My call with Michael yesterday pops into my head and I look down at the river, narrowing my eyes to see if I can spot any of those tiny vampire fish. They can't be real, can they? I shudder at the thought of them. "Say, Thiago, is that thing about the vampire fish true?"

He looks over at me and nods. "Probably. The local people have been telling stories about them for hundreds of years. In fact, they used to tie off their penises when they would go fishing, but the chances of having one invade your urethra is very slim, especially if you're wearing underwear."

Well, that's not exactly comforting. "How slim?"

"Are you wearing underwear?"

"Yes."

"You'll be fine. Besides, you're not going to be in the river. You're going to be on the river in a canoe. Totally safe."

"Right."

"Honestly, I'd be more worried about piranhas than vampire fish if I were you. They're far more dangerous," he says. "Where is your buddy? We're all supposed to travel in one group."

"She'll be right back. You guys go ahead."

He gives me a skeptical look. "Do you even know how to canoe?"

"I went to summer camp." Once and I hated it.

"Did they teach you how to canoe at summer camp?"

"Yes," I tell him.

"On a fast-flowing river filled with crocodiles and piranhas?"

"Er, not exactly, but don't worry. I've got it covered."

"Maybe Rohan and you should switch. He's an experienced canoer and so am I."

No way. I need time alone with Gwen. "Apparently Gwen is really experienced."

He raises one eyebrow. "She is?"

"Oh yeah. She basically grew up in a canoe."

"This isn't going to be a problem, is it?" he asks, narrowing his eyes at me.

"Nope. Definitely not. Because the last thing you need right now is more problems."

"Exactly," he says. "Now, you have the map, yes?"

"Yes," I say, reaching into the canoe and holding it up. "Go ahead. There's only one direction we can go, right? Downstream?"

"Yes, but it's not so simple. There are areas with big rocks to avoid."

"Avoid the rocks. Got it," I say. "Don't worry. We'll catch up with you in a few minutes, I'm sure."

He and Rohan push off and disappear down the river while I wait for Gwen, who comes rushing down a moment later. "Sorry about that. It's a long hike from here to the out—" She stops and looks around for the others. "I take it they left."

"It's okay, we'll catch up in no time."

"I hope so because I don't know the first thing about canoeing. Or camping," she says, getting into the canoe and settling herself on the front bench seat. "Do you?"

"Oh yeah, no problem," I tell her, offering her a confident smile. "Thiago said as long as we avoid the rocks, we'll be fine."

"Okay, well, since I'm at the front, I'll keep an eye out."

"Perfect." I push the canoe away from the shore, then hold onto both sides and hop in (as seen on TV). The canoe tips from left to right violently, but luckily it doesn't go over. We both start to paddle, and it takes me a minute to realize we're both paddling on the left side, which means the canoe takes a sharp right back toward shore. I dip my paddle in the water and hold it in place to turn the canoe. "Might work better if we're paddling on different sides," I say.

She turns and gives me a look. "Are you sure you know how to do this?"

"I'm a little rusty, but it'll all come back to me," I answer. Total lies. Rusty would mean I had the skills to begin with but let them languish. I don't have the first freaking clue what we're doing.

"Listen, Gwen, I wanted to apologize about what I said to you yesterday. It was … harsh of me and I'm really sorry."

She stops, mid-paddle, and turns to look over her shoulder. "It's okay. I've had people say much worse."

My gut tightens at the thought of people being mean to her. "It's not okay. It was uncalled for and mean and I'm sorry I said it."

"All right, well, thank you. I appreciate you saying that. I know I was frustrating you and I won't do it again. This whole trip has had me doing and saying things I normally wouldn't."

"I'm sure it has. Last night when I wasn't sleeping I was thinking about the pressure you must be under. Your entire team is counting on you to do the impossible, so of course you're going to do whatever you have to do to save them."

She dips her paddle in the water again and propels us forward but doesn't say anything. I wish she would talk. Hell, I'd even take yelling, because this version of Gwen seems to have lost her spark.

We glide along in silence for a minute until she says, "It

wasn't just about the funding. When I went after Niles and Karen yesterday."

"Okay," I answer, wanting to understand. "What was it about then?"

She turns her head to the side. "I wanted you to respect me."

"I do respect you. You're a highly educated, highly intelligent person, and you could argue the shoes off a mule."

Her lips quirk up in a smile I can only see half of from here and I find myself frustrated, wanting to see the whole thing. "Is that supposed to be a compliment?"

I chuckle a little. "I think so, why? Was it insulting?"

She laughs. "I honestly don't know."

"Well, take it as a compliment. It means I have the utmost faith in your ability to argue, which in the right situation, is an incredible asset."

"I probably missed my calling. I should've been a lawyer."

I shudder, then say, "Eww, God no. Awful people."

"Are they even worse than heartless CEOs?" she asks, sounding more like herself.

I laugh. "Who do you think we get all our evil ideas from?"

Gwen lets out a loud laugh that echoes off the water and I feel a wave of relief wash over me. Maybe we can salvage the rest of this trip and enjoy our time together, even though, in my mind, I know it's going to be far too brief. "What if we start over? Forget about the foundation and just be two buddies out here on the Amazon trying to avoid rocks and keep crocodiles from climbing into our canoe?"

Gwen looks back at me and smiles. "Sure, I'd like that."

"Good. First thing we should do is catch up with the group because like you, I don't know the first thing about camping. Or canoeing."

She laughs again, the wonderful sound filling my ears. "Okay, we better catch them because if not, Thiago is going to be right about us."

We both start to paddle a little harder, and soon we're moving swiftly down the river. Now that things feel better between us, I find myself glancing at her bottom, well, not so much glancing as gazing intently. God, that's a nice, nice ass. Even in cargo pants. I should not be staring at it so much. And yet…

A splash to our right snaps me out of my trance. When I look up, I see a pink dolphin surfacing, then another following close behind.

"Look!" Gwen says.

"Wow, they really are pink."

"Right?"

We both stop paddling and watch the pair play in the water nearby.

"If you ask me, there are far too few pink animals on the planet," I tell her.

"True. You've got your flamingos, I guess."

"These are better. Flamingos are too showy."

"Agreed," she says, grinning at me. "And they have weird knobby knees. But these guys are so graceful."

"And beautiful."

And distracting. Because neither of us sees the big rock up ahead…

23

Thiago is a Psychic Wizard...

Gwen

"Oh, fuck!" Ty yells, as the canoe smashes into the rock and splits down the middle.

"Shit!" Water immediately starts filling the vessel, soaking my feet and legs. Like a total idiot, I'm still paddling, hoping that if we go fast enough, we can outrun the water.

"Grab our gear," Ty says. "It's sinking."

My heart pounds wildly and a surge of adrenaline courses through me as panic sets in. I clutch my paddle with one hand and reach for my backpack with the other.

"Drop the paddle! It's of no use now," Ty yells.

"I can use it to fight off a crocodile!"

With the canoe now under me, I pull myself to my left to get to the nearest shore, only to realize I'm going to have to fight with everything in me just to keep my head above water. Half of the broken canoe pops back up and rushes away from us, propelled by the swift current. In the distance, I hear the trill of a dolphin.

The dolphins! They'll save us. "Help, Flipper! Help!!!" I scream.

"What?"

Ignoring Ty, I shout, "Pink dolphins! I command you to save us!"

"I don't think that's how it works," Ty says, and I suddenly realize he's right behind me. He grabs me around my waist and yanks me to the left while I grip my bag and the paddle with everything in me.

Okay, this is okay. Ty's got me. I'm going to live. I pull it together and start to kick my legs to help get us to shore. Finally, I let go of the paddle so I can use my free arm as well. Something brushes against my leg and I shout, "Did you feel that? It's a croc!"

"That was me," he says. "Try to calm down."

"I am calm!" I shout. "You calm down!"

We're just about to shore when he yells, "Fuck! Vampire fish!"

"Vampire fish?!" I scream, scrambling to the sandy beach. I crawl as far away from the water as possible before my body goes completely numb and I collapse. When I turn, I half expect Ty to be in a full-on wrestling match with some sort of massive fish with huge teeth but he's not. He heaves himself out of the river, dropping the bags on the shore. He pauses for a second, glancing up at the sky, then says, "Never mind. I'm fine."

"What?"

"No vampire fish. All is well," he says, nodding at me reassuringly. I can tell by the sheepish look on his face that he's totally embarrassed.

He flops onto the ground next to me, panting. "We made it."

"Yeah, thank God."

We're both silent while we watch the remains of our

canoe and one of the backpacks disappear around a bend in the distance, then Ty says, "You didn't tell me you had the power to summon wild animals."

I close my eyes and scrunch up my face.

Ty mimics my voice. "Pink dolphins, I command you to save us!"

We both burst out laughing. When we stop, I look over at him. "I *really* wanted to believe I could do it."

"I love your optimism. Truly noteworthy."

I grin at him, my heart pattering at the fact that he loves something about me. "Insanity is more like it."

"It's understandable. You were panicking, so…"

"And you weren't?" I ask.

"No, I was busy getting us and as much of our gear as possible to shore."

"Right up until the bit when you thought you were being attacked by a … what was it? Werewolf fish?"

"Vampire fish," he murmurs. "It's just something Michael told me about on the phone. But obviously they're not real and I'm fine. Say, was it me, or did it seem like those dolphins were totally laughing at us?"

I chuckle at him. "Changing the subject?"

"I'd prefer to, yes," he answers.

"All right. I won't ask, but only because you saved my life."

"Excellent. I'll consider us even." He grins at me. "Now, about those pink dolphins. Who knew they were such assholes?"

"Not me, but they totally are."

"It's one thing for them to ignore your command, but to laugh at us? Uncalled for."

"I actually think I prefer flamingos now," I answer, my stomach doing that flippy thing it does when he smiles at me, which definitely shouldn't be happening, given the fact that we capsized and are now stranded in the middle of the Amazon rainforest.

I have to say, Ty's hair isn't the only thing about him that's McDreamy-esque. His natural protective instincts are spot on. He got to me in record time and held me tightly around my waist while he fought the current and got us to shore. How he did that with two backpacks on is beyond me.

We're both quiet for a minute as the reality of what just happened sets in.

"That was crazy," he says.

"It was. This whole thing is crazy," I tell him. "You were amazing, by the way. You not only saved me, but you managed to keep most of our supplies too."

"Well, we lost one of the packs, which means we're down to one tent and one sleeping bag," Ty answers. He sighs and shakes his head. "I really should've been able to grab that one too."

"Don't feel bad. I managed to lose a bag at the airport." Pausing for a second, I glance over at Ty. "Oh my God, we *are* the problem. Thiago is going to be so pissed at us"

"*So* pissed," Ty says. "When he sees that piece of canoe coming down the river, he's going to blow a fuse."

I chew my lip for a second, looking around and realizing how alone we are. "They will see it, right?"

Ty gives me a confident nod. "Oh yeah, definitely."

"I mean, how could they miss it, right?"

"They won't," he says. "That would be absurd. It's going to keep on going right past them."

"Yeah," I answer. "It'll probably be a lot quicker without all the weight too."

Ty clicks his tongue a few times, then says, "Unless it sinks."

"Right. That's a distinct possibility, isn't it?" I say, my heart dropping a little. "Or maybe the backpack will stay afloat?"

"Yeah, let's hope for that."

"Because otherwise we're … kind of stranded, aren't we?"

"Yeah, and given the fact that we're on the opposite side of the river from where we started, it's not like we can walk back," he says. "Maybe we should try to hike along the shore until we find them?"

I shake my head. "They say if you get lost in the wilderness to stay put so you can be rescued. Besides, I'm guessing it would take days to hike as far as they're going by canoe."

"So, stranded, it is." His gaze is doing all sorts of things to me that it shouldn't be.

Clearing my throat, I stand up. "I guess we should hang up all these wet things while the sun is still high."

Ty stands too. "And here you said you don't know anything about camping."

I chuckle, then say, "You don't happen to have some secret survival skills they didn't mention in *GQ*, do you?"

"Sadly, I have no attributes when it comes to camping or camping-related fields," he says, pulling the tent out of its bag. "Other than having the proper travel vaccines, that is, but they probably won't come in too handy when it comes to starting a fire."

"True," I answer, grinning at him.

"They will keep me from getting, what was it you were saying the first time I saw you?" He taps his lips with his index finger. "Oh yeah, unbearable abdominal pains, bleeding gums, and rapid breathing?"

"I really know how to make a first impression, don't I?"

"I'll never forget it."

He stares at me a moment too long, then we both seem to come to our senses and get back to work while I silently lecture my lady bits to settle it down. Nothing is going to happen out here. Nothing. Yes, he's the hottest man I've ever laid eyes on. Yes, he's completely sexy, fun as hell, and ridiculously manly, what with the saving of my life earlier. Yes, he also seems like a loyal and loving brother. Wait, was I talking myself *out* of sleeping with him just now?

Right, yes. It's a no. For several reasons that have completely slipped my mind, but I know are important.

Once everything has been hung to dry, I turn in time to see Ty peeling off his wet t-shirt. Wow. Nothing about that sight says no.

He hangs it on a nearby branch, then grabs his swim trunks. "I'm going to go throw these on."

"I'll try not to peek," I say, even though I will most definitely be peeking.

Damn, he's too far into the trees.

Oh my God, Gwen, get it together already! Pathetic. Just pathetic.

I grab my bikini off the log I set it on a few minutes ago and find a spot behind a tree to change out of my wet clothes. Soon, we're both back on the beach together, completely alone with no distractions, no devices, and nothing to do. Ty sits down on the sand, then stretches out his long legs, looking totally relaxed. "Come take a load off, Ms. Fox. We might as well relax while everything dries."

I do as he suggested, laying down a respectable distance away from him (despite a very strong urge to straddle his lap). Feeling the heat of the sun on my skin, I tell myself to relax, even though I know the chances of that are slim to none.

"What would you be doing, if you weren't here?" I ask him.

"It's what? Tuesday morning?"

"That sounds about right."

"I'd be at the office in a meeting. Or answering emails. I get roughly three hundred a day, and those are just the ones that Donna, my assistant, passes through to me. She deals with all the unimportant ones."

"Wow. Three hundred?"

He nods. "It'll be a lot more right now though because of losing Richard. More meetings too. I'm going to be swamped when I get back, trying to reassure our largest clients that it'll be business as usual. And then there's the shareholders. I had a Zoom call with them the morning we left for Peru, but a lot of the bigger ones will want to see me face-to-face. And then there's our new COO, Anika. She's amazing, but she's going to need my help as she fully steps into the role. Our accounting and legal teams will have stacks of paperwork for me to go over and sign as well."

"Sounds … overwhelming."

"It can be, but it's what I wanted so I'm not going to start complaining now that I've got it," he says. "What about you? What would you be doing?"

"I'd be in the radio room monitoring dozens of screens for any activity they might pick up."

"Sounds…" He trails off, so I finish his sentence for him.

"Boring?"

He chuckles. "I didn't want to say it."

"No, I get it. Most people would find it boring, and it can be. I actually knit while I'm in there because it's something you can do with your hands and you don't have to look down very often."

"You knit?" he asks, looking amused. "What kind of things do you make?"

"Oh, the usual—scarves, beanies, blankets. Right now, I'm working on a blanket for my bed at my new house. I've been working on it for months."

He narrows his eyebrows and I can tell he looks worried about something, but I have no idea what it could be. "That sounds like a good use of your time."

Huh, a good use of my time. I'm tempted to ask him if that's as opposed to my actual job, but I don't want to. I'm too tired to debate right now, and I really don't want to spoil the moment. "Do you think they'll find us soon?" I ask.

"Do you want me to be honest or do you want me to make you feel better?"

"Honest, always."

"All right then, no, I don't," he says. "I'd actually be surprised if they come back today at all."

"Really?" I ask, turning my head to face him.

He looks over at me. "Richard said we'd be out on the river until close to dark, so the way I figure it, they're going to spend that entire day assuming we're a few minutes behind them. By the time they figure out we're not coming, it'll be nightfall. Then they'll need to get a motor boat because they'll have to go up-current to get here. Either that, or they'll have to get a hold of someone upstream to come find us."

I chew my lip while I let the reality set in. We're alone in the jungle. Well, technically we're surrounded by all sorts of things that could kill us, which means we're not really alone. But there aren't other humans around. I should be panicking. I should be coming up with some sort of plan to get us out of here. But I'm not. Instead, I'm lying here thinking about what it would feel like to kiss Ty Sterling.

"You okay?" he asks, rolling onto his side and propping his head up on his hand.

"Yes, fine. You?"

He nods. "We're both intelligent, capable people. I have every faith we can figure this out."

"Huh, imagine that—Ty Sterling, world's biggest skeptic, having faith in something."

"Don't get too excited," he tells me. "I could be just saying that so you don't start to panic."

I grin at him for a second, then say, "Nope. You have faith in us."

"Yeah, well, don't start thinking you're going to turn me into some sort of believer or something because that is *not* about to happen. You and I are going to spend the rest of the day and most likely the night out here, where we will figure out how to start a fire, set up a tent, and make ourselves something to eat. And tomorrow morning, I shall resume my regularly scheduled program of being a total cynic."

Shrugging, I say, "We'll see about that."

24

The Other Way to a Man's Heart...

Ty

"HAVE you ever seen a show called Swiss Family Robinson?" I ask.

"Is it about a family from Switzerland?" Gwen says, stepping back to look at the tiny tent we just managed to erect.

"How'd you guess?" I ask, grabbing the now-dry sleeping bag off the branch it was hanging from and shaking it off.

"I'm psychic. Now tell me about the show," she says, taking the sleeping bag from me and crouching at the entrance of the tent. She crawls inside (still dressed in her bikini) while I watch, suddenly every bit as erect as that tent. Thank God I'm wearing my cargo pants again because those swim trunks do nothing to hide even the slightest show of appreciation.

A second later she pokes her head out. "Hello? You were going to tell me about some show with some Swiss people."

Oh right, I was talking about something. "It was before our time, but somehow my brother, Michael, came across it on YouTube and got totally obsessed for a while. It was about a family of handsome blonds that got stranded on an island. They made the world's best tree house with all sorts of inventions for getting water to the top floor and washing clothes and crushing things. Mostly out of coconuts."

Gwen laughs and disappears into the tent again. "Sounds very wholesome."

"Oh, it was the height of wholesomeness," I tell her. "Anyway, I was thinking if we don't get rescued, we should follow their lead. Make a proper house, dig a well, fashion machines that can crush stuff … that sort of thing."

She pokes her head out of the tent. "How about we take it one step at a time? Maybe see if we can get a fire going first?"

"Sure, I suppose that's a good idea too," I say, looking around and realizing that it's going to be dark soon. I check the palm leaves and pieces of wood we gathered earlier this afternoon and find they're finally dry. Picking up the kindling, I carry it over to a spot near the tent, then set to work digging a shallow hole and setting up what I hope will be the base for a good fire.

Luckily our survival kit included some chemical fire starter and a box of waterproof matches, because otherwise, we'd be screwed. Just as I've got the fire going, Gwen crawls out of the tent, fully dressed again, much to my disappointment.

"Hey, not bad," she tells me, pointing to the fire.

"It's small, but it's got potential," I say.

She gives me a smirk that says her mind went to a dirty place just now, and I roll my eyes at her. "That wasn't a metaphor or anything. I'm literally talking about the fire."

"Right, good to know," she says, unpacking the food from the plastic storage bags. "Okay, so on tonight's menu, we've got freeze-dried Spanish paella that our chef will serve to you in our upscale brown bag. I suggest pairing that with some lukewarm river water that has been treated with water purification tablets. We will follow that with some delicious chocolate freeze-dried ice cream popular at planetariums around the globe."

"Ooh, sounds amazing. You can count on a five-star review later."

"That's what I was hoping to hear," she says, grabbing the small pot.

The sky grows dark and the fire grows hotter and bigger. Soon, Gwen is pouring the boiling water into the packet, and a few minutes later, we're sitting side-by-side on a towel, taking turns dipping our forks into the bag. It's a strangely intimate thing to be doing—to share food like this, with our arms touching as we eat. The warmth of her skin against mine does more to fill me up than the food.

"Not bad," I tell her.

"Thanks, it's actually my first time making paella."

"You must be very talented in the kitchen because I've heard it's a difficult dish to master."

She smiles up at me, and something pops into my mind about the way into a man's heart being his stomach. I won't say it though because my heart is now, and will forever, be off-limits. But the thought was there none-theless.

I offer her the last bite, and she shakes her head. "No, thanks, I'm full."

"It's all yours."

"You should have it. It takes a lot of calories to maintain all that muscle," she says.

"I insist. Either you eat it or it goes in the fire."

She pulls a face, then takes the bag from my hand. "Stubborn man."

"Is that nerd for thank you?" I ask.

She laughs, then has the last bite. "Yes, thank you."

Taking the bag from her, I put on an extra deep voice and say, "Here, little lady. You cooked. I'll do the dishes." I toss the bag into the fire and watch as it lights up.

"Aww, you're the best husband I've ever had," she says. "You're also the worst one, but…"

I burst out laughing and she joins in, then after a few seconds, I say, "Why *aren't* you married?"

She blinks quickly, looking surprised by the question, so I quickly follow it with, "I don't mean to pry or suggest you *should* be married. I just mean that you're obviously very beautiful, you're fun as hell, and you're really amazing. I can't figure out why some guy hasn't snapped you up yet."

Giving me a sassy look, she says, "I could ask you the same thing."

"In my case, it's because I'm not gay."

"You know what I meant."

"Fine, in my case it's because I don't ever want to be married," I answer, feeling a strange ache in my chest that I'm going to ignore. "And you?"

She stares at the fire and shrugs, her expression suddenly pensive. "I don't know. I just haven't met the right guy."

"But you'd like to be someone's wife one day?"

"God, you're nosy."

Grinning, I say, "Not normally." I pick up a small log and toss it on the fire. "In fact, I usually avoid finding out personal details about people. But for some reason, I'm very curious about you."

She blushes a little and glances up at the sky. "Curious like a zoologist studying a new species?"

Before I can stop myself, I say, "Curious like a man who wants to figure you out."

Swallowing hard, Gwen looks at me, her face growing serious. "Oh…" Her voice is thick with emotion as she says, "Well that's a very different form of curiosity."

"It really is, isn't it?" I ask, knowing I should not be going down this road. I shouldn't even know where it is on the map.

"Yeah," she says, glancing at my lips. "But back to you. Why don't you ever want to be married? You've already told me you're not a player who goes through women like we're paper napkins. Why *not* add a wife to your quiet evenings hanging out at home?"

"It's surprisingly hard to find someone I can trust," I tell her, shocking myself with my answer. "The money seems to get in the way."

She doesn't scoff at what I just said. She doesn't laugh, or mock me for feeling sorry for myself. Instead, Gwen just nods. "I could see that. How could you ever know if it's you they love or it's what you can buy for them?"

"Exactly," I tell her. "Not that I was a big fan of the institution before I made my money. It's just gotten worse is all."

We stare at each other with an intensity I can't describe, then, before I'm ready, she looks away. I follow her gaze to the sky and notice how very bright the strip of stars we can see between the treetops are. There's a full moon shining down, reflecting off the river as it hurries along. If I were the marrying type, I'd probably want to set up a scene exactly like this for the woman I loved.

Picking up the bag of freeze-dried ice cream, Gwen says, "Can I interest you in dessert?"

Not if it's food. "Sure, why not?"

I watch as she rips the bag open and hands me a piece, then gets one for herself. "Cheers."

We both take a bite and I stare up at the moon again while it melts on my tongue. "Huh, it's a little…"

"Dry?"

"Yeah. Bring your own saliva."

She laughs and wrinkles up her nose.

"Oh, was that too gross for Ms. Bleeding Gums?"

"Hey, that was purely to save those women's lives…"

"Right, I almost forgot. Gwendolyn Fox, patron saint of the unvaccinated."

Rolling her eyes, she lets out a little chuckle, then takes another bite.

I watch her, suddenly realizing how much fun I'm having.

When she looks at me again, she narrows her eyes a little. "What?"

"I didn't say anything."

"I know that. I meant what's that expression about."

"What expression?"

"I don't know. You have a goofy smile on your face."

"I don't have a goofy smile," I tell her, putting on a faux frown to prove her wrong.

"You did a second ago," she says with a sideways grin.

Shaking my head, I say, "No, I've never had a goofy smile before."

"Never?"

"Not once. Not even as a young child."

"I know a goofy smile when I see one, and *that*, sir, was a goofy smile. So, fess up. What's so funny?"

I stare at her, desperately wanting to pull her onto my lap and kiss her hard on the mouth. "I don't know. I guess I was just realizing that … I'm having fun here. With you. Which is surprising, really, because it's not something I do very often. And given the circumstances, I wouldn't have thought it would be possible at all."

"You mean the 'being stranded in the jungle with a woman who only wants you for one thing?'" she asks.

"Yes," I say, my gaze flicking down to her mouth and back up. "Although I would suppose it would matter what that one thing was, because depending on the answer, this would be exactly the type of situation where a person could have an incredible time."

"Incredible?" Her cheeks flush a little.

"Yes, depending on what she wanted me for." The tension between us grows thick.

"What if she only wanted you for your body?"

"Then I can guarantee it would be a night to remember."

25

It's Kind of Steamy in this Jungle...

Gwen

HE WANTS ME. And it's been so very long since someone wanted me. *So* long. Like I'm pretty sure I'm revirginated at this point. Let's face it, I want him right back. I want to feel him against me and inside me and on top of me and under me. I want to taste his kisses and his skin and to feel the way he moves. There's a silent alarm going off in the back of my mind, trying to tell me this is a terrible idea. It's saying something about betraying my work family and risking my heart with a man who literally just told me he has no interest in happily ever after with anyone.

And yet…

Here we are, two consenting adults, completely alone and absolutely wanting to do this. I stare up at him, taking in his chiseled jawline, his stubble, his dark eyes that are undressing me right now. My heart pounds in my chest, my body hums with excitement. "A night to remember? That's a bold prediction," I say in a breathy voice I don't even recognize.

"I'm confident I can back it up," he tells me, lowering his face to mine.

He leaves just the smallest space between our mouths. Enough that I can feel his breath and can almost feel his lips against mine. It's less than an inch and yet it's infinitely far away because there's still time for me to say no. To get up and walk away without allowing anything to happen. We could go back to whatever we were a minute ago. Just two people stuck out here alone together passing the time. That would be the smart thing to do—to get up and walk away because he is the very last man I should want like this.

But he's also the man I've wanted like no other. The desire I have for him is all that matters in this moment. There is nothing, no one else on this planet that means anything to me right now. There's no future, no past. It's just the two of us here in this perfect moment.

I close my eyes and leap, letting my lips brush against his. The warmth of his kiss draws me in and the alarm in my mind shuts off completely as I allow myself to get lost in the feeling of his mouth against mine. He lifts one hand and brushes his thumb against my cheek, setting the skin on fire there. Cupping my jaw, he tilts my head and my lips part even more, begging his tongue to find its way inside. When it finally does, I let out a loud moan, then I open my eyes and pull back to see if he's laughing at what just one little kiss can do to me.

But he's not laughing. He's giving me the most intense look I've ever seen. His eyes devour me in the moonlight. "You okay?"

I nod, my brain short-circuiting. "Yes, I just … got a little excited there, then I was worried that you'd think I was too excited."

His lips quirk up a little. "No such thing."

"Is this a bad idea?" I ask. "I mean, I know it'll be ..."

"Incredible?"

"Yeah, that," I whisper. "But is it reckless?" *No! Why did I ask that? Shut up, Gwen. Just shut up or you're going to ruin everything.*

"I don't think so. Unless you won't respect me in the morning," he says. "Because I couldn't live with that."

"Oh, I'll respect you," I answer. "I'll respect the hell out of you."

There's that half grin again that could dissolve panties all over the globe. "Then I say we allow ourselves this one night of not thinking about anything and just let ourselves have something incredible." He lowers his face to my neck and gives me a slow, soft kiss. "There are no decisions to make. No responsibilities. No loyalties. Only us. Out here. Alone. Wanting this."

His lips brush against my collar bone, then he makes his way up my neck. Nipping gently on my ear lobe, he whispers, "I want you, Gwendolyn Fox. I want you so badly it hurts."

His words and his lips against my skin are waking up parts of me that have been asleep for years. Maybe forever.

"I've wanted you since the moment I first saw you in that little black skirt."

"But I had vomit in my hair," I whisper. *Vomit? Seriously shut up.*

He lifts his face up so he's staring at me, those eyes doing *all* the things to me again. "You were still the sexiest woman I've ever seen."

"Really?" I squeak out.

"Really. And I've sat front row at the Victoria's Secret show."

I purse my lips together, then scoff. "Come on. There's no way I'm the sexiest woman you've ever seen."

"You absolutely…" Kiss. "One-hundred-percent…" Kiss. "Are." Kiss. "The sexiest woman I've ever seen and if you don't believe me, I'd be more than happy to spend all night proving it."

Swallowing hard, I say, "All right, but I'm quite skeptical so you've got your work cut out for you."

He grins at me again. "Good."

He pulls me onto his lap, his hands cupping my bottom as I straddle him. It's even better than I imagined, the feeling of being pressed up against him like this. He's harder, warmer, *more* than I thought he'd be. I'm so caught up in exploring his arms and his chest with my hands that I barely notice my shirt being lifted over my head, or my bra being unlatched until the cool, humid air hits my nipples, making them pucker. His large hands cup my breasts, making them tingle even more. Lowering his face over my right breast, he captures my nipple in his mouth, teasing it until I can barely take it. I let out another moan, louder this time, realizing I don't have to be quiet out here. He moves over to my other breast and gives it the same careful treatment, making me desperate for more.

I tug at the hem of his shirt, somehow managing to get it off him despite having no coordination right now. Pulling back, I take in the view of him like this—shirtless in the pale light of the moon. Perfection. He is utter perfection and the fact that he wants me blows my mind.

"Wow," I whisper, my hands everywhere and my mouth following as I taste his skin and breathe in the scent of him. He's teakwood and citrus, he's oak and spice, he's delicious and he damn well knows it.

A surge of irritation rushes through me. I'm suddenly unreasonably frustrated by the fabric of our remaining clothes. Fumbling with the button on his pants, I finally manage to get it undone, only to realize I'm going to have to climb off him to get him naked. In a frenzy of quick, sharp movements, he pulls me up so we're both standing and we manage to strip ourselves and each other. My eyes rake over his perfect nude form, excitement building in me as I realize I get to touch that. I get to *feel* that.

He's smiling as he looks me over, and there's not a hint of self-consciousness for me, like I've felt with other guys. Because the expression he's wearing is one of pure adoration. It's like he's worshiping my body. I've never felt sexier than I do in this moment with this man gazing at me in the moonlight. Unable to wait any longer, I press myself against him, crush my mouth against his, feeling the heat of his touch as he wraps me up in his strong arms and pulls me close. Our bodies fit together perfectly, like they've always known each other.

Our tongues move together in perfect unison, as though they've always danced together. An unrelenting need throbs inside me. I want this. I want him. I want to be wanted like this. Worshipped like this. Adored the way he adores me. Even if it is just for this one night. Even if things are so complicated in the real world that we never see each other again. I know deep in my bones that one night with him would be better than ten thousand nights with anyone else.

His hands float down my back and onto my bottom and just when I'm ready to start begging, he lifts me up, my legs wrapping around his waist as if they've always known they were meant to be around *this* waist. His hard length presses against my wet core and I wiggle my hips, inviting him inside.

He doesn't take me up on the offer though. Instead, he pulls back and looks at me. "Are you sure?"

"I've literally never been more sure of anything in my

life," I say, planting a hard kiss on him. My voice is raspy, my breathing ragged. "I want you, Ty. I want you now."

"I'm going to take my time with you," he says, nipping my bottom lip. "Don't forget, I've got something to prove."

I kiss him hard, desperation taking over. "You mean that thing about me being the sexiest woman? That's okay. I believe you. Let's *do* this."

He laughs, a full, deep sound that I feel inside. "Patience, Ms. Fox. We've got all night."

"What if we don't?" I ask. "What if a rescue boat shows up in like … five minutes? I say we just do this right fucking now, just in case."

I wiggle my hips insistently, lining up the tip of his smooth, perfect cock with the place I want to feel it most. "Ahhh, yes," I whisper, feeling him up against my clit.

"I want to taste you first," he says, carrying me to the tent while we kiss some more.

He sets me down onto the sand and instead of crawling inside, I yank the sleeping bag out and spread it out. "We're going to need a lot more room for this," I tell him.

Laying down on my back, I watch as he lowers himself over me, the power of him evident in each flexing muscle. I grip his taut ass, trying to pull him to me, but he resists, giving me a long, deep, slow kiss before he works his way down my body, his mouth leaving a trail of hot, wet kisses along my skin, awakening every nerve ending.

"God, you're perfect." He spreads my legs with his hands, then gently kisses and licks me, his tongue finding its way inside and doing all sorts of things I didn't know I wanted. I wriggle and writhe under him, the tension building in me, tightening until I can't hold out. Clutching the sleeping bag with both hands, I lift my hips off the ground, gasping and shaking with the sudden force of my release. "Yes," I call out as he gives me the most intense pleasure of my life. "Right there. Yes."

He stays there until I stop bucking and moving against his mouth, then slowly, carefully, makes his way back up, planting sweet kisses of adoration all over my body. This isn't just a guy wanting to get some. He isn't some selfish bastard who doesn't care about anyone but himself. This is a man who *wants* to give me pleasure. It's there in every brush of his fingertips, in every kiss, in every groan and every sigh.

I want to stay right here forever, letting him do what he's doing to me. I don't ever want him to stop. I don't ever need to eat again or drink. I just need this.

He captures my mouth with his, and I can taste myself on his lips, taste the pleasure he just gave me. It was full and complete and perfect, and somehow left me wanting more. Because I haven't had *him* yet. And I need that like I need air.

26

Pillow Talk and Proof of Love...

Ty

I HAVE NEVER BEEN SO TURNED on in my life as I am right now. I've been riding the edge of losing control since our first kiss. She's perfection itself. She's everything. She's letting me take control and take my time and do all the things she deserves. And I intend to show her how incredible she really is and how she should be treated. I may not be able to offer her more than tonight, but I want her to walk away from this with a confidence that will stay with her forever. If I believed in love, I would say this was it. But it's not. It's just two people wanting each other.

Very badly.

She lifts her hand to the back of my head, running her fingers through my hair as she kisses my neck. Somehow she finds an undiscovered spot right behind my ear that drives me wild. I let out a groan that comes from deep within me, pressing myself against her, trying to hold myself back. Her skin is silk against mine, her scent, the world's most seductive perfume, her gaze, the sexiest thing I've ever seen.

Tilting her hips, she opens herself to me, whispering, "I want you now, Ty."

I slide inside her, feeling her tight, wet warmth surrounding my cock, taking it all. She moans, the sound of it nearly undoing me, but I manage to put the brakes on, moving slowly, carefully, feeling her body respond with each movement. The tension between us builds until it's almost more than either of us can take. Smiling down at her, I say, "You're perfect, Gwen." What I mean is she's *my* perfect Gwen, but I can hardly put that thought out into the world.

She grins up at me. "Oh, you talk a good game."

"I mean it." I kiss her hard on the mouth as I thrust into her. "You're perfect. Just like this."

When I pull back, I look down to see her eyes are closed, her lips parted, and I know she's ready. The sight of it is enough to tip me over the edge. She arches her back, bringing me in deeper and we both let ourselves succumb to the frenzied euphoria that has been growing with each passing second since we met.

"Yes, right there," she pants. "Just like that."

I give her exactly what she asked for, my movements more forceful, faster, harder as we build to the climax we've both been needing. She tightens around me, drawing out a release like I've never felt before—something wild and so powerful I feel it in every cell of my body. We both groan with abandon, allowing ourselves to give in to this perfect moment with no care of anyone hearing or anyone knowing. "Gwen."

"I can feel you coming," she gasps, writhing under me, drawing out my orgasm. "Oh God, Ty, yes, yes, yes!"

I press my forehead to hers as the last few spasms come

over me, my breathing ragged, my body completely satisfied as I kiss her softly on the lips. I try to think of the perfect thing to say, but my brain isn't functioning at the moment so all I manage is to say, "Wow."

"Yeah, *wow*. That was…" She trails off, then kisses me again, nipping my bottom lip with her teeth. "Incredible."

Giving her a half grin, I say, "Told you."

"You did." She smiles up at me, her legs still wrapped around my back, holding me here. "You definitely didn't over-promise and under-deliver."

"I'm glad," I tell her, nuzzling her neck. Lifting my face so I can look at her again, I say, "So, do you believe me?"

"About what?" she asks, her words floating into the night air.

"That you're the sexiest woman I've ever seen?"

Giving me a mischievous smile, she says, "I don't know about that. I may require more proof."

We laugh and collapse into a heap of satisfaction. "More proof?"

"Yes, all experiments must be replicated in order to be proved."

I chuckle some more and wrap the sleeping bag around us. "Give me a few minutes and I'll be sure to replicate the results."

"Mmm, perfect."

"I'm glad you had fun."

"So much fun, I don't care if we ever get rescued. We can stay right here and become those Swiss people with the coconut inventions."

I smile and kiss her forehead, my heart tugging at the fact that we will, indeed, get rescued, and this moment will be lost to us forever. As much as I know it's how it has to be, the thought of it is … not something I can deal with right now. Right now, I need to be here with her, connected like this, wrapped up in each other, feeling nothing but pleasure and satisfaction.

She lets out a contented sigh.

"Are you happy?" I ask.

"Are you kidding?" Gwen says. "I could make a thousand batches of cookies right now."

I chuckle and kiss her again. "If only we had a kitchen."

———

After proving my theory twice more, we make our way into the tent, both of us physically spent. We cuddle up together in the sleeping bag, still naked. I'm on my back and she's laying with her head on my chest, lazily running her fingertips up and down my body, leaving a happy trail wherever she touches me.

"I wish we could stay here," I tell her. "This is by far the most relaxed I think I've ever been."

"Me too," she says, snuggling closer. "Somehow—and this makes no sense whatsoever because it should be the exact opposite—it feels … easy with you."

"It really does, doesn't it?" I ask, marveling at that fact.

"It's probably because we barely know each other."

It's because it just feels right. "Probably. No baggage, not like with family or people you've known your entire life."

"They know too much," she says in an ominous tone.

I chuckle a little, then kiss her on her forehead. "I think it's because humans are capable of hurting the ones who love them the most."

"That's sort of a dark way of looking at it."

"Is it?" I ask. "Take your family, for example. You obviously love them. Otherwise, you wouldn't put yourself through the constant rejection. And instead of accepting you the way you are and encouraging you, they make you feel stupid. I'm not sure why you put up with it, to be honest."

Her hand stills and she doesn't respond for a moment, long enough to make me worry I've said too much. But then she says, "They're my family."

"Exactly, which means they're supposed to take you as you are, warts and all."

"Okay, for the record, I don't have any warts," she says. "But, I get what you mean."

"Do you?" I ask. "Because it seems to me that you give them a giant pass when you should really be putting your foot down."

"How could you possibly know that? Maybe I'm ruthless with them."

"You're not," I tell her. "You're someone who spends every holiday with her family, and if I had to guess, I'd say you probably spend most of it wishing they'd just learn to accept that you love what you do and just drop it already."

"You're partly right. I do wish for that, but I'm not some poor, meek, put-upon woman. I'm actually hellbent on proving them wrong. It's that thought that causes me to throw my covers off every morning and start my day."

"Really? That's why you work in SETI?"

"Obviously I believe in what we're doing, but proving them wrong is also definitely one of the reasons I'm going to stick with it."

"Even though you know it's a total long shot?"

"Yes. I just have to do it."

"But why? I mean, really, what does it matter if you can prove them wrong or not? Why not just agree to disagree and go on with your life?"

She lets out a long sigh. "Because they think I'm crazy, and I'm not, and I really need them to know it."

"Crazy? Your job is a little … out there, sure, but you're certainly not insane."

She stares at me for a second, as if trying to decide how much to say, then lets out a sigh. "The other night, I didn't answer the question about the defining moment in your life, because it was too hard for me to share with the whole group," she says. "Not with everything that had already happened with them. And once you hear it, you're going to think the word hypocrite fits me perfectly."

"I doubt that very much."

"No, it does," she says. "Because I laugh at Karen for believing in Yetis, when in actual fact, when I was twelve, I saw a U.F.O."

I freeze long enough for her to say, "See? Crazy, right?"

"No, you were a kid. Kids sometimes mistake things they see for other things. Besides, I'm sure there's an explanation for what you saw."

She shakes her head. "Not for this. I was biking home from my friend's house. It was late in the evening in the summertime. And I saw a big, triangular thing coming down from the sky. Like, really big. Bigger than anything I've ever seen in the sky before or since. It had these bright lights around the outside. It hovered over a field in the distance, then after a few seconds it just shot up into the sky. Straight up until it disappeared."

"Could it have been a helicopter?"

"No, it really couldn't. I'm telling you, it was the size of a school. I rushed home, peddling as hard as my legs could go, and ran into the house to tell my parents. I was all wound up, thinking the world was being invaded, and my parents just laughed at me. No matter how hard I insisted, they came back with their own perfectly logical arguments," she says, staring up at the tent for a second. "It went on for weeks—me trying to convince them and them telling me I didn't see what I thought I saw. I spent my evenings over at that field, watching and waiting with my camera in hand."

"So, *that's* why you went to work for the SETI team in the first place," I say gently.

Nodding, she says, "I've dedicated my entire life to proving my parents wrong, and I know it's not healthy, but I just really need to be able to go back home and say, 'Suck it. I was right all along.'" She lifts her head and looks me in the eye. "Now that I think about it, I guess I do have some warts, only mine are psychological. I'm a petty hypocrite, and I might possibly be insane as well."

Offering her a small smile, I say, "There are worse things you could be."

She rests her head on my chest again. "Tell that to my parents."

"What about your brother? Did he believe you?"

"Privately, he would make it sound like he did, but when my parents were around, he joined the 'make fun of Gwen' team."

"Wow, that's shitty," I tell her.

"Yeah, it wasn't great."

"Do they still bug you about it?"

"No, nobody mentions it, but it's always the elephant in the room. I'm sure it would go away if I had a different job, but I just can't bring myself to give up."

I run my fingertips along her arm, wishing I could make it all better, wishing I could find someone who could explain what she saw.

"I've never told anyone that before," she says. "Not even my best friend, Allie."

"Thank you for telling me," I answer, reaching down

and tucking a lock of hair behind her ear. "I'm honored that you would trust me like this."

"Now you have to tell me your deepest secret."

"No, I don't," I answer, laughing a little.

"According to the Ty Sterling etiquette book, you do," she says, lifting her head off me and propping it up on her hand. "Remember our first night together? When you insisted I share something personal because you had?"

"The couch and the cookies?" I ask.

"Yes."

Shaking my head, I say, "That's not the same thing as your biggest secret."

"Of course it is," she says, sounding incredulous.

"I would've had to agree to the terms *before* you shared yours, but since I didn't, I'm under no obligation."

Narrowing her eyes, she says, "I only shared because I assumed we were working under the terms you laid out when we first met, now out with it. Biggest secret, go!"

"Or what?" I ask, grinning at her.

"Or, I'll … I won't let you do that thing you did again."

"Which thing?" I ask, my mind going over all the things we did.

"You know which thing, and you clearly loved it based on how loud you were."

I glance up at the tent, then back at her. "I did really love that."

"So?"

"All right, I'll tell you one. You're not the only petty person in this tiny tent."

"I'm not?"

"No. The truth is, I've always dreamed of taking away the only thing my father has ever given a shit about." I stare at her for a moment before continuing on, then I start to talk, telling her things I've never told another living soul.

"When I was a little kid, my father and I used to watch football together every Sunday. Apparently right from when I was a baby. It was really the only time he spent with me, so I loved it. I'd sit right next to him on the couch, watching every second, cheering when he cheered, even though I didn't have the first clue what was going on." I let out a sigh, then keep going. "When Michael came along, it wasn't long before we realized he was overly sensitive to certain sounds. Football was one of them. He'd just cry and cry when it was on, so my dad would turn it up louder. So he would cry louder. My mom would try to keep him in another room, but she certainly couldn't do that all day. She had to cook and clean up and do laundry, and the whole time, Michael would be on her hip, crying away. My father decided screaming at him to stop was the right move."

"Good lord," she says, looking disgusted.

"Yeah, he was a real winner. My mom yelled at him to just grow up and turn the sound off. He did it, and the crying stopped, but then my father was miserable. The next week, he decided to spend Sundays at the bar, which meant the only thing we ever did together had come to an end."

"I'm sorry, Ty. He sounds awful."

"He really was. He was unbelievably selfish, which would have been bad enough, but the way he was with Michael…" My gut churns thinking about it, but I force myself to go on, knowing I need to tell her everything. "He couldn't accept Michael the way he was. He always wanted him to 'snap out of it' and start acting like a 'normal kid,'" I say, my mind going back to our little bungalow on Pine Street. "Thankfully, he finally left. Moved to Dallas when I was ten and Michael was three so he could spend any given Sunday at the stadium. We were better off without him, except, financially, things were much, much worse. My mom had to work two jobs to keep a roof over our heads, but it was extremely difficult because Michael wasn't the kind of kid you could just drop off at a regular daycare. Every month, she scraped together just enough to pay the rent and put food on the table, but there was never anything left over."

Gwen rubs my arm with her hand, and even though her hand is so small against me, it provides a comfort so strong, it spreads through my whole body. "I'm sorry you had to go through all of that, and I'm sorry about your mom."

"She deserved so much better than to work herself into an early grave while my father was off pretending we didn't exist." I pause, my heart aching as it always does when I think of her. Brushing the pain aside, I say, "So, since I was young, I've always wished I could find a way to ruin the only thing he loved. Make him hurt the way we hurt." Shaking my head, I say, "I know it sounds stupid, but there it is."

"I don't get it. How could you take football away from him?"

"Not the game. The football club. In my … revenge fantasy, I'd buy the team and ban him from the stadium forever." I stop short of telling her I'm actually doing those things. I don't tell her I'm planning to pose in lots of pictures with the players and have them splashed all over the sports news pages, so he can die knowing if he'd only been good to us, he would've had his biggest dream come true. There's no way I can admit any of that out loud. Not just because she's got every reason to use it against me, but because I know it would change the way she sees me, and I can't have that.

"That would be one way to get his attention," she says.

"The last thing I'd ever want is his attention," I answer.

"Are you sure about that?" Gwen asks gently. Before I can respond, she adds, "It would be perfectly natural if part of you wanted him to see you—to know you exist and that he hurt you deeply. That's how it is with parents and children; no matter how much we wish we could stop caring, we can't."

Setting my jaw, I say, "Believe me, I stopped caring about that man a long time ago. Anyway, as you can see, I have my petty side too."

"It's not the same thing as spending every day of your life in pursuit of the ability to say I was right and you were wrong."

"Sure it is."

"Not even close," Gwen says, tracing my jaw with her fingertip. "For one thing, you're just fantasizing it, whereas I'm actively pursuing my childhood fantasy."

Oh, the guilt. I should tell her the truth, but there's no way I can. Not without jeopardizing the entire thing.

"And for another thing, what you're talking about would be a way to get justice for your mother and your brother. It's very noble of you to want to do that."

Shaking my head, I say, "That's the last word anyone should use to describe me."

She stares at me, her gaze intent. "No, it fits. The way you look after your brother and protect him from the world. How you kept your company going while Dr. Napper was off pursuing his dreams. You're noble, Ty Sterling. I'm sorry, but it's true."

She kisses me on the lips, letting her mouth linger long enough to cause whatever counterargument I had brewing to disappear completely. "You're a good man and that's got nothing to do with your bank account."

"Thank you," I say, kissing her gently on the lips. "And

you're a good woman. I hope someday you can stop letting your family make you feel less than. You're amazing. Screw them if they can't see it."

She scoffs. "I'm not amazing."

"You really are," I say, rubbing my thumb across her cheek. "And if I could wish one thing for you, it would be that you'd stop believing them. You've got this beautiful combination of intelligence and passion for what you do. I admire that about you, Gwen. And I don't admire anyone."

She raises one eyebrow. "Really? No one?"

Glancing up at the canvas above, I say, "I suppose that's not true, but I can honestly say that other than you, I can count the people I admire on three fingers. Hmm, make that four."

"Four? That's a tiny group."

"It's very exclusive."

"Who made the cut?"

"My brother, my mom, Richard, and … Ryan Reynolds."

"The *Deadpool* guy?"

"That's the one," I tell her, acting proud even though I'm feeling slightly sheepish. "He's a hell of a businessman—smart, ambitious, makes all the right moves. Somehow, he's managed to turn his self-deprecating humor and his emotional intelligence into an empire."

"Huh, I guess I never thought of him that way."

"Well, it's true. So you're in very good company."

"Thank you, Ty." She shakes her head a little and smiles at me, narrowing her eyes.

"What?"

"I just can't believe any of this is happening. If someone had told me a week ago that I'd be here with you doing what we're doing, I'd have told them they had the wrong girl."

"And yet, here we are," I say, capturing her mouth for a passionate kiss. The truth is, she's most definitely the right girl.

Which means I really must be out of my ever-loving mind…

27

Rescue Me

Gwen

I'M CINDERELLA—ONLY without the gown, the glass slippers, and the carriage that's about to turn back into a pumpkin at midnight. I'm completely nude, we have no mode of transportation, and there's no orchestra playing. There are, however, the sounds of the river rushing by and the birds singing, and a very naked, delicious man that I'm snuggled up against. And, like Cinderella, there's a ticking clock that is steadily getting closer to the end of the best night of my freaking life. (So, I guess I'm not really like Cinderella at all, other than that desperate sense of urgency she must have felt when she was dancing in Prince Charming's arms all evening.)

Anyway, the point is, I want to drink in every millisecond of this night together. I want to inhale him, memorize every ridge of his abdomen, every eyelash, every sound he makes, every sigh. I want the scent of him bottled up forever so I can bring myself right back here to this moment of being adored, accepted, personality warts and all, and well … loved, I guess. Isn't that what it is when someone sees you—like *really sees* you—and understands you and wants the very best things for you? I think it might be. And I'm not saying he loves me, because I know he doesn't. He can't. It's not in his nature, and even if it were, someone as guarded as Ty Sterling certainly isn't about to fall in love with someone like me in a matter of a few days. That won't happen. It's not happening. But it certainly *feels* like it's happening.

We just made love again. It all got started when he kissed me after I said that thing about being the wrong girl. It was like he wanted to prove to me I'm the right one, even though he can't say it out loud. It felt exactly like he needed me to know. The way he gazed at me and moved his body over mine and held me in a way that was both gentle and intense at the same time. The way he's holding me right now, still buried inside me even though we're both completely spent. The way he's kissing my temples and caressing my hair, as though he can't get enough of me, which is precisely how I feel about him.

It's magic.

It's every girl's fantasy.

It's going to end as soon as I wake up tomorrow morning.

So, I've decided I'm not going to sleep. I'm going to stay awake all night, fighting to keep my eyes open so I can make this last as long as possible.

"You must be exhausted," he murmurs. "It must be almost light out."

"I'm not. I just…" *Never want this night to end.* "… am really enjoying myself."

"Good." He kisses me again. "But if you're not careful, you're going to turn into a night owl like me."

"It wouldn't be so bad," I tell him. "If being a night owl comes with all those orgasms."

"It rarely does," he says, closing his eyes.

His breathing becomes steady and I watch his beautiful face while I trace my finger over his cheeks and nose and jaw and forehead. His lips part and soon, he's fast asleep, still holding me close.

I give him the gentlest of all gentle kisses on his forehead, and smile to myself, a sense of pride coming over me for managing to do the impossible—get him to sleep when he's not in his own bed.

My mind wanders lazily through everything that has happened since we got stranded here on the beach. Working together to set up a camp and gather firewood, laying in the sun to dry off, building a fire and sharing a meal, and then ... all the incredible sexy sex. My first thought is I can't wait to tell Allie, but then I realize the last thing I can do is tell Allie. I'm going to have to keep this secret to myself, which is not something I've done since we started working together.

My gut churns a little and I push the thought of betraying my team away. I know it'll come crashing down on me soon enough. For tonight, I'm going to allow myself to just be right here in this moment with this man. I deserve to have one night like this in my life. Just one.

I think about everything he told me, about his family, and his father. I can see him as a little kid, sitting on the couch with his huge brown eyes and long lashes, staring up at a man who didn't care about him in the slightest. My heart aches for him and for his brother and mom, even though I've never met them. How any man could love a football team more than his own children is beyond comprehension.

And that's when it hits me. Football club. He's not just

fantasizing about buying the Dallas Destroyers. He *is* buying it. That Muffy person he's having followed is the person who owns it, and he must need to make sure she's not meeting with other buyers or the entire thing could go up in smoke.

I freeze in place, my heart stopping for a second while I take it all in. I have what I need to get what I want. All I have to do is threaten to go public with it. He'd have to give our team the funding to avoid a bidding war. A paltry one hundred million would be a bargain compared to what the team would cost if there were other bidders.

But I can't do that, can I? Not with everything we've just done. Not with the way he's opened himself up to me and told me things he's never told anyone. For a man like him—someone so cynical and unable to trust—allowing himself to be this vulnerable is huge. I can't just betray him to get what I want.

But if I don't, I'll screw over not only myself, but my work family. And I can't do that either. I'll lose my job, the house I haven't even moved into yet, and my people, all in one fell swoop.

I close my eyes to shut out the thoughts I don't want rolling around in my brain. I'm not going to think about that tonight. That's future Gwen's problem. Today's Gwen is going to let herself lay here in the safe, strong arms of a man she has most definitely fallen for. Tonight, I'm going to let myself feel loved and adored and special. I'm going to lay here listening to him sleep, feeling his skin against mine, feeling the love flow back and forth between us—two people, as close as can be.

I'm going to stay awake so I can remember every second of this moment, because when tomorrow comes, it's all going to come to a crashing end. And there's no part of me that wants that to happen. Who knows? Maybe I'll get really lucky and we'll never get rescued and we can live here in the jungle forever, foraging for food and having sex all day.

Yes, that's totally possible. I'm going to hope for that. Although I would miss Starbucks. And my friends. Oh, and Christmas—all the songs and the lights. And sitting on my couch instead of on the ground. We would eventually fashion furniture out of trees or something, but it's not like we're going to find memory foam out here.

I snuggle in and take a deep breath, inhaling the scent of his skin. Honestly, at this moment, I think I'd be willing to trade it all for him. But that's not going to happen. We're going to be rescued, and when we are, this is going to be over. This smell will be a distant memory that eventually will be so tucked away in the back of my brain, I'll completely forget it. So, I'm going to stay awake all night so I can be conscious for every second of this…

———

I wake to the sound of a man's voice. "There's the tent. And … those look to be their clothes strewn all over the ground."

That's Rohan.

"Oh my God, maybe they were attacked!"

And that's Thiago.

We're being rescued. Unfortunately, we're trapped inside this tent without a stitch of clothing between us. I try to sit up, but Ty—who, as it turns out, is an extremely sound sleeper when he actually does it—pulls me closer. He looks so peaceful, I almost want to let him sleep, but I really can't, can I?

"Hello!" Thiago says. "Knock, knock! Are you alive in there?"

I freeze in place, not daring to breathe, even though we're caught, so I should just say something because in a few seconds they're going to find out anyway. Gah! The sleeping bag is under us and there's no way I'm going to be able to pull it out from under him. Damn my weak upper body. I have got to start lifting weights.

Thiago's voice grows quiet, but I hear him say, "What if they're not in there? What if they got attacked and they're dead and I'm going to wind up losing my job and getting sued because some billionaire convinced me to let him canoe alone?"

"I'm sure they're fine," Rohan answers. "From the looks of their clothes, they *chose* to take them off."

Oh God, this is awful. Embarrassing. Humiliating. Beyond bad.

"How can you possibly tell that?"

"Because a wild animal wouldn't remove your clothing before ripping you to shreds with their teeth. They just leave it on and go to town."

Geez, Rohan, that's a little dark. Accurate, but dark.

I tap on Ty's shoulder and whisper, "Wake up! We're being rescued."

He grunts a little and keeps right on sleeping.

"Did you hear that?" Thiago asks. "It was a whisper. They're probably so weak they can't yell for help."

The sound of the zipper makes my heart pound even harder than it already was. They're about to see me fully nude. In the bright sunlight. Wrapped up in the arms of a man I'm supposed to hate. Panicking, I shout, "Occupied!"

Occupied? This isn't a truck stop ladies' room.

The zipper stops and I let out a sigh of relief.

"See? They're fine," Rohan says. "Gwen? Is Ty with you in there?"

"Uh-huh," I squeak. "He's… right here."

"You two all right?"

"Um, yup. Great. Nobody got ripped apart by wild boars or anything. He's sound asleep actually."

"Would you like me to gather up your clothes and hand them in to you?" Rohan asks.

"That would be delightful, thank you," I answer, now sounding British for some reason.

Not that a British accent is going to salvage any remaining shreds of dignity I may have had when I arrived in Peru. Although, now that I think about everything that's happened, I'm relatively certain I left my dignity at the airport right around the time I picked up that baby…

28

Psychedelics and Public Confessions...

Ty

IT REALLY IS the little things in life that matter. Like being able to have a hot shower, which is what I'm doing now. Or getting a good night's sleep, which happened last night. How the hell I managed to do that on the hard ground in a tiny tent is beyond me. That is literally the first time that has happened. I'm telling myself it's because of all the fresh air and orgasms, but way deep down inside, I know that's bullshit. I've been on plenty of trips with fresh air and orgasms before and never slept a wink on any of them.

It's her. It's Gwen—the way she touches me, how she seems to understand me in a way no one has before, the feeling of her body against mine. We just fit together, like mashed potatoes and gravy or peanut butter and jam. Or Tweedledee and Tweedledum, because falling for someone is nothing, if not dumb.

I stand under the spray, trying to get my head on straight. I cannot fall in love with Gwendolyn Fox, SETI researcher, woman who loves to doodle on my face and throw darts at me. I will not spend my life with a person who sings nasty songs about me on karaoke night. It's not going to happen. Last night was just a night. It was the circumstances that caused us to … do all the things we did to each other. Every delicious movement, every touch, every kiss was solely due to us being two consenting adults alone with nothing else to do. I can see why people back in the day had so many children. They were bored.

Yes, it was boredom. In our case, the thrill of uncertainty.

I think.

Whatever it was, it's over. It ended the moment Thiago and Rohan showed up. We both knew it too. As soon as I opened my eyes and saw her scrambling to get her clothes on, whatever spell we were under was broken. It was a very long, very awkward boat ride all the way to a luxury eco-resort in the heart of the jungle (which has no damn phones and no internet reception, by the way). By the time we arrived, it was almost nightfall, which meant Thiago blew an entire day of the trip rescuing us. The only good thing about it was catching Gwen staring at me from time to time and smiling at each other—the look of two kids who got caught with their hands in the proverbial cookie jar.

We just sat there while Thiago lectured us about being not just the problem, but the '*biggest* problem he's ever had on any trip.' Apparently he's thinking of going to work for his brother-in-law who owns a fish canning company, just so he won't have to deal with tourists anymore. Yikes. I don't blame him for being mad though. He was up half the night arranging for a boat to come pick them up at their camping spot at first light. The entire time, he had no idea if we were alive or dead, and if we were dead, if they'd ever recover our bodies. So imagine his irritation when he discovered we were fine and had just been happily shagging all night—because they totally know that's what we were doing. There's no denying it. I can only hope neither of them tells anyone. I don't care for my own sake, but in these types of situations, it seems like the woman winds up taking any criticism, which is the last thing Gwen needs.

I shut off the water and hurry to dry off and get dressed. We're late for whatever Richard had planned for this evening. I'm not looking forward to it, other than that I'll be able to see Gwen. My heart picks up its pace a little as I rush out of my room and hurry along the plank sidewalk to the open-air studio where the ceremony is to take place.

I search for her as soon as I walk into the large room, but she's not here yet. The space is lit by candles and there are mats and pillows in a circle on the floor. The rest of the group has already taken their places on the mats and have left two spots next to each other for Gwen and me.

I hurry to sit down, under the watchful glare of Thiago. He's standing next to the oldest man I've ever seen, who's dressed in jeans, a Hawaiian shirt, and flip-flops. In the center of the circle sits Richard's urn, reminding me once again of what we're doing out here. My gut aches a little as I stare at it. When it finally sinks in that he's really gone, I'm going to have a hard time getting over it. I'm alone in the world. I have Michael of course, but I no longer have a partner.

Speaking of partners, I'm about to suggest that I go look for Gwen when she appears, dressed in a flowy skirt and a tank top, her wavy hair down. God, she's beautiful. I should stop staring because that'll only make the group suspicious about what happened last night.

"Okay, now that the straggler has arrived, we can get started," Thiago says.

I watch as she rushes to the mat next to mine and sits down, offering me a shy smile that does something to me. I give her a head nod, hoping that everyone else will think we're just two buddies who definitely didn't have sex five times last night.

Thiago clears his throat. "First we will watch the video from Dr. Napper, then we will get started."

He turns on his iPad and once again, Richard's smiling face appears. "Well done everyone for taking on the survival challenge. I hope at least something went wrong that forced you to test your limits and find out what you're made of."

Gwen and I glance at each other. She shrugs and whispers, "No, nothing."

I snort laugh quietly, then get back to watching the video.

"Tonight, you will expand your consciousness with the help of my dear friend, Don Romulo Luna. I assume he will outlive me due to his lifestyle, but if not, his son, Don Romulo Luna Jr., must be here. Both are highly respected *curanderos*, or healers. Tonight, he will take you on a journey of the mind, so you can dream your deepest dreams, open up a world of possibilities you never imagined, and wake up tomorrow refreshed, renewed, and truly alive in a way I was, in a way few people really are."

"Oh God, I bet it's an ayahuasca ceremony," Gwen whispers to me.

"Don't worry about it. Ayahuasca only affects people with weak minds. You'll be fine." And so will I because there is no way I'm going to wind up speaking in tongues or rolling around on the floor. I glance at the man in the flip-flops, guessing that he's the senior version of Don

Romulo Luna, based on the fact that I'm pretty sure you could store your iPhone in his wrinkles.

On the screen, Richard is talking about how this world should be a place for dreamers. "But the world has grown skeptical, fearful, afraid of what we don't know. We live our comfortable lives in our comfortable bubbles, terrified of stepping outside them to see what else is out there. Instead, we stare at our screens, scrolling mindlessly, not really living, but not dead either. Tonight, you will find the dreamer in you. And please don't just do this for yourself. Do it for humanity because if there's anything the world needs, it's more dreamers. Ty, I'm right about this, and I hope this journey will show you why. The entire reason I backed the types of projects that other people reject is because they do what so few people on this planet do— they hope. They believe. They have faith in what can't be seen. That is how we get better as a species. That is how change and growth happen—through the fearless pursuit of the unknown. I love the fact that you're all out there inspiring others to explore and embrace the mysteries of our planet, the universe, and ourselves. It thrills me to know that you—the dreamers of the world—have each other, even if you never find what you're looking for. You're doing important work together. You're giving others hope. And who knows? Maybe you're right.

"Now, Don Romulo is going to pass around the special herbal tea that will help take you to a place of pure honesty, where the deepest desires of your heart will be unearthed for you. Please drink up and let yourselves go on a journey to the farthest reaches of your own mind. And Ty, you have to do it. It's my last wish."

How many frigging last wishes did he have?

The video stops and Thiago points to the man. "It is a great honor to be here tonight with Don Romulo Luna. He is one of the leading healers in all of Peru. Politicians and celebrities come to him for help. He doesn't speak English, but you will understand what he is saying, believe me. He is going to pass around the special tea and then we will begin."

I hold up one hand, then say, "I don't want to be a problem, Thiago, but I'm not going to drink something unless I know what it is."

Thiago rolls his eyes. "Don't want to be a problem," he mutters. "Of course you do. It's herbs, okay? It's not going to make you sick or paralyze you."

"Well, that's comforting," I say, watching as Don Romulo walks around with a tray of small cups.

When he reaches me, I take a cup then watch as Gwen does the same, my gut tightening at the thought of her taking something that might make her sick. I give it a whiff, then whisper, "Does this smell like ayahuasca?"

"I have no idea," she says. "Does ayahuasca smell boozy?"

I shake my head and stare into the cup at the amber liquid. "I'm not sure I want to expand my consciousness. Do you?"

"I don't know. On the one hand, it could be really amazing. But on the other..."

I glance up, only to see Don Romulo watching us. He smiles and offers me an encouraging nod, then says something in Spanish.

"Do you speak Spanish?" I murmur to Gwen.

"A few words but they have to be spoken really slowly and they have to be about the days of the week or trips to the grocery store."

Thiago calls from across the room to us. "He said it's very safe. He would give this to his granddaughter."

"Oh well then," I mutter.

"I'm doing it," Gwen says. "Don Romulo is a highly respected healer. He's not going to risk his reputation by making someone like you sick."

"Someone like me?"

"Someone with deep pockets who can sue his ass off. But more importantly, I trust Dr. Napper, and if he thought this would be good for us, I believe it will be." With that, she tips back the cup. When she sets it down, she says, "That was pretty tasty, actually. Not even a hint of poison."

I chuckle a little and shake my head at what I'm about to do. She's right—Richard would never risk any of our lives. "Okay, fine. It's not going to affect me anyway."

"Exactly, we might feel a little tipsy is all."

I drink it down, only to find out that Gwen was right. It does taste nice—like warm spices and rum. "Huh, it kind of tasted like Christmas."

Don Romulo smiles around at all of us and says something to Thiago, who translates. "He says relax and listen to his song. By the end of it, your deepest desires and your core truth will come to the surface."

"Not likely," I mutter.

He starts to sing, and I lay back, listening to the melody as it ebbs and flows. I lose all track of time while he's singing. It could be five minutes or it could be hours, but by the time he's done, I find myself obsessed with one relentless thought: I'm in love with Gwen Fox. So clearly, whatever I just took is affecting me somehow because that's not possible.

Around the circle, I hear the voices of the rest of the group as people start talking to each other. Niles is saying something about how he watched the movie *Ghost* a hundred times and, every time, he cries like a baby when Demi Moore says 'ditto' at the end.

"Same!" Karen yells. "And how they say 'see yah' instead of goodbye because they know they'll be together again."

She reaches for Niles and they clutch hands and talk about how perfect that movie was. I turn to Gwen. "Wow, that certainly hit them hard."

"That's for sure."

"Makes sense though because they're both highly impressionable," I tell her.

"Do you feel anything?"

Shaking my head, I say, "Nothing. You?"

"No."

Savannah holds up her hand and says, "I can't get out of debt because I'm obsessed with Beanie Babies. I wish I could stop but I love them too much to quit. My house is full of them. Like, totally full. They're taking over my life. I think I need to get help."

"Oh wow," Gwen mutters.

Don Romulo says something to Thiago, who translates. "Good. This is good. Let the truth come forward and you will heal yourself tonight."

"I will?" Savannah asks. "Does this mean when I get home, I'll be able to finally shut off my Beanie Baby E-Bay notifications?"

Don Romulo nods and smiles at her, patting her on the hands.

"Oh, thank God," she answers.

"Say, how did he know what she was saying if he doesn't speak English?" Gwen asks me.

"Good question. Maybe he understands it but won't speak it?" I offer, noticing that she looks like an angel with a bright light around her. I lean in, staring at her and feel myself swaying a little. "Do you feel anything yet?"

"Maybe a little," she says. "You?"

"Nah. It's not going to affect me."

I sit, listening while Rohan talks about how he secretly hates his job—not Richard, of course, but the unpredictability of it, and that in some ways, it's a relief that he'll be moving onto something else, even though he'll miss him horribly. His biggest wish is to do something important with his life, to be a leader, and also to meet Cher. Karen starts to talk about getting into the pageant circuit again, only she wants to go for Mrs. Universe this time because you can be over twenty-five to win. But she desperately needs a Mr. Universe to make it happen. I can't even concentrate on her words because the only thing I can hear is my own heart, telling me I love Gwen Fox. And now it's telling me she has to know. I look over at her. That bright light is still surrounding her. She's laying on the mat with her eyes closed, looking like the most perfect version of Sleeping Beauty ever. I wobble a little, reaching out and touching her hand. "Gwen. Gwen, wake up."

She opens her eyes and smiles at me. "I'm awake. Isn't this great? I feel so relaxed."

"Yeah, it's terrific. Listen, I have to tell you something," I say, scooting over to her mat and kneeling beside her. "You have to listen to me. It's the most important thing I'll ever say to anyone."

She sits up and faces me, focusing in with intensity. "What is it?"

My tongue feels thick and my heart is pounding. "You're the person I've been waiting for my whole life. I'm in love with you. I want to marry you and have babies who look just like us and grow old together and carry you around when you're too weak to walk anymore."

Her mouth drops and somewhere in the back of my mind, I notice that everyone has stopped talking and they're all listening to me. But I don't care, not in the least, because I have to say this. Right now. "I'm in love with you and I'm pretty sure if you don't love me back, I'll die right here because my heart will shatter completely and I'll be dead. You can hear me, right? I'm actually saying these things out loud and not just thinking them?"

"You're saying them," she tells me, reaching out her hands and taking mine in hers.

"So? What do you think, Gwenny? Do you want to get married and have babies and grow old with me?"

Nodding, she breaks out into a wide grin. "Yes, I do, Ty. I really, really do."

"Let's do it then. Let's get married right now," I tell her, lifting her hands to my mouth so I can plant kisses on her knuckles. "Right here, tonight. Let's get married and be together forever."

"Okay," she says, letting go of my hands and wrapping her arms around my neck. She kisses me hard on the lips and after a few seconds, she falls back and I go with her, laying on top of her while we kiss some more. When we stop, she says, "I don't ever want to be away from you. Not even for a minute. I'd even use the bathroom with you. With anyone else, that would be a total turn off for me. But with you, I'd do it just so we don't have to be apart for even a few minutes."

"Yes, Gwen, yes, let's do that. We can sleep together and shower together and eat together and pee together. It's going to be amazing," I tell her, kissing her again.

"It'll be incredible, like last night," she answers.

We start making out again, only for me to feel a persistent tapping on my shoulder. I totally ignore it because I'm trying to get Gwen's shirt off over her head. "Hey, you two, you better stop this," Thiago says.

"Are we being a problem?" Gwen asks him.

"For your own sakes, you should stop. Maybe … go to one of your rooms. But you can't do this here."

I push myself off of Gwen, a distant part of me knowing what he's saying makes a lot of sense. Then I stand and pull her up. Wrapping my arm over her shoulder, I look at Thiago. "Say, you're not a registered minister, are you? Or how about Don there? Is he maybe a priest? We'd really like to get married now."

Thiago shakes his head and says something about it being a good idea to take it slow, but I'm really not paying attention because my hand has moved down to Gwen's perfect bottom and I'm totally focused on that right now.

"Maybe wait until morning and see if this still seems like a good idea."

"Oh, it will," I tell him, glancing down at Gwen. "She's my person. My buddy. My ride-or-die. I want to buy her everything she's ever wanted and build a rocket ship so we can go find her alien friends and go see movies with her and have sex with her on the kitchen counter."

"Oh, babe? Really?" Gwen says, looking up at me. "You want to go find aliens with me?"

"I do. I never wanted to go to space before, but if that's what you want, I'll go. I'll build the best spaceship ever made and we'll go together," I say, turning to her and wrapping my arms around her.

She tilts her head up so we can kiss some more. "You're the best," she says.

"No, you're the best. The best person who ever lived and I'm so fucking lucky to have you." I turn and look at Richard's urn. Pointing to it, I say, "Thank you, Richard. Thank you for introducing me to the best person who ever lived. I'm going to put babies in her right away. As many as possible, all at once."

"Okay, you two," Thiago says, putting his hands on our backs. "Let's get you back to your room."

"Sure, yeah," I tell him, only vaguely aware that everyone else is staring at us like we're insane.

"Good night, all," Gwen says. "See you in the morning, when I'm fully pregnant with his babies."

As we walk down the path to the lodge, I hold Gwen's hand and she rests her head on my shoulder. I look up at the stars above us and let out a happy sigh. "Look at the stars, Gwenny. Just look. They're shining there for you."

She looks up, then at me. "I had no idea you could be so romantic."

"I didn't either. No clue whatsoever. But you bring it out in me. Only you can." I lower my mouth to hers and we kiss some more until the sound of a throat clearing interrupts.

"Keep going," Thiago says.

"Okay," I answer, thrilled to get the go ahead. I pick Gwen up by her ass and kiss her hard.

"No, no. Keep going back to your cabin," he snaps.

"Right, that makes more sense," Gwen tells me.

We burst out laughing and I carry her to my cabin and set her down so I can unlock the door. "Do you think we said anything embarrassing back there?" she asks me.

"No way," I say, opening the door and lifting her up to carry her over the threshold. "I'm never going to change my mind about anything I said to you. In fact, I'm *proud* I said all those things because they're true. I was speaking from my heart, and I never do that. Never. I only use my mind. But tonight, all heart. All truth."

"I'm proud of you too, babe," she says. "You're so brave. My big, strong, brave Ty. I love you, Ty. I love you with every breath. With every heartbeat. I love you with every cell in my body."

"That's exactly how I feel about you," I answer, setting her down gently. "Let's make love all night and tomorrow morning, we'll get married."

"Yes, it's going to be amazing," she says, tugging my shirt over my head. "I can't wait to be your wife."

"And I can't wait to be your husband," I tell her, yanking her skirt off.

"We're never going to change our minds because this is forever."

"Yes, it is. Gwen and Ty forever."

29

Truth, More Truth, and Even More Lies...

Gwen

HE WANTS TO MARRY ME. My big, brave, strong Ty wants to spend every minute of every day with me. Mmm, the breeze from the fan feels so nice against my skin. Oh, and he's down on his knees, kissing my stomach. No one has ever done that to me before, but I love it. Just like I love him. Imagine loving someone I spent so much time and energy hating. I run my hands through his dreamy hair, my heart feeling like it could explode. That's how much love I have for him. Not hate at all.

Oh my God, I have to tell him the truth! Although, what he's doing down there is completely distracting...

No, Gwen. Tell him!

"Wait!" I say, pulling back from him. "I can't marry you until you know the truth about me."

His eyes grow wide. "What?"

Don't do it. He's going to be so hurt and he'll stop loving you. No, I have to. It's the right thing to do. "It might make you hate me, but you deserve to know." Gesturing to the bed, I say, "You might want to sit down."

He gets up and walks over to the bed, taking a seat. Reaching out, he rests his hands on my hips. "I want you to know you can tell me anything."

"Thank you, babe," I say. "And I want you to know you can tell me anything too."

"Thanks. Go ahead. Tell me. I'm ready."

"Okay," I say, my heart pounding. "Keep in mind, I didn't know you until this week."

"Gotcha."

"Well, back home, in my job … I sort of used to—and I want you to know I'm never going to do it again, okay?"

"Okay…"

"But I used to print off photos of you and…"

"And draw nasty pictures on them, I know," he says.

I freeze, my jaw dropping. "You know?"

He shrugs and pulls me closer, planting kisses just under my breasts. "Yeah, I know. I've known the whole time. You also used to dedicate 'You're So Vain' to me on karaoke night. You hated my guts."

I stand perfectly still as he runs his big, warm hands up and down my sides and kisses me some more. "You knew? How did you know?"

"I had our security team look into everyone who was coming on the trip."

Shock vibrates through me. He knew. And yet…? "Wait. Why did you … why weren't you…?"

He looks up at me. "Why wasn't I an asshole to you?"

"Yeah," I say, cupping his face in both hands. "How could you be so wonderful to someone who has said and done such awful things about you?"

"I didn't take it personally," he says. "It's not like you knew me. If you had known me and still hated me, that would be totally different. But in this case, it was sort of flattering in a weird way. Like I was some sort of super villain in your story."

He's kissing my abdomen again and dammit if it doesn't feel so good, I'm completely forgetting what we were talking about… Oh right, my big confession. I drop to my knees in front of him, needing to look him in the eye. "It's true. I didn't know you at all. Only what I saw in interviews. But I'm so sorry about what I did. It was awful, especially because you're the most amazing man I've ever met. Even the fact that you could forgive me so easily shows how wonderful you are. You're so mature to not take any of that personally."

Smiling at me, he says, "It doesn't hurt that you're so hot."

I kiss him hard on the mouth. "You're the best. I want to run home right now and tear up all those photos I drew on and tell my work family the truth, that I love you and that I'm going to spend the rest of my life with you even though it'll mean they'll hate me forever, and then I want to hurry down to the bar and dedicate some gorgeous love song to you. I'm not sure which one yet—probably something by Celine Dion…" I kiss him again, my heart swelling with emotion. "I can't believe you forgave me. I'm so relieved."

"Of course I forgave you. I'm in love with you. You could never do anything that I wouldn't forgive."

"Really? Do you mean it?"

"Yes."

"Same with you. Except, you know, cheating on me or leaving me for another woman."

"I'd never do that."

"I'd never do that either. Cause I am your lady. And you are my man."

"Wait. Is that a Celine Dion song?"

"I think it's from a cover she did."

"About the power of love?" he asks.

"Yup. That's the one."

"That's our song, babe," Ty says. "That's our song. 'The Power of Love.'"

"It's perfect. Let's dance to it at our wedding tomorrow."

"Yes, let's do that."

"Thank God we took that drug because I am never going to regret this."

"Me either."

———

You know when you do something so embarrassing, you'd rather die than face the people you did it around? Yeah, that's me right now. Whatever the hell we took last night doesn't affect your memory in the slightest, which, if you ask me, is a total crime. It strips you of any and every inhibition you have, only to cause you to make a total ass of yourself and suffer the pain of remembering every humiliating second of it the next morning.

Although, I'm also able to remember every delicious moment of what happened when we got back to Ty's room, so at least there's that. The sex was beyond incredible. It was like every single cell in my body climaxed for hours, which I know isn't possible, but trust me, it happened.

Only now, I'm lying in Ty's bed, watching him sleep while I freak the fuck out. He couldn't have meant what he said and neither did I. I mean, there's no man on earth I'd want to poop in front of, thank you very much. Not even him. *Especially* not him. No way. And we absolutely can't get married today. We've never even met each other's people or seen where the other one lives. What if he's a total slob? What if he's got some sort of weird sex room at his house and would expect me to join him in there every night? Or worse, what if he chews ice cubes?

The truth is, we don't even know each other. I mean, it *feels* like we know each other, but we really don't. I definitely don't want him to 'put as many babies in me as possible all at once.' Yuck. That sounds awful. No way he wants that either. All of that adds up to the fact that we were drugged into saying a bunch of shit we didn't mean.

Publicly.

So there's only one thing a girl can do in a situation like this—pretend she can't remember a thing. Yes, that's the only solution. It'll take us both off the hook, because let's face it, it'll do no good to acknowledge what we said last night. No good at all. It was all nonsense anyway. So, we should just pretend it never happened.

Unless…

What if he *does* want to marry me and have babies that look like us and grow old together and carry me around when I'm too weak to walk? Because I could totally get on board for all of that. Especially the being carried around part. I'm already sick of walking, I know I won't want to do it when I'm old. I stare at his face, a thrill running through me at the idea of being his wife. Well, so long as he's not an ice cube chewer with a sex room.

No, idiot, that's not going to happen. I have to trust everything he's told me when he's *not* completely whacked out of his mind on drugs. He doesn't want to get married. He doesn't want children, and he sure as hell doesn't want someone like me. I need to get out of here a.s.a.p.—it's my only chance to save my poor heart. And also to save my sanity and keep my work family, because if I come home married to Ty Sterling, the devil himself, they'll all hate me forever. Not that he wants to marry me, because he definitely doesn't.

I wiggle away from him and go in search of my clothes, which are strewn around the cabin. Quickly getting dressed, I then take one last look at him, just to torture myself. God, he's perfect. I'm tempted to crawl back into bed and continue snuggling his perfect, warm, naked body. But I can't. I have to get the hell out of here. Fast. I slip out the door and hurry to my cabin, hoping no one sees me.

An hour later, I've showered, put on some makeup and done my hair up in a bun, hoping to erase the memory of last night's Boho Gwen in her flowing skirt with her hair down and her inhibitions nowhere to be seen.

I throw on my cargo pants and a T-shirt and make my way down to the open-air restaurant for breakfast. My heart pounds in my chest as I walk along the wood path through the trees. My feet slow down because they know exactly how embarrassing it's going to be when I get there. But I have to go. It's not like I can hide in my cabin for the rest of the trip.

When I arrive, I see the rest of the gang eating already, except Ty, who is at the buffet. "Oh God," I mutter, my stomach flipping.

I lift my chin, throw my shoulders back, and walk across the restaurant with as much confidence as I can muster. Yes, this will work. This is how I'll convince everyone I don't remember any of it. I pick up a plate and offer Ty a bland smile. "Good morning."

"Good morning," he says, looking slightly wary.

Damn, that's not the expression of a man who wants to marry me. Oh, wait, not that I want to marry him either. Because, no way. "The eggs look good today," I tell him, thinking of making a joke about how they look 'unfertil-ized, just like I like 'em.'

"Yes, very good," he says, scooping some onto his plate.

"So, last night was weird, wasn't it?" I ask, my heart thumping. Before he can say anything, I add, "I totally blacked out right after that thing Karen was saying about being Mrs. Universe."

Ty gives me a knowing look and I can tell he's going to go along. "That *is* weird because I don't remember anything after that either."

"It must have hit us both at the same time," I say, piling some fruit next to my eggs.

"I guess it makes sense since we drank it at the same time."

"Exactly. So, do you know what's on the agenda today?" *Oh, that's good, Gwen. Casually change the subject.*

"Not a clue, but I'm assuming we'll find out right after breakfast," Ty says, gesturing for me to lead the way back to the table.

I give him a polite nod, then start to walk back, hyper-aware of the fact that he's right behind me and what I really want is for him to reach his hand around my waist and pull me to him, then plant kisses down my neck.

"*Da* dum da dum, *da* dum da dum!" Karen sings.

"Here comes the bride," Savannah says.

"Are you fully pregnant, Gwen?" Niles asks.

Oh fuck. They're not going to let us off the hook, are they? Setting my plate down, I give them a blank look, then say, "What? What's that about?"

I take a seat, then look at Karen with an innocent expression.

Ty, who sits next to me, says, "Yeah, what are you talking about?"

He's good. He's scary good at looking innocent, actually. Mental note: do not trust this man.

"Come on, you know what happened last night," Karen says. "You two were adorable by the way. I mean, it's a little fast for you to be pledging your undying love to each other, but hey, sometimes love at first sight happens."

"Pledging our … *pfft*," I say, shaking my head. "I don't recall that. Ty, do you recall that?"

"Nope. Never happened. Maybe you imagined it, Karen," he says.

"Well, if it never happened, why do I remember it too?" Niles asks. "I distinctly remember you saying you were going to get married this morning and spend every second of the rest of your lives together, including in the bathroom."

"Eww," I say. "That's both weird and gross."

"You totally said it. I heard it with my own ears," Savannah says.

"Maybe it was some sort of group hallucination," I tell them, grasping at the very last available straw. "That was some powerful stuff they gave us."

They all burst out laughing while Ty and I stare at them.

"What's so funny?" he asks.

"It was bourbon and tea with some spices in it," Niles says. "Thiago told us this morning."

"And it was only half a shot of bourbon," Savannah laughs. "We were all basically sober."

"No, that's not possible," Ty says, shaking his head. "Because I'd never black out if I were sober."

"Same here," I say. "The spices in it must have been … super powerful."

"Nope. Just a bit of cinnamon, some nutmeg, and cloves."

Ty shakes his head and scoffs. "There's no way that's true. It was clearly a very powerful psychedelic."

"No, it really wasn't," Savannah says. "We all were able to abandon our inhibitions because of the environment and the power of suggestion. The whole thing was entirely placebo. We all felt the effects because we wanted to."

"And we said things we wanted to say," Niles adds.

Fuuuucccck. Also, somehow, yay! Because he must have feelings for me. Oh my God, I'm so confused. I need to go lie down.

"Which means you two actually *do* want to get married and you, Ty, want to put … how did he put it?" Savannah asks.

"As many babies inside her as possible," Karen answers. They all start laughing again while Ty and I sit red-faced and totally busted.

Thiago walks over to the table. Oh, thank God for Thiago. He's going to save us. "I'm sorry to interrupt the fun this morning, but we have a long day ahead." He pauses and sneers at Ty and me. "If we're going to fit in a wedding ceremony as well, we'll need to really hustle."

Apparently he's *not* going to save us. He's going to join in the fun instead.

"Nope, that's fine," Ty says. "We're definitely not getting married."

I wait for him to say the word 'today,' but he doesn't, and somehow that one little missing word causes me to abandon all hope.

"Oh, so you had a change of heart," Thiago says.

"Yup," I mutter, wishing a giant fish bowl with blades would land right now so I could climb on and get the hell out of here.

"Excellent," Thiago says. "Because a wedding would've been a problem."

"Obviously we're not going to have a wedding in the middle of a funeral," I say, as though the idea were Thiago's to begin with.

"Well, you seemed so certain of the idea last night, I wasn't entirely sure you'd have come to your senses this morning," he says. "Anyway, today we're going on a long hike. It's going to rain so dress accordingly." Thiago sets the urn down next to Ty's plate and hangs the Baby Bjorn on the back of his chair. "You're taking Dr. Napper today. It's your turn. Plus, it'll be good practice for when you and Ms. Fox have all those babies."

———

"You know, they really shouldn't be allowed to pretend to drug people," Ty says.

"Agreed," I pant, walking next to him as we climb the steep, slippery path. We're behind the rest of the pack again and are making our way up a mountain in the rain. Normally, I'd be looking around in awe, taking in as much of the lush scenery as possible so I wouldn't forget it. But I'm too angry to notice any of it. Screw the rainforest. I'm beyond humiliated and I'm over the top pissed off. "It's got to be unethical, no?"

"Definitely," he answers. "We should report them to … someone."

"Yeah, like the board that oversees shaman." Pant, pant. "Oh, or maybe TripAdvisor."

He snaps his fingers and points at me. "Good one, that would do it."

"Honestly, I don't even believe we *weren't* drugged. There was probably something in that incense that made us all super high."

"Exactly, because there's no way I would have said any of those things if I weren't supremely high," Ty says.

"Same," I scoff. "That bathroom stuff? No freaking way would I ever be down with that, and the very fact that I even said it proves that nothing I said was true, because that certainly wasn't."

"That totally makes sense. I've *never* in my life wanted to put babies inside someone. I cringe even at the thought of saying something so ridiculous, so yeah, whatever that was, it messed us both up but good."

"I bet he only drugged the two of us so they could all have a laugh."

"That has got to be it. Who knew shaman were such assholes?" Ty says, adjusting the straps on the Baby Bjorn. "They're even worse than pink dolphins."

How is he not out of breath? I mean seriously, my lungs are on fire and I'm not even carrying anything? He's got the world's heaviest urn, and a backpack with both our waters.

"And the rest of those yahoos, laughing it up?" I say. "I could do without them for the rest of my life."

"Agreed. I mean, obviously we both said some things we didn't mean last night, but is it really so funny?" he asks. "It's like all those stupid videos people post when their kids are coming off anesthetic."

"It's really the lowest form of humor," I say. "To make fun of someone who doesn't have all their faculties." God, my lungs are seriously burning. I have *got* to start doing some cardio when I get home.

"Obviously, neither of us meant what we said. We barely know each other, and even if we did, we're not compatible."

Not compatible? What? "I don't know, we did do pretty well when we were stranded overnight together."

"Yes, but that was just out of necessity. It wasn't like we *chose* to be out there alone."

"True, but we made the best of it and we worked together quite well."

"Sure, but I would've acted that way with anyone," he says.

He would've acted that way with anyone? Grrrrr... "I'd say we did a lot more than just work together." Irritation scratches at my already irritated chest. "And there were certainly *things* we did that night that I wouldn't do with just anyone."

Ty stops walking and stares down at me for a second. "It was sex, Gwen. I thought we were both on the same page about that. What happens in the jungle stays in the jungle?"

My face heats up and I can't stand to look at him. Not when he's basically telling me I mean nothing to him. So I turn and keep walking. "Of course I know that," I say curtly.

"Are you upset with me?" he asks.

"No. Why would I be?"

"Because you seem upset."

"I'm not upset. I have no reason to be. You and I both knew what we were doing out there ... and last night. Although last night was a little different on account of us being under the influence." I pick up my pace, wanting to get away from him.

"Then why did you snap at me?"

"I'm insulted that you'd assume I thought it meant more than it did."

"It was a fair assumption based on what you were saying."

"Was it? Or was it an assumption based on the fact that I'm a woman?" I ask, even though I know that's not true.

He's not sexist. He's cynical, closed-off, and close-minded, but he's not sexist.

"It absolutely wasn't because you're a woman, and quite frankly, *I'm* insulted at the accusation."

I stop in my tracks, my head snapping back. "You're insulted? Last night it was all 'I love you, Gwen, I want to spend the rest of my life with you and carry you around when you're too old to walk,' and this morning, you're saying you would've done all that stuff with any rando who happened your way."

He stares down at me, and I force myself to meet his gaze. I can't appear weak. Not right now. Not with him. "Gwen, I thought we both agreed that the stuff we said last night wasn't true. Are you actually trying to say that in less than a week, you decided to get married and have a family with *me*, of all people? The guy whose photo you've been defacing for years?"

"No, obviously not."

"Then what's the problem?"

"I just can't help but object to the fact that you would've done ... *what we did* ... with just anyone."

"I didn't mean I would've done *all the stuff* with anyone. I was talking about compatibility. I meant I would've *worked* with whoever I was with to survive," he says. "But even so, I don't want to lead you on here. I need to make it really clear that whatever we're doing here isn't going to become a permanent thing."

Oh, that hurts. It really hurts so much more than it should. "Good," I say, shrugging. "Because that's the last thing I'd want. The entire thing is actually making me feel pretty icky, because I'm basically betraying my work family."

Ha! His head snapped back a little when I said the word 'icky.' It's *his* turn to feel hurt. "Well, I wouldn't want that."

"Neither would I. They're everything to me."

I turn away from him and keep climbing, grabbing hold of a branch to help pull me up, then letting it go so it snaps back.

"Ouch."

"Oh, did I get you?" I ask, over my shoulder. "Sorry about that." Not sorry, actually. That felt fucking great.

"Look, I get that you're embarrassed about what happened. I'm embarrassed too. But turning on each other isn't going to help anything."

Damn him for being so reasonable when I want to fight. "I'm not turning on you. I'm just…" *Hurt.* "In a bad mood. Ignore me. And don't worry about it. I'm not interested in marrying you or having your babies. I'm not hurt that you don't want to do that either. I'm fine. I'm just grumpy right now and want to go home."

"Okay, good. Because the last thing I'd want is to hurt your feelings," he says. "I really like you, Gwen."

Oh, come on. Do not say stuff like that. Please. My heart can't take it. "I know. I'm on your tiny list of people you admire."

"You really are."

"I'm honored," I say, my tone bordering on sarcastic.

"I don't expect you to be honored, but I do want you to believe me, because it's true."

"I believe you."

"I hope so. If I were someone else—someone who wanted to be in a committed relationship—I'd definitely pick someone like you."

Bastard. "You know what? You really shouldn't say things like that."

"I shouldn't *compliment* you?"

"No, you shouldn't. I know you think you're being nice, but it's really quite mean."

"Quite mean?"

"Yeah. *Really* quite mean. Because that's the sort of compliment that can make a girl think something more is possible than what's possible."

He grabs my arm and I spin around, slipping a little in the mud, but he steadies me. My heart pounds in my chest and I want nothing more than for him to kiss me and tell me he does want more. Even though there are other people just up ahead. Even though this whole situation is crazy and he's wearing his business partner strapped to his chest for God's sake. I want it anyway.

But he doesn't. Narrowing his eyes at me, he says, "But you don't want more to be possible."

Lifting my chin, I say, "No, I don't."

"So then what's the problem?"

"The problem is that you're a tease."

"I'm a tease?" he scoffs. "I believe I've delivered on any and all teasing."

"Yeah, you delivered all right," I say, pulling out of his grip on my arm and continuing on. "But the things you say —you shouldn't. Because if you said them to the wrong woman, she'd get hurt. Not me, obviously. I know the score here and I'm more than happy with the rule of the game as-is. But some other, more sensitive woman would really get hurt."

He catches up with me. "So, you're just trying to give me life advice."

"Exactly," I tell him with a firm nod. "Pretty solid life advice too, if you don't want to go around hurting people."

"But I didn't hurt you."

"Not at all. You couldn't. Because someone like me would never fall for someone like you."

30

A Few Words Before You Go...

Ty

SOMEONE like her could never fall for someone like me? What the hell is that supposed to mean? And why does it feel so shitty to hear that when I don't want to be with her in the first place? I don't have time to find out because we've arrived at a clearing in the jungle and everyone is here waiting for us. The sound of rushing water draws my attention to a waterfall coming from a cliff about fifty feet up from where I'm standing.

Gwen rushes ahead, clearly trying to get away from me, while I slow down. It takes me a second to realize the rain has stopped. A voice in the back of my mind tells me to take note of this moment because it's important, and I'm not sure if it's the somber look on Rohan's face or the fact that my feelings are all stirred up, but I know without a doubt I'm going to remember this place. There's a patch of blue sky and the sun is peeking out, shining on the misty air surrounding us. I'm soaked through but I'm not cold.

When I join the rest of the group, I see that Karen looks like she's about to cry.

"What happened?" I ask.

Rohan offers me a sad smile. "This is where we leave Dr. Napper."

His words are like a punch to the gut, even though this shouldn't be a surprise. It's the reason we've come all this way. "Here?"

He nods.

"But this is so sudden," Gwen says.

"It's how he wanted it," Rohan answers.

I open my mouth to protest, to question the sanity of leaving the urn up here, but then I remember it's Richard and he had a plan all along, so I unbuckle the Baby Bjorn and set it down on a large slab of rock.

"Are we scattering his ashes?" Niles asks.

"No," Rohan answers. "The urn will be left nearby, but Dr. Napper only wanted Ty to take him there. The rest of us say goodbye here." His voice cracks and I feel my nose tickle a little with emotion.

I take a few steps away from the urn, wanting to give people some privacy, but even more, wanting to avoid hearing what they have to say to him. The last thing I want today is some big emotional scene.

I stare up at the sky, feeling the sun on my face and doing my best not to overhear Savannah thanking him for taking a chance on someone like her, and for giving her meaningful employment for all these years. Niles wishes him a peaceful afterlife and says that he'll always be on the lookout for him wherever he goes. "How about if our codeword is picarone? I'll know it's you."

Huh, I had no desire to roll my eyes just now. That's weird because normally I'd be laughing my ass off inside at that.

Gwen steps up and places both hands on the top of the urn and says, "It was a pleasure to meet you, sir. I'll be forever grateful that you believed in us and you gave us a chance. I'm sorry we didn't make contact while you were alive, but like you said to me, 'it'll happen. Maybe a hundred years from now, or maybe tomorrow.' Thank you."

When Rohan walks up, all I hear are some loud sobs, some whispering, then more sobs. A lump forms in my throat and I do my best to swallow it, but it won't budge.

Thiago walks over to me. "Are you all right?"

"Fine," I croak.

"This is hard. I get it," he says, patting me on the shoulder. He hands me the iPad. "He has a last video, but it's only for you. He said you're to take this and the urn and walk along the ledge behind the waterfall until you reach his final resting place. You'll know it when you see it."

Rohan walks over, carrying the urn, his eyes red and swollen.

"Why don't you come with me?" I ask. "You were the closest person to him these last few years."

He shakes his head and smiles at me. "It was his final last wish."

I smile back and take the urn. "You sure?"

"No, not really. I have no idea what he's going to say in that video."

"Perfect," I say with a little chuckle.

"He was himself to the very end, wasn't he?" Rohan says.

"He certainly was. And there will never be another one like him."

"I'm not sure if it's a good thing or a bad one."

"It's bad. The world needed Richard." And now he's gone.

"Here," Rohan says, flipping the iPad open and turning on the flashlight. "I have a feeling you're going to need this."

"Awesome." I take a deep breath and glance at Gwen, who's looking at me like her heart might break. I give her a nod, then start across the clearing.

This is real. This is actually happening. Richard is really gone.

I grip the urn and my eyes well up. I find myself feeling grateful for the mist off the water as I creep along the ledge behind the waterfall. Not that anyone else is here to see me right now, but this way I can hide my reaction from myself too. I finally get to an opening in the rock and shine the light into it, only to see it leads to a large cave. As soon as I take a few steps inside, the sound of the water grows more faint. I glance around, in awe of what I'm seeing—ornate carvings of a bird in flight, each one showing the wings in a different position as it seems to fly to the center of the cave. On the far wall, carvings of a condor, a snake, and a puma hover over a gold altar just big enough for the urn. I shake my head and laugh a little. "You son of a bitch," I mutter. Of course this would be his final resting place.

I carefully approach the altar, imagining some sort of booby trap *a la* Indiana Jones, but of course nothing happens. I set the urn down carefully on top of it, then stare at it for a second before starting the video.

"Hello Ty," Richard says with a smile. "What do you think? Is it over the top? I assume you'll think it's totally over the top. I bet you laughed when you saw it, but for me, this is the perfect place to rest for eternity, listening to the peaceful sounds of the water. I wanted you to be the last one to be with me, since you were the first one with me as I morphed into the man I became. The truth is, you were the most important person in my life."

"No, I wasn't. That was you," I mutter.

"Although, I'm sure you think *I* was the most important person in my life, and maybe these last few years I have been, as I've been off experiencing life and squeezing in every adventure possible. But the truth is, no one knew me like you did. No one believed in me the way you did when we were first starting out. Those years in college—eating ramen noodles every day, hanging out with you and Michael in our tiny basement suite, and dreaming of what was to come—was the best time of my entire life. I mean it. And that should really say something because I've *really* lived. I've seen it all and done it all. But hanging out with you was better than all of it. From the start, you were right there—trusting me and encouraging me—and without you, I wouldn't have achieved … well, maybe anything. We really did create something wonderful together, didn't we? It was because we trusted each other, but more than that, we had faith in each other. Where everyone else thought I was a total screw-up, a joke even, you saw a dreamer with potential, and, even more important, you made *me* see it too. So, thank you for that, Ty. Thank you for having faith in me and accepting me as I was because that has made all the difference."

I let out a sob, then blink quickly, trying to get myself under control.

"I want you to know I still have every faith in you. I always have. That faith was the reason I was able to go off and do everything I've done—because I knew you were back home holding down the fort. I owe you an apology for leaving you to handle it all. Running the company and the foundation is a massive undertaking. It's all been on your shoulders for so long and even though you do it so well, I know it weighs on you. I told myself that you need to stay home for Michael anyway, so one of us might as well be off exploring. But the truth is, I just needed to be free."

"I know you did," I say, wishing we could've had this conversation while he was still alive.

"I'm sorry, Ty. I really am. You're a good friend and you've got a huge heart, even though you keep it tucked away from almost everyone who meets you. My wish for you is that you finally find peace. Real peace. The kind that can only come from forgiving and letting go. Let your heart open up again. Let people see you for who you really are, because that guy—my best friend from college—was incredible. The greatest. Maybe sell the corporation and find something you love to do all day. Paint or do macramé or grow orchids. I don't know. Something that's just for you, because so far, you've spent your entire life living for other people. You've done an amazing job with Michael. You've given him more than anyone else could've. And it's long past time for you to give yourself something more too. My wish for you is that you'll let yourself really live. Have the courage to be vulnerable. *Love* someone. Yes, you might get hurt, but what if you don't?"

Gwen's face pops into my mind and his words vibrate through me. What if I don't get hurt? The thought gives me a flicker of warm light deep inside.

"All right, so this is it. The final goodbye. I love you, man. You were my best friend, my brother, and my partner. Thank you. Be good to yourself for a change. You deserve it. Oh, and don't worry, you're not going to have a huge boulder chase you when you leave or anything." Richard holds up one hand and smiles. "Take care, my friend. And for God's sake, try to have some fun."

The screen goes black and I let the tears roll down my cheeks, sniffling as the reality of what's happening overwhelms me. I wipe away the tears and place a hand on his urn. "Look, I don't believe you're really here listening so I know I'm saying this just for myself. We had a complicated relationship, especially these last few years, but I'm sorry you're gone. I'm sorry to lose you because you really were my best friend. You believed in me too and together, we took this amazing ride, getting farther than either of us dared to imagine we would. We didn't see eye-to-eye on much, but you're right, we created something incredible. We had it all. We really did. Somehow, I think we both lost our way a little." My voice cracks and I let a few more tears out before I keep going. "And I have to hand it to you, these last few days have done what you wanted them to do —made me question how I'm living and what I'm doing. I wish you were here right now so I could ask your opinion on buying the team because I'm suddenly not sure it's the right thing to do. And as far as the foundation goes, I finally get it. After spending time with some of the people out here, I understand what you were trying to do. What you did. You gave a bunch of dreamers a place where they could feel accepted and where they could keep their hope alive. It was a beautiful thing you did, Richard. I only hope Skip will keep it going."

I pause and let my shoulders drop, not wanting to walk away just yet. "Thank you, my friend. Thank you for everything."

31

Just the Two of Us...

Gwen

"HE'S BEEN GONE QUITE A WHILE," Savannah says. "Should we go look for him?"

I shake my head. "I think he just needs time to do this."

A look of understanding crosses her face. "Yeah, probably."

"Maybe we should move on to the last challenge," Thiago says. "I can take you over there and come back for Ty after I get you started." He gestures to a path through the trees and says, "Come on."

"I'll wait here," I say, my heart squeezing a little when I think about what he must be going through. "I don't want him to think we abandoned him and since I'm his buddy, I should be the one to stay."

Also, because I'm shagging him, but we don't need to bring that up, do we?

Thiago nods and offers me a rare smile. "Thank you. I'll be back for you soon."

I wander over to the pool and sit down on a rock, watching the waterfall, waiting for any sign of him and hoping he's all right.

My chest is heavy and I'm exhausted emotionally and physically. I've never been so mixed up or messed up in my entire life. I love him. I hate him. I want him. I want to push him away. I'm like a toddler who needs a nap. Actually, I'm like a terrified woman in love who needs to go home and talk to her best friend. Only I can't talk to Allie. Not about him.

I close my eyes, feeling the warmth of the sun on my face and noticing how all I can see is bright yellow and little flecks of black dancing across my lids like the flecks on the screen when you watch a really old movie.

My life back home feels like it's a million miles from here. It feels like it's been years since I sat at my desk or curled up on my couch when it's only been a matter of days. But I've lived more and done more and seen more in these last few days than I have in my entire life.

A shadow blocks out the sun and I see Ty standing over me, clutching the iPad with a somber look on his face. When my eyes adjust to the brightness again, I notice his skin is a little blotchy and his eyes are red. Standing up, I reach for him, not caring about our conversation right before we got here. I hug him tightly, knowing that is what he needs right now. Not words. Not banter. Just the warmth of another human who wants to ease his pain a little.

He places the iPad on the rock, then wraps his arms around me and holds me close. And suddenly, our lives, our reality, our egos don't matter. All that matters is this. The two of us together. Caring for each other. I rub his back with my hands, hoping to soothe him in what must be an impossible moment of his life. We stay this way for a long time until he pulls back a little, far sooner than I'm ready. Ty rests his forehead on mine and lets out a deep sigh.

"You okay?" I whisper, a lump in my throat.

He doesn't say no, even though I know that's the truth. Instead, he says, "That was a lot harder than I thought it would be."

"I'm sure it was."

"He was my best friend."

"I know."

"He could also make things so hard sometimes."

"I know."

"But so could I."

"I know that too," I answer. By heart. "We're all like that, I think. It's part of the human condition."

He lifts his forehead off of mine. "We're all just a bunch of hot messes, aren't we? Running around making life so much more complicated than it needs to be."

I offer him a sad smile. "That is one-hundred-percent accurate."

He glances around, then says, "Where is everyone?"

"They went on to the final challenge. Thiago is coming back for us."

"Let me guess, they made you wait because you're my buddy?"

Shaking my head, I say, "I wanted to be here for you."

He stares at me for a second, his eyes flicking down to my mouth, but he doesn't do what I'm silently begging him to do. He doesn't kiss me. Instead, he nods. "Thank you. I appreciate it."

I pull him close and hug him again, wishing I could tell him how I feel, wishing I could tell him I meant what I said last night. Well, the not-gross parts, anyway. The big parts. The fact that I'm in love with him and I do want to spend my life with him. But this moment isn't about me. It's about Ty and it's about his best friend and it's about him finally allowing himself to feel the pain of the loss he's just suffered. "This is a perfect place to stay for all eternity."

"Yeah, he chose well," Ty answers. "It's really something in that cave. Very peaceful."

"And well-hidden."

"That too."

"He was a remarkable person, wasn't he?" I ask.

"The best. Such a visionary," he says, running his hand up and down my spine in a way I can only describe as hypnotic. "I wish I had understood him better when he was here. I was just so … angry about so many things he was doing."

"You had reason to be," I say, reaching up and running my hand through his hair. "He left you holding the bag for a long time."

"Permanently, as it turns out. But he had his own demons he was running from. He and I aren't that different in that way."

I lift myself onto my tippy toes and gently kiss his cheek. "You're both good men. You're the same in that way too."

Ty stares down at me, lifting his hand to my chin. "Thank you, Gwen. There's no one else I would want with me right now."

"There's nowhere else I'd rather be."

He lowers his face to mine and I close my eyes, waiting for him to kiss me. But instead, I hear a throat clearing behind me. Thiago, the world's biggest beaver dammer, has arrived.

32

A Leap of Faith

Ty

"I'M SORRY TO INTERRUPT," Thiago says. And this time, he really does look sorry. Not angry or annoyed or impatient. "The others have completed the last challenge. Are you ready to leave?"

I nod, then look back at the waterfall one last time, knowing I'll never be back here again. I take it all in: the smell of the air, the sounds of the birds and the rushing water, the warmth of Gwen's small hand on my back.

"Follow me then," Thiago tells us, turning and disappearing into the trees.

Gwen offers for me to go in first, but I shake my head, not wanting to have her go last in case an animal comes up behind us. We trek silently along through the thick brush until we reach a fast-flowing stream. Following it, we arrive at the top of a cliff where the stream seems to drop off into nowhere. Gwen peers over the ledge and I instinctively reach out and wrap my arm around her waist, my heart skipping a beat at the thought of her falling.

Thiago turns to us. "This is the leap of faith—a rite of passage for the Shipibo-Conibo people who lived here. You cannot see the bottom, but you must trust that when you jump, you make it."

"Jump?" Gwen asks. "But, it's just black down there. How do we know what we're jumping into?"

"You don't. That's why it's called a leap of faith," Thiago answers. "It not only proves your trust in the others who have gone before you, it also proves your faith in yourself—to get through whatever challenges life brings you. Once you do this, you will know you have the courage to do what must be done."

Gwen and I look at each other, then back over the edge. "Why would anyone do this?" she asks.

"My question is who the hell was the first one to jump?"

"Excellent point." Looking at Thiago, she says. "So, the rest of the group did this already?"

"Yes."

"And they survived?" I ask.

"Yes, of course. It's totally safe," he says, looking insulted.

"How about you go first?" I ask Thiago.

He shakes his head. "I have to be the last one. Just in case one of you hens out."

"Hens out?" I ask.

"You know, like a chicken?" Gwen says.

"Chickens out," Thiago says, snapping his fingers. "I always get those mixed up."

"Don't worry about it. Your English is a hell of a lot better than my Spanish will ever be," I tell him. Glancing at Gwen, I say, "I don't much care if people think I'm a hen. How about you?"

"Well, I don't love the idea of being thought of as a

chicken, but I also don't love the idea of dying. What if we don't do it?" Gwen says.

"Then the three of us have a long hike back down the way we came and, instead of going back to Lima this afternoon, we'll have to stay one more night at the lodge."

Gwen raises her eyebrows at me. "Oh, high stakes."

Shit. We look at each other and nod. "We gotta do it," I say. "I have to get home."

"I know."

"Okay, I'll go first," I tell her. "That way if it goes south, I can yell up to you not to come."

"Theoretically. So long as you're not dead."

Thiago lets out a huff. "You won't be dead. Now, stand right here, on that part of the ledge. You're going to step off and fall. Don't try to jump far from the edge. Just step off, got it?"

I move so I'm standing where he said to. "Yep. Got it."

"And whatever you do, don't try to catch her. You'll just end up breaking your back."

"Hey, I resent that remark," Gwen says.

I chuckle a little, then smile at her. "See you on the other side?"

"I'll be there."

I look down, my heart pounding so hard I can feel my pulse in my ear drums. My hands go clammy, my muscles tense up. I force my right foot into the air. Then I set it back down. "You're sure this is safe?" I ask.

"Completely."

"Because I really can't afford to die. I have a lot of people counting on me back home. My little brother, my employees… I can't let them down."

"You won't. But if you don't jump, you'll be letting yourself down."

I turn and look at him. "I'm kind of okay with that,

actually. My regular life doesn't require random acts of bravery, so…"

"Everyone's life demands random acts of bravery," he says. "Without them, we don't truly live."

"Shit, you've got me there, don't you, Thiago?"

He nods solemnly. I look back at Gwen and sigh through my nostrils. "He's got me there."

"He makes a very compelling argument."

"Plus, I really do need to get back home. Michael's probably a wreck by now."

"Then go, Ty. I'll see you in a minute," Gwen says. "I promise."

I turn back and without thinking, I shut my eyes and step off the edge.

I expect to free fall until my heart is in my throat. I expect to feel the wind whizzing past. I expect to land hard in a deep pool of water. But I don't. Instead, I drop down what feels like only a few feet, and I land on a patch of grass. The rest of the group is waiting and they all clap when they see me.

Bursting out laughing, I call back up. "It's fine, Gwen! Come on down so we can go home!"

33

A Guide to Letting Go When You Really Freaking Don't Want to Let Go...

Gwen

I DON'T WANT to go home. Not a bit, even though it's the only thing I've wanted since I got off that plane in Lima. I don't want to face my work family and tell them I failed. I don't want to have to hide so many really huge things from Allie. But most of all, I don't want to say goodbye to Ty and never see him again.

But that's exactly what's going to happen in just over an hour. After the leap of faith, it was a surprisingly short walk to the road where two Jeeps were waiting to take us back to the lodge where we showered, ate one last meal as a group, and talked about the adventure we'd just had. Now we're on a chartered plane to Lima, where we'll all go our separate ways.

Ty and I are sitting together—he gave me the window seat. Damn him for being a gentleman. He's making this so much harder than it has to be. Rohan is across the aisle from us with Niles next to him. Karen and Savannah are in front of us. Thiago is fast asleep across a row at the front.

There's no Wi-Fi on the plane, so instead of diving into the thousands of emails waiting for him, Ty has been chatting with Rohan for a while. I've been resting my eyes and trying not to eavesdrop but at this point, I really can't shut it off. Ty asked Rohan what he's going to do now that Richard is gone and Rohan just told him he has no idea.

"Do you want another executive assistant job?"

"I don't know. I'd kind of like to stretch my wings a little. Maybe try something bigger."

"Good, you should do that, Rohan. You're definitely capable," Ty tells him. "If you want to stay on at the company, let me know and we'll see what we can find for you."

"I'd appreciate that, sir," Rohan answers, and even though I'm not allowing myself to look over at him (because I'm giving them their privacy), I can tell by his voice he's honestly touched.

"And I want you to know I feel bad about chasing away so many people at the start of the trip," Ty says.

"I understand why you did it."

"It was selfish of me. I should've let Richard have his send-off the way he wanted it."

Ty Sterling, you son of a bitch. You're going to make me fall even more in love with you.

"I want to have a memorial for him in a few weeks. Something over the top," Ty says. "Bring in people who knew him from all over the globe, get some A-list celebrities to sing."

"That sounds like something he would've loved," Rohan says.

"I think so too. And I'm wondering if you wouldn't mind heading it up."

"I'd be honored."

"Excellent. Let's set up a meeting for the end of the week so we can throw a few ideas around," Ty tells him.

They're quiet for a moment, then Rohan says, "Can I ask you a question?"

"Sure."

"Why do you call him Richard when everyone else calls him Dick?"

Ty pauses for a second, then says, "What makes you ask that?"

"I don't know. I always thought maybe it was to bug him a little. You know, get under his skin since he did such a good job of getting under yours."

"I could see why you'd think that, but that's not why I did it," Ty says. "I called him Richard because it's easy to laugh at a guy named Dick. A lot of people did, especially when we were in college. But he was never a joke to me."

His words hang in the air for a moment and I feel a lump in my throat as I take them in. I can feel the swell of emotions that I know he's experiencing right now as he thinks about his friend. His partner. His loss.

"If you don't mind me saying, I really had you figured wrong all these years," Rohan says.

"You mean you thought I was a total asshole."

Rohan laughs. "Well, not *total*, but … yeah."

"Yeah, I know I can give off that impression," Ty says. "In fact, sometimes I am one. I know that."

"Well, it's been a privilege to get to know this side of you."

"Thank you, Rohan. I appreciate you saying that."

They chat for a few minutes longer, then Rohan says he's going to have a quick nap before the flight lands. Karen and Savannah have both gone quiet as well, so I assume they're asleep. I open my eyes, only to see Ty looking over at me, a smile on his face.

"Did you catch all that?" he asks.

"What? I was sleeping," I tell him.

"Liar," he says. "You were awake that whole time."

"Okay, maybe, but I was trying not to listen, I swear." Giving him a little grin, I say, "That was really sweet, what you said about Richard."

Ty chuckles and shakes his head at me.

"What? It's an occupational hazard." We stare at each other for a second, both of us knowing this is the end. Nope. Don't want to think about that. "Are you excited to be on your way home?" I already know the answer, but some part of me wants him to say no, that he doesn't want to leave because it'll mean we won't be together anymore and he doesn't know if he can stand that.

"Yeah, it'll be good for Michael, and for the company."

"That's not what I asked," I say, pursing my lips.

"There will be things I'm going to miss about Peru," he says, resting his hand on mine. "A lot."

He gives my hand a little squeeze and it warms me from my toes to the top of my head. "What about you?"

"Same." I chew on my lip for a second to stop myself from leaning over and planting a huge kiss on his mouth. "This has been crazy, hasn't it?"

"Yes." He grins. "Strangest five days of my life."

"Agreed. I actually think Dr. Napper was right though. I definitely did grow and learned a lot about myself."

He nods. "Yeah, who knew you were so good at making paella?"

I laugh quietly, then look down at our hands. I flip mine over and interlace my fingers with his, wanting this moment to last forever. "Or that you were so good at rescuing women from fast-flowing, vampire-fish-filled rivers?"

"I certainly didn't know that about myself."

I let my smile fade. "And this trip forced me to face a side of myself I'd rather not know about. The judgmental side, and the petty side of me too."

"You're not nearly as bad as you think you are," he says.

Shaking my head, I say, "I won't be anymore, and I have to say a lot of it is because of you."

His eyebrows raise. "Really?"

"Yeah. What you said about not letting my family make me feel like less. That stuck with me. It's going to take some work, but I can see the truth now. I don't need to prove myself anymore. I sure as hell don't need to explain myself to people who won't understand anyway." I let out a contented sigh. "I'm going to let that all go and stop trying to fight to be the smartest person in the room all the time. Just think of all the time and energy I'll have for important things."

He smiles at me, his gaze doing all the things it always does, and reminding me of how much I'm going to miss this when we get off this plane. "I'm glad for you, Gwen. That's going to make you so much happier, and if anyone deserves to be happy, it's you."

"You do too," I tell him. "You're not who I thought you were."

Giving me a half grin, he says, "I hope not."

"You're not. Not a bit," I tell him, needing him to know how wonderful he really is. "You've changed so much from the person I met at the start of this trip. You've opened up, and I know you won't want to hear this, but you've become a bit of a believer."

Narrowing his eyes, he says, "I have not."

"Sure you have. You let yourself get pretty 'drugged' at the ceremony."

"If you'll remember, you did too."

"Oh, I know, but I wasn't the one insisting that it wouldn't affect me."

He chuckles. "That really worked on us both, didn't it? Two people with such strong minds."

"Who turned out to be the biggest idiots in the pack," I tell him with a grin.

"That we did," he says, his eyes flicking down to my lips again. "But I still think they gave the two of us something much stronger than they gave everyone else."

"Of course you do," I answer.

"Which means, I'm not some big believer now."

"I don't know … you at least partially believed the story about the vampire fish, if I recall."

His face turns slightly red. "Yup. You got me there."

"And you took the leap of faith, which required what?"

Rolling his eyes, he says, "Faith."

"Exactly. I'd say you made some remarkable progress. In fact, I don't think you hold the title of the world's most cynical man anymore."

"Damn. I really liked being the reigning champion of something."

"You'll have to find a new thing to be king of."

"I suppose so, now that I'm a disgrace to skeptics everywhere."

The pilot announces that we're making our descent into Lima. Ty rubs my thumb with his absentmindedly, then his face grows serious. "What are you going to do? You know… after?"

"When I get home? Sleep for a month."

"No, when you lose your job."

His words feel like a gut punch, even though I've known it's been coming for days. "Skip won't…?"

He shakes his head. "Not a chance."

"In that case, I don't know. Honestly, I'm not ready to think about that. The team is still working to find the funding and I'm going to go home and throw myself into that, and hope that we can find a way."

"It's an impossible amount of money," he tells me.

My heart drops to my feet and I nod a little, unable to think of anything to say to that.

"My advice would be to start looking for something else."

"Yeah, I guess I should do that at the same time, just in case."

The plane touches down, and as it does, Ty grips my hand a little harder. "Say, why don't I give you a lift back to California? We're pretty much going to the same place."

I stare at him for a second, wanting so badly to take him up on it, just to have a few more hours with him. But I shake my head, knowing it's only going to make things harder. "Thanks, but I think I need to get back to reality. I also want to see if I can find my bag at the airport."

He nods, looking disappointed. "Yeah, that makes sense. Besides, what would all your work friends think if you came home with the enemy?"

"Exactly. They'd be totally pissed at me."

"I wouldn't want that. It's probably for the best anyway. I'm going to have to work the whole time."

"I'm sure you are," I say, as the plane comes to a stop. The other passengers start to gather their things while Ty and I just stare at each other, our hands still intertwined.

Come on, Gwen. You have to let go. You can't have this man. I try to pull my hand away, but he tightens his grip just a bit.

"Gwen, this has been… I just want you to know…" He pauses, and my heart picks up its pace, while my lady bits start to wake up, hoping for something really wonderful to happen. "I want to say thank you. For being here for me. This whole thing would've been so much harder if I had to go through it alone."

Oh. Gratitude. Awesome. "You're welcome."

He lets go of my hand, leaving it suddenly cold, and we both take off our seat belts and gather our things.

When we're standing on the tarmac, he turns to me. "Okay, well, I'm heading this way," he says, pointing to a hanger nearby.

"I have to go into the main terminal. Find my backpack."

"Good luck with that."

"Thanks," I say, turning to leave. Then I quickly turn back. "Oh, Ty, I need to get your number so I can send you the money I owe you."

Shaking his head, he says, "You don't owe me anything."

"I do. It's important to me to pay you back," I tell him, opening my contact app on my cell phone. I hand it to him. "Don't worry. I won't booty call you in the middle of the night or anything."

"No?" he asks, raising one eyebrow. "That's a shame."

He puts his number into my phone, then hands it back, our fingers brushing. "You take care, Gwen."

"You too, Ty. Thanks for everything." I lift myself onto my tippy toes and give him a soft kiss on the cheek.

"You sure you don't want to come with me?" he asks. "It's a really nice jet."

Laughing, I shake my head, hating like hell that I'm passing up the opportunity. "I really, really want to say yes, which is exactly why I shouldn't."

Ty looks down at me one last time, then gives me a gentle kiss on the forehead. "It's been a pleasure getting to know you, Ms. Fox. I hope you make some alien friends someday."

34

A Fast Freight Train to Nowhere...

Ty

DONNA

Good news on the yacht. Made the deal this morning. You're out $432,000,000, but Muffy is thrilled. So thrilled, she's considering not entertaining that other offer.

DONNA

I hope you're all right down there in Peru. Yacht delivered to Tampa, where Muffy and her friends will board for their "50th b-day repeat." In a stroke of creative genius, I've arranged a surprise performance by The Thunder from Down Under. If you're not familiar with them, they're male strippers from Australia. Fingers crossed the show will be a hit.

MUFFY

Ty, darling, I am aboard the world's most beautiful boat and according to my friends, I look gorgeous. We're taking it on a ride around the Bahamas for a few days, but I wanted to send some bikini pics of the gang as a thank you. Enjoy!

DONNA

Muffy has called twice to see if you got the bikini pics?! I've explained that you're deep in the jungle somewhere but that I'm sure you'll be very pleased when you get cell reception. I apologize in advance for what you will see when you get out of there.

MUFFY

Ty, darling, thanks ever so much for sending the Thunder. I think I'm falling for a young gentleman from Perth named Diesel who has a thing for older women. I thought I'd give you a heads up in case you're thinking things between us might turn into more than a business deal and some sexual banter.

DONNA

Okay, boss, when you look in your inbox, try not to blow a fuse. Yes, there are 1576 emails to answer, 1000 of them marked urgent, but I have every faith you can blow through at least 500 on the flight home. (I'm holding the rest for now, so as not to overwhelm you, but thought you should know there are more coming.)

MUFFY

Ty, darling, I'm afraid I have news that might break your heart. Last night, in a sunset ceremony, the yacht's captain married Diesel and me. It was beautiful. He wept openly. I may or may not have told him I'm 47, but don't worry, I have a plan. I'm going to see if I can convince him he's got number dyslexia and that he mixed up the fact that I'm 74. The things we'll do for love…

DONNA

Muffy checked in to see if she broke your heart. Apparently she married a stripper? The good news is she feels so bad about upsetting you, she told the other buyer the team has been sold, so I guess congratulations are in order. You're about to become the sole owner of the Dallas Destroyers. I hope it makes you happy.

———

"ALL RIGHT, TY, WHAT'S WRONG?" Michael asks, pausing the show. "And don't tell me it's because you have another 843 emails to respond to by morning because you quite often have hundreds of emails and you're never in this bad a mood."

I've been home for two hours now, and even though I thought I was doing a pretty decent job of pretending I'm fine, I must be failing miserably. We're sitting in the living room with Planet Earth on while I work. "I'm fine, Michael. I'm just busy."

He raises one eyebrow at me and takes another cookie from the plate on the coffee table. "That's not true. You're grouchy and you've only eaten one cookie even though this is definitely a top-notch batch by Greta. Usually you'd have had four by now."

"Four? No," I say, shaking my head as I press send. "Three maybe, but never four."

"Come on. What's wrong? Is it because you didn't sleep?"

I open an email from Anika, my new COO. "I actually slept like a log. Well, the last two nights, anyway." The last two nights, tangled up with a very naked, completely comforting, absolutely lovely Gwen Fox.

"Really? That's never happened before."

"I know," I tell him, keeping my eyes on my screen even though I'm not able to concentrate on a word of what's in front of me.

"Was it a particularly comfortable bed or something?"

"No, the first night was in a tent on a beach next to the Amazon. No bed at all."

"And the second?"

"Comfortable bed in a lodge in the rain forest."

"So, was it the sounds of the rain forest that helped you sleep?"

My face warms up. "Um, no. I don't think so. I've been to jungles before."

"Interesting. We should try to figure out what was the difference so you'll be able to do it again when you go on business trips," Michael says. He takes a bite of cookie, then, after chewing and swallowing, he says, "Although, you've never come home this grumpy so maybe it's better if you *don't* sleep."

I go back to reading Anika's email, only to be interrupted again. "Did something bad happen out there?"

"No, nothing bad happened. I'm fine."

"You're not fine," Michael tells me. "I can tell, and in case you forgot, I have autism, which makes it difficult for me to read body language and facial expressions. If *I* can tell, it's got to be pretty bad."

I chuckle a little, then shake my head and sit back against the couch. "All right, you got me. I'm a little upset. Well, confused, maybe. Remember that friend I told you about? Gwen?"

"Yes. She's the one who told you about the Geminid meteor shower."

"That's right. Anyway, I spent a lot of time with her when I was there. A lot of time. And I really enjoyed it, but now that we're home, we can't ... spend more time together anymore."

"Do you mean intercourse, Ty?"

I sputter, then remember he's thirty-four, not eight. "Yeah, well, that was part of it."

"I see. So I was right when I guessed you wanted to date her."

Nodding, I let out a sigh. "Yeah, you were right. But it's not going to work out."

"Why not?"

"Because I'm about to do something that will hurt her

and all the people she cares about."

"Why would you want to hurt them?"

"I don't want to. It's just … inevitable. She works for the foundation, which Richard was going to take over. But because he's gone, I have to shut it down, which means they're all going to lose their jobs."

"They can find new jobs, can't they?"

"Yes, but they won't like their new jobs as much."

"Why not?"

"Because the foundation is a place for people who have unusual interests. For example, there's one team searching for Yetis."

"That's ridiculous. Yetis don't exist. Why would you pay people to look for something that doesn't exist. It's a massive waste of time and money."

"I know, and honestly, I never understood why Richard did that," I say. "Until I spent some time with the people who worked on some of the teams over these last few days. Suddenly, it made sense."

"I don't understand. Are you saying Yetis exist, Ty? Because I assure you, they don't."

"No, I'm not saying that. What I'm saying is the foundation isn't like a normal business where the focus is on making money. It's more like a charity. Sort of. Richard set it up because he wanted to give people somewhere to go every day where they could spend time with like-minded people who believe things that others might make fun of," I say, my gut tightening.

"Well, I know what it feels like when people make fun of you. It's not very pleasant," Michael says with a firm nod. He stares at me for a second, then says, "Do people make fun of your friend, Gwen?"

"No." *Only her parents.* My muscles tense with anger. "Her job isn't as easy to make fun of as some of the other teams. She's on a team trying to contact intelligent life-forms from other planets."

"Ah, yes, I've heard of that," Michael says. "And she enjoys her work."

"Very much," I tell him. "As much as you enjoy learning about dinosaurs."

He frowns at me. "So, don't take away their money. Then she'll be happy and you can have lots of intercourse and sleep well."

"It's not that simple," I say. "I need the money to buy the football team."

"Ah, yes, the football team. I have something to say about that," he says, pointing to the air. "It's a terrible idea. While you were away, I researched the duties of a team owner. I'm not sure if you know this, Ty, but it will be a lot of work."

"I'm hiring a president to run everything for me."

"That's very wise indeed, but much of the responsibilities will still depend on you. Did you know the owners meet regularly to make decisions about the league?"

I nod, feeling irritated. "Yeah, I know. A few times a year."

"Correct me if I'm wrong, but I don't think you can send someone else to those meetings. And what if you need to build a new stadium? It's a major undertaking that will require you to be in Dallas for much of it, making decisions."

I sigh, feeling completely worn out. "Michael, I know what I'm getting myself into. Running a successful organization is all about hiring the right people to do the right things. It's not my first rodeo."

"What are you talking about? You've literally never been to a rodeo."

"It's an expression. It means I know what I'm doing.

I'm experienced."

"Why not just say that then?" he asks, looking completely exasperated.

"Right. I should have," I answer. "Anyway, the point is, don't worry about me. I know what I'm doing. I know all about what it'll mean to own the team."

"I have a very bad feeling you're going to have to be away a lot and I don't think it'll be worth it, especially if buying the team means you have to shut down the foundation and that you'll lose this woman Gwen, who I assume you want to have more intercourse with."

"Michael, I'd prefer if we don't talk about the intercourse, okay?"

"Why? Does it make you uncomfortable, Ty? Because it shouldn't. It's a natural thing that all animals do. Well, other than a few species of lizards, wasps, and crustaceans, where the female of the species is capable of reproducing using a process known as parthenogenesis, or self-fertilizing. But humans require a mate."

"Yes, I know that."

"Then why are you uncomfortable talking about it?"

"Because … it's just different when we're talking about a specific person."

He narrows his eyes and I know he needs me to explain.

"Gwen. It's different for us to talk about Gwen. It feels … wrong."

"Why? Was the intercourse wrong?"

"No, it wasn't. In fact, it was … very nice. It's just that when two people are in a relationship, it feels wrong to talk about *those* parts of the relationship with someone else."

"But you're not in a relationship with her. You said so yourself."

"I know that."

"So why don't you want to talk about it?"

Rubbing the bridge of my nose, I say, "Some things are private, Michael."

"Private? Like when you got your penis stuck in your zipper before your junior prom and you didn't want to tell Mom about it?"

I close my eyes, my embarrassment fresh even though it happened decades ago. "Yes, like that."

"I see."

"Okay, good, because I really don't want to talk about it." I stare at my laptop even though the screen has gone black. "It's too late. I've already agreed to the deal and I've put down a large down payment. I can't change my mind now."

"Hmm, well, that is unfortunate then. It seems to me like you've made a choice that you will regret deeply for a long time."

The alarm on his watch goes off. Michael shuts off the TV and stands up. "Time for bed. I have to be up at seven a.m. to go to the museum tomorrow."

"All right, Michael. Have a good sleep."

"You too, Ty."

He leaves me sitting on the couch, thinking about how I'm about to make the biggest mistake of my life. Well, according to him anyway. He can't be right about it though. It's not like he's ever even had a girlfriend. He doesn't understand the finer nuances of romantic relationships or how fucking terrifying it is to open yourself up to that kind of pain.

No, Michael is wrong. There's no way I'm going to regret this 'deeply for a long time.' I'll be fine. Totally fine. I don't need someone like Gwen Fox to be happy. I can be perfectly happy all on my own.

Only I'm not, am I?

35

The Fork in the Road...

Gwen

Fox Family Chat

> Just got home. Exhausted. I'll call you soon.

MOM

> How'd it go with Sterling? Did you make any headway?

> No, and I really don't want to talk about it.

CARLA

> Gwen, it's when we don't want to talk about something that we most need to. Please feel free to call me anytime. You sound like you have a lot to unpack.

> I do have a lot to unpack, but it's mostly just clothes and some hiking gear. Haha.

CARLA

Using humor to mask your true feelings
isn't healthy, Gwen.

BEN

Gwen, I suggest taking Carla up on her
offer for help. She's an expert.

Carla, thank you for the offer. I appreciate it,
but I'm seriously fine. For real. I promise I'm
in touch with my feelings, unlike my mom
who refuses to admit she has any.

DAD

Gwen, that wasn't very nice. Glad you're
home safe and sound though. Get some
sleep.

Thanks, Dad. I'm going to have a shower,
then drop into bed.

MOM

Call me when you're not going to be so
rude. We should develop a plan for your
future employment.

Texting with Allie:

Just got home. Struck out with Sterling. So
freaking tired I want to cry.

ALLIE

You struck out?

Sadly, yes.

ALLIE

Did you at least get your backpack back?

Yes. Turns out it was at the airport the whole time. Apparently, the guy took longer than expected to unload that part of the plane, so I missed it by about thirty seconds. The guy at the counter thought it was hilarious. Any luck with Skip?

ALLIE:

Hard no. He's a total creep. I'll tell you all about it at work tomorrow.

I was thinking of taking the day off to sleep. I've been through the shit.

ALLIE:

Blerg, Keenan's counting on you to be there. We're starting the day with a big meeting to discuss the project's future. Everyone is dying to find out what happened.

Okay, I'll be there.

ALLIE

I'll bring strong coffee.

You're the best. Crawling into bed. Good night.

———

I'm on no sleep. None. I wonder if insomnia is a sexually-transmitted disease, because Ty had it, and we had lots of sex, and now I have it. Yes, that's probably what happened and it's got nothing to do with the fact that I'm completely torn up inside about what I'm going to do with the information I have. If that's the case, all I have to do is sleep with some unsuspecting guy and pass the insomnia to him, which would obviously be totally evil if it were possible.

But if it were possible, I'd choose someone truly evil. Or maybe Chad.

Last night, I Googled the Dallas Destroyers. According to Wikipedia, it's owned by a person named Muffy Tillington, but in a matter of days, her name will be deleted and Ty Sterling's will be inserted. I also learned that football teams are worth an insane amount of money. This one is estimated to be worth five billion dollars. That's a lot of freaking zeros. Nine to be exact. And that's after the five. I cannot wrap my head around the fact that a building that doesn't even have a roof, some uniforms, and a bunch of men in tight pants can possibly fetch such a price.

But I digress, and I really need to focus because I'm faced with two futures, both incredibly clear. I can either be the hero—not only for my team, but all the other teams in the foundation—or I can be just another victim.

If I leak that Ty is buying the Destroyers, it will most likely spark a bidding war, and if he loses, he'll have a surplus of cash on his hands. There's a chance—albeit tiny —that he'd decide to use some of that money to keep the foundation going. Maybe, just maybe, what happened on the trip would be enough to make him rethink his position and make him want to help us. But maybe not. If he is successful in buying the team, even with a bidding war, he'll have had to spend a lot more money to get it, so even though we won't get what we want, neither will he. In this scenario, I walk away looking like a hero (and like the smartest person in the room for figuring out what he was up to). We'll all still be jobless, but at least we'd walk away knowing he's not happy either, my team will know I remained loyal, and we can still be friends forever, even if we wind up scattered all over the country.

On the other hand, if I keep what I know a secret, I'm trading my dream for his. And let's face it, his dream is *not* going to make him happy. Even if he does get it for the bargain price of $5,000,000,000. (See? SO many zeros!) That's a hell of a lot of radio telescopes.

I pull up in front of the dark building. The parking lot is empty, which makes sense because it's only six-thirty and we don't start until eight. I decided to come in because I do my best thinking in my office. And my best thinking I must do right now.

I grab my bag of airport gifts I bought for the team and hurry to the front door, the air chilly on my cheeks. When I get inside and turn on the lights, I'm greeted by the sight of Christmas decorations. The tree is in the corner and the cheap, plastic gold garland is hanging from the reception desk. I've always hated that garland, but right now, my heart tugs at the fact that this is the last year I'll be seeing it. Walking over to the tree, I plug it in, then take a moment to stare at the colorful lights.

"Oh God, Christmas tree, I don't know what to do."

The tree doesn't answer me (obviously), so I head for the lunch room to take down Ty's photo. I grab the stack of pictures off the table and stare at his face, which still looks gorgeous even with his blacked-out teeth. I throw them all in the recycle bin, then trudge to my office. Flipping on the lights, I see that Allie has decorated already, including a little Grinch tree on my desk. I put my hand over my heart, guilt weighing me down as I think about my feelings for Ty and the fact that I'm keeping a huge secret from my bestie. Well, several huge secrets really.

I sit down and grab a piece of paper, then do what any girl would do when she finds herself in this situation. I write out a pros and cons list.

Pros of Screwing Over Ty

- Potentially stop sale of the team, thus freeing up money for foundation.
- Will be a hero, even if just to make us feel better when we're shut down (karmic payback for all the crappy things he's said about us in public)
- Screwing over Ty will actually help him, since obviously buying the team won't get back the love his dad should've given him.
- It's what he would do if he were me.
- Won't be screwing over team.

Cons of Screwing Over Ty

- Highly unlikely he'll back us anyway, even if he has the money.
- Complicated if he stays on as my boss and we get married because he'll be furious with me, most likely for a long time.
- Also complicated if he stays on as my boss, *isn't* angry, but team hates me for falling in love with our arch nemesis.
- I'm in love with him and I'd never want to hurt him.

I stare at the page. Instead of my mind charging forward in one clear direction, it continues to move in useless circles, getting me no closer to making a decision than I was before. Who knew falling in love with your arch nemesis would be so complicated?

———

"So, to recap, Skip Napper is *not* going to make good on his uncle's wishes, and in fact, plans to sue for the money that is currently in the foundation's trust fund," Keenan says, glancing around the table at the team. "We've also struck out so far in finding a new backer, but please don't think of it as not having made progress because getting a no is better than not knowing. Also, we aren't yet at the bottom of our list of billionaires to reach out to." Keenan looks down at the paper he's holding. "Tina, how many people are left to contact?"

"Four, and based on our results so far, it's about a 0.00001% chance that we'll get a yes. All the billionaires already have foundations and right now, nobody's looking for more."

"I see," he says, pursing his lips. Smiling at me, Keenan says, "And this brings us to Gwen, who looks exhausted. Gwen, how'd you make out?"

This is it. Do or die time. The moment of truth. I shake my head. "I tried, believe me, but he was never going to change his mind." Feeling disloyal to Ty, I add, "I mean, maybe if the money wasn't already spoken for, but with the situation he's in, he can't back out even if he wanted to."

Groans come from all sides of me and I shrink a little more in my chair.

"So, based on that, it sounds like he didn't want to," Virgil says.

"I really tried, as did the other team representatives."

Chad scoffs. "Yeah, but as if any of those idiots could've convinced him."

Feeling defensive on their behalf, I sit up a little. "Actually, Chad. I think we've been wrong about them. They're not idiots. They're … dreamers, kind of like us."

"Only they're dreaming about fictional things."

"Maybe, yeah," I say. "But you know what? After getting to know them I realized I've been judging them too harshly. Besides, they're not hurting anyone so who are we to say they should be doing something else with their lives?"

Allie narrows her eyes at me, but she's smiling. "Okay, who are you and what have you done with the real Gwen Fox?"

I chuckle, relief washing over me to be sitting here with my best friend. Who I'm lying to. Gah! "It's still me, but maybe I'm more like Gwen 2.0. New and improved. More open-minded, less judgmental, less argumentative."

"Did they drug you out there?" Tina asks. "I've heard psychedelics can cause personality changes."

"No, they didn't drug me." I tap my lip, going for a playful thinking expression. "At least I don't think they did." Dropping my hand, I offer Tina a genuine smile. "Honestly, it was a transformative trip, which was what Dr. Napper wanted. He had all sorts of challenges set out for us and wanted us to think about leadership, legacy, and taking risks... It was amazing, really. I'm different. I feel different and I want to be a different person. Someone better than I was before."

"Wow, Gwen, I'm so excited for you," Keenan says, and I can tell by his smile that he means it.

"Thank you." I glance around the table to see that not everyone looks so happy for me. But of course they don't. We're about to lose our jobs. "Obviously, I wish I could've transformed Ty into someone who'd give us the money, but ... that would've been a miracle."

"Did you at least manage to get any leads on that Muffy club thing?" Chad asks.

"He's not the kind of man who goes around spilling the tea," I answer, hoping no one notices that I'm not saying no. "I'm sorry, everyone. I really did try my best to get through to him."

"I'm sure you did," Keenan says with a bright smile that makes me feel about one inch tall. Dammit, why does he have to be so trusting and awesome?

"This is why we should've sent me," Chad mutters.

"Oh, shut up, Chad," Allie says. "It's not like you and I did any better with Skippy."

"I'm sure she did her best," Tina adds. "And it was a long shot to begin with."

Guilt. Oh, the guilt. "I did bring some presents for everyone," I say, as though that's going to make anyone feel better. "I left them at my desk. I'll go grab them."

Allie stands. "I'll go. You're wiped from your trip."

"Thank you, Allie. It's the gray bag on my desk," I tell her as she hurries out of the meeting room. "Look, I know it's disappointing, everyone. I'm disappointed too, but let's not give up. We've got some of the best minds in the country in this room. If we put our heads together, I bet we can come up with a plan."

Keenan stands up and picks up a marker. Taking the lid off, he holds it up to the whiteboard. "Excellent idea, Gwen. Let's do some brainstorming."

"What if we start a PleaseFundMe campaign?" Edward asks.

"Good, I like that," Keenan says, writing it down.

"Or we start a YouTube channel showing people what we do," Tina says. "We could make it really funny to get views."

"Okay, love that one."

Allie returns to the room with the bag. I smile up at her, but she doesn't smile back. In fact, I can tell she's near tears as she sits next to me.

"Allie, we're doing some brainstorming for ways to get funding," Keenan tells her. "No idea is a bad idea."

She offers him a purse-lipped smile. "Sure. Yeah."

"Oh! What about an Only Fans page?" Edward says.

Keenan's eyes grow wide. "Okay, well, I should clarify. There is such a thing as a bad idea."

I lean over to Allie and whisper, "What's wrong?"

She glares at me. "I saw your pros and cons list. You probably shouldn't have left it out."

Oh, butt nuggets…

Three Days Later

Okay, so life since I've arrived back home has been absolute crap. Our team has made exactly zero progress in finding funding (on a scale of zero to a thousand progresses). I still can't sleep. And Allie is furious with me for being a disloyal cow who's been putting herself ahead of her people. Okay, so that's not exactly what she said. She said she's 'disappointed beyond all imagination that I would protect Ty Sterling, of all people, over our team.' She followed that with repeated versions of 'I can't believe you kept this all from me,' and wrapped up with the worst one of all—'I thought you were my ride or die.'

Lucky for me, she hasn't told anyone else on the team because I was able to convince her that it won't help to go public anyway (which it probably won't).

But I can fix this. I have to. I've been wracking my brain for an answer, and the only way I can make things right again is to get us the funding. But I don't want to just have our team get the money. I want *all* the teams in the foundation to be flush with cash. And for that to happen, I need to come up with a cool billion, which feels every bit as impossible as it is.

The truth is, there's only one person I know who knows

how to get his hands on that kind of cash. Ty. I've spent what feels like hours staring at his number on my phone, trying to force myself to use it.

Come on, Gwen. Call him. You need his help. Desperately.

I stare at my list of talking points I've written out so as not to seem like I'm hoping he'll change his mind about wanting to spend his life with someone. (Me, obviously.)

I look over at the throw pillow on my couch and pretend it's him.

"Hey, Ty, sorry to bother you. I know you're busy so I won't take up much of your time."

"This is a business call actually, but how've you been?"

"Oh, that's good. Have you been sleeping well since you got home?"

"Me too. Just great. Never better. Anyhoo, I was hoping to get some financial advice. I just have one quick question, then I'll let you go. If you were me and you needed to come up with a quick billion, what would you do?"

Nodding, I pick up my phone again. "I'm ready."

More importantly, I have to do this or things between Allie and I will never be the same again.

36

Evicting Mind Squatters Who Make Giant Fucking Messes...

Ty

I FINALLY UNDERSTAND what it means to feel like you're just going through the motions. I consider myself an 'in the moment' type of guy so that phrase has never really hit home with me before. But since I got back, I'm numb. Disconnected. Not all here, which is weird because my entire life, I've been all here all the time. But right now? Not so much. Part of me is a few weeks back in time when Richard was still alive and life felt so simple. Part of me is still back in Peru with Gwen. Part of me is in a future where I own the Destroyers and my father is utterly destroyed. Is future me happy? I wish I could say he was.

Dammit, Michael, why'd you have to put all those doubts in my head?

But maybe I don't have any real doubts. Maybe this indescribable yucky feeling is just me feeling concerned about spending so much money all at once. It's the most I'll ever lay down in one go.

I've removed my half from the holding account, which means I'm officially separated from The Dick Napper and Ty Sterling Foundation forever. And just in time, too, because Skip the asshat has decided to sue to get 'his' money out. His money. What a joke since he hasn't actually earned a penny of it.

I'm back in Dallas, heading to the stadium to meet up with Muffy and her 'gorgeous new hubby, Diesel.' We're going to watch the game in the owner's box, then sign the paperwork. It's the very final hurdle in a life-long marathon full of them. Then it'll be done. My gut tightens at the thought because let's face it, I've now crossed the line and am hurting a lot of innocent people. I can try to tell myself it's just the cost of doing business or that it's unfortunate timing and that I'm not actually to blame, but the truth is, I'm to blame.

Gwen's face pops into my mind for the millionth time over the last few days. Her smile. Her laugh. Her naked. She's going to be devastated, and there's no coming back from that, is there? You can't totally fuck over the woman of your dreams, then swing back around and say, "Hey, baby, what're you doing later?"

That's not how it works, no matter how much I wish it were the case.

The limo passes by The Ripley's Museum, and I stare at the brightly lit building. Maybe, Ripley. Maybe some of it's true.

My phone rings. It's a number I don't recognize so I let it go to voicemail, hoping whoever it is has the good sense not to actually leave a message because who the hell wants to have to check their voicemail?

After a minute, I hear a beep indicating that yes, whoever it was did, in fact, leave a message. Rolling my eyes, I listen to the message.

"Oh, hi, Mr. Sterling, um … Ty. It's Gwen. You're probably not answering because you don't recognize my number, or maybe you suspect it's me and you're not answering anyway. Either thing makes sense. I'm sorry to bother you. Shit. I should've hung up instead of leaving a message which means you have to call your voicemail, which I know is totally annoying. It defeats the purpose because the last thing I want to do is bother you. I already said that, didn't I? I do have a question. Don't worry. I'm not pregnant or anything. Dammit, that sounded funnier in my head. Anyway, I'm calling about a business-related thing—don't worry I'm not calling to ask you for money. Umm … hopefully you'll have time to call me back. I know you're swamped. You probably still have four thousand or so emails to—BEEP."

I replay the message twice, just to hear her voice, then I save it and sit for a minute. Setting my phone on the seat next to me, I stare out the window at the buildings whizzing by. I'm not going to call her back. That would be the stupid thing to do.

But she sounded so desperate. I can't really leave her like that, can I? Wham, bam, wham, wham, bam, bam, thank you, ma'am?

Oh, fuck it.

I pick up my phone and call her before I can change my mind. As soon as she answers, I say, "I can't believe you made me check my voicemail."

"I know, right? That's the worst," she says.

We both laugh, and it's the first time since we were on the plane to Lima that things have felt right. Brushing that thought aside, I say, "How've you been?"

"Good, yeah," she says. "Well, actually not that good, really. I think I caught your insomnia. And we got word today that Skip is going to sue the foundation so … that's not awesome. I'm also not super popular with my team on account of coming home empty-handed. Well, I bought them all little trinkets from the airport, but … you know. Anyway, that's not why I called. I do have a reason. It wasn't like I just wanted to hear your voice or something."

"I'm sure it wasn't," I say, realizing I've been listening to her ramble on with my eyes closed so I can concentrate on every word. "You said you have a business question. How can I help?"

"So, obviously, we're still trying to figure out a way to get funding, and I realized that people who have money know how to get more of it."

"That's true. We do."

"I'm hoping you can tell me how, so I can get some and keep the foundation going."

"You mean keep your project going," I say.

"No, the whole thing. I really want to help everyone out, which means I need to come up with a cool billion, so not exactly the kind of money you get from hosting bake sales or setting up a PleaseFundMe page."

"True," I answer. "A billion, huh? That's … a lot trickier than coming up with a hundred million, which is what you need for your team."

"Yes, it's ten times harder. We've been cold-calling billionaires, but you can guess how well that's going over." Gwen pauses, then adds, "I'm hoping you might have a couple of ideas that you'd be willing to share?"

Letting out a heavy sigh, I say, "Gwen, I wish I did. Honestly, it's just so much money that you're talking about. So, so much."

"Well, we don't need all of it upfront. Just enough to get us all through the next year. That would give us time to keep fundraising."

Oh God, she sounds so damn hopeful, it's breaking my

cold, cold heart. "Off the top of my head, I can't think of a way to do it, but I promise if I come up with something, I'll let you know."

"Sure," she says, her tone overly bright. "Thank you. That's all I can ask."

"Okay."

"I should let you go."

"Yeah, I should probably go, because … business calls and whatnot." Business calls? That didn't even make any sense. "I'm … um, in Dallas at the moment."

"Oh, Dallas, right. Is it going to work out then? Buying the team?"

I freeze for a second, my mind scrambling.

Before I can try to pretend I don't know what she's talking about, Gwen says, "I figured out that you weren't just talking about a hypothetical."

"You did?"

"Yeah, you left a pretty clear trail of breadcrumbs."

Shit. "I guess I did."

"Don't worry. I haven't told anyone. Well, my best friend Allie knows, but I didn't tell her. She saw my list of pros and cons on my desk, but don't worry because I didn't write the team name down on it so she doesn't have enough to go public with the story before the deal is done," Gwen says. "Which I'm assuming has happened already since you're in Dallas."

"Not yet, but it'll be done in a couple of hours."

"Right, well, congratulations. I hope it's what you want."

"It is."

"Good. Yeah, excellent. Okay I should let you go."

"All right. I'll call you if I think of anything to help you," I tell her, my chest aching at the thought that this might be our last conversation. "Take care of yourself, Gwen."

"You too, Ty."

"You're going to land on your feet. I know it."

"Thanks. I appreciate your confidence in me."

"I'm right about that. Some lucky organization is going to snap you up really quickly."

She lets out the least enthusiastic chuckle I've ever heard. "I hope so."

"Okay, take care," I say, needing to get off the phone before I tell her I might love her.

"You too, Ty," she says.

I'm about to hang up when I hear her voice again. "Ty? Are you still there?"

"Yeah."

"Look, I know you're probably super excited about your big acquisition and I don't want to put a damper on that, but I just … wanted to tell you I'm worried about you."

"Why? I'm great. Better than great. About to close a chapter on my life that should've been over a long time ago."

"Are you? I mean, really?"

"Yes, I am."

"Hmph. Okay. But, can I just tell you one thing first?"

"Sure."

"Do you know how one of the biggest arguments *for* the death penalty is that it'll bring closure and peace to the victim's family?"

"Jesus, I'm not killing anyone," I tell her. "I'm buying a sports team."

"Bear with me because I am going somewhere with this."

"All right."

"So, they've done studies on how the victim's families feel before and after their loved one's killer is put to death, and it turns out that it doesn't help. Generally speaking, they don't get closure. They don't feel better."

"Again, I'm not killing anyone."

"I'm not saying you're killing anyone. But he hurt you, and Michael, and your mom, so more than anything, you want to hurt him right back."

"Exactly."

"But it won't make you feel better. I'm not trying to talk you out of buying the team, because maybe you'll really love owning the Destroyers. Maybe that'll be the most fulfilling thing in your entire life and it'll light you up for the next fifty years or so. I have no idea," she says, her words rolling out fast. "But if that's not the case, don't do it. You've already let this excuse for a human being take up way too much of your precious time and energy. Don't let him have any more."

"So you think I should just walk away from the whole thing and let him get away with it all?"

"No, I think you should find him and have one quick conversation with him. Tell him who you've become, in case he doesn't already know. Tell him how awesome Michael turned out to be. Let him see what he's missing out on and then … let him go."

"You make it sound so simple."

"The truth is, you get to decide how simple it is. You have all the power now and he has none."

The limo stops in front of the stadium, and a moment later, the driver opens the door. I get out and step onto the busy sidewalk. A group of college-aged guys walks by shouting about how the Destroyers are going to destroy.

"I can hear that you're already there, so I'll let you go," Gwen says. "Whatever you decide tonight, just know that you're a really good person with a big heart. And maybe, if he had stayed, you wouldn't have turned out that way."

I stand in the cold night air, listening to her, knowing deep in my bones that she's right about all of it. Knowing she could've screwed me over so badly, but she didn't. Knowing she's the person I can trust. Knowing that I don't want this anymore. All I want now is her.

But it's too late to do anything about it now.

Only maybe it's not…

———

I walk into the stadium, but instead of taking the elevator to the owner's box where Muffy and her man are waiting, I take the steps to the top of the stadium, unbuttoning my wool overcoat despite the cold. It's still ten minutes until kickoff, but I know he'll be here already. My feet slow and my heart pounds as I walk up the last few rows until I reach section 445, row 27, seat 2.

And there he is. Patrick Sterling. After over a quarter of a century, I still know his face, even though it's lined with wrinkles now and his dark hair has gone grey. He looks old, small, weak, and broke in a Destroyer's jersey that has a rip on the collar. He's not the larger-than-life man who I used to look up to when I was too young to know any better. For the first time, I see him for what he is —a weak human being. Someone lacking character and destined to disappoint.

He looks up at me, and for a second, I'm tempted to turn and walk away. But I don't. I have to do this, even if it makes me want to vomit. "Hell of a night for a game, isn't it?" I ask.

He grins at me. "You said it, buddy. There's nothing better than Monday night football."

"Nothing at all?" I ask, raising one eyebrow. "Not, say, the love of a good woman or maybe your family?"

He narrows his eyes at me. "Do I know you?"

"No, you don't."

"You sure, because you look very familiar."

"That's because I'm your son."

37

Family Hurdles and Christmas Miracles...

Gwen - One Week Later

"I DON'T UNDERSTAND. The money has run out. You can't stay if there's no money," my mother says.

"Yes, but we're smart people. We're going to find a way to get the money," I answer, wishing I'd just lied to her and told her it was all sorted out already. I tug on the itchy collar of my ugly Christmas sweater, noticing one of the tiny lights on the tree is out.

"I don't think you are."

"Well, you would be *wrong*, Mom," I say, making a growly face. I glance up, only to see Keenan dressed in a T-shirt that looks like an elf uniform. He's standing outside my open door looking at me with a curious expression on his face. My skin heats up and I offer him an 'I'm okay' wave.

He smiles and gives me a thumbs up, which is exactly what I need because my mom is saying, "Gwendolyn, you sound just like you did when you thought you saw a UFO. Do you need more attention from Dad and me? Is that what this is? Or … did you hit your head again? Because I don't understand how you can honestly think it's not over."

I glance over at my Grinch tree, my heart tugging at how disappointed Allie is in me. She actually went out and bought a *new* ugly Christmas sweater instead of wearing our matching ones again for our annual 'last day of work before Christmas holidays work family Christmas party.' Not that I blame her. "I'm counting on a Christmas miracle."

"What?! That's it. I'm booking a flight to come see you."

"Relax. I was being sarcastic, Mom," I say, noticing that Allie is standing next to Keenan in the hall, both of them watching me intently. "Look, I can't explain it, but somehow I just know. We've been so fixated on having all the money upfront, but I realized we don't need it all now. We really only need enough to get us through the next few months. Then the next few after that. With social media, I think we could probably manage to get a lot of public support, and once that happens, someone will step in so they can look like a hero."

"That's not a plan, Gwendolyn. That's a pipe dream."

"Well, it may be, but I have to try. And given the fact that I have a fairly symmetrical face, it's worth a shot." I shrug at Allie, who gives me a nod that says 'that totally makes sense.'

"A symmetrical face? Oh my God, you finally lost it. Your father didn't think it would happen, but here we are," she says. "I'll be there by tomorrow at the latest to sort you out. First thing we need to do is get you out of that house deal. You certainly can't pay your mortgage with a promissory note that says, 'Somehow I just know.'"

My fists ball up and I feel my blood pumping through my veins. "You know what, Mom? There is nothing wrong with me, and I'm not stupid. I'm actually extremely bright, and I don't need you to come here to 'sort me out' because I'm fine. I already had my realtor find a way to back out of the deal. I'm working on a plan to keep the project going, and I'm going to find a way."

"Just please, give it up already," Mom tells me. "I talked to Ben this morning and he can get you on at the Goddard Institute. You can stay with him and Carla until you get your feet under you again, but you're going to have to let him know right away because there's a very narrow window for him to squeeze you in."

Standing up, I start to pace the tiny room. "I'm not moving to New York. I'm not abandoning my team. I'm going to stay on and keep fighting to live another day because that's what teams do."

"But you could be part of a new team—a much better one that does real work."

"I do real work," I grind out, exchanging eye rolls with Allie.

"You know what I mean—work that will yield real results, instead of spending your entire life waiting for something that won't happen for another four hundred years, if it even happens at all," she says, sounding totally exasperated. "This is your chance, Gwendolyn. You can finally do something important with your life."

I think about what she said, and suddenly Ty pops into my mind, and what he said to me about my parents. "You know what, Mom? It's sad to me that you can't see me for who I really am because I'm fucking amazing."

Keenan's eyes pop open but he nods and mouths, "That's true."

"Gwendolyn! Language!"

"I'll swear if I fucking want to, Mom, because I'm an adult," I say, standing up straighter. "And you know what else? I have a rare combination of high-functioning logical reasoning, intelligence, and optimism. I'm a dreamer, and I'm not ashamed of that because you know who else was a dreamer? Einstein. And Carl Sagan and Stephen Hawking—all of whom were convinced that there is intelligent life on other planets. And I'm not saying I'm a genius, so don't think you have to set me straight on that because you don't. I'm just saying I'm in pretty damn good company."

Bringing up Einstein, her hero, is definitely going to ruffle her feathers, but you know what? Good. I want to ruffle them.

"Einstein *never* explicitly said he believed in alien life forms."

"He basically did," I tell her, glancing at the poster of him sticking his tongue out. "In 1920, when he posed the question, 'Why should the earth be the only planet supporting human life? It is not singular in any other respect.' He was most definitely open to the possibility, and since he was the G.O.A.T., I'd think that would be enough to open your very closed mind," I say, quickly following that with, "G.O.A.T. stands for greatest of all—"

"I know what it stands for," she snaps.

"Good," I say, realizing I've fallen back into the trap of trying to argue her into believing in what I do. I sigh, and flop down into my chair. "You know what? This conversation is over. Forever. You can either accept that your daughter has a respectable career as an astrobiologist, or don't. I don't really care because it's my life and it makes me happy. I'm not going to spend the rest of my days trying to convince you. You can be disappointed in me if you want, like your mom was that you only had two children instead of eight like she did. That's up to you. But I'm done trying to prove myself to you." Tears fill my eyes as I say, "I like me. I believe in what I do. I'm excited for my future, and that's all that matters."

There's silence on the line, then, after a moment, she says, "Well, good, I guess."

"Seriously?" I ask.

"Yes. I'll stop trying to talk you out of your job."

"You're not just saying that because you believe it's coming to an end?" I ask, scared to believe her.

"Maybe a little, but I promise I won't say anything if you do somehow manage to keep things going."

My heart lifts and I feel suddenly lighter. "Really? Why would you do that?"

She sighs. "Because you're my daughter and I love you, and, according to Carla, I've been unnecessarily hard on you."

Wow, score one for Carla, my new favorite sister-in-law. "Okay, good."

"I know you're smart, Gwendolyn. I've never thought otherwise," Mom says. "Which is why I fought you so hard on your career. If I didn't think you had incredible potential, I wouldn't have bothered."

"Well, in that case, thank you, but no thank you. I've got it covered."

"I'll do my best to keep that in mind," she says. "Now, are you still coming home for Christmas?"

"No, but not because I'm upset. It's because we have a tough job ahead of us and a very tight deadline."

"I understand. It won't be the same without you, but we'll be rooting for you," Mom says, adding, "Well, you know, sort of."

I let out a laugh and she joins in, and suddenly, I feel closer to her than I have in years. The distance between us wasn't just in miles, it was in keeping each other at arm's length emotionally. "I love you, Mom."

"I love you too, Gwendolyn." Her voice wobbles a bit as she says, "And even more than that, I'm proud of you. You have more determination than your father and I put together."

My face scrunches up in an ugly cry and tears roll down my cheeks. My voice cracks and I say, "Thank you. I needed to hear that."

"No, you didn't," she tells me. "Because you've got it covered. You really do."

As soon as I end the call, I look up to see a group of people smiling at me. Keenan, Allie, Tina, Edward, and Chad. They're all in bright green, red, and white tacky clothing, and they all start to clap, even Chad.

"Well done, Gwen," Keenan says. "Family hurdles are the toughest ones to cross."

Allie holds her arms out for a hug, and I stand, relief washing over me.

"Are we okay?" I whisper.

"Yes, we'll be fine," she whispers, squeezing me tightly. "I'm so proud of you."

I pull back and smile at her. "I really said all the things, didn't I?"

"You really did," she says, and I hug her again.

Out in the hall, I hear Chad murmur, "Oh my God, what is *he* doing here?"

Allie and I let go of each other and I look at her with wide eyes because there's really only one 'he' that Chad could be referring to.

Ty.

"Mr. Sterling, what a surprise to see you here," Keenan says.

Oh. My. God. It *is* Ty.

"I'm here to see Gwen Fox," he says, sounding all sexy and in charge, of course.

"How do I look?" I ask. "Is my face all blotchy?"

She winces and tilts her head, but says, "You look beautiful." Grabbing a couple of tissues out of the box on her desk, she says, "But let's just get some of the snot off your face." She wipes under my nose, just as Ty steps into my office, looking devastatingly perfect in a dark grey suit.

My face flames. My body hums with excitement at the sight of him, while I simultaneously wish I could blink my eyes and be in a little black dress and sexy heels instead of a light-up sweater, jeans, and elf slippers that have bells on them. *Okay, Gwen, act casual.* "Oh hey, Ty. Nice to see you again."

Good. Very breezy.

He glances down at my outfit, his lips quirking up in a grin. "I see you've kept the bright colors in your wardrobe."

"Well, Marisol did say red was my color, so…"

He stares at me for a second, his eyebrows knitting together. "You all right? You look like you've been crying."

"Happy tears," I tell him. "I just had a very meaningful conversation with my mother. Someone told me I should stop letting my parents make me feel less than, and I decided to take his advice."

"Whoever that was sounds wise," he tells me.

Allie, who is standing between us, glancing back and forth at us, says, "He does sound wise. Who told you t—" She pauses, her face lighting up. "Oh, he did."

Without breaking eye contact with Ty, I grin and nod. "Yup."

She clears her throat. "How about we give you two a few moments alone?"

"You must be Allie," Ty says, holding out his hand to her.

She takes it and they shake while she smiles up at him, her cheeks bright pink. "Uh-huh."

"It's nice to meet you, Allie. Gwen's told me lots of wonderful things about you."

"She has?"

"Yes," he answers with a small chuckle.

"Um, Allie, remember when you said that thing about giving us a minute alone?" I ask.

She shakes her head a little, seeming to snap out of her daze. "Right. Yes. Sorry."

"Don't be sorry, he has that effect on people," I mutter.

"Yeah, I can see that," she says, before muttering, "All is forgiven."

She hurries out the door, closing it behind her.

"What did she mean by that?"

"Oh, just … nothing," I answer, because if ever there was a time to be vague, it is definitely right now. "What brings you by today?"

Please say it's because you want to marry me. Or because you're giving us the money. Either thing will make me equally happy. Well, one more than the other.

"I need you to show me around."

"Show you around the building?"

"Yes." He takes a couple of steps toward me, glancing at my lips. "Because if I'm going to back your project for the next decade, I need to understand what you do, and how."

"Don't forget why," I say, my voice going all breathy.

He glances up at the ceiling, then back at me. "I feel like I've already got a handle on that one."

"Wait, you said *if* you're going to back us."

"Yes, I did."

"The emphasis being on the word 'if,' as in you haven't made up your mind?" I ask. "Or did you mean that you *are* planning to back us, but you were trying to sound sort of casual and sexy about it?"

Chuckling, Ty says, "The second one. Is that how I came off?"

"Is that how you were hoping to come off?"

"Yes."

"Then, yes. Definitely very sexy," I say, my temperature going up a full five degrees.

"But maybe not all that clear, since I left you wondering."

"True," I answer, stepping closer to him, the bells on my slippers jingling.

"I should work on that."

Nodding, I say, "It's hard to be clear and sexy at the same time."

"I suppose if I have to pick one, I should choose clear. It's the only way people get what they really want."

"What do you want?" I ask, my heart pounding.

"I'd rather tell you what I don't want."

I glance down at his lips. "So, do that."

"I don't want to be a coward who hides behind skepticism. I don't want to own a stupid football team, and I don't want to spend the rest of my life letting a sad, little man stop me from putting my trust in the right person."

"Good, because who would want any of those things?" I ask, my voice thick with emotion.

"Not me. Not anymore, anyway," Ty tells me, reaching for my waist and pulling me closer. "I want better things from now on."

His mouth is so very close to mine, I can feel his breath on my skin. *Come on, kiss me. Just do it.* "I want to spend my days and nights with someone honest enough to call me on my bullshit and stop me from making the biggest mistakes of my life. Someone I can have a good argument with and still go to bed happy. Someone I admire for her blend of intelligence and passion."

Why, oh why, am I wearing this stupid sweater for the most romantic moment of my life? "I seem to recall you describing me that way."

"That's because I did," he tells me, lowering his mouth to mine. "And I wasn't even hopped up on psychedelics at the time."

"No?" I ask, swallowing hard.

I close my eyes but can feel his smile as he says, "I was totally sober."

"Then you must have meant it," I tell him.

"I must have." He finally kisses me, and it's anything but gentle. It's a toe-curling, 'I'm all-in and I want you forever' kiss. It's everything I've been waiting for my entire life, it's what I've been craving since we went our separate ways. It's the beginning of something wonderful. It's a new start, as fresh as the fallen snow.

His arms are wrapped around me, and he's holding me close, warming me up with every movement of his hands, with every kiss. I kiss him right back, needing him to know I'm all-in too. Needing him to know he can trust me to be by his side through the good, the bad, and the ugly. Needing him to know I'm proud to be the one he chose. My heart is as full as it could ever be. I feel like I could explode with joy.

We both pull back panting and smiling at each other. "I have a confession to make," I tell him. "Before we go any farther."

His smile fades. "What?"

"I meant everything I said when we were hopped up on tea and bourbon. Except … obviously not the bathroom stuff."

Ty grins at me. "Obviously."

"But the rest of it. I'm in love with you, Ty Sterling, and I can safely say until I met you, I didn't have the first clue what that meant, but I do now," I tell him. "I want to hang out with you and play cards with you and Michael, who will hopefully like me. I want to test out cookie recipes together and watch documentaries and kiss you good night and wake up with you next to me and do all the things with you, and the truth is, I don't think I'll ever want to stop wanting that, so if that freaks you out, I'm sorry, but that's just the way it is and I'd rather be upfront about it now."

"It doesn't freak me out," he says, smiling down at me. "It probably should, but it doesn't."

"Well, good then." I give him a firm nod.

"Good." He narrows his eyes a little. "Do you think your work family is going to be mad at you for sleeping with the boss?"

"Are you kidding? They're going to be thrilled to even have a boss," I tell him, giving him a hard kiss. "Wait. But do you just mean our project or all the projects?"

"All the projects."

"Really? All of them?"

"Yup. I just couldn't stand the thought of tearing down what Richard had built. Not after I understood why he built it and what it meant for the people who work here."

"Oh my God, you really are perfect."

"No, but I'm going to try."

We kiss again, and just when things are about to get a lot more 'not suitable for work,' I pull back, a thought popping into my head. "Fuck me, there really was a Christmas miracle," I mutter. "I have to call my mom."

And They Lived Happily Ever After...

Ty - Six Months Later

I WAS WRONG. About timing being everything. About life being all about grinding it out relentlessly until you achieve your dreams. I was wrong that there's no such thing as luck or the stars aligning. I was wrong to judge all those people who understood that life is for living and enjoying, not just for working. I was wrong about Richard, who knew all of this and made it his last wish (the real one) to try to teach me.

Richard figured it out, and that's what made him a great man. Not his inventions, although those were pretty damn amazing too. But the way he lived his life was the real work of art. And my new biggest goal is to make my life a work of art too. I started out by thanking my father for leaving us because if he had stayed, I wouldn't have become the man I am today, and Michael would have suffered every day. I told him I forgive him and that I know he did the best he could, and that it's sad that his best was just so little. I wished him well and walked away, knowing I was just starting my journey of being half the man Niles is but twice the man my father will ever be. I went directly up to the owner's box and was just about to tell Muffy the deal was off when she told me the team was no longer for sale. Apparently Diesel (who one hundred percent thinks she's in her forties) has always dreamed of owning a major sports franchise, so they're keeping it, and she's having the owner's box refitted by the same guys who did the lighting on the yacht (which she paid me back for). I guess she had the money all along, she just wanted to see if she could get me to buy it for her.

The next few weeks were spent working on a big farewell memorial service for Richard. Rohan managed to get Elton John to rewrite a version of Candle in the Wind, and he sang as video clips of Richard doing daring things played. There wasn't a dry eye in the house. I hired Rohan, who is not only smart and loyal, but was always destined for bigger things, to run the foundation. He's doing a bang-up job of it so far, and I have every faith he'll be able to continue it. Between him and the people on the SETI team, they've come up with ways to fundraise so they can increase funding for all the projects, and I have to say, their efforts have yielded impressive results. All the cash goes back into the trust, where I'm turning it into some really big money for them. Gwen's work family doesn't hate me anymore, and in fact, I've been invited to karaoke night, at which, Gwen and I get up and sing "The Power of Love" as a horrible duet. I do all the really high parts, but only for comic value.

And every day, I wake up and silently thank Richard for helping me see what was truly important in life. Thank God I finally got the message before it was too late, because if I hadn't, I'd be missing out on all of it. I'd have missed out on *Gwen*, and that would have been the tragedy of a lifetime.

Michael would have missed out on her too, which would've been a total loss for him because the two of them are true allies. She won him over pretty much instantly by showing up at the house with a fresh batch of chocolate chip cookies (which are so much better than gingerbread, even though I pretend they aren't just to get a rise out of her). Three months later, she moved in with us and I can honestly say neither of us have ever been this happy. She's the missing piece to our family puzzle.

Tonight is Friday game night and since it's a warm summer's evening, Michael is setting up the games on the patio table. We're starting with Exploding Kittens, then moving onto Catan, followed by Trivial Pursuit - Wildlife Edition, during which he's obviously going to wipe the floor with us.

Gwen and I are just cleaning up the dishes while two batches of cookies finish baking, one of each. I wait until she's got her hands in the soapy water before walking up behind her and kissing a little spot on the crook of her neck that she can't resist. She stops what she's doing and lets out a small moan while I wrap my arms around her waist.

"Mmm, you smell so good," I tell her, breathing in the scent of her skin.

"That's the cookies."

"No, it's not. It's you."

She turns her face and I capture her mouth with a lingering kiss. When I let her go, she says, "I love Friday nights."

"Me too," I murmur, brushing my lips against her skin. "If you're not doing anything after Michael beats us at everything, I'd love to get you naked and do all the things you like."

"That sounds like the perfect way to end an evening."

"Doesn't it?"

"Much better than worrying about a football team," I tell her.

"So, you're happy with how things turned out?"

"Ecstatic."

"Great word."

"It's also highly accurate."

"Well, you know how much I love accuracy," she says, leaning her back against me.

Michael clears his throat. "I am sorry to interrupt you but I believe we are scheduled to play games now, which would require you to stop … canoodling and finish the dishes."

I let go of Gwen and we both laugh. She smiles at Michael. "Sorry about that. Your brother distracted me."

"I've noticed he does that a lot," Michael says, shaking his head. "Ty, please. We won't be able to get through all three games if you keep distracting Gwen like that."

The oven timer goes off and I pick up the oven mitts and put them on. "All right, I'll try not to, but no promises."

Michael and Gwen exchange a look and she winks at him. "Well, I, for one, promise to keep my hands to myself and stay focused."

"Thank you, Gwen," Michael says with a small bow.

Grinning at him, she says, "It's the only way I can vanquish you both."

Michael laughs, then says, "Ha! That will never happen."

Pulling the plug in the sink, she then wipes her hands

on a dish towel. "Oh, I'm going to win tonight. I'm feeling lucky."

I quickly move the cookies from the sheets to a cooling rack, then grab a plate to put some on while Michael and Gwen talk trash about my lack of Catan abilities. I laugh along, my heart full as I take a second to enjoy the simplicity of this moment.

This is what life is meant to be. It's not about how many commas are in your bank account or whether your name is on a building. It's about the little moments spent with the people you love, having fun and making memories.

Later that night, after we make love, I smile down at Gwen in the dim moonlit room. "Thank you."

"Thank you? Believe me, I should be thanking you after that," she says with a grin.

"No, I mean thank you for being you, for showing me what life is all about. Thank you for being fearlessly honest and for loving me and for loving Michael and making this place feel like a home."

She lifts her head off the pillow and kisses me. "Oh, that. You're welcome."

"I'm serious. You're the best person I know, Gwen. You're my person."

"Your ride-or-die?"

"That too," I say with a grin. "You wouldn't want to marry me, would you?"

Her eyes grow round. "Are you actually asking or is this just a hypothetical?"

"I'm asking. Well, I guess I was sort of pre-asking to see if I have a shot before I ask you properly, you know, like somewhere romantic with a big, fat diamond in my pocket."

"Well, if you're pre-asking, my advice would be to go ahead and buy the big, fat diamond."

I lower my head and give her a lingering kiss. "In that case, maybe I will."

"Perfect. Maybe I'll say yes."

We both laugh, then kiss some more. When we stop, I grin down at her again. "Say, I have to go to the bathroom. Can you bear to be without me for a minute alone or do you want to come with?"

She bursts out laughing. "I think I'll wait here."

"Suit yourself, Ms. Fox, but the offer stands."

THE END

Want more Ty and Gwen? Well, you're in luck then because I've popped three hilarious deleted scenes into a booklet for you. To get to the free download page for the Deleted Scenes Bonus Booklet, go here:

https://BookHip.com/PGLFCRK

Coming Soon: Love Signals

It's time to unlock the greatest mystery of the universe: true love.

Allegra Cammareri's life is on hold. As a SETI researcher, she's been waiting a whole decade for signs of intelligent life, and so far…nothing. She still lives with her big Italian family (none of whom believe in a little thing called 'privacy'). And her love life is the ultimate cosmic joke.

But that's all about to change, because Hollywood A-lister, Hudson Finch, is coming to Mountain View to job-shadow Allie for six weeks. *Hudson Freaking Finch*. The man himself. America's heartthrob and Allie's secret celebrity crush, who's been sent to prepare for an upcoming movie role.

What begins as an awkward dance between science and celebrity quickly turns into something she never could've predicted, and soon Allie finds herself caught in the orbit of America's most sought-after leading man. From the close quarters of the research lab to a night stranded together in a secluded cabin, the unlikely pair discovers that maybe opposites really do attract.

Will the stars align for this unlikely couple? Or will theirs be just a fleeting encounter in the chaos that is modern love?

*** Love Signals is an irresistibly charming, deliciously dishy, banter-filled tale about an ordinary woman and the superstar who falls her. With a crazy cast—including a father who's sure no one will ever be good enough for his littler girl—there's sure to be plenty of cringe-worthy moments, lots of laughs, and even a few tears. It's a stand-alone rom-com with a few tablespoons of extra spice than a regular Melanie Summers book.***

WHAT TO EXPECT:

- Opposites attract
- S.T.E.M. romance
- Powerful, rich celebrity meets a strong, smartie pants regular girl
- Romantic settings, lots of banter, embarrassing mishaps, and oh, so much tension
- Forced Proximity/Stranded alone together with only one bed

Pre-order your copy of Love Signals today!

Acknowledgments

It takes a village to publish a novel. Seriously. A freaking village of patient, organized, supportive, amazing people. I am so very grateful for the many sets of eyes, helpful hands, and sharp minds who helped make Ty and Gwen's story the best it could be. From plotting to editing to proofreading, every novel takes months' of work and many friends along the way to help guide the process and keep me on track.

This book has been scrubbed and helped along by two hard-working editors: Kristi Yanta, who handles my developmental edits with patience, kindness, and a keen eye, and Melissa Martin, my dear friend/PA/copy editor/formatter/graphics designer/rememberer of all the million details I tend to forget. Melissa is my go-to person for ALL the things, and I am so grateful she's willing to go on this journey with me.

I also have an amazing proofing team including Laura Albert, Kellie Porth-Bagne, and of course, my very sweet and funny mom, Nevia Brudnicki, who swears like a sailor.

And while I'm on the topic of my mom, I need to thank you for bringing me into this world, raising me to be my best and to care for others, and for *everything* you do for us. And a big thank you to my dad, who is no longer with us and I miss every day. Thanks for teaching me to work hard and dream big, Dad.

Huge hugs and thanks to my very dear friend Kelly Collins of Colorado, who is an AMAZING author and savvy businesswoman. Her no-nonsense support, and unwavering faith in my abilities is often the difference between me putting out my next book and closing my laptop to go in search of a real job.

Special thanks to the ab fab Jenn Falls. Jenn is my plotting/branding buddy and my most excellent friend who continually reminds me to keep it simple.

Huge thanks to my dear friend, Whitney Dineen, with whom I wrote nine whole books with in 2021 and 2022 (and they're really freaking good ones, at that)! Thank you for your continued support and for making me laugh as we both continue on in our journeys.

To my very dear writer friends: Kate O'Keeffe, Delancey Stewart, Pippa Grant, Aven Ellis, and Tracie Banister. I wish you all good health, wealth, and much success in the future. To my girls I grew up with: Nikki, Karlee, Kristyn, Kelly, Judy, Laureen, and Jenny – much love to you all.

And thank you so much to every fantastic blogger and reader out there who has supported my career. YOU are why I write. If it weren't for you, I'd just be a crazy woman in her pajamas talking to imaginary friends. But because of you, I'm called an *author* (which just sounds so much better).

To my kiddos, for keeping me humble and helping me keep up with the world (well, sort of), thanks, you three. Love you to the moon and back. As always, I need to thank my smart, witty, ridiculously handsome husband, Jeremy, for your steadfast love and support, for all the laughter and fun, and for all evenings when you make supper alone and all the days you drive the kids to all their things so I can get caught up (because I am always, *always* behind). I promise to take you on that trip around the world when this book is turned into a movie and we're finally rich. 😉

About the Author

Melanie Summers is a multi-award-winning, Amazon best-selling author of romantic comedies and women's fiction. She's written over thirty books for people who have 'had it up to here' with the real world and need to laugh, feel good, and sigh happily. When she's not writing or reading, she's usually out for a walk with her two adorable dogs, hanging out on the beach with her husband and their three teenagers, or curled up on the couch for family movie night. Melanie resides on Vancouver Island, Canada where her life goal is to become one of those fabulous people who take daily ice baths in the ocean. So far, she can get in up to her ankles, which is not awful, thank you very much.

If you'd like to find out about her upcoming releases, sign up for her newsletter on www.melaniesummersbook s.com.